THE ADMIRAL'S BATHS

DANA GYNTHER

*For my husband
Carlos García Aranda,
a native Valencian,
and his father
José García Fenollera
who, as a post-war law student,
occasionally bathed in the
Admiral's Baths.*

Reconstruction

May 2011

I sat back from the window, listening to the sound of the wheels folding back into the body of the plane. Today, that low mechanical hum, the wheeze of an aging robot, reminded me of an albatross. A huge ungainly bird who, once airborne, tucks its stubby legs up to its belly and stretches its wings into a long glide. That image, so wholesome and peaceful—one I'd surely seen in some sleepy documentary—made me smile. I was nearly moved by my own calm. Before today, I used to have a flying phobia.

Even when I was too young to grasp the concept of mortality, I'd had an instinctive fear of flying; right now, however, I found myself looking back on that fear with a certain nostalgia: the sweaty palms, the pounding heart, the rash purchases of exorbitant bottles of mini-Absolut. Every landing had come without incident and yet, achy and tired, I'd descended from the airplane in semi-astonishment that I was still alive. Since the week before, however, it all seemed somewhat contrived: a middle-class, peace-time attempt at an adrenaline buzz. A week ago, I'd learned something about fear: like everything else, it's relative.

"Ms..." A flight attendant was suddenly kneeling at my side, checking the paper in her hand. "Ms. Rachel Cardon?"

"Yes?" I glanced over to find her looking at me with anxious curiosity. "What?"

"We just want to offer our assistance." She was using a conspiratorial whisper. "In case you need anything."

I blinked in confusion. Was this a new publicity campaign? "Uh, thanks," I said with a polite little nod.

With a searching stare, she bored into my eyes—first one, then the other—and looked back at the paper. "Excuse me, ma'am. It says here that you're blind?"

"Oh." It came out in two syllables. "Well, I'm not."

"That's strange," she said, turning pink. "We always get a printout of our handicapped passengers. For some reason, you're marked here as blind."

"It must be a mistake. Really"—I smiled, trying to erase her embarrassment—"you don't need to worry about me."

A nervous laugh tumbled from her lips. "Right, then. Sorry to have disturbed you."

I watched her scuttle back down the aisle, back to her home turf of strange metal bins and coffee makers. Blind. The error was unusually apt. For the past week, I'd been like a kid in a perpetual game of pin the tail on the donkey: spinning around and unable to see.

It wasn't that there hadn't been any warning. For days, meteorologists had been predicting extreme weather for the southern states. On April twenty-fifth, the tornado outbreak began, hitting Arkansas especially hard; two days later, swarms of twisters were touching down everywhere.

I'd been watching the Weather Channel like some kind of reality show—mildly entertaining, shocking at times, but nothing to do with *me*—unwilling to imagine a tornado could possibly head in my direction. I wasn't even considering it. My head was too full of the noisy buzz of having just been dumped.

Three days before and out of the blue, Todd Russell, my boyfriend of nearly a year, had up and moved—one week before our summer-long trip to Spain. I felt detached from anything outside my own pain; sick with anger and hurt, I'd barely eaten since he left. I was standing at the ironing board, absently watching a monster funnel attack a hospital in Cullman, Alabama. Although it was only a hundred miles north, for me it could have been on the moon. Half an eye on the storm, I jabbed the iron around the pockets of a shirt, cursing myself for my attraction to natural fibers, to unpredictable hipsters. Then, I noticed the ticker tape at the bottom of the television screen: tornado warnings in Tuscaloosa County.

As I leaned over the ironing board, trying to see out the dark, streaky windows, I heard the siren's jarring screech. It had gone off several times in the last week or two, already forcing me to decide on the safest place in the house. Like many southern homes built on red clay, this one had no basement, and the storage space under the stairs was already jam-packed with suitcases, holiday decorations, and my son's old skateboards and soccer balls. During a pause in the siren, the serious tone of the weathercaster's voice got my attention: *If you are in the vicinity of the city of Tuscaloosa, take shelter immediately. A dangerous storm is expected to hit the downtown area.* I turned off the iron, picked up my cell phone and, once again, took refuge in the windowless half-bath next to the kitchen.

I'd been sitting on the bathroom floor for some twenty minutes, my bottom cold and numb, staring down at my phone. Its wallpaper was still an adorable couple shot, Todd and me at Gulf Shores, bathed in pastels, pale blue water and a pink sunset behind happy faces. I was resisting the urge to call him when the lights went out. The blackness made me gasp, instant panic. Did the dark make the wind seem louder? Was that the infamous freight train sound? My ears popped from the pressure; the house creaked and groaned. A violent crash above and I threw myself against the floor. Covering my head with my hands, eyes squeezed shut, heart lashing wildly, I chanted a stream of mumbles: "Please God no, please God no, please God no, please God no..." despite the fact I'd never believed in Him. Was this it? Was I going to die alone, in a bathroom, at the age of forty-seven?

After several minutes paralyzed on the bathroom tiles, fear muffling my ears, I suddenly noticed the quiet. I sat up and reached for the knob, then pushed the door open with my foot. A dim light came in from the hall. From my place on the floor, I could just see the kitchen table, a bowl of golden apples undisturbed in its center. It was over. I had survived. Pulling a towel down from the rack, I cried into it, hard sobs of relief, of thankfulness.

When I was finally able to stand, I left my refuge and went to the living room, intending to begin an inspection of the house. I immediately saw that the garden—indeed, all the vegetation from the yard—was pressed up against the windows. Peering in, the bushes seemed hostile, overly curious about life indoors. It was if all my well-loved plants had turned on me, taking me hostage. My heart sank, thinking of all the sections I'd painstakingly developed out there over the years: the Mediterranean corner, the butterfly garden, the little Buddha fountain...

I cracked open the door and squinted. Sunlight was unexpected. It glistened off the jumble of plant scraps and the wayward junk which had landed there like an unwanted yard sale. The tall, slender birches and crepe myrtles were missing and, wondering where they'd gone off to, I suddenly remembered the huge pecan tree on the other side of the house. The crash! Cold and shaking, I kicked aside someone else's lawn chair and walked out into the yard, taking giant steps over debris like a child playing Simon-says. Rounding the house, I saw it. The gnarled trunk of the lovely old pecan was askew, half-uprooted. I gazed up, a huge knot tying securely inside my throat. Its biggest bough had smashed the roof of my study—my sanctum sanctorum—while various other branches were plowing through the windows of my bedroom.

I'd gawked at the side of my broken house, mouth open, arms out tense, until I became aware of the sound of voices. Was someone calling my name? For the first time, it occurred to me to look around, down the street. It was like a war zone, like we'd been pummeled by bombs, a Blitzkrieg. Trees hung in rags, brick houses had holes, the split-level at the end of the circle was a pile of sticks. Glass was everywhere. And neighbors. After the storm, they had also been drawn out into the light.

"Hey, Rachel! Are you alright?" one cried.

I nodded blankly, watching a group of teenagers carry Felix, the elderly man who lived diagonally from me, out of his splintered home on top of his front door. Some people were bleeding, others limping. Remnants of centennial oaks and spiry pines lay scattered on the yards and street, making passage impossible. How would they get to the hospital? I stood rooted in the yard, light-headed and unable to catch my breath. I wanted to help someone—I was fine, after all—but couldn't speak or move. Suddenly, everything went black.

When I came to, I was on the grass face to face with Mike Wilson, a large, bearded, be-capped neighbor that, before that moment, I'd only exchanged hellos with.

"I think you're in shock, Rachel," he'd said. "Try to breathe slowly. In, out... in, out... That's better. Here, let me get you inside."

With one massive arm around me, he'd helped me through the mess that had once been my garden, now filled with broken limbs and wet trash: a child's twisted tricycle, a beach towel, roof shingles, a fender. He lowered me onto my sofa and brought me some water in a plastic Mardi Gras cup that I'd never used before. Where had he even found it?

"I'm going back outside," Mike had said, peering out the window at the unlikely glow. "Funny how the tornado seems to have swept up the rain and taken it along for the ride. Listen," he added, patting my head in an awkward parting gesture, "if you need anything, just holler."

He'd let himself out while I lay on the couch, slightly less dizzy, frowning at the memory of Todd pointing Mike out one morning and calling him the "living definition of a 'rube.'"

In, out... in, out... I used to practice controlled breathing during take-offs, but this time I'd forgotten all about it. I slid off my shoes. Tucking my feet up on the empty seat beside me, I was glad for the first time Todd hadn't come. What would he have done in Valencia anyway? While I was busy doing research and working on my article, how might he have spent his free time?

"Anything to drink, ma'am?" The flight attendant from before blushed at me.

"Yes, I'll have a beer." I considered making a joke—maybe something about her turning a blind eye or me getting blind drunk—but she quickly handed me a squat can of Heineken and a bag of peanuts and the moment slipped away. I nodded my thanks and, struggling to open the peanut packet, continued checking off idioms in my head: blind as a bat, blind side, blind leading the blind, love is blind—I stopped cold. Love is blind. I looked at the empty place beside me, my bare toes next to the unused red blanket, still in its plastic bag. And here we are, back to Todd.

Our relationship had seemed so promising. After the first few weeks, in the flood of discovery of common loves and interests—fine food and photography, folk singers and handmade pottery—I'd felt a connection with him like I hadn't had for years, not since Jeff, my ex-husband. Without ever giving up the lease on his own place, he'd begun spending more and more time at mine. And not just to share the bed—there he was, helping with the garden, changing the odd light bulb, making a Sunday-morning run to the Krispy Kreme— and six months later, it felt... consolidated.

My son Nick, off studying Architecture across the state, had been indifferent about this new relationship whenever I mentioned it on the phone. At best, vaguely pleased for me. But during his trip home at Thanksgiving, something changed. On Wednesday, the initial contact between boyfriend and son had gone smoothly enough and on the feast day, we didn't even see him. Nick and I celebrated together while Todd, a chef, was busy at the restaurant, preparing Cornish hens and roasted quail, miniature turkeys for traditionally-minded folks who didn't want the mess. The following day, we'd had our annual get together for the Auburn-Alabama game. None of us were big football fans, but for the last four years, ever since Nick had begun his studies at Auburn, we'd been enjoying a lighthearted school rivalry. A half-dozen people had come over—a few of Nick's old buddies from high school, a couple of strays from the History department—and everyone was in good spirits, drinking and snacking to the sports commentators' breakneck prose.

At some point during half-time, Nick dragged me into the kitchen. His face was red, his mouth a straight line.

"Your boyfriend's drunk," he said.

I glanced at Todd, perched on the arm of the sofa, a beer in his hand, his eyes half-closed.

"Everyone drinks a little too much sometimes." I shrugged.

"No," he said, still heated. "That guy's such a loser. You need to get rid of him."

"Why do you say that?" I asked, becoming concerned. "What did he do?"

"He's talking bullshit, Mom," he said. He avoided my eyes, looking instead at the television screen.

"What, about the game?" I asked with a little smile.

"Yeah, right," he said, the sarcasm dripping from his lips. "You know how sensitive I am about football."

"Well, what then?"

He looked into my face. "You can do better, Mom. Seriously."

I sighed. This was my first real relationship since the divorce ten years earlier; before Todd, I'd been completely absorbed by my son and my career. I knew Nick was unused to the idea of me dating—it had been just the two of us for ages—but I still didn't understand this sudden selfishness. Was it latent adolescence? A misguided Oedipal complex?

"I think you might be overacting, Nick," I said, my voice quiet.

"I'll tell you one thing," he said, "while he's around, I won't be."

Taken aback, I watched him put on his jacket and tell his friends he had to go, that something had come up. Feeling stiff and slightly hollow, I sat down on the couch, imagining Nick's drive through Tuscaloosa's empty streets. The whole town was in the stadium or in front of their TVs. I stared at my own screen unseeing, the beer growing warm in my hand. Todd slowly slid off the arm of the sofa, squeezing in beside me. He nuzzled my neck. "Hey, you," he mumbled into my ear, his breath smelling faintly of tobacco. I reached up and grazed his stubbly chin. "Hey," I whispered back, debating whether or not to ask him about it. As Auburn made a dramatic comeback victory to a roomful of exasperated cursing and shouting, I quietly reflected over what had come over my son.

Not wanting to make things worse, I decided not to mention Nick's outburst to Todd. I assumed he'd get over it, that the close relationship we'd always enjoyed as a single mother and an only child would soon be restored. But, it wasn't. He didn't phone or visit. He spent an unprecedented Christmas in Atlanta with his father's new family, then Spring Break with his girlfriend, Allison. At first, I was upset by his cold reception on those rare occasions when he even picked up his phone and was tempted to drive the three hours to see him, to finally talk it out. But, then I became angry myself, furious at his babyish silent treatment, the emotional blackmail.

Breathing out in a slow stream, I peered down at the Atlantic Ocean, now thirty-five thousand feet below, then plunked down the window shade—the clouds outside were blinding—and closed my eyes.

I hadn't even had the time (or the energy? The guts?) to tell Nick that Todd had left before the storm came through. I hadn't told anyone. It happened on Easter Sunday. I was making coffee when Todd came downstairs to find a little basket on the table: a chocolate bunny and some marshmallow chicks. I turned around, expecting a smile, but instead he'd plopped down in the chair, flicked the basket onto its side, and proclaimed, "I can't do this anymore."

This. What was *this?*

He began packing his things—some toiletries, t-shirts and boxers, a few books, and his fancy-pants corkscrew (it shocked me to see that his 'moving out' required only a gym bag)—and announced he was heading to New Orleans. In ten minutes, he was gone. I sat at the table, my coffee grown cold, silently gouging the beady black eyes out of those cute yellow chicks. I knew we'd been riding on inertia for a while—in fact, I'd been hoping the trip to Spain would reenergize our relationship, bring it back to its initial levels of camaraderie and sex—but this had come out of nowhere. Was he no longer attracted to me? Was there someone else? I spent three days in a simmering stew of rejection, abandonment, and wounded pride, all topped with the noxious sensation of rapid ageing. The third day brought the tornado. *Flying* in the most primitive, the most terrifying sense possible. A thousand people were injured, hundreds missing, nearly fifty dead. The breakup no longer seemed so important.

"Pasta or chicken?" the flight attendant asked again, touching me lightly on the arm; she looked only tired now, all awkwardness gone.

"Uh..." Nick had always joked that the question was pointless, as they basically tasted the same. "The pasta. With red wine, please."

A tray on my lap, I unscrewed the individual wine bottle and tore open the plastic cutlery pouch. I glanced up at the small, ill-lit screen—a political thriller, by the look of it—but couldn't be bothered to put on the headphones. Really, even without flight anxiety, twenty-first century travel was pathetic.

I took a sip of the mediocre wine, winced, and thought of the last wine I'd drunk: an aged *La Pesquera*, a fine Spanish red that I'd stashed away for a special occasion.

About an hour after the tornado had passed, when I was finally steady on my feet, I braved the upstairs of my house. The windows smashed, the ceiling fan on the floor, the tree's mossy limbs had become part of the bedroom. I'd seen photos like this in some of Nick's avant-garde architecture magazines: big trees growing in houses instead of little houses wrapped around trees. However, these branches were tangled up in waterlogged clothes, bedding and drapes, taking away any pretense of minimalistic elegance.

I tried to get into my study, the outward reflection of my inner self, but the doorframe was crushed. I got on tiptoes and tried to peek through a broken slat, but, it was impossible to see anything. I'd spent the whole morning in there, grading final papers on the Spanish Civil War and taking occasional breaks to google Valencian cuisine: rice dishes, Moorish sweets, *horchata*, trying to encourage my post-breakup appetite. All morning that room had been the same bastion of organized chaos it had always been: shelves overflowing with books and punctuated with curios. Framed photographs, from the sepia portraits of my ancestors to my own artwork; an international array of wooden masks; fossils and shells; an antique mandolin; a collection of handcrafted animals. My favorites: the Inuit walrus carved in blubbery stone, the terracotta bird from a Mexican honeymoon, the golden-glazed horse, a family heirloom. I stood in silence scouring the shelves in my mind, wondering if any of these fragile things had pulled through.

Now, through the gap, I could only make out a mysterious, organic space, unrecognizable as part of a human dwelling. Strange sounds, rustling and muffled chirps, came from the inside, as if squirrels and owls were already roosting, claiming my haven as their own.

My eyes flooded with tears at the thought of all the treasures lost or destroyed, but then I guiltily remembered the razed split-level at the end of the circle and my neighbor Felix, lying prone on his door. I was alive, unhurt, with *most* of a roof still over my head. Really, I had no right to bemoan any losses. Clutching the rail, I carefully went back downstairs to pour myself a glass of wine.

After a maddening search for my old corkscrew, I pulled the nicest bottle of wine out of the pantry. If this wasn't a special occasion, what was? I poured a burgundy stream into the Mardi Gras cup and savored the taste in my mouth. With candles lit and new batteries in the radio, I sat back on the couch as it began to get dark. Although tipsy—one glass did me in, what with my jangled nerves and empty stomach—I was responsible enough to think I should make some calls. Check on local friends as well as reassure my far-flung loved ones. But I couldn't recall where I'd put my phone. Lying down, I listened to the radio blast out death tolls and destruction sites: Forest Lake, Hackberry Lane, McFarland Boulevard—but I couldn't bear to hear my own street listed. I changed the station to classic rock and, to a Jim Croce tribute, sobbed myself to sleep.

The growl of chain saws woke me up around dawn. I climbed up on the couch to look out a patch of window; a group of neighbors and volunteers were already trying to clear the street. Ashamed at having kept to myself after the storm, I picked up the bowl of apples to offer the workers. I opened the door and ran smack into Nick. His face broke apart when he saw me, a muddled combination of happiness, relief and vexation.

"God *damn* it, Mom," he cried, as he shoved the fruit bowl onto the table and picked me up in a big bear hug. "Why didn't you answer your phone?"

Gulping back tears, I held on to my son (when had he gotten so strong?), unprepared for the overwhelming surge of comfort and healing that came from his arms.

After a minute, finally peeling my hands off his neck, Nick told me about his frenzied trip up from Auburn. The evening before, he had sat in front of his television in a panicked silence, watching the tornado live. For once the weather commentators did not have to exaggerate to make a good story: the twister that ransacked Tuscaloosa was up to a *mile and a half* wide, with winds up to a *hundred and ninety miles* per hour, and had left a trail *eighty miles* long. Nick had left at three o'clock in the morning, when he thought it was safe to get on the road, and headed northwest. In the pre-dawn shadows, he could see other pockets of tornado paths along his way. When he got into Tuscaloosa, the fallen debris made it impossible to drive. He parked his car on the side of the main road and walked the rest of the way home. The closer he got to our damaged neighborhood, the more frightened he became. He ran the last half-mile.

Still standing in the doorway, I told him about the storm from the bathroom vantage point, the crash, the garden, the kind neighbor Mike.

"You were alone during all this?" he asked. His concerned voice took on a snarky edge. "Where was Todd?"

"I don't know. New Orleans, maybe?" I shrugged. "He and I aren't together anymore."

"Thanks for telling me." Nick was cross again.

"He left just the other day. Easter Sunday. It still hasn't really sunk in. But, hey, you're here. And there's no one in the world I'd rather see right now."

I threw my arm around my grown son, so much taller than me, and looked up into his face.

"I'm glad to see you too," he said. "God, when I was watching the tornado last night..." He stopped and bit his lip, unable to continue. Clearly, the violent storm had restored a sense of perspective, bringing our five-month estrangement to a brisk end. "I saw the roof," he said, clearing his throat and changing the subject. "Looks like your study was hit pretty hard. What's the plan?"

"Plan?" I blinked. The next step, the practical notion of reconstruction, had not yet occurred to me. I was still in a swamp of devastation coupled with gratitude.

Following Nick upstairs, I watched him assessing the damage with an educated eye. His mental note-taking was almost visible. He yanked at the unyielding study door.

"I'm going to need a crowbar to get in there," he said. "It looks bad, but it could be worse. When's your trip to Spain?"

"Spain?" I stammered.

What had the storm done to my brain? I'd forgotten all about the arrangements to spend the summer abroad, housesitting for friends in Valencia, writing that article... "Uh... May second," I managed. "The tickets. They're for the second. When is that? What day is today?"

"That's next Monday. You've got five days. Counting today."

"I can't go to Spain, Nick. Look around you."

"Mom, I can take care of this. Why do you think you've been writing those checks for me to go to college?" He smiled. "Hell, maybe I can write up an Independent Study project for this. Or at least weasel out some extra credit."

"Are you serious? Could you really put this back together? Looks to me like all the kings' horses and all the kings' men—"

He put up his hand—a polite shut-up gesture—and took out his phone. He woke up Erik, then Mitchell, the two engineering students he'd worked construction with for the past two summers. After discussing the project with them ("You *will* pay us, right Mom?") and giving them a list of supplies, he called Allison.

"Hey, there," he murmured, clearly still besotted, though they'd been together since they met in ARCH 1000 their Freshman year. "You want to spend the summer in Tuscaloosa? I've got a free place to stay."

Having our city destroyed brought the people of Tuscaloosa closer. Unable to carry out normal routines—the university cancelled final exams and postponed graduation; many schools and stores were closed—neighbors worked together to rebuild our lives. With chain saws and community spirit, main streets were slowly cleared, towers of debris building up along the sides. President Obama, after declaring a State of Emergency, visited Tuscaloosa two days after the tornado to see the destruction for himself. Erik, Mitchell and Allison arrived that same day, already able to park Erik's pickup, filled with tools and equipment, glass panes and lumber—valuable commodities in short supply—right in front of the house.

We spent the day cleaning out the backyard and that evening, we had a barbeque, cooking all the meat that had been slowly thawing inside my freezer. As I grilled the filet mignon and sirloin steaks that Todd had bought weeks before, I toasted Nick and his friends, and we finished off the bottle of *La Pesquera.*

"Thank you all." I was misty-eyed again.

"Uh, Dr. Cardon." Erik had known me for years, but still preferred to use my title. Was it some modern-day irony? "I've worked with these two on many a house and, well, with these guys, you never know *what* you'll end up with. You might want to reserve those thanks till it's done."

The three days after the cook-out were a blur. As I packed for the trip—thank god all my favorite clothes had been in the ironing basket and not upstairs in my weather-beaten bedroom—Nick and his crew began cutting down the old pecan tree, freeing the house from its grip. While I organized travel documents, e-tickets, contact information and project notes, they covered the damaged roof and broken windows with blue tarp. Early that morning on May second, getting into the car for Nick to drive me to the airport, I noticed that most of the houses on my street were now wrapped up in that blue plastic, the color and sheen of a swimming pool. It gave the place a strangely festive air.

As we drove out of town, I was blown away by its unfamiliarity. Tuscaloosa lay in heaps, horizontal. Entrails poured from stores; rumpled, upended cars were sprinkled about; springtime trees had turned into poles, boughs and branches snapped off. It was this lack of trees that was most disorienting. Before, a large part of the view had been lush green foliage and, without it, the light was peculiar, excessive even. Formerly hidden objects—a rickety water tower, the hospital—were now exposed, seemingly brand new and overly large.

We got to Birmingham early since I had to replace the computer left stranded in my study. After buying the same model and a travel case, Nick and I grabbed a quick lunch. It seemed odd that there, just an hour north of Tuscaloosa, everything was business-as-usual. The people around us were nonchalantly shopping for electronics, driving too fast, eating burgers and fries, unaware that their houses were fragile, barely conscious of the fact that life was precious. It almost hurt my feelings.

"Nick," I said, moving my chair to avoid looking at the other diners. "I feel terrible about leaving you with all this responsibility. The reconstruction, the insurance claims…the whole mess."

"I can handle it," he said. I looked at the set of his jaw, the seriousness in his playful green eyes, the same color as my own. Had he matured that much in the last few days? "I really can. And I think you really need to take a break from all this. I want you to have a great time in Valencia. Say hi to Hector and bring me back some *jamón*. Deal?"

During the journey—on the flight to New York, during the brief stopover in JFK, and now on the transatlantic trip—I had gradually become accustomed to seeing people who hadn't experienced a recent tragedy, who hadn't undergone disaster. Watching them fiddle with their phones and blow on their lattes, bored or tired but certainly not on the verge of breaking down, little by little, I no longer found them offensive. Just clueless. And luckier than they knew.

"Store your tray tables and put your seats in an upright position," a flight attendant announced in Spanish, Catalan and English. "We are now beginning our descent to Valencia."

As the plane positioned itself for landing, I peeked down on the shining Mediterranean, finally excited about being back in Spain. I'd spent a year teaching English in Madrid after finishing my BA and had fallen in love with all of it: the culture, food, language, geography, lifestyle. On every visit back, it almost felt like I was in my twenties again, that same excitement, that same energy. Nick was right; I needed this.

I looked down on the dusty fields surrounding the Valencia airport and rubbed my hands together, anxious to be on land with my old friend, Hector Ballester. Fellow historians, we'd been close friends for some fifteen years. Our first books had come out within weeks of each other and, sharing the same publisher in the UK, we were thrown together for a short lecture and book signing circuit around Britain: London, Birmingham, Manchester and Edinburgh.

Almost immediately, we discovered professional similarities. Both of us, in fact, were considered outsiders within our own History departments; we were each more interested in everyday life than in royal houses, world wars, or turning points in ancient civilizations. Hector focused his research on homosexuality, transgender and transvestism, whereas I specialized in the history of clothing, cosmetics and hygiene. We each enjoyed a certain success writing culture and history features for mainstream magazines and suffered the wrath of jealous colleagues who wrote dry articles for pompous journals only read by a handful of PhDs. We were both invariably referred to as 'lay historians'— or worse.

On our first day in London, Hector and I signed a complimentary copy of our books for one other. Mine: *The Dark Arts: Beauty Techniques in Medieval Europe*. And his: *The Molly Houses of the 18th Century, London's First Gay Bars*. We read them while on the tour, each delighted with the clever, lighthearted style of the other. By the time we'd reached Edinburgh, mutual respect and sheer enjoyment—at the readings, restaurants, bars, and one modern-day Molly house as well—had come together to form a solid friendship. Over the years, we'd visited each other several times, both in Spain and in the States, and written each other incessant emails. Communicating in a Spanglish only comprehensible to those who had a mastery of both languages, we discussed the minutiae of our lives: we talked shop, enthusiastically outlining new projects as well as grumbling about our more conservative colleagues; chatted about books and films; gave newsy accounts of friends and family; and vented about our respective partners (a minor element in our correspondence which took on Olympic proportions during my divorce from Jeff).

After everything I'd been through these last ten days—from the breakup with Todd to Nick's goodbye hug at the airport—I regretted the fact I wouldn't be spending the summer with Hector. He had offered me the use of his flat (along with the obligations of watering his plants and taking care of Molly, his skinny housecat) while he and his longtime partner, an Irish painter named Fergal, went to Tangier for three months. It was supposed to be a romantic summer abroad with Todd—morning swims at the beach, wine-laden paella lunches, long siestas on the breezy terrace of Hector's rooftop apartment—with light rations of work added in. Now, it seemed that my article and Molly the cat would be my only summer companions.

When I stepped out of baggage claim, Hector immediately jumped up from a bench. "Rachel, darling." A few gray hairs at his temples, a new pair of glasses, and he looked the same as always. He enveloped me in a warm hug; I happily breathed in his expensive cologne. He took my bag—"Let's get out of here"— and led me out of the small airport to the line of taxis waiting outside. In the cab, I leaned my head on his shoulder.

"*Dios mio, chica.* How are you?" he asked unrhetorically, peeking down to scan my face.

"Oh, Hector. It's been so hard. At this very moment, well, I feel okay. Great to see you, of course, but—"

"When you called to say you were still coming, I couldn't believe it. That tornado was on national news here in Spain, you know. I nearly choked when I saw it."

"You have no idea. It was terrifying. During the storm, of course, but even after it was gone. Seeing everything—big, tough, *solid* things—in shambles. I don't know how to explain it. It changes your perspective. Even on the meanings of words. Take, for example, 'indestructible.' Or 'water-proof'—"

A truck whooshed by as the taxi barreled onto the six-lane highway leading into the city. I flinched and scooted away from the window. I'd forgotten about Spanish traffic. Or maybe these were lingering nerves left from the storm? Hector smiled at me and took my hand.

"I will say one thing, though," I added, wanting him to know. "It's renewed my faith in humanity. Seriously. Everyone really came together. All for one and one for all."

"I was so relieved when you told me that Nick showed up the next day. I was worried about you growing apart this year. He's such a great kid, and you've always been so close."

"I can't tell you how happy I was to see him. I guess I hadn't really realized how much I'd missed him." If I thought anymore about it, I would probably start crying. "Did I tell you that he's going to oversee the reconstruction of the house?"

"What? What is he now, about seventeen?"

"Twenty-two," I corrected. "And you know? I think he'll do a much better job than I would have. I've been useless lately."

"I'm sorry Todd didn't work out," he said gently, pushing up his glasses. "You were together nearly a year, weren't you?"

"Nearly a year," I repeated. "That doesn't sound like much, does it? I wonder why it hurts so bad."

"Oh, Rachel. It always does." He kissed my forehead, a soft peck.

Looking out the cab windows, now in the city proper, we fell into a momentary silence. Although the breakup was recent, it was already impossible to imagine Todd there alongside us. He would have hated the language barrier, relying on me to speak or pointing and gesturing to get his meaning across. A moody bastard, would he have spent the summer in a funk? Taken too much advantage of the good cheap wine? A Spanish expression popped into my head: *mejor solo que mal acompañado.* Better on your own than in bad company.

"So, tell me," Hector said, squeezing my hand to get my attention. "What will you be working on while you're here? You mentioned a piece on... What was it? Medieval bathing?"

"Ah, Work, my faithful companion." I smiled at my old friend. "Yes, I think you'll like this topic. It's steamy, with plenty of nudity and pangender contact."

"Sounds promising." He grinned.

"It deals with the influence of Muslim culture on Spanish hygiene in the Middle Ages and how long it took local ideas on bathing to change after the expulsion of the Moors and Jews. Though I'll have to come up with a snazzier title than all that."

"*Bien, bien, bien*" he murmured.

"As a focal point, I'm going to use that beautiful old *hammam* we visited the last time we were here, the Admiral's Baths?" I gestured out the window—we'd passed the old city gates, still scarred by Napoleon's cannon balls, and the streets were be-coming narrower—although I knew we were nowhere near the bathhouse.

"I remember how much Nick liked it," he said. "Though I suppose the notion of a public bath would appeal to the imagination of most teenage boys."

"There's that," I said with a smile. "But Nick's been a fan of Islamic design since Jeff and I took him to the Alhambra when he was just eight. I think he's even sneaking horseshoe arches into the drawings he's doing at school." I said that as if I knew what he was working on nowadays, as if I knew his plans for his final project. I took a deep breath, revisiting the tense, monosyl-labic conversations I'd had with him all winter. "At any rate, I'm going to research the old bathhouse and see if I can use its par-ticular history to make wider generalities."

"That's a great idea," he said. "The place is perfect. It's been around nearly the entire Christian era of Valencia."

"That's what attracted me to the idea. According to my notes, it was built in 1313 and closed for business in 1959. Imagine—cathedrals, castles, coliseums... those things were built to last, but a common bathhouse?"

Built to last. I was reminded again of all the construction in Tuscaloosa destroyed by the tornado. Was the New World more accident prone than the Old? Ill-fated, young and klutzy?

"A public bath, nearly seven hundred years old." Hector whis-tled. "If the walls could talk, you know they'd have some tales to tell."

The taxi snaked through the Barrio del Carmen which, centuries before, had been the Moorish Quarter. As we turned onto Hector's skinny street, he made a quick call to Fergal who came down to greet us on the sidewalk. We carried my bags up the four flights of stairs and went out to have an *aperitivo* on the terrace.

I sank down on a deck chair, took a sip of beer, and looked around. Spires and domes rose up through bougainvillea and hibiscus leaves while tiled rooftops, covered with lichen, could be seen below. The evening was cool; a sliver of moon shone in the light blue sky. With an exhausted smile, I raised my glass to my friends.

Three days later, Hector and Fergal set out for Tangier at day-break. We'd been having a lovely time: buying bagfuls of deli-cacies from the stalls at the Central Market; strolling down Caballeros Street, lined with palaces from centuries past; eating out at the trendy cafés in the old quarter; talking nonstop. A foolproof antidote to the anxiety and sorrow of the weeks before. But now, without them, I felt restless, uncomfortable in my skin. In the newfound silence, I pottered around their house, opening kitchen drawers filled with chic gadgets, examining the book-lined shelves, spinning a top, one of many in a lacquered bowl. Everything was clean, dusted, in its place. I couldn't help but feel a certain sadness here in this cozy flat, a couple's nest, sur-rounded by treasures that had not been wiped out by a natural disaster. From their designer armchair, I gazed up at Fergal's lat-est paintings: chiaroscuro portraits, they somehow managed to express agility, motion, humor. I stared at *Hector, laughing* until, finally, I broke into a grin.

"Jesus, I've got to get out of here."

I strapped on my sandals, packed up my laptop and went into the sunshine. Although I always got lost in the tangled streets of the Carmen, I decided against bringing a map. What was the hurry? I had the whole summer to find my way. Working on whim, I took a series of turns, past bakeries and bars, little plazas and huge converted convents, until I found a pleasant café. After ordering the *desayuno popular*—coffee, toast, and orange juice—I popped open my computer and pulled up the Admiral's Baths website.

I bookmarked it a few weeks prior—before any life-altering events—but hadn't had time to look at it carefully. I scrolled down, examining the various images of the baths through the years: there were a few nineteenth century engravings, including a very precise floor plan by a certain A. Laborde, and reproductions of delightful old postcards, sepia-toned photos, dating from the early twentieth century. At that time, the bathhouse had taken on a ritzy Arabian-Nights look, with potted palm trees, chandeliers and velvet benches. Further down, I clicked on the before and after photos of the recent restoration work: the wooden doorway, the pillars and arches, the vaulted rooftop and the star-shaped skylights.

I sat back, finishing my coffee, and stared at the last photo on the screen: eight-sided stars dug deep through the roof, their soft glow magical against the whitewash. The baths' chunky walls didn't surprise me, but the domes were also a foot thick—at least! And a foot of what, exactly? Stones and mortar? *Built to last.* I thought of my own roof. How many inches of wood and insulation had kept me safe, warm and dry? Three? Add another half-inch for the shingle?

The year before I'd done a series of altered photographs of ceilings. So evocative—our inner skies, our lids, our covers. I took photos of wooden ones with peeling paint, plaster ones with fanciful mold formations, a rundown porch ceiling with a rusted fan covered in kudzu. I had thought my own house's ceilings too humdrum for the project. And now, with their scars, branches and wildlife? I made a mental note to ask Nick to record the whole restoration process with photos. As for me, I would do a series of the baths, of those stars.

An hour later, after asking five different people how to find *los Baños del Almirante* (four, locals all, had no idea what I was even talking about), I was outside its Arabesque door. It was tucked away on a short, z-shaped street—probably the secret to its survival—on the way to nowhere. On the half-hour, a man in his mid-twenties with dark tousled hair and white eyeglasses opened the large door, let a few people out, and escorted me in for the video and museum tour.

"Shall we wait to see if anyone else is coming?" I asked, checking my watch. It was already five past.

"They can come for the next session," he said. "At eleven, we're expecting a group."

"Well, this is quite a luxury for me, having the place to myself," I said. "I've visited before, but this time, I've come to write an article about it. I'm a historian."

"Really?" He smiled. "I'm working on my doctorate in history. This tour guide thing is just temporary. At least, I hope so. But with the way the Spanish economy is going, you never know."

"Well, you don't go into History for the money, that's for sure." I smiled back, offering him my hand. "I'm Rachel, Rachel Cardon."

"Xavi Minguez," he said, shaking it. "Pleased to meet you. Let's go on in."

We stepped down into the vestibule, a large room lit from windows high above. For the first several centuries of the bathhouse's history, it had been a changing room. Nowadays tourists used the benches here to watch an explanatory video projected on the wall. To medieval music, the short film wordlessly showed two actresses—portraying a lady and her maid—going through the motions of bathing in a *hammam*: collecting buckets of water in the cold room, steaming off in the hot, relaxing in the warm room, sponging off grime, oiling and scraping the skin.

After the video, Xavi and I walked through the three rooms, the cold, warm and hot. In the first, Xavi pointed out the small patch of tiles left from the fourteenth century; the awkward slant of the floor to allow for drainage; the skylights, which, when new, had been covered with colored glass. He opened the double doors, and we stepped under the dome of the warm room. Against the walls, benches were decorated with sponges, ceramic pitchers and thin linen towels; this would have been the room for relaxing, chatting, even making business deals. In each room, small speakers sat on the floor, half-hidden by wooden buckets but still incongruent on the rustic tiles, piping out the sounds of water, the trickling and pouring of bucket-bathing.

We passed into the hot room where a smoke machine was filling the room with make-believe steam. "Nice touch," I said to Xavi, with a smile.

"Yes, but it's still too cool in here for it to have the right effect," he said. "It would have been as hot as a sauna in here, about fifty or sixty degrees Celsius. But these walls—they're about a meter thick—they keep in the chill. Without a working boiler, even in summer it's cool in here."

"I was looking at the before and after photos this morning on the internet. The restoration is first rate."

"It was complicated, due in part to the first renovation done back in the sixties." He threw the weight of sarcasm on the word 'renovation.'

We walked back into the warm room. The pillars were so homely— stone and marble assembled piecemeal, the bottom portion thinner than the top—I couldn't resist touching one, giving it a gentle stroke. Near its simple capital, I noticed a carving, softened by time but still visible in the ocher stone: **I i F**.

"What's this?"

"No one knows for sure," he answered, "but it's very old. Most agree it's as old as the pillar itself, which dates back to the baths' construction. Don't ask me how they know these things; it's something about the wear and color of the stone. It's most likely someone's initials. That little i there means 'and' in Catalan and is sometimes used to link family names. But, they have no idea whose. The original owner, back in the fourteenth century, was Pere de Vilarasa. No Is or Fs there. They think it might stand for the name of an important client, maybe put there to save his place."

"Interesting." I grazed the initials with a fingertip.

"You know, you may want to get in touch with the architect who carried out the restoration," he added. "His name is Paco Nogales. He could tell you more about the baths than anyone."

"Thanks, Xavi. I'll do that. But you haven't seen the last of me yet. In fact, I'll probably be back in a day or two to take some photos."

"I'll be here. For better or for worse," he said with a half-smile.

"By the way, are there any other carvings in the baths?"

I thought it could make an interesting aside for the article. Besides the little tag, perhaps there were some really interesting bits of graffiti that I'd missed: clever, medieval doodles, a scrawled insult, or lewd boasting in the style of Pompeii.

"No, that's the only one."

Too bad, I thought, walking out of the baths. No story there.

THE CARVING

1348

*In truth, had it been honestly
possible for me to guide you
whither by a road less rough than this be,
I would have gladly done so.*

GIOVANNI BOCCACCIO
IN HIS INTRODUCTION TO THE DECAMERON

Fatima twisted her long beige tunic behind her thighs as she hopped up on the potter's wheel. It was early April and already warm in the workshop. She wet her hands in the bucket and set the wheel in motion with her foot. Singing to herself, she centered the mound of clay, opened it and began its transformation. She brought it up into a tall vessel, then down again, broadening the mouth and folding the edges with the perfect tool between the thumb and the forefinger. After several minutes and various shapes, she took her foot off the large, lower wheel and the smaller one on top slowly came to a stop. With a cotton string, she cut a perfect urn free from the wheel.

Fatima liked being in the workshop early in the morning, just after the prayers of daybreak. Before anyone else arrived, it was hers. In an hour's time, it would be loud and hectic, with her brothers and cousins working the wheels and firing the ovens outside, her father shouting orders to the apprentices, her uncle grumbling and getting in everyone's way. It would become a noisy, manly space, where she was tolerated only because she was the daughter of the master potter, Azmet Aben Calip.

She picked up another mound of clay—Fatima had always loved the feel of it—and slapped it onto the wheel. As a small child she used to sit next to the pit of gray clay behind the workshop, making long coils, balls of different sizes, and flat discs which reflected every line in her palm. She would toss her leather slippers to the side of the pit, put her feet in the watery clay, and squeeze it hard between her toes. Giving the large wooden wheel a sweeping kick, she wondered again if her mother, who had died just few hours after she was born, would have allowed her to do such things. Her father, however, took great delight in his only daughter's love of clay, pottery, his life's work.

Azmet often joked that Fatima, his youngest child, was the finest work ever created by a Paterna potter: her skin was the lovely, sandy brown of his unvarnished work; her eyes, a surprising transparent green like the glaze he made from copper; and her lips and brows were perfect, as if he had painted them on himself. He had named her Fatima, not only for the daughter of Mohammed, but for his signature motif, the Hand of Fatima, an ancient symbol of a raised hand which he often painted on his work.

Fatima embraced the clay with one slippery hand while widening the opening with the other. She knew that, in other Muslim families, she would be expected to spend her days with the women, weaving, cooking, washing. But, since her grandmother Aisha died the previous year, she was the only woman left in the family. At seventeen, the lady of the house. Perhaps it was for this reason that her father allowed her to stay with the men, both in the workshop and at home. Or maybe it was because he enjoyed having his favorite by his side. Whichever it was, the privilege earned her disapproving remarks from Muzaffar, her father's younger brother, and raised eyebrows from others in the Muslim community.

She was playing with the clay, up and down, when she heard someone come through the door. It was the new apprentice, a lanky boy with enormous dark eyes, bringing fresh buckets in from the pit. When he caught sight of her, bent over the wheel with her calves exposed, her long fingers dripping with water and her mouth open in song, he dropped both buckets, spilling the sludgy clay.

"Oh," he murmured in a tongue-tied blush.

She jiggled her legs to let her tunic fall to the floor as she stopped the wheel. "Good morning," she said, with a nod. "I didn't mean to startle you. You must be the new boy."

"Yes, I'm Azan," he replied shyly. He was unable to look at Fatima directly but couldn't resist stealing glances. "I just… I've never seen a woman at the wheel."

"I'm Azmet's daughter Fatima. It's true that, as a general rule, women aren't permitted to make pots. But I've been working clay since I was a child and now"—she paused to wet her hands—"there is much to be done."

She put her hands on the clay—which she'd left in a nondescript cylinder—and quickly turned it into an elegant rounded bowl.

"It's beautiful," he blurted out.

"Oh, it's nothing," she said. She dried her hands on a rag before lifting it off with a delicate touch.

Azan was staring at her, his feet in a puddle of gray mud.

"You might want to clean that up." She smiled.

The master potters of Paterna had made names for themselves all over the Mediterranean and that of Azmet Aben Calip was the most renowned. He and the other potters belonged to a community of Mudejares, which in Arabic meant "those allowed to stay." Christian forces had defeated the Muslims over a century before, ending the five-hundred years of Islamic domination in that region of Spain. After their victory, they expelled most of the Muslims and the city was repopulated with the families of the knights and soldiers who had conquered the land. However, almost all of the potting families in Paterna, a village two leagues north of the walls of Valencia, stayed. Their work was valued and they were protected by the king.

Some of these potters made functional, uncelebrated pieces with scarcely any decoration: cooking pots and enormous storage vessels for oil and grain, or roofing tiles, water pipes, and gutters. With all the relocating and construction taking place in Valencia, these were necessary, practical pieces in high demand. Azmet and his family concentrated their efforts on finer work, painted with care. They used glazes of green, cobalt blue, and the most spectacular of all, the golden glaze, made from copper and silver.

This work was then shipped to France, Italy and Northern Africa and had become fashionable with the nobility. In fact, Azmet had recently received a surprising commission. The Pope, Clement VI, had ordered a sumptuous set of dishes to celebrate the renovation of the Papal Palace in Avignon. Azmet thought it a glorious irony to work for the Pope, who paid exceptionally well.

Fatima was still at the wheel a few minutes later—straw now on the floor, buckets refilled, and the new apprentice nowhere to be seen—when Miriam walked into the workshop. She was the midwife of the community and had been present when Fatima was born. Although she was known for her great knowledge of medicine, she had been unable to save neither Fatima's mother nor her aunt from the dangers of childbirth. She had been a close friend of her grandmother Aisha, who used to shake her head in wonder at Miriam's youthful appearance. Although she was well over fifty, her hair was still dark, and her body, slim.

"Good morning, Fatima," Miriam called out with a smile. "Are you working for the Pope this morning?"

"Miriam!" Fatima stepped down from the wheel to greet her, quickly wiping her hands; since her grandmother's death, she had seen her only rarely. "You've heard about the papal commission?"

"The whole community is talking about it. A curious honor for a follower of Allah, wouldn't you say?" She raised her brow in a playful way, her dark eyes shining.

"Perhaps it is." Fatima couldn't resist Miriam's smile. "Though they say that Clement VI is more Prince than Pope, famous for his extravagant banquets where beautiful women are always welcome. Which is why, I suppose, we are all working so hard." She drew back a linen cloth from the side table to show Miriam the finished wares. "I'm mostly doing the painting."

For the Pope's table, each piece was to be different, decorated with the traditional motifs of Moorish potters: the Tree of Life, flowers and fruit, stylized animals, arabesque lettering. Fatima was by far the best painter in the family and, in her hand, these symbols and designs became elaborate artistic creations.

"It's beautiful," Miriam murmured, picking up a plate with a racing hare. "Worthy of any palace. Your work always is." She said it without flattery. "I was wondering, though, do you have time to throw some jars for me? This summer I hope to widen my store of roots and herbs."

"It would be my pleasure," Fatima said, with a respectful nod. "Although it seems unlikely that you could add anything else to your collection." Going to Miriam's house with her grandmother as a girl, she was always intrigued by the rows of pots filled with dried leaves, tubers and bulbs, balms, elixirs, unrecognizable things. "What remedies could you possibly not have?"

"Well, several, it seems. Yesterday I talked to some Valencian healers who were passing through. They spoke of medicines that were new to me." Miriam's voice became serious. "They also told me about a strange sickness out on the islands, killing people by the score. They say it's caused by a poisonous cloud out at sea."

Fatima shivered in spite of the warmth in the room. "Let's hope it stays out on the water."

"I'm sure it will," Miriam said reassuringly, then brightened, changing the subject. "Tell me, what will your family be doing tonight for Muharram?"

It was the celebration of the Muslim New Year.

"We will have the family feast, as we usually do. But this year, without grandmother here..." Fatima bit her lip. "I've been thinking about her ever since I got up this morning."

Since her grandmother's death, Fatima had often felt lost. Grandmother Aisha was the only woman in her life, caring for her from the time she was born, both mother and friend. She was patient and loving, with a quick smile that was charming in spite of missing teeth. It was her grandmother who taught her to play the psaltery and sing the old songs of the poets of Islamic Spain; it was Aisha who comforted her when her monthly cycle began and explained to her the mysteries of being a woman; it was she who had shown her how to make the dishes for feast days. This year, Fatima was responsible for the family meal and the idea was making her feel even lonelier.

"I miss her too," Miriam said softly, taking Fatima's hand.

They smiled sadly at one another before Miriam made to leave.

"Well, we both have much to do. Make me the jars when you can spare a moment from His Sanctity," she said with a laugh. "Oh, and use the green glaze—it reminds me of you."

When she was alone again, Fatima went over to the shelf where she had hidden a small piece she'd been working on, a gift for her father to celebrate the New Year. Azmet was extremely fond of the game of chess and had made himself an extraordinary chess set several years before. The squares of the board were green and white, and the chess pieces were all stylized men with turbans and mustaches. He often spent the evening hours in their court-yard playing long games with old friends, other Mudejar potters, some of whom his children called uncle. Occasionally he played with their real uncle, although Muzaffar took the game far too seriously. A month before, in his frustration, Muzaffar broke one of the pieces, the *alferza,* the councilor, who stood at the green king's side.

Fatima had made her father a new chess piece, but not mere-ly a replacement; instead of another councilor, she'd fashioned the green king a queen. She knew that her uncle would be scan-dalized to see the figure of a woman on a chessboard, but she thought her father would approve. Looking at the beautiful face painted on the small figure, Fatima was sure that this queen would give the green side an exceptional advantage.

After wiping the piece clean of dust, she wrapped it in a strip of silk and put it in her bag. She looked out the window; the men would be filling the workshop at any moment. Today, however, she was to spend the day cooking, helping the servants with her grandmother's recipes.

Singing softly—*Three Moorish maids, such beauties they, went to pick olives one by one...*—she followed the quiet dirt path home. Entering the courtyard, she breathed deeply; the jasmine vines were in full bloom, a striking contrast to the smell of the dusty street scattered with dung. The large patio, which was both garden and room, was the center of their home; all the rooms of the house opened onto it and, in the middle, a twisted old olive tree grew. At the well, she could see Zaida and Kadiga, the two sisters who worked as their servant girls. They were ten and thirteen, the daughters of a widowed neighbor.

"Come, girls," she called them. "We have a busy day ahead."

Zaida had just scrubbed the tile floor of the courtyard and the three of them sat crossed-legged, surrounded by baskets and large clay platters. Zaida ground lamb for meatballs, which would later be grilled on embers, while Kadiga patted dough into flat loaves, which would be cooked in the small adobe oven in the corner of the patio. The sisters settled down to their tasks and began to gossip.

"Have you seen the new apprentice?" Kadiga asked her sister. "He's good-looking."

"I met him this morning," Zaida replied. "Azan's his name. He's from Valencia."

"How old do you think he is?" asked the little sister.

"I don't know," Zaida said. "He might be sixteen."

"A good age to marry—maybe he's the one for you." Kadiga teased Zaida, who made a slight effort to feign annoyance, but giggled in spite of herself.

Fatima, mildly envious of the companionship the sisters shared, tried to ignore the girls' chatter. Humming to herself, she started making *alcorza*, her father's favorite dessert. She pitted a pile of dates, mashed them in the stone mortar, then added chopped walnuts, almonds and honey. As she was pressing the sticky mixture into little tortes, her father walked into the house.

"We'll eat well tonight, I see," said Azmet.

"Oh, Father, I don't know. I'm afraid the dishes won't taste the same without grandmother here."

"Your labor always bears good fruit, Fatima. Look at those tortes—you've made such charming shapes. Crescents? Your grandmother never did such things."

As usual, her father's kind words put Fatima's mind to rest.

As the sun went down, the family gathered in the courtyard to perform their ablution and the prayers of sunset. When they finished this ritual, Fatima, in her grandmother's place, formally motioned to Zaida and Kadiga to bring the trays to where the men sat on cushions. Azmet presided over the meal, which he shared with his sons, Mahomet and Aben, his brother Muzaffar, and his three young nephews. Azan, the new apprentice was also there, sitting against the wall, waiting his turn.

He had arrived from the Moorish Quarter of Valencia two days before, and was now sleeping on a pallet in the workshop while learning the new trade. Azmet had invited the boy to join in on the family festivities but Azan did not want to appear too bold and had not yet approached their circle. The aroma of the fresh roasted lamb, however, was making his mouth water.

With an effort at ceremony, the young servants brought out the food, all arranged on the finest ceramics of a master potter. Bowls filled with olives, goat cheese, almonds and cucumber were followed by large platters of lamb, meatballs and grilled vegetables. Afterwards, they brought the stews over, aromatic dishes of rabbit, spinach and chickpeas, and the cloths containing warm bread. The men immediately began to eat, taking the food gracefully with their fingertips.

"What a wonderful feast, Fatima," her father called out.

"Yes, you've pulled it off." Her older brother Mahomet laughed.

Conversation came to a lull as they ate. Kadiga and Zaida brought out jugs of wine and water flavored with pomegranate seeds and, although they tried to remain serious as they poured the wine into earthenware goblets, the sisters couldn't resist peeking over at Azan in his place near the jasmine vines. Azmet, curious as to the cause of the girls' attentions, saw his young apprentice by the wall and invited him to join them. There was still plenty left and none would go to waste.

Now almost dark, Kadiga went round, lighting oil lamps and clay lanterns, which cast whimsical shadows around the patio. The stars were slowly emerging overhead, and the air was becoming cooler.

Fatima wiped her hands after eating—her appetite had been scant—and brought out the psaltery. She placed it on her lap, and slowly began to pluck the strings. She sang:

Come, whoever you may be
Think upon it until you see
What I intend and what I feel
And thus you will understand me

Together with the moon and sun
Seven the stars which turn above
And there my own nocturnal star
Revolving with them in the sky...

All of a sudden she could not continue; a lump had formed in her throat. Singing the old song made her even more aware of her grandmother's absence. With tears in her eyes, she managed to continue plucking the strings, keeping the melody. The others, who were now engaged in business talk, discussing the papal commission, did not notice. Only her father looked over, worried, curious; she sadly mouthed the word "Aisha."

Her father rose, patted his daughter's head, and called to Zaida to bring out the desserts.

"Come, Fatima, put down the psaltery," Azmet said with a smile. "I want to try your *alcorza*. I've been thinking about it all afternoon."

Zaida offered date tortes and quince turnovers to the men as her sister refilled their wine glasses.

"Look, Fatima's made the tortes into moons," said Tariq, her youngest cousin, who was only eight.

"It isn't enough for you to make shapes with clay—you must do it with our food as well." Aben teased her. Understanding this to be a brotherly compliment, she grinned back at him.

After having eaten one last torte, Azmet gave Fatima a small bundle. "A token for you, my daughter, to celebrate the New Year and to wish you good fortune."

Fatima took the gift with care, and slowly unwrapped the cloth. It was a beautifully sculpted ceramic horse painted with the golden glaze.

"Oh, it's perfect," she began, but her brother Aben broke in.

"Father!" he exclaimed with a laugh. "Fatima doesn't need a toy, she needs a husband!"

"It's true," added Mahomet, almost serious. "She isn't a child anymore. She's almost eighteen. She should have her own child by now."

"Yes, yes, I know that your sister is now a woman. Her beauty as well as her painting skills have brought her many offers from the young potters of Paterna. But I have decided to keep her with me for another year."

He looked over at Fatima, who smiled at him. She had no desire to leave her father's house, to become part of a new, unknown family. A husband would surely not permit her to work with clay or even to sit in the company of men (would that include her brothers?). She knew that she held a unique position in her all-male family which others in the Muslim community—especially the women—viewed as overindulged.

"Perhaps I will marry you two off first," Azmet joked. His sons laughingly protested, but fell quiet as their father held up his hand. "But for now, I have a different task for you. You two are no longer children either, and I have decided to let you accompany the papal commission to the port of Valencia."

Mahomet and Aben looked at each other in surprise. For years they had been asking their father to let them go to the city, to the port, to be responsible for taking the wares to the merchants and receiving their payments. Between themselves, they often spoke of their desire to leave the dirty clay to the apprentices and to become tradesmen.

"Thank you, Father."

"We're ready for this, you'll see."

"The shipment should be ready in a month's time. You will take it by mule cart to the port, where you will meet the representative from Avignon. He will pay you partially in silver but also in Flemish cloth. Which reminds me, my young merchants will need new robes. Tomorrow, we will buy some fine cloth."

By the time Zaida and Kadiga cleared the last dishes away and left for their own home, the family had fallen into a comfortable silence. Fatima was playing a quiet tune on the psaltery while the others reclined on cushions, looking at the stars, exchanging a few words, taking another sip of wine. She looked affectionately at the men in her family: her older brothers, tall and handsome, ready to be independent; her father, his graying beard, the warmth in his eyes, content to let his daughter remain a child. Her eyes fell on the lovely golden horse he had crafted to surprise her. Finally, she was ready to give him her gift. She put down her instrument and went to her room to get it.

"Father, I've also made something for you. To celebrate the New Year."

He took the figure in both hands and removed the silk. "Fatima, she is exquisite."

"Do you know what she is? What she's for?"

"Tell me, my daughter."

"She's to take the place of the broken councilor in your chess set. She is the green king's queen. I think she'll bring you luck."

Azmet threw back his head and laughed.

"Poor Muzaffar! You'll have difficulty beating me now." He showed his brother the piece. "My king has this wise woman to give him advice on where to go and what to do."

But Muzaffar was not amused.

"This is absurd! A woman on a field of battle?" He shook his head. "Surely you do not intend to use this piece."

Azmet's smile faded. "Of course I do. It's a splendid gift and I'll use it with pride."

"I don't understand how you coddle this daughter of yours," his brother continued. "She does what she pleases in this house. She is always here, in the presence of men. It was one thing when she was a child, chasing after her brothers as if she were a boy. But now that she's grown..."

Muzaffar looked over at Fatima, his eyes traveling all over her body, coming to rest on her breasts. With a sudden jerk, his gaze shifted back to his brother, who was eyeing him warily.

"You let her throw pots of all things," he continued. "Not a seemly task for a woman."

"My brother, you know yourself that Fatima is a very skilled potter. Better than many men I know," he added, looking at his brother in a way that made his meaning clear.

"That's not the point!" he shouted, his face red with anger. "I have seen her in the workshop, her legs bare under the wheel, singing to the clay as if it were a lover—it's disgusting."

Fatima quickly looked down. Her face burning with shame, she picked up the psaltery and held it against her body, wishing again that her grandmother were there. Her brothers and cousins looked from Muzaffar to Azmet and back again, shocked, not daring to enter into the argument themselves. As for Azan, he tried to make himself invisible, knowing that he should not have been privy to a family dispute. However, he had seen Fatima at the wheel just that morning, and far from disgusting, he'd found her admirable, flawless. He would have loved to have been her champion, but knew that would not only be inappropriate, but ridiculous.

Azmet looked at his brother for a long moment of self-contained rage. Finally, a long sigh softened his face.

"You are not used to drinking wine, little brother. It does not become you. I must ask you to leave now and to go to bed. In the morning you can make amends to my daughter and myself."

With these words, the feast ended. Muzaffar and his sons silently walked out of the courtyard, to their own home, next door. Azan slipped out the door as well, hoping he had been forgotten, and made his way back to the workshop.

"Boys, you go on to bed," Azmet said wearily. "I'd like to talk to Fatima alone."

She looked at her father, waiting for him to speak. He picked up the jug to pour out the last of the wine, but found it empty. He put it down and wiped his eyes.

"We both know that Muzaffar is a fool," he said finally. "He inherited none of Aisha's courage or wisdom. But, he is not the only one in the community who thinks it wrong that I let you work the wheel. It's true, Fatima, it's a man's job."

"Father, it was you who taught me. I learned together with Mahomet and Aben. And, well, wouldn't you agree I'm as good as they are?"

Azmet chuckled sadly. "We both know you are far better than either one of them. But, from now on, I'd like you to limit your activities to painting. And perhaps you could work here in the patio? The workshop is always filled with men. Really, it's not a suitable place for a young woman."

Fatima nodded her head. She was upset by his words but knew she could not contest them. She was not really angry with her father—she understood that he had disregarded tradition for years, letting her work alongside her brothers—but she was disappointed.

"Father, I'm tired now. If there's nothing else?"

"Of course, my daughter," he smiled at her fondly. "Get to bed. And truly, the feast was wonderful. Your grandmother would have been so proud."

When Fatima was alone, lying on her straw mattress, she began to cry. Even at Aisha's side, she had never enjoyed the women's duties; she'd always been happiest when working with her brothers. Perhaps with time, after the argument with Muzaffar had been forgotten, he would let her back into the workshop? Surely, this wouldn't last forever.

The next day Muzaffar made formal apologizes to Azmet, the patriarch of the family. However, the brothers, having never been close, now had no desire to spend time with one another. And playing chess together was simply out of the question.

The most elaborate commission ever made by the workshop of Azmet Aben Calip, tableware for a party of fifty, crafted and painted for the Pope himself, was finally finished. They carefully wrapped the pieces in linen, packed them into large clay vessels, and arranged them on the mule cart. Mahomet and Aben, elegant in their new tunics, were setting off after dawn prayers. Nasir, their father's journeyman, was to accompany them. He had worked with the family for years and was appreciated for his loyalty and his strength. Big and burly, he was known locally for winning the wrestling competitions during town festivals. It was thought that if they met up with thieves along the road, with Nasir's help, they would be able to defend their expensive cargo.

"Now, you won't forget anything I told you last night, will you?" their father asked nervously. "About making contact with don Martín? And how to avoid being swindled?"

His three children all exchanged a look and smiled. The night before, their father had once again repeated his instructions and advice—on travel, negotiation, life at port—using the same words as the day before, and the day before that.

"Yes, Father, we'll remember," Mahomet said.

Both he and his brother were trying to downplay their excitement as they casually tied long pieces of linen into loose turbans, letting the ends fall onto their shoulders. Their hands seemed controlled, but their feet were nearly dancing.

"We should be getting on the road," Nasir called from the cart.

"Here, knowing your appetites, I made you this." Fatima handed Aben a large canvas bag, filled with boiled eggs, cheese, apples, figs and several discs of bread, which she had made before daybreak.

"Thanks, little sister." He grinned, already ripping off a piece of bread and stuffing it into his mouth.

"That's for later, you goose! You've just had your breakfast," she scolded him with a smile.

After Fatima and their father gave Mahomet and Aben warm hugs, they jumped onto the cart and waved. "Farewell!"

"Salaam! Let Allah protect you! Have a good journey!"

Azmet came over and put his arm around the shoulders of his youngest as they watched the mules begin the difficult, uneven walk to sea. Fatima looked up at her father's face and saw pride blend with worry.

Now that the important commission had been finished, activity at the workshop went into a lull. With her brothers and Nasir gone and her uncle keeping to his own house, the shop was nearly empty; only the young apprentices were there, practicing throwing and firing under Azmet's expert tutelage.

A few days after her brothers had left, Fatima came into the workshop and found her father there alone at the wheel, throwing a pot for his own pleasure.

"Father," Fatima began slowly. "I'd almost forgotten. A few weeks back Miriam came into the shop and asked me to make her some jars. I promised her that I would. She was such a dear friend to grandmother. Could I please make them?"

She looked at her father—her lips clamped with hope, her eyes pleading—until he began to laugh.

"Ah, Fatima," he said, shaking his head. "You love this old mud as much as I do. Yes, you may fulfill your promise to Miriam and make her pots. But, any future work must be discussed between us beforehand, do you hear?"

"Yes, of course," she said, grinning at the idea of future work. "Thank you, father."

She dug her hands into the clay and squeezed it hard like she had as a child. She'd missed it; it was a part of her. She kneaded it carefully then formed a dozen squat pyramids. She sat at the wheel, determined to be more modest since the rift-causing argument at New Year. She kept her tunic hanging down to her feet but couldn't stop herself from humming.

After a half-hour or so her father approached her. He eyed her work. Fatima had already made four tall jars, perfectly uniform. No small task.

"Nice work, my child," Azmet smiled admiringly. He pulled out a cloth and wiped his brow. "It's hot in here, isn't it?"

"Oh, not too bad for May," she replied.

"I've had enough of mud for one day," he said. "I'm going over to see Malik."

"Give my love to him and his family," she replied, her eyes fixed on the clay. "I'm sure they miss Nasir as we do Mahomet and Aben."

As he walked out, Azan walked in with the other apprentices. Fatima had not seen him since the feast, when he'd sat near the olive tree, stuffing himself with meatballs.

"The ovens are hot," said Hassan, the oldest of her father's apprentices. "Which pieces need to be fired this morning?"

She pointed her chin towards a shelf full of bowls and jugs; the boys loaded the pieces onto a board to take outside to the large adobe oven next to the clay pit. Azan, a large amphora in his hands, paused in front of her, staring at the motion of her wet hands on the clay.

She looked up at him, surprised by his attention. When he caught sight of her light green eyes looking into his, he began to stammer.

"Oh, sorry! I don't mean to bother you. It's just, your work, it's so, so good."

As he spoke, his hands spun nervously like a wheel, then mimicked hers, lifting the clay into jars.

Fatima laughed; she liked the way he talked with his hands. Although she was used to the apprentices peeking over at her, whispering about her amongst themselves, this one was different, timid and humble. She also felt sorry for him, sleeping in the dusty workshop, far from his family.

"I understand you're from Valencia, Azan," she said. "How do you like living here in Paterna?"

He gave her an awkward smile, made a few noncommittal gestures, said "yes" several times, and walked out the door.

The next day, Fatima sat at the wheel next to Azan and offered him advice to improve his technique. As they worked the clay, side by side, they slowly began to talk and, once he got over his shyness, Fatima found that she enjoyed his conversation.

"In Valencia, we are more than twenty living together in the family house. It's large, of course, with many rooms built one on top of the other, at every possible angle." He took his hands off the clay to make a collection of crooked boxes in the air. "And the noise! There's always someone shouting, a baby crying, roosters crowing. There's never silence." Azan smiled at Fatima, then looked at her with curiosity. "The quiet here in the village has been hard for me to get used to. And I've never seen a family as small as yours. And you, the only woman? It's very strange to me."

"Most families in Paterna are like yours, large, with grand-parents caring for babies, everyone living together. We have not been so lucky. My mother died when I was born, then we lost my aunt when she had my little cousin Tariq. It was my grandmother who raised me, and now she's gone too."

Their conversation stalled for a few minutes. Fatima could have added that her father had never wanted to remarry, his broken heart rendering him impractical; or that her uncle had not been able to find another woman in their small community gullible enough to be coaxed into his arms. Love and marriage were certainly not topics to be broached with a boy, an outsider at that.

After a moment, Azan began telling her about the Moorish Quarter in Valencia: its twisted streets and gardens, the mosque where the men gathered, the busy souk, the public baths. He described the different jobs of his neighbors, the smiths, the knife-makers, the tanners, and, his father's profession, the glass-blower. Fatima watched his hands, making coarse, brusque movements to depict the men who worked with hides, and thin, delicate ones for those who made glass, and wondered if it were possible for a tanner to have long, fine fingers like Azan.

"Didn't you want to be a glass blower?" she asked.

"I'm the third son, Fatima. My parents thought I should learn a different trade. They were so pleased when it was decided I would be an apprentice for Azmet Aben Calip."

Fatima smiled, looking down at wheel. She didn't want Azan to see the pride in her face.

A week later, Fatima finished Miriam's jars. A set of twelve with well-fitting lids, each one painted with a fanciful animal— a smiling dragon, a sea snake, a cat with wings. That way, the mid-wife could distinguish between them. Fatima no longer had an excuse to be in the workshop.

That afternoon she climbed up into the adobe dovecot on the hill and looked out. She searched the path to Valencia, past the subtle waves of the wheat fields and the vineyards' straight rows, hoping to see her brothers return. She picked up a plump pigeon and stroked it as she looked towards the sea. There were several people walking, others with carts or donkeys, but it would be three more days until Mahomet and Aben came home.

When her older brother walked in the door, dirty and exhausted, Fatima ran out to welcome him.

"Look!" She grinned. "It's the triumphant return of our world-renowned merchant."

"Hello, Fatima," Mahomet said with a brief smile that was far from enthusiastic. "Where's father?"

"I'm right here," Azmet called as he rushed into the courtyard to greet his son. When he saw the serious look on Mahomet's face, he became worried. "What's wrong? Did you have trouble at port? Was don Martín not there?"

"He was there, Father," Mahomet said. "He praised the work and paid us as agreed. Here is the silver." He handed him a heavy leather pouch. "Aben is bringing in the cloth, which is fine indeed."

"Did you stay to make sure the cargo was loaded?" Azmet asked, still trying to discern the problem.

"Yes, Father," he continued patiently. "We watched them put it on a skiff and take it out to a large galley ship in the harbor. We even waited on the pier until they set sail for Marseilles."

As Azmet breathed a sigh of satisfaction, Aben walked into the patio, carrying several bolts of cloth, shiny red, yellow and blue.

"Has Mahomet told you the news?" he asked. Aben was wearing the same expression of anxious concern as his brother.

Azmet looked at both his sons in confusion.

"It's Nasir," Aben said. "He got sick in Valencia. When we took him home just now he couldn't even walk. Mahomet, Malik and I had to carry him inside."

Fatima covered her gasp with her hands. She couldn't imagine the strongest boy in the village too weak to walk.

"He fell ill a few days ago—headaches and nausea—and we didn't think it was serious. But on the journey home, he was miserable." Mahomet shook his head. "We made a bed for him in the back of the cart, padding the wooden slats with the Flemish cloth." He shrugged. "I'm sorry, Father, but we had no choice. He was wrapped in his blanket, huddled up in a ball, burning hot and trembling at the same time. We stopped in Campanar to sleep and a kind woman gave us bread and soup. But Nasir couldn't eat—he could barely lift his head."

"When we got up this morning—it was long before daybreak; none of us could sleep—that's when we saw his neck. During the night, a big bubble had grown there," Aben said, touching his own throat. He paused a moment, then looked up at his father. "I don't know if he's going to make it."

Azmet had been listening to his sons wordlessly, taking in the news. "I can't believe it," he now cried. "You weren't gone ten days. And now Nasir is diseased? And you think he's dying?" He looked from one son to the other; they could barely return his gaze. "I will go see him myself," he muttered as he left the courtyard.

Left alone with her brothers, she gave them hugs. "I'm sorry about Nasir, but it's good to have you two home. Are you hungry? Can I get you something?"

"No," they said as they slumped down on the patio floor. "We feel terrible, like it's our fault."

"That's impossible," Fatima said.

"I don't know," said Mahomet. "You see, the French galley ship wasn't at port when we arrived and we had to wait a few days. At night, Aben and I had a room in an inn—"

"It was so dirty—and smelled of Christian tradesmen." Aben wrinkled his nose.

"But not Nasir. We asked him to sleep under the cart to protect the wares from thieves. He complained. It was chilly and damp."

"Almost every night he was woken up by rats, scurrying about and sniffing his body."

"That must have been horrible," she agreed. "So, you think he got an illness from sleeping on the wet ground? I suppose it's possible." Something Miriam had told her was nagging at her, trying to resurface. "Tell me, what did you do during the day?"

"The days were long, but interesting enough," Mahomet said with a shrug. "We saw sailors and tradesmen from every seaport imaginable. We watched rich Venetians bargaining their cotton for olive oil, Catalan sailors packing up sacks of raisins, bound for Tunisia—"

"And slave merchants," said Aben. "The slaves had the saddest eyes you've ever seen."

"One day, we left the village and went to the beach," Mahomet said. "We took off our slippers and walked on the sand, letting the waves wash our feet—"

"That's it," Fatima said, finally remembering. "Miriam told me that there's a new sickness which comes from a poisonous sea cloud. Lots of people are dying on the islands."

"There was no cloud there, little sister," Aben said, shaking his head. "The sky was bright, sunny, blue. And the smell"—he closed his eyes and breathed in—"was fresh and pure. Really, not sickly at all."

"Well, I think I'll have a talk with Miriam and ask her what she knows. I'll go by her house tomorrow. I need to deliver her jars anyway."

At that moment Azmet came back into the courtyard, shaken and pale.

"Nasir's dead," he said.

His three children jumped to their feet, then waited motionless, expecting their father to continue, to give them information or instructions. But their father just stood there, bewildered.

"Should we go pay our respects, Father?" Mahomet finally asked.

"No," he said, his eyes cast down, his voice tired and old. "His mother's grief is too great. Wait until tomorrow." He looked up at his sons and nodded at them with a grim smile. "You did well, very well. And I imagine that now you two need some rest. I'm all too familiar with that dry, bumpy path to port. Go lie down. You'll feel better when you get up." With those words, their father retired to his own quarters and lay down himself.

That evening, rested and comfortable after supper, in their own home, in the company of their father and sister, Mahomet and Aben suddenly realized that they too felt unwell.

When Fatima went to her brothers' room to rouse them for morning prayers, she found them both sound asleep.

"Wake up, you two. It's daybreak," she called; but they didn't respond.

She went to Mahomet's side to give him a nudge, but quickly drew back. He was lying face down and a putrid smell was coming from his body. She hesitantly touched his arm; it was overly warm. She turned to Aben, who was sleeping on his back. She gently stroked his forehead. It too felt feverish.

"Mahomet, Aben" she said softly. "Hey, it's already morning."

Aben's eyelids fluttered then finally opened. She sat beside him and took his hand. Despite the fetid odor, she managed a smile.

"Fatima," he said slowly. "I feel terrible." He shifted on the mattress and winced. "It hurts to move. And my head is pounding."

Mahomet rolled onto his side and looked at them; there was fear in his eyes.

"Me too," he said nervously, reaching up to feel his smooth neck. "Aben, do you think it's the illness that killed Nasir?"

"I'm going to Miriam's," Fatima said, her voice flat. "She'll know what to do. I'm sure of it."

"I hope so," Mahomet looked up at her. "We saw Nasir change in just a few days. The fever ate him away."

In an attempt to make her brothers more comfortable, Fatima rounded up all of the cushions and blankets from around the house. She padded and tucked them in as best she could. She was about to leave when she noticed tears on her younger brother's cheeks.

"I'm afraid," Aben said, knowing they would not mock him.

Fatima wrapped the herb jars in cloth and packed them into the large hemp bags tied to the flanks of the mule. On her way to Miriam's house, which was slightly outside the village, she couldn't stop thinking of her brothers. She had seen them several times with flu or fever, but it was never like this.

When she led the mule into the midwife's courtyard, she found Miriam hanging laurel leaves to dry. Her long, dark braid divided her narrow back in two.

"Hello there, Fatima." Miriam turned with a smile, and gave the mule's muzzle a friendly pat. "Are you done with my jars?"

"Yes, I've got them here."

She carefully unpacked her wares, setting them on a nearby bench. Miriam looked at each jar with delight.

"Oh, I love the minotaur. And this dragon? It looks too sweet to be dangerous." Laughing, she handed Fatima two silver coins.

"I'm glad you like them," Fatima said. "But really, I've come for your help."

"What's the matter?" she asked, putting the jar down to give Fatima her full attention.

"My father's journeyman, Nasir. He died yesterday."

"Malik's son? The wrestler?" Miriam asked, surprised. "Did he have an accident?"

"No, it was a strange illness. He went to port with my brothers and, after a few days sleeping on the ground, he complained of headache and fever. They said that, by yesterday morning, a ball had grown on his neck. He was dead in a matter of days." Looking hopefully into Miriam's eyes, trusting her ability to heal, Fatima said, "Now my brothers have the same fever."

"You say that they have been to port? They must have breathed in the poison of the miasma."

"I remember you mentioning it when you came by the workshop. But Mahomet and Aben told me they didn't see any clouds there. They said the coast was beautiful, purifying even."

"Well, you wouldn't expect to *see* such a cloud, would you?" Miriam retorted, as if her knowledge was being questioned.

"How do you cure it?" Fatima asked.

"Once the corruption enters the body it is very difficult to remove."

"What are you saying? That there's nothing I can do? Miriam, they're in pain." Fatima's voice, about to break, grew soft. "Isn't there anything that will make my brothers well?"

The midwife paused a moment, looking around the courtyard, trying to think of practical solutions. When she finally spoke, her words were solid.

"Your brothers will have great thirst with the fever, so give them plenty of water. Good smells will help... burn rosemary in the rooms. To drive the poison away, you must cleanse the house. I think this is the most important thing. Wash the floor down with vinegar and throw juniper on the fire. Keep their bodies as clean as you can."

She thanked the midwife and was leaving when Miriam called out after her.

"Fatima! After you tend to them, don't forget to cleanse yourself."

Eager to begin these chores, she headed quickly back. After returning the mule to the pen, she ran to the house.

"Zaida, Kadiga!" she called, her eyes scanning the empty patio. She went from room to room, but found her brothers home alone, shivering in their beds.

"Brothers," Fatima whispered to them, trying to get their attention but not react to the foul odor in the room. "I've talked to Miriam and she's told me what to do to cure you. Have you see Zaida or Kadiga? I need their help."

They shook their heads, too weary to speak. She felt their hot brows and fetched them some water from the well. With a promise to return promptly, she ran up to the workshop, to see if the maids were there on an errand for her father. As she entered the shop, Fatima was surprised to see Azan by himself, idly modeling some clay.

"You're here alone? Where is everyone?"

Ill at ease, Azan looked up at Fatima; his fingers, like spiders, were weaving the clay into useless strands.

"Hassan and the other apprentices have left and, well," he said slowly, his sheepish face going red, "they say they're not coming back."

"What? Why?" Fatima stared at Azan. On top of everything else, there were problems at the workshop?

"They say that Allah is displeased with this house. That it's cursed."

"What do you mean?" Fatima was incredulous. "We're good Muslims here. How can they say that?"

"I heard them talking." Azan's words were gathering speed and the rest came tumbling out. "They blame your father for Nasir's death. They say it was caused by his pride and ambition. That, working for the Pope, he sold his faith for silver. They say that's why Nasir died and why your brothers are sick. They're afraid of Allah's anger and will not come back to this house."

"That is ridiculous!" Fatima cried. "The midwife told me that, at the port, they were poisoned by the sea. It's not the vengeance of Allah, it's poison."

"I'm sorry, Fatima." Azan balled the thin coils into a lump and put it on the table. "I'm just telling you what they said."

"And Zaida and Kadiga?" Fatima did not look hopeful.

"The same. They all left this morning while you were out."

"This is terrible. Father will be devastated. Has he heard?"

"I don't know. I haven't been to your house. I didn't know what to tell him."

"Neither do I." Fatima hesitated for a moment, then became decisive. "Listen, there is much to be done. I have to clean the house, to drive out the poison. Azan, please, will you help me?"

"Of course, I will. I'll do whatever I can."

Azan rose from his stool and Fatima gave him a grateful smile. "Let's hurry then."

Fatima and Azan carried out the midwife's instructions and soon the house filled with the smells of vinegar, herbs and burning wood. It was now time to cleanse her brothers' bodies.

She heated a bucket of water and put a thin gauze veil over her nose and mouth to avoid breathing in their smell too deeply. Nervous, she walked back into their room. She had never touched their bodies before nor had seen them without clothes; it was their grandmother who had always taken care of them when they were ill. She was somewhat relieved to find both brothers deep in a feverish sleep.

She sat down next to Aben and dunked a clean rag in the water. She began washing the parts of his body that she knew: his hands, face, arms. This made him stir, peek at her through heavy lids, and nod off again. Mastering her embarrassment, she opened his tunic. When Fatima found he was too exhausted to wake—there was no modesty, no joking words; he did not protest or tease her—she knew he was seriously ill. As she cleaned his broad chest, she found welts in his armpits, boils the size of eggs. She lightly ran her fingers over them, making him recoil in pain. Alarmed, she got up and went to the door.

"Azan," she called.

When he came in from the patio, she showed him the boils.

"This must be like the bubble Nasir had on his neck," she said. "Could you go to Miriam? Ask her what to do about them. Tell her that they hurt."

While Azan was away, she continued washing Aben, grateful his eyes remained closed. Not only would she feel uncomfortable with him watching her touch his discolored skin—his belly, his groin, his legs—but she didn't want him to see her crying. When she'd finished, she rinsed the rag and went over to Mahomet's bed.

"Hey," she cooed. "I'm going to wash you now. I'll try to be gentle."

He nodded slightly, but he too kept his eyes closed. Although he was older, he was smaller and thinner. Again, she started with the public parts of his body, then shyly made her way up his arms, down his blotchy legs. She found boils in his inner thigh, budding next to his scrotum. She turned her head away, shame coloring her face, disgust rising up from her belly. She heard footsteps outside and quickly covered him up.

Breathless from running, Azan came into the room, his face grave and pale.

"That was quick," Fatima said. "What did she say?"

"When I told her your brothers had those bumps, she seemed frightened. She called them buboes and said that people..." He stopped in mid-sentence, his fingers churning in the air.

"What?" she asked, twisting the rag into the bucket. "Tell me."

"That people rarely survive them."

"Well." Fatima breathed deeply. "Did she give you any advice about what to do about them? Any cures?"

"She said you could try making a small slit at the side of each boil to drain it, then cover it with fresh dung," While giving these practical instructions, he was actually able to look her in the face. "As the dung dries, it sucks out the poison. But, Fatima." He paused, looking away again. "Miriam didn't want me anywhere near her... and has asked that you not return to her house."

Fatima stopped washing her brother and looked at Azan.

"What?" she asked, stung by hurt and confusion. "And why not? Does she think we will bring the sickness to her on our hands? On our very breath?

She threw the rag into the bucket, bewildered by Miriam's entreaty to stay away. Her grandmother's old friend often faced illness, wounds, death. Why would she not treat her brothers? Because of these boils? Fatima also wondered where her father could be. Surely he would know what to do. She bit her lip, trying to calm down, to think.

"Dung?" She shook her head. "No, clay will work much better. It's cleaner, of course, and dries quickly. We are potters, and we will use clay to cure my brothers."

Fatima sent Azan to the workshop and went out to the patio and gathered jasmine for their room. She was filling the narrow aisle between the two small mattresses with flowers—hoping it would mask their smell, if only for a moment—when Azan came in with a bucket of clay and a handful of knives and needles, those usually used to mold, trim and decorate clay.

Fatima decided to begin with Aben, since his buboes were in the armpits, an area more familiar to her. After staring at the lumps for some time, she swallowed, then finally, made a cut in the first one. Wide-eyed, she gasped for breath as it oozed pus and blood. In a panic, she tried to flatten it like the balls of clay she had shaped as a child, hoping to make it disappear. He writhed in pain, clamping his eyes shut and groaning.

"I'm sorry," Fatima said, grimacing in sympathy. "I'll be more careful."

One by one, she slit open the boils, wiped away their putrid juices, and packed them with clay. Staring down at Aben shivering, his underarms covered in cold, wet mud, she got a lump in her throat.

"It'll dry soon," she managed, covering him with a blanket. Combing his hair with her fingers, she slowly smoothed down the strands plastered to his forehead. "Without all the pus and corruption inside you, I know you'll get better." She tried to sound confident.

Reluctantly, she moved on to Mahomet. Breathing slowly, she told herself that a man's leg was like a large arm, a limb, nothing more. She lifted his tunic and, with her eyes half-closed, spread his thighs apart and shifted his genitals away from the buboes. She picked up the small knife, to discover her hand was shaking. She looked up at her older brother's face—his slightly-parted mouth, his eyes, already hollow—and her sorrow gave her will.

She slit the large bubo first, now prepared with a rag for its spill; she sopped up the smelly pus so it would not soil the mattress. She'd burn these rags later. Her jaw set firm, she continued on with the other four. When she was finished—Mahomet's groin packed in clay and covered in blankets—Fatima got up and picked up the bucket.

"Get some sleep," she murmured to them, unnecessary words.

She was in the patio washing her hands with their rough homemade soap when her father walked in the door.

"How are your brothers, Fatima?" he asked.

"Oh, Father." Tired and sad, she was relieved to see him. "I think the disease has become worse. They both have boils as big as fruit. I have just applied the cure." Wiping her hands dry, she looked into his troubled face, and decided not to tell him about Miriam, her outlook on the boys' condition or her abandonment. "Where have you been? I've been worried about you all day."

"I have been to see my old friends, my fellow potters." His voice was despondent. "None of them would talk to me. They all believe that I've brought affliction to the community." He shook his head. "Even worse, Malik thinks I've caused his son's death. He wouldn't let me near his house. Fatima, he threw stones at me!"

She went over to embrace her father, and as she did so, she felt that he too was unusually warm. In his eyes, she saw the glassy look of fever. She did not understand; her father had not been to the sea, he had not breathed the miasma. How was it possible that he too was ill?

She looked down at her hands, and began washing them again.

With the realization that her father was also ill, the following day Fatima made up her mind to speak to her uncle Muzaffar. Although their houses were side by side, they had barely seen each other since the New Year celebration the month before. She was not looking forward to it—she had no desire to ask him for *anything*—but knew that she could use his help. Taking slow, deep breaths, she went over to his house and stepped into the courtyard.

"Muzaffar, cousins," she called. "It's me, Fatima. Peace be upon you."

There was no answer. She walked into the house and saw that it was empty; not only was no one home, but their belongings were also gone. Uneasy, Fatima went up to the workshop and saw that the mules and cart were missing and all the finished wares stored in the shop had disappeared as well. Her uncle and his sons had left, and it was clear they meant to be gone for a long time.

Later that evening, her brothers fell into fitful sleep, bits of dried clay still stuck to their body hair. Their father also took to his room, his friends' ostracism weighing heavily on his mind; he blamed his weariness and nausea on this. Fatima sat with Azan in the courtyard. Although she was tired, she did not want to be alone. She offered him some bread and fruit and brought out her psaltery. She tried to sing a song to compose herself, to remind herself of what life had been like before everything started falling apart. He watched her plucking the strings without even looking at them.

"You play so well, Fatima, and you have such a pretty voice." His fingers moved as if he too were playing an instrument. "I love hearing you sing while you're at the wheel. You practice two arts at the same time."

"You are very kind, Azan, but, more often than not, I can't stop myself from singing. It flows from my heart."

He smiled at her and looked away with a blush. "Muzaffar came to the workshop early this morning," he began. He took a deep breath, uncomfortable. "I watched him and his boys load the cart with pottery and tools. He didn't ask for my help and I stood out of his way. He said to tell your father that he was taking his half of the shop, his inheritance. That he and his sons were going away. He didn't say if they were coming back."

"Yes, I went to his house today and saw that they had left. Oh, Azan, I feel that I am partly to blame. What will I tell Father?"

"Wait until your brothers are better to discuss such matters. How are they faring?"

"I don't want to lose hope, but I see no improvement. The cures don't seem to do anything. I haven't been able to help them, or even lessen their pain. If anything, I make them feel worse. I'm afraid they're dying, like Nasir." She swallowed hard, trying not to break down. "And, my father. He also has the fever."

"Your father, too?" Azan was taken aback.

"I don't understand it either but somehow, without even going to port, he has breathed the same poison. I've been thinking. Is it possible that this disease is carried from one person to the next? Is that why Miriam is afraid to be near us?" She put down the psaltery and looked at her friend. "If this is so, you must leave, Azan."

"No." He shook his head, waving fear away. "Don't worry about me, Fatima. I'll stay here with you. Really, you can't do this alone. It's too much for one person. I'll stay and help you."

"No, Azan. Go back to Valencia, go home to your family. I want you to live." She took a deep breath and looked into his eyes, "You are my only friend. Please, Azan. I want you to live."

"But, Fatima," he said quietly, staring back at her. "I want to help you."

"Then you will do as I ask. Go. Now."

He searched her face for a sign of insincerity, for any excuse to stay, but found none. He stood to leave and clasped her hand in his.

"When all this is over, you can find me in the Moorish Quarter," he said. "You will always be welcome with the family of Yusuf, the glass-blower."

Fatima nodded her thanks and watched him leave. She felt alone and afraid without him there, but was satisfied that he would be spared. She played the tune of an ancient love song on the psaltery, but had no voice to sing.

Fatima was exhausted. For two days, she had tried, single-handedly, to take care of her father and brothers, expecting, at any moment, to fall ill herself. She was constantly occupied: making broth and trying to feed them; emptying their chamber pots, filled with thick, reddish urine; washing their rancid-smelling bodies—now a matter of routine, their manhood no longer frightening or embarrassing her—and piercing and packing their buboes with clay. Even with all of these practical matters to attend to, Fatima did not forget her prayers. Five times a day she earnestly performed the ritual. Facing Mecca, prostrate on the floor, her nose breathed in fumes of vinegar as she begged Allah for the lives of her loved ones.

Washing her father in silence, Fatima counted in her head the days since her brothers had returned from the port of Valencia. Six. It had only been six days. She shook her head in disbelief.

Gently, she maneuvered the rag around the large, painful welts on his neck and underarms. Fatima had decided not to cut any more buboes; it caused them all such pain and to no apparent advantage. As she was rearranging his robes to cover his dark, blemished skin, Azmet asked for his brother.

"I want to see Muzaffar. It has been some time since we have spoken. Perhaps I have been too harsh with him. Go, Fatima, fetch your uncle. I need to speak to him. It's urgent."

At a loss for words, Fatima hesitated a moment, trying to think of a lie, to invent a story that would not hurt her father.

"Muzaffar?" she asked, too brightly. "Oh, he is very busy at the moment. There's work—"

"Fatima, stop," he said, taking her hand. "You have never been good at falsehood. Tell me, where is my brother?"

"He's gone," she said, giving up. "I went to his house for help when you fell ill, and found it empty. He's taken the mules and everything from the shop he could carry. I'm sorry, Father."

Azmet sighed, closed his eyes, and murmured to himself. "Muzaffar, you have always been a coward."

He asked Fatima to leave him alone for a while, to go and check on her brothers. As she walked into their room, she was alarmed by Mahomet's wide, frightened eyes.

"A-aben." He choked out the word, "Fatima, he's no longer breathing."

She ran toward his bed and put her hand on Aben's head, now cold after days of fever. She looked at Mahomet—having his dead brother lying just a few feet away had shaken him greatly—and knew she had to remove Aben immediately. With great difficulty, she dragged his lifeless form out of the bed onto his blanket, and pulled him into the courtyard. Catching her breath, Fatima remembered the funeral rites performed for her grandmother the year before, and rotated the body to face Mecca. She knew that the body should be carefully washed, its orifices stuffed with cotton, then sprinkled with rosewater and camphor. However, now it was more important to take care of the living. She would come back later and perform the rituals as best she could. The burial itself, she thought grimly, was going to be much more difficult.

Still panting from the effort of moving his corpse, Fatima kissed her brother gently on the forehead and quickly went back in to see how Mahomet was dealing with the shock. Now he seemed much calmer; in those few moments alone, he had resigned himself to his fate. Fatima lit another sprig of rosemary and approached the bed, trying to ignore the smell.

"Did he have any last words?"

"No, he had not spoken for a long time. He went out slowly, like an ember."

They sat in silence. She could see that her brother was completely drained and suffering terribly. Trying to make him forget his pain, she decided to share memories of themselves as children.

"Do you remember when we were little, how we would go into the open fields near the workshop and chase the pigeons? Aben would wave his arms like a great bird, cawing as loudly as he could, pretending to be a hawk."

"And you, little sister, would whirl your arms like windmills, thinking it would make you run faster. How you wanted to keep up with your big brothers."

"And I usually could. Remember our first lessons in Father's workshop? He was so patient with us, as we learned to throw pots and paint—"

"Until I upset his precious glaze pot and spilt the golden glaze. I have never seen him so angry, to this day."

"It was Aisha who wanted to get angry with us, but never could. Whenever she caught us sneaking raisins or figs, she would start to scold us and we would give her such looks, she would begin laughing instead."

Mahomet reached for her hand and closed his eyes; she could see he needed rest. Softly, she sang to him, a song from their childhood, one they had all liked.

If you should see the mouse
Sitting in the corner
Shelling his little walnuts
Sharing with his little sisters.

If you should see the frog
Sitting by the stove
Frying her tasty fritters
Sharing with her little sisters

She wiped his brow. Looking down at her older brother's face, she knew that, like Aben, he too would soon be gone. She would then be little sister to no one.

"Mahomet," she asked quietly, "Tell me again about Mother."

"Oh, Fatima," he sighed. "You know I was only five when she died."

"Yes, I know. But, please, tell me again what you remember."

As a small child, when she was afraid or when their father was absent, Fatima used to beg Mahomet to remember what he could about their mother, images that brought her comfort. It had been years since she had asked him for these stories. He opened his eyes and looked at his younger sister with great affection. Slowly, he began to recite his vague memory.

"She had a long, thick braid of black hair. She let me play with it. I would wrap it around my hands..."

Smiling, she looked into her brother's face, only to see it twist in a convulsion, then stop, unnaturally still. She sat staring at him—her smile frozen—horrified at the realization that she had just heard the last words he would ever speak. Her childhood, personified by her brothers, was gone. A huge choking sob erupted from her throat, but then, in terror, she immediately remembered her father and ran to his room.

From the door she saw his unmoving face—his eyes were closed and his mouth ajar—but, as she nervously crept over to the bed, his chest rose silently. With a sigh of relief, she crouched down next to him, watching him breathe, studying the lift and fall of his ribcage, the subtle movements around his mouth and nose. She perched on the edge of his mattress and tried to breathe in time with him. In out, in out... It was difficult to keep the sluggish pace of a sleeping man grown weak with disease.

Inhaling with exaggerated slowness, she examined the face of her father, the only parent she had ever known. Handsome just days before, it was now ravaged by pain and poison; she would not have recognized those features outside their home. She lightly grazed his warm palm, worn smooth from a lifetime of water and clay, and wondered how to tell a man that he'd lost his sons. Mahomet, Aben. With a shiver, she thought of their unattended bodies; one alone in his bed, the other out in the courtyard. What should be done with them? Even ill, her father would be able to help plan their burial, or at least tell her what to do. In out, in out... She was concentrating on the movement of her father's chest—Would this breathing stop? Would she be left all alone?—when she suddenly heard his voice.

"Fatima," he whispered.

"Father," she returned, looking into his face. Watching his feeble mouth trying to smile, her eyes welled with tears. She controlled the urge to cry, her nose a burning tickle inside, and asked, "What can I get you? What do you need?"

"Just you," he said. "I need nothing else."

She stroked his hand in silence, stringing words together in her head, and finally spoke.

"Father, I have bad news," she began then, as he clenched his eyes in expectation, faltered. She found courage and said carefully: "Mahomet and Aben, your sons, have both passed away."

"I must go to them," he stammered, trying to pull himself up. Azmet made an enormous effort to rise, but his body was too heavy for his limbs. He fell back on the mattress, exhausted and forlorn, then broke into sobs. "Why? Why did I send them to port?" he muttered through tears. "I should have gone myself."

"You couldn't have known the danger," Fatima said, shaking her head. "No one knew."

He wiped his face with his hands, swabbing his eyes, and began rubbing them together, wishing for strength.

"Did you say the prayers for them, Fatima? Did you wrap them in clean sheets?"

Seeing the agitation in his face, the panic, she nodded slowly. She knew then that she could not trouble him about the burials.

"There's nothing to worry about, Father. Everything will be done as it should."

As he lay shivering in silence in the late spring afternoon, Fatima sat at his side. Knowing she had little time left with him, she no longer shied away from his smell, but breathed it in deeply; she filled her lungs with her father's odor, now the strongest part of him. He dozed off and on, mumbling with closed eyes, and she remained there, watching her living father, unable to imagine life without him. As the light in the room grew thin, he woke and took her hand.

"Your uncle is gone, your brothers are gone, and I will soon follow. It breaks my heart to leave you. You have been my greatest joy." He tried to smile again, but grimaced in pain instead. Looking at his face, her eyes shone with fear. "You must be provided for, my daughter. Look in that jar, the green one decorated with the Hand of Fatima."

She slid a leather pouch out of the jar and opened its strings. A shower of copper, silver and gold—the money from the Avignon Pope as well as years of other work—fell onto her palm.

"This money is yours," he said, covering her hand with his own. "Find a good man to care for you and use it as a dowry."

She kissed his sunken cheeks but could not voice words of thanks. She did not want this money, she thought, as she dropped it back into the pouch. She wanted her family. Fatima looked at her dying parent and felt like a small child.

"Please Baba," she begged, using the name she hadn't called him for years. "Baba, don't leave me. Please don't go."

Knowing these words, and all others, were useless, she closed her mouth tight to keep in the sobs.

"Ah, my daughter. You have the tree of life within you. Your hands, trust in your hands."

Azmet smiled at Fatima for the last time.

Breathing in and out, imitating the slow pulse of her father's last hours, Fatima stared into his face, his glazed eyes, his open mouth. This body had held her father. Finally she reached over and closed his lids. She shuddered, then vomited some bile into her hand, realizing in passing that she had not eaten that day. She got up, sluggish, walked out to the well, drew a bucket of cold water and began washing her hands. She scrubbed them with the abrasive soap of ashes and oil, between the fingers, over the nails, again and again, trying to rid them of the smell, the touch, of death. When Fatima looked down, her hands were red and sore—her palms were raw and her veins stood out. She hadn't been able to stop.

Weak from fatigue and little food, Fatima slowly changed into her white tunic, the Muslim dress of mourning, which she had made the year before when her grandmother died. For days she had barely slept, frantically caring for others, and now felt strangely idle. Alone in that house with three corpses, she curled up in the darkness with her eyes wide open, incapable of tears or sleep.

What would happen tomorrow? Her loved ones' bodies needed preparing and burying. Who would help her with these tasks now? Miriam didn't want her near and her father's old friends had turned on him, blaming him for the sickness that killed him. A mere week before, her family had been respected, happy and prosperous; now no one would touch them.

Before the sickness, she had still been grieving over the loss of her grandmother and suddenly, she found herself with no family at all. Memories of the life they shared together swiftly passed through her head: laughing with her brothers in the workshop, Aben inevitably throwing a clump of wet clay at her; her grandmother, patiently teaching her how to play the psaltery when her fingers were still short and stubby; her father watching her work, beaming with pride. How could they all be gone?

Among the practical concerns and the sorrow of loss, the most persistent thought she had, the one that dominated all others, was why? She could grasp that she had lost her family to this monstrous sickness, but what she could not understand was why she was alive. She had not been able to save them (Should she have put dung on their buboes instead of clay? Would they have lived then?) and, inexplicably, she herself had been saved. Was this good luck? Or the very worst kind?

Consumed with her thoughts, Fatima had been lying in silence for hours, when she heard a noise. There were voices in the courtyard, and she could see the soft glow of torchlight making shadows on the wall. Her body—grown numb with grief—awoke, all of her senses suddenly alert. The hair prickling on the back of her neck, she did not breathe, but listened to the intruders as intensely as she could.

A voice cried out.

"My God! There's a dead body at my feet! Here in the patio!"

"Be quiet, imbecile," said a second voice, "you knew we'd find Death in this house. That's why we're here." It took on a sarcastic tone. "To take the things they no longer need."

"Yeah," said a third, "This was the Moor who worked for the Pope. There'll be riches here somewhere."

With her body pressed up against the wall, covered in cold sweat, she listened to the looters; they went noisily from room to room, opening trunks, emptying pots and jars, filling their bags with her family's possessions and making rude comments about the odor. One of the men made startled cries each time he found a corpse in the house, first Mahomet, then her father. What would they do when they found her? Terrified, she looked wildly around the room trying to decide what to do. Should she defend herself? Run?

As one of the men approached her room, she grabbed the money pouch and the clay horse. Clutching them to her, she darted out to the patio. The thief, a fat man with a hairless face, screamed when he saw her coming at him—a green-eyed spirit dressed in white—and dropped his torch. Fatima heard the men shouting at each other as she ran out into the street; afraid they would follow her, she quickly made her way to her father's workshop in the darkness.

The workshop was so silent and black that, for the first time in her life, it gave her a chill. She stood in the doorway, peering inside, trying to make out the shapes. Her uncle had neglected to take the wheels and unfinished wares; perhaps the thieves might come here too. That is, if someone wasn't already inside, waiting in a corner, watching her now! Shaking, Fatima backed away from the door and quietly crept behind the workshop to the large firing oven, a much better hiding place. As she passed the pit, she dunked a hand into the mud and picked up a wad of watery clay. She entered the mouth of the oven and lay stiffly on the ledge, drawing her legs and arms in towards her chest. Her heart continued to race as her nervous fingers began rolling the clay into balls, buboes.

After a long hour lying uncomfortably in the oven—agonizing about her house and her dead, but afraid of what might lay in wait outside—Fatima began to smell smoke. Impossible, she thought, there's no fire here, only a decade's worth of old ashes. As the smell grew stronger, she crawled out of the oven to see what was burning. Over the pines and cypresses, she saw smoke coming from the direction of her family home. Cautiously, she made her way along the dirt path and, from a distance, saw a few neighbors watching her house burn. Undoubtedly they would not imagine this the fault of Christian thieves, but another sign of Allah's displeasure. Fatima stood hidden in the trees, motionless, as the flames consumed their home. The wooden beams, the straw mattresses, the cushions, rugs, the olive tree—and the bodies of Azmet, Mahomet and Aben.

Fatima awoke from a short, fitful sleep and, for a moment, was confused to find herself in the firing oven. An hour or two before daybreak, when the fire began to die out, she had come back to her refuge and dozed off. She considered returning to the house now, with the daylight, to see what was left among the charred plaster and soot. Shivering, she imagined discovering her loved ones' half-burnt bodies: disfigured, with empty eye sockets and open, pleading mouths. Biting her lip, her eyes flooding with tears, she prayed that they had been turned to cinders, that their ashes had been carried on the wind to Paradise, because she knew she couldn't bear to go back and look. She wiped her eyes on her long sleeve, climbed out of the oven, and stretched, lost as what to do next.

Looking at the orangey-pink Eastern sky, in the direction of the sea, in the direction of Mecca, she began to kneel down. To say her morning prayers as she had done every morning for as long as could remember. But, as she was crouching down, her body stiffened. Fatima rose up again, holding herself as straight and tall as she could. All of the praying she had done this last week—not only the ritual recitations of the Qur'an, but the humble entreaties for His help whispered constantly under her breath—all of it had changed nothing. Orphaned, homeless, without friends, she felt hollow, devoid of faith. She would no longer pray to this God who had taken everything from her; she no longer owed Him anything.

Without a family, without a God, Fatima stumbled into her father's workshop, familiar again by day. Mechanically, she reached for some clay, kneaded it into a wedge and put in on the wheel. She climbed onto her favorite one, the one with a view out a small, crooked window. Staring out, she saw three skeletal trees barely moving as a thin breeze slipped through them; the smell of fire was still in the air. She kicked the wheel into motion and wet her hands. This is what her family did.

In a trance, she brought the clay in, up, down, until it was docile. With long fingers, she raised the clay into a herb jar, like those she had made for Miriam, the last pots she threw. Her father had admired them, not two weeks before. She widened the jar into a bowl, an urn, down into a plate—then smashed it into the spinning wheel, letting daubs fly. What was she doing? She slumped down, her dripping hands hanging between her knees. None of this made sense; it had all happened too quickly. What was she expected to do now?

She looked around the workshop, hoping for an answer. Fatima had spent most of her life here, from when she was a toddler playing underfoot, to when she began to learn the trade. She had always liked the early morning in the shop, before it filled with men. And now, they would not come. Their steps would not be heard, their hearty voices would never fill this room.

Weeping, her face creased in sorrow, she squinted at the wheels and tables, blurred by tears. There were her father's half-empty glaze pots, green, blue, gold; the shelves her uncle had cleared, helping himself to the all best wares and tools (Had flight granted them survival?); the little stools she and her brothers had used as children, gathering dust under a bench; and Azan's imperfect pots, the gray clay now bone dry.

She couldn't just sit there. With sudden resolve, she got up, washed the mud off her hands, and began looking for useful items. Here in her hometown, nothing was left for her. She spotted a canvas bag and quickly began filling it with things she would need for a journey: an old shawl, a knife, a small sack of roasted almonds left behind by one of the apprentices. She packed the money pouch and the ceramic horse, the only remaining memento of her father. She'd made up her mind to find Azan, and would be leaving immediately.

Closing the door to the workshop (Would she ever come back?), she looked towards her family home. Wisps of smoke, thin and ghostly, were still rising from beyond the trees. She put the tattered, gray shawl over her hair, struck by the idea that everything she owned could now fit in a shoulder bag. Between thievery and fire, she had lost all the things she'd loved: her grandmother's psaltery, her father's chess set, the embroidered slippers which had belonged to her mother. Things she thought she would have forever were now destroyed, gone. With a few deep breaths, she set out for Valencia.

Fatima had never been out of her village before, but she had often heard about the well-traveled road to the city. As she was leaving Paterna, she passed the midwife's house. She paused in front of it. Did Miriam truly not want to see her again? Might she too throw stones? Was she alive? She kept moving decidedly ahead. She gathered some ripe apricots from a tree and put one in her mouth, whole.

In a daze, Fatima followed the path. She had the strange sensation that a part of her body was missing, that a piece had somehow been severed away. She tried to determine which. It was evidently not her legs, which she was using to walk, nor her arms, which she could sense swinging lightly at her sides. It couldn't be her head, she reasoned, as she could hear and see. She decided that there must be a huge, gaping hole, in her torso where her heart used to be. She breathed in sharply and, indeed, found the space inside empty.

Unmindful of her surroundings—the vegetable gardens, fields, clumps of trees—by mid-morning she nonetheless reached the Guadalaviar river, which hugged the path almost to the city. Fatima had been walking in silence for quite a while—she'd lost all notion of time, unable to say if she were even hungry—and had seen no other people. Suddenly, she was startled by the sound of dogs growling and barking. On the other side of the river, a pack of hounds was fighting over a large, dead animal; the body's long hairless legs had the same blotchy appearance of her brothers' limbs. Suddenly, she realized. The animal was a woman.

Horrified, Fatima started running. As hard as she could, through an orchard, down a hill, she did not stop until she tripped and fell, completely winded. Flat on the ground, she began crying, great heaving sobs. The scenes of the last days repeated again and again in her mind: her loved ones' bodies, reeking and hideously transformed; their pain and fear; her father's final moments. She had not saved them. She had not saved them.

In time, she began breathing again. Her face red and distorted, she walked over to an immense carob tree next to a canal. Under its sheltering boughs, she decided to wash herself. Fatima unbraided her hair, surprised to find she could still smell the rancid odor of the dying in it. Wondering again why she had not become sick, she kneaded her skin under her arms and around her inner thighs—checking for buboes for the dozenth time— terrified of carrying the disease to Azan's family. No boils, no fever, no bruises, no pain. Suffering, she thought, was another matter. She rinsed herself with water, then wrapped herself in the shawl and lay down in the grass under the tree. There she slept, a long dreamless sleep, for the first time in days.

When Fatima awoke, it was the next morning. She slowly opened her eyes and, looking up into the slender branches of the tree, she noticed a nest. Baby birds were crying out for food, chirping as loudly as they could. She watched the mother bird fly back to feed her young and, as she lit on the nest, Fatima started again to weep. Alone, with no family, she was nobody. Nothing.

Suddenly, she heard the sound of people coming toward her. Wiping her eyes, she scrambled to her feet. A large ox was struggling to pull a cart piled with trunks, chairs, a bedstead and several children perched on top. Three adults walked alongside the cart, talking nervously.

"Please," Fatima called to them as they came near. "Are you coming from Valencia?"

They all turned to her voice at the same time, the same expression of panic on their faces.

"Stay away, you!" cried a portly man, brandishing the pole he'd been using to encourage the ox.

"I mean you no harm," said Fatima, holding out her open palms.

"Death is all around us," he replied. "No telling whose cloak he's wearing."

"Is the sickness in Valencia?" she asked. "Are they dying?"

"By the score," he said, softening towards her a bit, poking again at the ox. "That's why we're heading for the country. I wouldn't go to the city if I were you."

"It's unclean," chirped the woman next to him, shaking her head in disgust. "Smells of rot."

By this time, they had passed Fatima, in direction of Paterna.

"God be with you," the man called over his shoulder.

She hesitated a moment, watching their backs walking quickly away, then picked up her bag and continued towards Valencia. When she arrived to the bridge at Campanar, she saw several groups of people, on packed carts, astride animals or on foot, heading out of the city in a rush. They were all wearing the same hostile, fearful expressions as the man and his family. Keeping her distance, she crossed the river and followed the Na Rovella canal, the city's source for drinking, mill wheels, and sewage, all the way to the gates of Valencia.

Normally, a woman traveling alone would have been highly suspect, an anomaly, but in a few short weeks, this disease had completely changed the norms of society. As it spread through the city and the countryside, through homes and families, these small details lost their importance. The sentinel at the gate barely looked at Fatima as she walked in.

After the river path, listening to running water and giving a wide berth to any others on her way, the entrance into Valencia was a shock. The square inside the city doors was the noisiest, dirtiest, most chaotic place imaginable. Instead of talking, the people all seemed to shout; dozens of conversations, in various dialects and languages, could be heard at once. Although her community had always spoken in Arabic amongst themselves, they had no trouble understanding Romance, the Spaniards' tongue. As Fatima looked around, she caught phrases from all sides.

"Come, bed us both!" Fatima heard behind her.

She whirled around to see a threesome of dirty revelers, drunk and laughing; two men were pawing a woman, grinning toothlessly while exposing her breasts right there in the street. Next to them, a solemn group of men wearing broad-brimmed hats and carrying long staffs, were readying themselves for the long, dangerous pilgrimage to the shrine of Santiago de Compostela.

"Go with God's blessing," said a weeping woman, as she handed a pilgrim a sack of provisions. "And come back."

In front of her, worried city officials were talking about the plight of the island of Majorca; the miasma had wiped out half its population leaving it vulnerable to complete devastation by pirates.

"They'll look Death straight in the eye to line their pockets," said one.

Fatima stood awkwardly in the middle of the square gawking at the spectacle around her. She was desperate to get away from this crowd, so unlike the small Muslim community she'd been raised in. She spotted a group of bearded men speaking Arabic in low tones and decided to follow them, hoping they would lead her to the Moorish Quarter.

Hugging the wall, her head bowed low, she went behind them at a discreet distance. They swept down narrow, twisted streets in their loose turbans and ample tunics and into a different enclosed neighborhood. This place felt more familiar. In fact, Fatima could almost recognize it from Azan's descriptions: the foul-smelling tannery, the mill wheel, the disorderly souk and, in the middle of it all, the mosque. Thinking back on their conversations, the idea of seeing him again made her happy for the first time in ages. She stopped to ask the local butcher for directions.

"Excuse me, sir? Could you tell me how to find the home of Yusup the glass-blower?"

Closing one eye to better his aim, he pointed at a large, rambling house at the end of the street. When Fatima caught sight of it, she smiled, remembering how Azan had constructed it with his hands. She thanked him and was turning to go, when the butcher called to her.

"Take caution, young lady. They've had the sickness in that house."

Alarmed, she ran to the entrance of the large family compound and called inside, "Azan, Azan!"

An older woman, thin and haggard, came to the doorway.

"Who are you, calling after my son?" She glowered. "A girl alone?"

"Forgive me, madam." She bowed with respect. "I am Fatima, daughter of Azmet Aben Calip, master potter of Paterna. Azan was an apprentice in my father's workshop. I've come to see him. He said I would always be welcome in the house of Yusup."

Azan's mother looked at her coldly. "When my son arrived from your father's house, he was weak with fever. He died the following day."

Fatima looked at her, stunned, unbelieving.

"No," she cried. "I sent him away so that he would live."

His mother, unimpressed by such heroism, continued to speak, pointing at Fatima, her finger jabbing the air.

"After that, the babies got sick. A pathetic sight, that was. Big welts on tiny bodies. Then my mother, an old woman, fell to the disease." With an angry sneer unsoftened by sorrow, she continued, "Azan carried Death on his back from your house to mine. No, daughter of Azmet Aben Calip, you are not welcome here."

Azan's mother turned her back on Fatima, leaving her dumbstruck on the street. Frozen, she stood before the closed doorway, her mouth agape, her eyes already brimming with tears. She had not saved any of them.

With a small shake of her head, she turned from the house to make her way out of the crowded Moorish Quarter. Her head was ringing with the sounds of the vendors' cries and the beggars' wails; the familiarity of their tongue made them louder still. Passing the mosque, she quickened her step; it only served as a grim reminder of His deafness to her prayers.

She went back through the walls, into the city proper. Taking arbitrary turns, she tried to formulate some kind of plan, but could not even answer the simplest questions: where to go, what to do? Adrift in a jumble of narrow streets, Fatima finally surfaced on a small square. There, next to a tall, wiry palm tree, a bakery was emitting the first pleasant aroma she'd smelled since her arrival into the city. Breathing in deeply, she realized she was hungry; for a day and a half, she had only eaten almonds and apricots. She walked inside and took a look at the puffy round loaves. Before now, she had only eaten flat bread, freshly baked in her small adobe oven.

"Yes, miss?" asked the man behind the counter, his face as pale and puffy as his wares. "Can I get you something?"

"One, please," she said shyly, pointing at the bread.

With the loaf tucked under her arm, she was fishing a coin out of her money pouch, when a short, lean man came bustling into the shop and bumped into her. The leather pouch flew from her hands and all its contents rained down. There, on the bakery floor, lay a fortune. She looked up at the men, obviously astonished to see such riches come out of the purse of a young, unkempt Muslim woman. As Fatima nervously began gathering the coins, the small man stared at her with bloodshot eyes. He bent over and picked up a piece of gold that had rolled between his feet. He handed it to her and gave her a crusty wink.

"You'll want to be more careful, Miss," he said with a grin.

Outside again, berating herself for her clumsiness, she trotted quickly up the street, holding her bag close to her chest while stuffing bread into her mouth.

The narrow lane opened up onto a large square, where an enormous cathedral was under construction. Fatima gasped, briefly forgetting her sorrows. Despite the scaffolding, piles of quarry stones, and thick dust, it was the most spectacular building she had ever seen. She sat down on a block of yellowish stone—the clanging of mallets and chisels composing a discordant tune around her—and continued eating her bread, slowly now. Staring up, she studied the detailed carvings surrounding the huge wooden doors, certain her father could have made such figures from clay.

Moments later, a group of men made their way into the square, marching in a uniform gait, two by two, forming a straight line. They walked in silence—at least twelve or fifteen pairs of them—with serious expressions on their faces. They came together in the dusty plaza right in front of Fatima and stopped. The stonemasons must have noticed them too; only a single hammer played on. The other people in the square began to crowd around to see what they would do.

After forming a circle, Fatima was surprised to see them strip down to the waist, there in public, all together. With a timid glance at their exposed chests—some thin, some fat, some muscular like Aben's—she thought perhaps they were acrobats or jugglers, though they didn't look festive or amusing like those she'd seen at the fair. She noticed that they were all carrying small whips, each one tipped with sharp iron spikes. They stood expectant, waiting for a signal from their leader who stood barefoot in the middle of the circle. At his cry, Fatima was astounded to see them begin beating their backs and breasts with the whips. Back and forth, front and back, they moved as one, rhythmically whipping themselves and praying in tempo. Occasionally, the spikes would get caught in the skin, requiring a sharp tug that would make them bleed.

Fatima looked around her, to see if the other people were as surprised as she. Surely this wasn't normal in the city of Valencia? People stared at them, wearing a host of expressions from horror to respect, from glee to disgust. Swarming closer, the crowd raised their hands to the heavens, wept, shouted out: "Save us!" "Forgive me, God!" "Help us, Jesus!" "Amen!"

Was this a Christian practice? The mob was encouraging them, groaning in sympathy, chanting prayers, touching themselves, as if they too felt the pain. They seemed to hope that the men's penitence would save them. That another's suffering would somehow be enough to do away with the terrifying sickness threatening them all.

Fatima, enveloped by the throng, was unable to move. Jostled and pressed against strangers, she pulled herself in, trying to keep her distance—especially from the men—but it was impossible. Nauseous, sweaty, holding her shawl tightly around her head, she wanted to turn away, but watched in spite of herself. The flagellants quickened their pace. Scanning the crowd for a way out, she saw, at her side, the small man from the bakery. Grinning at the grotesque exhibition before them, he was wedged beside her, straining to see. Then, he slowly turned towards her and his pink-eyed stare met her gaze. She cringed and covered her mouth.

The penitents began whipping themselves into a frenzy; the mob, in response, became more and more excited: jubilant, aroused, delirious. Trapped, surrounded by death and madness, Fatima could no longer bear it. She pushed her way out and ran.

She moved quickly, gulping for air, willing herself to think of something beautiful, something pleasant. At once she recalled Azan's enormous eyes looking into hers with love. What had he looked like as he was dying, what forms had his hands traced in the air? She bit her lip, fighting back tears—the knot in her throat was painful now—trying not to break down in public. She did not know it mattered little; heartbreaking displays of grief had become commonplace in the streets of Valencia.

Unable to think straight, she walked down a smelly street, through another noisy square, and turned into a small alleyway, searching for quiet. It was a cul-de-sac. At the end, she found a small public bathhouse.

Although Fatima always kept herself clean, bathing often at home in addition to the daily ablutions, she had never been to a public bath. She remembered Azan's description of the baths in the Moorish Quarter: how the men and women alternated days to bathe, how clean one got in the stifling steam, the camaraderie the men shared. She looked down; her white mourning dress was filthy, stained with soot and dirt and now speckled with flecks of blood. Looking closer, she saw it still had bits of dried clay from her father's workshop. Was that just yesterday morning?

Two women and a handful of children filed out of the bathhouse and each one in turn gave Fatima a passing look, of curiosity, wariness, distaste. Did they stare because she look unbalanced, her face contorted and wide-eyed? Or because she looked like a dirty beggar? Or simply a Muslim in Christian quarters?

She ventured in and was relieved to find that, because of its thick walls, the vestibule was cool and the noises from outside, inaudible. The room was empty; no one was there to collect her money. No matter, she would pay later.

Basking in the silence, her first tranquil moment since she'd passed through the city gates, she sat on one of the benches that lined the long room. A soft light floated down from a lantern skylight held aloft by thin pillars. She closed her eyes for a moment, sniffing the clean in the air, and slid the old shawl off her head.

Glancing at the gray cloth, she imagined her grandmother's disapproval; she would never have let her leave the house wearing such a thing. She bent down to remove her leather sandals—the insides were coated in damp grit—and kicked them under the bench. After a few deep breaths (she had never undressed in public before), she took off the squalid funereal tunic. She hung it on a peg and, with her canvas bag slung over her shoulder, opened the small wooden door that led into the first bath chamber.

Once inside, she heard the musical sound of water trickling into a basin, its gurgle and tinkle, and saw, to her surprise, sunlight streaming through star-shaped skylights. Some of them were covered in colored glass, making red, yellow or blue reflections on the whitewashed walls and tiled floors. Fatima caught her breath. She had made such stars on clay lanterns for candlelight to shine through, but had never thought to add glass. She held her palms underneath the different colored rays, to capture light like a butterfly.

The wet tile was cool under her tired feet. She stretched her aching limbs and splashed her face with cold water. Looking for a bucket, she peeked behind a muslin curtain. There in the store-room, a wizened slave woman was stacking cakes of soap. With a glare and an angry grunt, she pointed Fatima to the buckets piled up in the corner, and sharply pulled the curtain back. Her wonder at the bathhouse—its music and colors—was broken by the hostile apparition. She picked up a bucket, dunked it into the basin and, trying not to spill, opened the double doors—one after the other, to keep the heat in—to the next bath chamber.

The second room was luxuriously warm. A dome rose in the middle where, again, colored star-light shone through. She sat on a wooden bench, put the bucket on the floor, her bag next to her, and closed her eyes, trying to relax. It was impossible. Fatima's body was stiff from the long walk and sleeping in strange places, and when she closed her eyes for more than a moment, night-mare images—blackened buboes, flames, flagellants—jumped into view. Fatima dipped her hands in the bucket and, for the first time, noticed the other women in the room. One was ly-ing on her belly on a bench on the other side of the dome; her servant was massaging her back with oil. The woman's head was turned toward her, leisurely staring at her with half-open eyes. As Fatima stood to go into the steam room, the woman sat up and addressed her.

"Young lady," she said, "Do you not have clogs? The floor in there is extremely hot."

"I didn't know, my lady. This is the first time I've been to a bathhouse."

"You will hurt your feet if you go in there barefoot. Anna," she said, turning to her servant, a woman at least twice her age. "Get this girl some clogs and a towel."

"Thank you, my lady." Even though she was nude, Fatima could tell that she was noble, by the way she held herself, the look on her face. She was lovely, with thick, dark hair piled up on top of her head and a body of beautiful curves. Fatima did not know quite what to say next. "Do you come to the baths often?"

"These are the Admiral's Baths and I am the Admiral's wife." The noblewoman said, and smiled at her. "Yes, I like coming here. I find it soothing and peaceful. Especially now."

The servant came back with a sponge, soap, a linen towel, and clogs. As she was putting them on, the Admiral's wife in-structed Fatima that, to make steam, she only needed to pour water onto the scorching tile floor. Tottering in the unfamiliar wooden shoes, Fatima went through the last set of double doors and into the suffocating heat.

She scooped a bucketful from the boiler and splashed it to the floor. The water sizzled and steamed. Suddenly, Fatima could smell all of the odors of the past week: vinegar, rosemary, smoke, rot. They were streaming off her skin and hair. She stood in the center of the room, erect and still, immersed in heat. Breathing in the burning air, she tried to detect her loved ones' stench, the smells of her brothers and father. She filled her lungs, but choked and coughed, unable to hold it. When she tossed more water on the floor, all the odors disappeared, vanishing into raw heat. Fatima didn't know if she felt purified or emptier still.

After a few minutes, when her face was bright red and she could no longer abide the intense temperature, she filled a bucket with hot water and went back into the warm room. She saw that the noblewoman was still there; her servant was now scraping the oil and dirt from her skin with a smooth wooden knife. Fatima sat down and mixed the hot water in the bucket with the cold, and slowly, meticulously began to wash herself, in no hurry to finish.

Again the noblewoman spoke to Fatima. "I can see by your carriage that you are a woman of refinement. How is it that you do not have a servant girl to help you?"

"I have just come to Valencia. I am alone here."

"What? You have no relatives here?" Her voice now expressed more concern than curiosity.

Fatima was afraid to reveal her true circumstances—that everyone else in her family had perished from the sickness; that now, she was unwelcome in her own community. She didn't want this woman to react like Azan's mother; she didn't want to be thrown out into the street, wet and half-washed.

"My father sent me here to take care of my aunt and cousins," she began. The lie crept slowly out of her mouth as she eagerly invented an aunt to take the place of the uncle she had never liked. "But when I arrived at her house, they weren't there. Their neighbors said they'd left the city." Her voice trailed off, not knowing what to say next.

"Yes." The noblewoman nodded. "Many have fled. One of my servant girls disappeared just a few days ago. She gathered her things early one morning and I haven't seen her since. Lord knows what's become of her." She closed her eyes for a moment, then focused again on Fatima. "What are your plans? Will you return to your father's house? Or stay at your aunt's and hope for their return?"

Fatima looked at the woman blankly. Her father was right; she was no good at falsehood. More importantly, with these words came the realization that, when she left the baths, she had nowhere to go. Despite the warmth in the room, a cold panic gripped her.

"I don't know," she stammered. "My aunt's house is, uh, closed and… my father… he won't be expecting me. The journey is far…"

Fatima paused a moment, afraid the noblewoman would ask where she was from. Paterna was too close, too accessible; she could even know someone there. Fatima was trying to think of a substitute hometown, but the lady's face did not question her. It merely urged her to continue.

"I suppose I will stay in an inn," Fatima concluded.

"A woman alone?" The Admiral's wife shook her head. "It's not safe. If you would like, you can find lodging in the servants' quarters of my house. It's right next door. Like I said, I now have an empty bed."

Fatima breathed out in relief, surprised by this display of kindness. She remembered Aben's description of their room at the port—bedbugs and bad smells—and didn't like the idea of facing an innkeeper on her own. Since the death of her father, she had only experienced violence and aggression. This stranger's thoughtfulness moved her.

"Thank you," she said, bowing her head, near tears. "But, I can pay you for your hospitality, my lady. My father did not leave me wanting."

"We can discuss these things later. What's your name?"

"I am Fatima," she said simply, offering nothing more.

If the Admiral's wife was surprised to hear a Muslim name, she did not show it.

"Pleased to make your acquaintance, Fatima. I am Isolda Rocamora y Maza de Vilarasa," she raised her chin slightly with each syllable, then brought it down with a smile, "but you can call me Isolda."

The two women, now clean, went into the vestibule to put on their clothes. Fatima looked at her dirty tunic unhappily, knowing that she had no choice but to put it back on. She had nothing else. Isolda looked at her clothes, then at her. Did she wonder why she was traveling without a proper bag?

"I can give you something clean to put on, Fatima," she said quietly.

"Thank you. I would be very grateful. Tomorrow I'll buy some cloth and make something new."

Fatima picked up her bag and began to feel around in it for her money pouch. Not able to put her hand on it, she sat on the bench and began taking out all its contents: the shawl, the nearly empty sack of almonds, the last of the bread, the knife, the ceramic horse. The blood drained from her face.

The copper, silver and gold, her entire inheritance from her father, was gone. She rose to her feet and looked at Isolda, panic-stricken, immobile.

"What is it? What's wrong?"

"My money," she whispered, hardly able to speak. "All my money... it's gone."

An hour later Fatima was fidgeting at a long wooden table, still unable to believe that she had lost her fortune. Had the pouch fallen to the street when she was running? Or had somebody taken it? She remembered the grinning man with the pink crusty eyes. Had he dipped his hand into her bag and helped himself to her future?

On her first day away from home, she'd managed to lose the Pope's silver, the same money which had brought her family infamy and death. At such tremendous cost to her father and brothers, she now had nothing. With no dowry, security, or independence, she could only hope for charity. What an idiot she was.

Thankfully, Isolda did not think it a ruse and still invited her home. Fatima found the house, a veritable palace, intimidating. Austere stone on the outside, it had a spacious inner courtyard flanked by impressive gothic arches, with a great outer staircase leading to the upper floors. The furniture in the main rooms was massive and richly carved and tapestries lined the walls. Isolda had given her a robe made of light, rose-colored wool, covered by a sky blue mantle; it was warmer and far less comfortable than the simple tunics she was used to. She fingered the flared sleeves, looking around the Admiral's kitchen. Here, surrounded by pots and pottery, Fatima felt more at home.

Isolda offered her a glass of wine and poured one for herself. Fatima rarely drank anything but water but, today, she appreciated the strong taste. As she took a sip at Isolda's side, she noticed an imperfection in her left eye. In the white, clear and bright as marble, there was a tiny spot, perfectly round and as brown as the iris. Staring into the dark eye with its small, unlikely offspring, she was reminded of the moon and the morning star. She was almost startled when its owner spoke.

"So, Fatima, you have no people here in Valencia?"

"No, I have no one," she said quietly. She blushed, remembering her deception: the unlikely tale of a man sending his young daughter to the city by herself. The words she had just spoken, however, were true.

"Life in Valencia is very dangerous for a woman without the protection of her family. I have heard of cases where women alone have been abducted, taken to be sold as slaves." Isolda paused a moment, then continued. "And most of these women— orphans, widows—end up in the *bordell*."

"What is that?" Fatima asked.

"It's a walled area in the city where men go for pleasure. I hear that the women who work there can't leave. They're trapped." Looking down, Isolda added, "They say that there are more Muslim women there than Christians."

Fatima shuddered, her fury at losing the money renewed. "Is there no place where I can find honest work?"

"You know, people are in movement now with this plague. Many are fleeing to the country, trying to run away from Death himself. I told you about the servant girl who left here, without a word to anyone. She worked at the bathhouse." Isolda looked at Fatima, thinking, considering, talking almost to herself. "Though it's also true that we have fewer bathers now. Some people are afraid that bathing will make them ill, that the miasma is in the water, the steam. Many of the bathhouses in Valencia have closed out of fear. But I think cleanliness will help keep the sickness away."

Fatima frowned, remembering her brothers, her father, and how she had washed them all lovingly, despite their putrid odor. How she had warmed the water on the fire, mixing in a bit of lemon, and had used clean linen rags. How she'd gently rubbed their blotchy, aching bodies, skirting carefully around the large pus-filled welts. And how they had died just the same.

"Fatima," Isolda said suddenly, "Would you like to work at the baths? It is hard work—scrubbing the walls and floors, mopping, bathing and massaging women—and it is undoubtedly beneath you. But it's yours if you want it. You can live here."

"My hands have never been idle, Isolda. I accept your offer with thanks."

That night, Fatima lay on a wool mattress in a stone room, listening to the snores of Elena, the wiry, puckered slave she'd seen earlier that day at the baths. Her eyes open in the dark, she stroked the smooth, glazed horse. Passing her fingers over every line of the piece, its long neck, strong back, elegant tail, she marveled that her father's hands had shaped it for her. He had given it to her to bring her good fortune at New Year. Good fortune! And now she had no family, no home, no money. She bit her lip, fighting away tears. Considering the circumstances, Fatima thought, she *was* lucky. She could easily be sleeping under a bridge, in the damp with the rats, like Nasir. Would she get the sickness then? How terrified she would be out there, alone in the dark. Dragging the horse across the sheet, a heavy, uninspired prance, she breathed deeply. Feeling an intense gratitude towards her noble patroness, she thought perhaps it was destiny which led her to the bathhouse. She put the horse away and, as she was falling asleep, tried not to thank Allah for this blessing.

The next morning, it was not a woman's day at the bathhouse, so Isolda asked Fatima to accompany her to the market. On the way, big woven baskets in hand, the older woman fell into easy conversation.

"I've always liked shopping at market. Although I could send servants, for me it's always been the perfect excuse to leave home. A lady's life doesn't often extend beyond her household: embroidery, prayer, children. For me, it's nice to get out."

She lifted her chin to the bright sunny sky.

"I love the colors there," she continued. "The big piles of fruit and vegetables, or the fowl, still in its feathers."

"Yes, I've always loved the market as well," Fatima agreed, trying to remember the last time she'd gone. Again, it seemed like the last ten days—from when her brothers fell ill until now—had passed in unparalleled slowness.

"Many of the stalls are empty now, since the sickness began to spread." Isolda sighed, her voice losing its brightness. "Plenty of vendors have left town and I suppose few people are still working the fields. The food prices have gone up as well. It's not easy, anymore, shopping for a household of eight. We'll see what we find today."

"Eight?" Fatima asked, surprised; she'd seen almost no one in the house since her arrival.

"Yes, eight. I have two daughters, Leonor and Inés. They're five and three, but old enough to recite the Pater Noster and do a few stitches." She smiled. "Their brother, Pere, is only four months old. He still lives with his wet nurse."

Fatima nodded, though she found it strange to allow one's baby to suckle at the breast of another woman.

"You've seen Elena, of course, the slave who sleeps in the room with you. We call her the Silent One because she doesn't speak Romance or any of the other languages common here in Valencia. She's Greek."

"Ah," Fatima said. She hadn't noticed the old woman's foreignness as she'd not heard her talk.

"Then there are Maria, Eva, and Anna, our servants," she concluded. "The maids, Maria and Eva, are cousins. They live at Eva's house, so they only join us for the midday meal. Anna is our cook, but she also accompanies me to the baths. You saw her yesterday. She's been with me since I was a child."

"Your household is made up only of women," Fatima said in wonder, having always been surrounded by men.

"When my husband isn't here," Isolda replied, "I suppose you're right; we *are* all women. My younger sister Alba used to live with us as well but I lost her to typhoid last year. How I've missed her." She frowned sadly, then looked Fatima in the face. "You look to be about her age."

They arrived to a large square where people were selling their wares. Although Fatima thought it was a big, bustling marketplace, Isolda shook her head.

"You see?" she said. "At least half the vendors are no longer here."

That day, Isolda only managed to fill their baskets with a leg of lamb, fresh onions, pine nuts, and two dozen sparrows. She was unable to find a cut of pork to her liking, which was a relief for Fatima. Although she no longer said her daily prayers, she didn't know if she could eat from the pig.

As they were walking home, they met a man leading an ox-driven cart. On it, five or six bodies had been piled, half-hidden by a blanket, their blackened limbs stretching out beseechingly. A powerful odor of spoiled meat rose up from the cart. Both women quickly covered their mouths and noses with their hands as they watched the cart pass. Isolda made the sign of the cross; Fatima stood still, mute.

"We've been fortunate in my house," Isolda said, when the cart had made its way down the street. "None of us has fallen ill. Some neighbors and a few friends have been lost to the pestilence, but thank Heaven, we are all still well."

"You have been lucky indeed, ma'am," Fatima said softly.

"A week or two ago, I decided not to let Inés and Leonor go out on the street anymore. It's for their own good—to keep them away from the terrible sights and smells. Though, sometimes I take them to the baths with me."

"Tell me about the baths," Fatima asked, eager to speak of other things. "How did your husband come to own them?"

"My husband's father, Pere de Vilarasa—God rest his soul—was on the Royal Council of King James II. As a reward for his loyalty, when an old Moorish complex was torn down, he was given the lot. He built a mansion of stone, which is where we live now. The king granted him permission to build a bathhouse and a bakery. They were built behind our home some thirty years ago. You see, both businesses share the same oven. Kindling is very dear in the city."

Back at the house, they emptied the baskets onto the kitchen table; Anna eyed the ingredients skeptically.

"This is the best we could do today," Isolda said with an apologetic smile.

"I'll go round to the bakery and pick up a few loaves," Anna said, peeking into the bag of piñones. "With a bit of bread, this will make a fine meal."

"Like all of your others," Isolda said fondly, patting her old servant's arm. She turned to Fatima. "Let's rest a moment." Out on the courtyard, they settled on a bench, their skirts overlapping on the stone.

Isolda picked up their former conversation. "My husband, the Admiral of Aragon, has never taken an interest in the affairs. So, the practical matters of running the business and keeping the books have fallen to me. I must admit, I enjoy it."

"Is the Admiral away at sea?" asked Fatima.

"No," Isolda shook her head. "He was a knight in his youth and spent years engaged in military campaigns in Sardinia and Cyprus. When we married, he was well past thirty. I suppose he's never become accustomed to home life. His passions are horsemanship and the hunt, and he can spend weeks—months!—away with his friends, his hounds, and his falcons. He left shortly after his son was born—in celebration, I suppose—and we haven't seen him since."

"Oh," Fatima said with a blush. She could not imagine an absent husband—what was the point?—and thought it must be shameful for the wife. "I'm sorry."

"I don't mind it. In fact, when he's here, he upsets our routine," Isolda said, shrugging slightly. "Now with the sickness, we expect he'll stay away from the city for a long while to come."

As Fatima looked away to hide her embarrassment, she saw a maid coming down the stone staircase with two small girls.

"Leonor, Inés," their mother called to her daughters. "I'd like you to meet Fatima, the newest member of our household."

"Hello," she said shyly. Fatima was unused to children, especially elegant little girls with carefully styled hair and rag dolls cradled in their arms.

The girls looked at Fatima with curiosity.

"Your green eyes," said Leonor. "They're so bright."

"Like a cat's," added Inés.

"A cat, you say?" Fatima arched her eyebrows. She plucked a long burnt stick from the brazier in the corner of the patio and, on a paving stone, drew a funny cat, with big eyes and long whiskers, a fish in one paw. The girls laughed and begged her to draw more animals.

"Now a bull," cried Leonor.

"A rabbit," said Inés.

In thirty minutes, the girls had a bestiary at their feet; the flat stones were covered with wild boar, deer, dogs, birds of all kinds. Not only did she now have the little girls in her pocket, but it was a pleasure for Fatima to make pictures again, to employ her craft.

"Where did you learn to draw like that?" Isolda asked, delighted.

"I used to paint pottery," she replied.

Somehow, however, her expression did not invite further inquiry.

When it was again the women's day to bathe, Isolda took Fatima over to the bathhouse to show her its inner workings.

"How does it get so hot?" Fatima asked. "I only see the one boiler."

"That boiler heats the whole place. Look here," she said gesturing to a chamber under the hot room. "The hot air from the boiler is piped under the floor and up into the walls. That's why you have to wear clogs in here," Isolda added. "The floor gets so hot that, when you pour water on it, it makes steam. It's quite ingenious, but in fact, it's a very old system. The Moors used it and the Romans before them."

Isolda showed her the storage room filled with bath products—oils, soaps, clogs, towels—that clients could use or buy for a few cents more. She pointed out the latrine, and explained what tasks needed doing and when. Back in the vestibule, she gave her a sheer linen shift to put on.

"Here, you can wear this," she said. "In anything else, you'd get too hot."

When Isolda had gone back to her house, Fatima, in the thin shift, walked back into the baths. No customers had arrived yet, and she was alone there with Elena, the old slave.

"Good morning," Fatima said with a friendly smile, but Elena scowled and turned away.

After she had worked with her an hour or so, Fatima wondered at the fact that Isolda called Elena the Silent One; she was constantly muttering and seemingly cursing everything around her. Although Fatima tried to help her, Elena resented her presence and was unpleasant to her, countering Fatima's attempts at courtesy with rude gestures and ugly-sounding words. Slave though she was, she intimidated Fatima, who decided it was best to avoid her.

Despite Elena, the bathhouse was a peaceful place in the morning and, unlike most of the city, it had a pleasant smell, of steam, musk and soap. Fatima still hadn't gotten used to the odors of Valencia: the urine-soaked walls where men routinely relieved themselves; the refuse collecting in corners; and the houses where people dared not enter due to the smell of rotting corpses. The bathhouse, with its thick walls and freshly-made steam, was a rare escape from the odor of Death in the city. Even the latrine didn't smell bad. It had an open water pipe underneath which constantly flowed directly to the sewers.

By midmorning, the bathhouse was bustling with activity. All different kinds of women came to the baths: nobles with their attendants; the wives and children of well-to-do merchants and artisans; the occasional baker's wife or woman from the marketplace. That first day, Fatima was surprised to discover that, once these women had removed their ample robes, they had an astonishing variety of body shapes. The only nude female form she'd ever before seen was her own. Well, and that of Isolda the other day. There, she saw an older, barrel-chested woman with surprisingly muscular calves; a bony woman whose breasts had never blossomed; a fleshy one who had survived birthing several children. Clothed, these women's bodies all looked quite similar, distinguished only by height and weight and the richness of their garments; nude, each one was completely different.

While Elena took the ladies' payment and kept an eye on the boiler, Fatima massaged, oiled and scraped them. She rubbed them gently, but with the strong hands of a potter. Her fingers absentmindedly tried to work shapes out of their pliant skin and, when using the wooden knife to scrape off impurities, she made designs on their fleshy backs: the Tree of Life, arabesque letters, the Hand of Fatima. She cleaned their hair and formed coil pots on their heads, rolling and twisting the thick strands. As she massaged them near their necks and underarms, she became nervous, terrified of finding buboes like the ones on her loved ones, the only other naked bodies she'd ever seen. She didn't find any, however. Perhaps those with the boils were already too sick to leave home.

At times, the bathers relaxed quietly: servants silently bathed their languid mistresses, mothers searched their children's scalps for lice. At other moments of the day, the women, nude or draped in linen towels, gathered in the warm room to talk. It reminded Fatima of the descriptions of the harem from the old songs and, again, she regretted not having sisters, cousins, aunts, a mother.

Away from men, the women felt free to discuss problems with their husbands, fathers, sons: the domineering ones who belittled them, the foolish ones in the process of losing their fortunes, the aggressive ones who would occasionally beat them. They commiserated with each other, offered advice or consolation; occasionally they had some sport, laughing about their husbands for their arrogance or vanity.

Moments of mirth were rare, however, as the dominant topic of discussion was the sickness. And each time it arose, the women were prompted to scrub themselves all the harder. These conversations were painful for Fatima, making her stomach clench and her breathing shallow. She listened to them talk—about their experiences, their knowledge, their horrors—but never said a word. She found that there in Valencia, surrounded by women, she had become the Silent One.

Caressing themselves with soapy rags and sponges, the women told woeful tales of abandonment, husbands leaving their wives to die, mothers running away from their sick children. Entire families leaving the city in hopes of salvation, only to be found dead on the road, a league away. And all the women had their own notions on how to protect themselves and their families from the plague.

"My father is a physician," began the woman Fatima was scraping. "He says the marital act overheats us and makes us more likely to get the fever. If our husbands insist, he recommends a good bleeding the next day to restore our humors to their proper balance."

"Oh, I'm not worried about that—my husband hasn't touched me in years." an older woman said with a snort. "But I do carry a vial of rosewater with me and sniff it as I walk in the street. The good aroma keeps the foul poison away."

"My sister believes the opposite. She thinks vile smells will keep her from getting ill."

"What's her reasoning there?" asked the older woman.

"She argues that bad counteracts bad. She's surrounded herself with squalor—dung and filth—and hovers over the latrine. She reeks of pigs. I will not get near her."

"Speaking of pigs, last Sunday, on my way to church, I saw two sows in the street. Their snouts were in the clothes of a man who had died of the fever. After mass, I passed that same spot and they were dead on the ground. I have lost my taste for pork, I tell you."

"We've stopped eating fish or anything else that comes from the sea. The miasma has poisoned it all."

Talk of food changed the course of the conversation, to new dishes, recipes, bad produce at the market. Talk of the market turned to a newborn seen there, his birthing, breastfeeding. Babies brought the conversation back to death and disease. It always resurfaced, again and again, throughout the day.

In the evening, the baths became quiet again. Elena and Fatima scrubbed the floors as the fire slowly went out. Little by little, the boiler stopped bubbling and the hot room lost its steam. Then, Fatima bathed herself, washing her hands with care, exploring the skin where buboes appear, trying to find solace in cleanliness.

Sleep was elusive, in spite of her exhausted body. Every night, she lay awake for hours, trying to ignore Elena's presence in the next bed. With her ceramic horse cradled in her hands, Fatima thought longingly about her family and had imaginary conversations with them. In her mind, she told them about her experiences, her trials, and tried to imagine their reactions to her new life. She could hear her grandmother's kindhearted advice about how to deal with Elena, and her brothers' playful comments about the naked women in the baths. Sadly, Fatima could almost see her father's bewildered disappointment, that his lovely, talented daughter was working in a common bathhouse, cleaning the latrine and scrubbing the backs of Christian ladies.

She thought of her family in Arabic, a language she had not used in days. She missed its beautiful mixture of guttural tones, strong consonants and soft shushing sounds. The last time Fatima had spoken Arabic was with Azan's mother, who had spit out accusing words and stared at her with loathing. She concentrated on the voices of her loved ones, conjuring up each of them in turn, even Azan's, which was just changing into a man's when he died. She thought of how they said her name. There was something different in the way Christians pronounced "Fatima," the Romance tongue changing it just a touch. She lay in the dark, in the silence of night, and imagined hearing her loved ones repeating her name, calling it loudly, whispering it, saying it in jest, love, or even anger. Then, inevitably, in agony as they lay dying. She wept quietly as she looked back on her life before the plague, now as remote to her as the old songs her grandmother had taught her, sweet poetry from the distant past.

Days went by. Mule carts, laden with corpses, drove their stinking cargo out of the city to dump into long trenches, as the living argued heatedly about what was causing the disease: the wrath of God, the miasma, or the ominous conjunction of Saturn, Jupiter and Mars. Whatever had brought it on, everyone was trying to cope in their own way: some people spent their days fasting and in prayer, alone in their houses, terrified of their neighbors; others scoffed and boasted they would drink and make merry until Death came for them. A few, and Isolda and Fatima were among these last, found comfort in work and routine. In fact, Fatima thought that if her hands were not constantly busy, she might lose her mind.

She began taking on more tasks. In the mornings, Fatima carried the bread from the Admiral's bakery to the market, wielding a big woven basket filled with large round loaves on her head. She helped more with the housework, especially after Maria and Eva unexpectedly quit coming to work in mid-July. Isolda also wanted her near, to accompany her to market or to entertain the children with her pictures. The girls continued playing happily in the sunny courtyard, oblivious to the black horror raging in the streets outside their home.

Even though the summer was hot and dry, as the days wore on, fewer people came to the bathhouse. Among the women who did come, their talk never strayed from the theme of pestilence. At home, each was so rapt in her personal saga of grief and fear, it felt as if she were struggling alone; in the warm room, however, some of the burden was alleviated. They were all together in this.

"My brother and his family were taken by the disease two days ago," began one sadly. "And his house has already been looted. Today, on my way here, I saw a man wearing his hat and tunic. It gave me such a shock. I can't imagine how even a thief could wear the clothes of the dead."

"Maybe that thief's not right in the head," said another. "You see so many madmen now, wandering the streets. Most in rags and half starved. There they are, listening to the monks sermonizing in the squares, with their mouths open, their eyes wild. Like they don't understand a word."

"Between the looters, the madmen and the priests announcing the end of the world—"

"Yes, Death is all around us now," said one. "The disease itself is no longer even necessary."

During these discussions there were often silent spells, when they all fell prey to their own terrible thoughts. At times, they wept. Then, suddenly, someone would voice a thought aloud; occasionally, another would respond. And the conversation jerked along.

"My husband has left us," a young woman softly confessed. "He doesn't work at the mill any longer. He doesn't see the point. He's taken up quarters in the *bordell.* "

"My husband's gone too," whispered another, looking down at her pregnant belly. "I don't know if he's taken flight or if he's dead. I don't even know which I prefer."

"So many people have left." An older woman shook her head. "Gone or dead. Valencia seems empty. Only ghosts live here now."

They fell quiet again and Fatima, finished with the pregnant woman's hair, went through the double doors, into the hot room. She stood in the stifling air, until her face became red and the sweat poured down, crying along with the steam.

In the weeks since she had come to stay at the Admiral's home, Isolda had begun treating Fatima as a companion rather than as a servant in her bathhouse. Perhaps it was because Fatima reminded her of the younger sister she had lost the year before; more likely, though, it was the bonds of plague: when fear and desperation forge friendships that would have never been made otherwise. Whatever the cause, in Isolda's home, like in her father's, the usual rules of society were overlooked for her. The Lady treated her as an equal. And though they spoke of many things, for the first couple of months, Fatima somehow managed to avoid speaking of her family, her past, her origins.

Towards the end of July, Isolda and Fatima were returning home from the market, dodging ownerless livestock—skinny cows and aggressive goats—that had come into the city looking for food in the filthy streets.

"I don't know why we bothered." Isolda shook her head.

Only a handful of vendors had been there that day but their prices were so high that Isolda spent all she had on a hare, a few pigeons, and a skinny head of Romaine.

"It's better than nothing," Fatima said.

Although Isolda had bartered and argued with the vendors, trying to get a nice, big cut of meat and plenty of greens for her household, Fatima knew it wasn't necessary. They needed much less food now than before. None of them had much of an appetite, due to grief, anxiety, or the putrid smell of death borne on the breezes in Valencia. They ate very little—Fatima was often satisfied by a chunk of bread—and they were all visibly thinner.

"I think the rats around the market would probably make a better stew than this hare," Isolda muttered with a frown.

"True, they've become quite plump." Fatima nodded. "And so bold."

As the two women were passing through the square by the cathedral, they saw a large, unruly group of men carrying torches and shouting. They had encircled a couple of Jewish families, distinctive-looking in their hooded robes with the bright yellow badges on the front. They had been on their way back to the Jewish Quarter, when they were stopped by this mob. The Christian men were taunting them, waving the torches in their faces, and the parents were frantically trying to protect their frightened children.

They could hear the leader of the group yelling furiously: "The Jews are responsible! They have brought Death to Valencia, poisoning the city wells to kill off us Christians. This filthy scum has caused the sickness!"

The mob shouted in agreement, making a tighter circle around the terrified Jews, who, in turn, crammed themselves together, pressing their children behind them, into the center. The leader went on shouting, brandishing his torch.

"We know your tricks, foul pigs, and we will burn you here and now. If we kill the Jews, the disease will go away!"

With his oily torch, he touched the beard of the man in front of him, who screamed, trying to put it out with his hands. The mob laughed loudly, one giant, heartless man.

Fatima looked at Isolda in horror. "These people are innocent—look at that woman, weeping in fear. At the children!

They have not brought this plague upon us—this is ridiculous. We must do something, Isolda. We must save these people."

"What are you saying? It's too dangerous!" Isolda exclaimed, shaking her head in surprise. "We cannot defend these Jews from that angry mob. Two women? And with what arms? A skinned rabbit and a few birds? They would laugh at us—or more! Who knows? Maybe they're right. Perhaps the Jews are poisoning the wells."

Fatima began to sob. She was furious at her own helplessness but mostly, at the disease itself. Not only had it robbed her of her family, but it had caused this madness, now a part of everyday life. And there was nothing she could do about it.

"What's wrong?" Isolda looked at her, worried and bewildered.

She allowed Isolda to lead her away. Behind them, the shouting from the mob became louder, followed by terrified shrieks. When they could smell the stench of burning hair, Fatima broke away from Isolda and began to run.

"Fatima!" Isolda, right behind her, grabbed her robes to slow her down. "Come back to the house with me. Please!"

Fatima stopped, hid her face in the crook of her arm, weeping; the basket of pigeons dangled from the other hand, forgotten. With her arm around Fatima's waist, Isolda helped her home. Once inside the courtyard, Fatima slumped down on the bottom step of the stone staircase, her head in her hands. Isolda gently rubbed her back, waiting for her to calm down, to speak.

"How can it possibly be the Jews?" Fatima burst out angrily, between sobs. "Think, Isolda! Are they out at sea? On the islands? Are they swarming through the countryside and villages like locusts? This sickness is everywhere, not just in the city, near these wells. And I'm sure the Jews are dying as well."

Fatima turned silent and looked into Isolda's eye, her beautiful eye with the morning star. It was now filled with worry, staring back into her face. After a moment's deliberation, she decided that Isolda, a true friend, her only friend, could be trusted. She took a deep breath.

"I know the Jews are innocent," she continued quietly, "because there were none in my house when my entire family died of plague."

Isolda looked at her in surprise, quickly stood up, and backed away.

"What are you saying? You told me your father sent you here to the city. Your aunt, you said she fled."

"I couldn't tell you the truth. Not that first day. You would have cast me out. I know what they say about those who survive... that we use witchcraft, that we have the evil eye. People are afraid, suspicious of those who live, when everyone around them dies. I don't know why I lived. I still don't understand it. And sometimes, I wish I hadn't."

She began sobbing again and Isolda took her in her arms, holding her close.

"I know you're not evil, Fatima," she whispered, stroking her hair. "Now, tell me what happened. I want to know."

With her voice breaking, Fatima described each member of her family in loving detail—her father Azmet, her brothers, Mahomet and Aben, her grandmother Aisha—bringing them to life, savoring the words. She talked about their lives as Mudejar potters, the papal commission, and how her proud brothers had personally taken the exquisite dinnerware to the port. And how everything changed when they returned.

"Nasir was the first in our community to die of the sickness. How were we to know that so many would follow?"

"No one could have imagined it." Isolda breathed out slowly. "But, what brought you here?"

"The night my loved ones died, looters came. I ran away to safety but, later that night, my house burnt to the ground. I don't know if the thieves set it on fire—Were they disappointed? Was all we had not enough for them?—or if it was an accident."

Isolda looked around her courtyard, unable to imagine being bereft of her home, of all her possessions, left to wander alone.

"I had no one left in Paterna, so I decided to come here to find my friend Azan," she continued, drawing out his name. "He was a kindhearted boy, one of my father's apprentices. But when I arrived, I was told he too had died. It was chance that brought me to the baths. I came to Valencia in search of a friend." Fatima looked up at Isolda with red-rimmed eyes. "And I found one."

"Yes, you did," Isolda murmured. "Oh, Fatima. I'm so glad you've told me about your life before you came here. Truly, know that you can tell me anything."

Isolda felt that now, finally, she understood Fatima. Her refined nature, her obvious talent, her silent suffering. Isolda also realized how much she cared for this young woman, and how lonely she had been before her arrival. The year after her sister died, she had barely spoken with anyone; since Pere's birth, she'd not even had a husband to bicker with. They sat on the stone steps, holding each other, long after both had fallen silent.

Isolda lost her infant son that August. He died in the arms of his wet nurse, who succumbed to the disease the following day. The wet nurse's husband, not yet affected, brought the small motionless body to Isolda. She put it on the bench in the courtyard and opened the blanket. It too had buboes and blackened limbs.

"Fatima, look at my little Pere," she cried, looking at her son's body. "Can you tell that he was a beautiful boy?"

"Yes, of course."

Fatima took Isolda's hand. She wanted to console her friend with reassuring words, but could think of none.

"I was his mother," she moaned. "I should have been there. Maybe I could have saved him."

"There's nothing you could have done," Fatima said, shaking her head. "Trust me. I washed my loved ones, fed them, applied cures, but nothing worked. Nothing."

"But you were there, Fatima," Isolda said sadly. "I had not yet gotten to know my son. It was his nurse who fed him, bathed him, kissed him. It was not I."

Fatima nodded. It was true. At least she had been with her loved ones at the end, doing whatever she could.

"It was she who watched him die," Isolda added with a sob. "It was not I."

Fatima held Isolda in silence.

The next day they buried the baby in the Vilarasa crypt and the parish priest came briefly to say a few words. The business of death—granting absolution, collecting offertories, delivering funeral masses, attending gravesides—was keeping his schedule extremely tight. In fact, he could only manage to perform the rites for the rich, those that made it worth his time. Isolda's husband, the Admiral of Aragon did not return for the funeral of his heir. She did not know where he was, or if he were even alive.

In September the temperatures began to cool and the number of deaths, to wane. The people of Valencia embraced autumn; hope was restored with rains and falling leaves. By the feast of Saint Luke in mid-October, the disease had disappeared, and with it, the visible fear, the charlatans selling cures, the public penitents, and the putrid smell of rotting corpses. Finally, some six months after it had begun, all that was left of the plague were gut-wrenching memories, nightmares, grief, mourning and a desperate desire to return to a normal life.

It seemed almost uncanny that, after months of living in the moment, experiencing daily tragedy, life could just go back to the way it was. People began to believe in the future again: to plan, to save, to plant crops. They resumed their old habits, came back to the city, back to work. More than anything, though, the survivors yearned for love—for affection and human contact— commitment, marriage, parenthood. They all had the need to be held and comforted and many, the instinctive urge to repopulate the land.

Isolda's cousin Beatriz, betrothed to the knight Jusep de Lluxent since the age of thirteen, suddenly, five years later, wanted to celebrate her wedding vows. She chose November first, All Saints' Day, thinking it would surely bring good fortune to honor all the saints at once. Beatriz came by the stone mansion to tell her cousin the news.

"I'm so happy for you," said Isolda, hoping that her cousin's marriage would be more successful than her own.

"Dear Isolda," Beatriz said, "I know you are still in mourning for your son and I am so sorry for your loss." She bowed slightly. "But I was hoping that you would let me have a gathering in the Admiral's Baths the day before the wedding ceremony. We ladies could come to the baths that evening, to beautify ourselves, to play music and dance, to have some wine—"

Isolda cut her off with an uncomfortable look. "Oh, I don't know, Beatriz. After all we've been through—"

"But that's precisely my point. To get together—just for pleasure. We haven't had a moment's diversion in months. People are worn out by their own unhappiness." She looked Isolda in the eye. "Couldn't you use a bit of fun, dear cousin?"

After her initial hesitation, Isolda finally agreed. She could not live in this gloom forever. When Beatriz had left, she found Fatima in the kitchen with Anna, peeling almonds.

"It seems that we're going to have a celebration in the bathhouse." She smiled at them both. "My cousin wants to have a prenuptial gathering with her women friends. It will require some work—preparing food, moving furniture—but I think it will be a nice change."

The baths were closed to the public the evening of the festivities. Ten noblewomen came, each one with her own handmaid. Isolda asked Fatima to attend her that night and Elena was also there to help serve. In the vestibule, the ladies were helped out of their many layers of clothing: from the capes and fur-trimmed mantles, to their long, colorful gowns, down to linen chemises and woolen hose. Finally, they slipped off their drawers and wrapped muslin cloths around their naked bodies. Leaving their pointed shoes in the vestibule, they put on wooden clogs and went through the double doors and into the baths.

The ladies first took a steam bath in the hot room, and then, while being oiled and massaged in the warm room, they enjoyed a long discussion about the wedding plans. What a delight it was for Fatima to hear cheerful talk: about the feast and the rings, the priest and the clothes, not to mention a detailed analysis of the groom.

Once the ladies' bodies were washed and scraped, their hair oiled and rebraided, Anna and Elena covered the warm room floor in rugs and cushions. Standing candelabras were lit, casting a golden glow around the room. Elena brought in jugs of wine and large baskets of bread and turnovers from the bakery; Anna served the ladies from trays filled with bowls of pomegranate seeds, sliced apples in honey, nuts and dried figs, and left the trays on the rugs, for the women to take what they pleased.

They sipped their wine and had some fruit, but continued to amuse themselves with their bodies, enjoying rarely performed beauty rituals to celebrate the occasion. One of the ladies had brought a Muslim slave, who was shaving all of their legs with a thin wire; another of the maids, with a pair of bronze tweezers, was busily thinning eyebrows. As they were admiring themselves in their hand mirrors, applying musk and kohl, the ladies joked with one another.

"Do you think I should shave my pubis as well?" the bride asked. "Or will Jusep think that I am still a little girl and take me back to my father?"

"With your breasts, Beatriz, I can't imagine him making that mistake." One laughed.

"Are you frightened about your wedding night?" another asked earnestly. "Do you think he will hurt you?"

"Only if he thinks I'm not a virgin!" Beatriz grinned, taking a bite of apple.

They began to sing and dance, some more awkwardly than others, some just leaping and tumbling. One of the women had brought a dulcimer and was striking the cords with the elegant little hammers as she sang love songs.

Nights, nights, beautiful nights
Nights are for falling in love

Oh what nights, o mother of mine
Those nights which never come

Tossing and turning in my bed
Like fishes in the sea

Fatima, still combing through Isolda's long hair, listened intently to the song, one she used to sing in her courtyard under the stars. She was thinking how thin the dulcimer sounded compared to the rich tones of the psaltery when suddenly it struck her: she had not sung a note since her family had passed away, she, who had never been able to stop. While throwing pots, painting, cooking, sewing, walking—there had always been song.

Listening to the noblewoman's strong, confident voice and watching her fingers manage the little hammers, Fatima realized that it had been stolen from her: she had been robbed of her voice the same night the thieves had come into her father's house. She was now a half-mute; no one in Valencia—not even Isolda—knew the sound of her singing voice. The thought made her feel heavy-hearted and alone.

The women amused themselves fully, free in the baths away from men, dancing and singing, laughing and drinking. Although they had all lost loved ones during the months of plague, they now welcomed the chance to forget their grief and to celebrate life. It was late when they finally took their leave. One by one, they left the cozy warm room and, with their attendants, went to reapply their many layers. They said their goodbyes, donned their headdresses and returned to husbands, fathers, brothers, and sons.

Beatriz was the last to leave. "Thank you for the lovely gathering, Isolda. I cannot imagine my wedding day being any better. See you tomorrow, dear cousin."

Isolda and Fatima were now the only two left in the warm room.

"Come, my friend." Isolda beckoned her to a cushion on the rug. "Sit with me. You look so sad. Here, have some figs and a glass a wine and tell me your sorrows."

Fatima joined Isolda on the carpet and took the glass. As she sat, she noticed that at night the star skylights were black.

"It was the music," she began slowly. "When I was a child, my grandmother taught me to play the psaltery. I used to sing the old songs and play." She sighed. "But that was all destroyed when my father's house burned down."

"The instrument was lost?"

"Not only that," she said, "but my song."

"Oh, come now, Fatima. You'll sing for me, won't you?"

"Please don't ask me," she said, near tears. "I don't think I can."

Isolda took her hand and they sat together in silent companionship.

"Bring some water," Isolda said finally. Her voice was quiet, her eyes half closed. "Tonight, I will bathe you."

Fatima looked into Isolda's face, surprised, but did as she was told. She felt a bit dizzy when she stood; the heat and wine had gone to her head. She brought a full bucket back to where Isolda was waiting and took off her shift. Isolda dipped the rag into the clean, warm water and used a lavender-scented soap that one of the ladies had left behind. She washed Fatima gently, taking her time, examining her body as she cleaned: her thin arms and fingers, her sharp hipbones, the nape behind her braid. Isolda put down the cloth and picked up her glass, sharing her wine with Fatima, holding it for her as if she were a child. As they were drinking, they looked at one another steadily; each woman found great beauty in the eyes of the other.

Isolda put some fine oil, perfumed with mountain herbs, into her hands, and began to rub Fatima's shoulders, her collar bone, her chest, then pulled her into a loving embrace. Both women reveled in the sensation of holding someone and being held; after all they had experienced in recent months, this feeling of closeness, comfort and love was so intense they could have wept in relief.

As they clung to one another, Isolda began exploring Fatima's body. She took her round breasts into her hands, caressing them, touching the hardened nipples with her finger tips. Isolda lowered her onto the cushion, taking her chin with one hand, and kissed her mouth, the silky, full mouth that she had never seen smile.

Fatima, who had never before felt desire, was flustered, confused. It seemed that her heart had dropped between her legs, that her whole body was tingling and alive. She kissed Isolda back, tasting honey on her lips, wine on her tongue, and ran her fingers through the thick hair that she had carefully combed earlier. Excited, she felt Isolda's warm, oiled skin against her own, and breathed in her scent. With a slight moan, she took Isolda's breasts in her hands, marveling at their softness.

Suddenly, the door flung open. Elena, her arms filled with muslin cloths, stopped short when she saw the women, naked and entwined. With a disgusted scowl, she dropped the cloths and barked out something incomprehensible, then spit, making herself perfectly clear. Fatima jumped up, put on her shift and began gathering the bowls, jugs and glasses to be taken back to the house. Isolda continued lying on the cushion, her eyes closed.

While Isolda spent the entire day at her cousin's wedding, attending the services, the feast, and the dance, Fatima and Elena worked at the baths. A completely different place from the night before, the carpets, cushions and candles were gone and sunlight streamed through the skylights. A few women were washing their young children, who gave the odd complaint, while others were scrubbing their underclothes in the buckets. Nothing there spoke of festivity, wine, song, desire.

If it weren't for Elena, perhaps Fatima might have wondered if she had only dreamed that Isolda had bathed her, kissed her, touched her. But every time their paths crossed that day, the ill-tempered slave took the opportunity to make obscene gestures at her, making Fatima nervous, even afraid. Towards closing, when she was mopping the floor of the cold room for the last time, Elena walked in. In her hand she held Fatima's golden horse, the last gift from her father, the only token left of her family. Before she could say a word, Elena, her expression filled with hatred, threw it into the latrine.

After the celebration in the baths, Fatima did not see Isolda for three days. She felt dejected and ashamed. Was she hiding from her now because of those moments they'd shared, holding each other in the warm room? She missed her company and wanted to talk to her, to reassure herself that they were still friends. But, for those three days, because she could do nothing else, Fatima carried on with her chores: working in the baths—touching women's bodies suddenly felt awkward—and taking bread from the Admiral's bakery to the market, which was steadily growing again. She helped Anna in the kitchen and played with the girls, but Isolda did not leave her rooms. As for Elena, Fatima could no longer look at her. Instead of going back to their room, for two nights now, she'd fallen asleep in the kitchen, her head nestled in her arms on the table.

Finally, Isolda came out of her room and went looking for Fatima. She found her in the cold room, staring down into the open hole of the latrine.

"Good morning, Fatima. Come. I need to talk to you."

Fatima followed her into the vestibule, where they sat together on a bench. Isolda took her hand; they were both trembling.

"I'm sorry I haven't seen you these last few days. I've been lost in thought. You see, I have news for you, my friend."

"News?" Fatima asked. "What's happened?"

"The day after my cousin's wedding, the baker's son, Carles, came to me and asked for your hand. I have decided to accept, and will pay your dowry."

Hurt and angry, Fatima looked at Isolda's downcast eyes. "So, I am like a slave, to be bought and sold?"

"No, of course not," she said, meeting her gaze. "You know I would keep you here with me if I could—how I've enjoyed your company. But, surely you understand, there's no future for you here. Working in a bathhouse, without a home or a family? To have honor in society, you must marry. A woman alone is an impossibility."

Fatima considered Isolda's words, knowing they were true. For a woman to be considered whole, she had to be connected to a man; at her age, that man had to be a husband.

"But, who is this person?"

"He's the son of Sara and Alonso, the chief baker who runs the Admiral's bakery. The boy's not too old, only twenty-two or three, and fine to look at. He's bright and ambitious—I think he means to open a bakery of his own. Truly, Fatima, he seems a good man."

"I don't understand... how could anyone want to marry me? I am nobody. A broken woman, with nothing to give."

"Fatima, you yourself know that is not true," Isolda shook her head. "You have much to offer."

"But I don't know him! I've never even noticed a young man at the bakery. And he doesn't know me." Fatima frowned. "It's ridiculous."

"He's seen you picking up the loaves for the market and has been struck by your beauty. Your green eyes have captivated him. Oh, Fatima. Perhaps this is a chance for you to start a new life, to begin living again."

"Here with you, this too has been a new life."

"But it's not enough."

Fatima thought of her father and how he too had told her to find a good man to marry. She nodded.

"Listen," Isolda added. "Before you can marry him, you must convert to Christianity. You know that unions are strictly forbidden between the faiths."

"Faith? I lost my faith when I lost my family. I believe in nothing, Isolda."

"Then, it will be all the easier for you. Just say the words, Fatima. The priest does not have to know what is in your heart."

"Whatever you think is best," Fatima said with a sigh.

"Oh, and another bit of news that may interest you." Isolda smiled now. "I've given my cousin Beatriz an extravagant wedding gift. Elena now belongs to her." Fatima looked at Isolda in surprise. "Until your marriage, you'll have your own room."

That night, back in her bed but with no small horse to hold, Fatima thought of men. With the exception of the old slave, she had very much enjoyed living in a society of women at Isolda's house; now, she would be back in the company of men. She took stock of what she knew about them. Her father and brothers, loving and kind, had treated her as one of them, but her Uncle Muzaffar was another matter. What if her husband was as small-minded as he? She considered Azan, so sweet and shy, then Isolda's husband—whose absence was considered a blessing. She nervously thought back on the different conversations she'd heard in the baths. For months she'd listened to women bathers discussing their husbands, disclosing their flaws, but never their virtues. Would this baker-man be foolish, vain, or violent like those men? She thought of the hard, angular bodies of men, their hairy chests and limbs, their strange appendages. She would be expected to lay with such a body. Unfortunately, she could not disassociate it from buboes, bad odors and loss. After tossing for hours, she fell asleep.

Isolda took Fatima to the church of Sant Joan the next day to see her parish priest. Inside, the church was dark, even at midday, and the smell of incense was heavy under the vaults. Fatima looked around. The bloody images of the crucifixion and martyred saints reminded her of the flagellants, whipping themselves into a frenzy on her first day in Valencia. Frightened, she clasped Isolda's hand.

The priest came out and greeted them. He was a young man, narrow and slim, with long, fine hands. These were in continual

motion, smoothing his black robes, from chest to thigh, again and again. Fatima watched him rubbing his elongated torso, slowly and deliberately, as if this contact with his gown was his only worldly pleasure. Distracted, she found it difficult to concentrate on what he was saying.

"The Moor wants to convert to the True Faith, I understand. Very good, very good. Come over here. That's right... Take this cross in your hand and swear to renounce your heathen god and take Jesus Christ our Lord as your savior."

Fatima, ill at ease, looked at Isolda anxiously, who calmly nodded back at her. She took the cross in her hand and, watching the priest stroke himself, softly swore to become a follower of Christ. He led her to the baptismal font, near the altar. He dipped his hand into the basin and wet his fingers.

"I baptize you in the name of the Father, the Son, and the Holy Ghost."

Mildly curious, Fatima was wondering what powerful form this spirit might take, when the priest dribbled the holy water onto her forehead. The cold trickle ran into her eye, making her blink repeatedly, but she resisted the urge to wipe it off with her sleeve. It rolled down her face like a tear.

"Now then," the priest continued, "there is the matter of changing your name. What is your full name?"

"Fatima, daughter of Azmet Aben Calip."

"Have you decided on a Christian name to adopt?"

"No," she answered slowly, "I haven't."

She had been unaware that this was an essential step in the conversion ritual and did not like the idea. Even though she no longer believed in Allah, she was still her father's daughter.

The priest, oblivious to her look of uncertainty, continued. "Well, Maria, the name of the Blessed Virgin, would be the best choice. As for surnames, many converts want to profess their new faith proudly, and choose names like Santangel or Perez, son of Peter."

"Pardon me, sir, but is it really necessary to change my name?" she asked the priest. "The name Fatima is all I have left from my father. May I please keep it? I'll take any surname you choose."

The priest's hands stopped mid-stroke. "You would keep your Moorish name after converting to Christ?" he asked, eyeing her suspiciously.

"My father was a good man. He died last summer, poisoned by the miasma. I would like to honor him, Moor that he was."

Fatima looked so sincere, so distressed, that the priest was moved. "Yes," he said softly, "Honor thy father and mother." He paused for a moment. "Since your first name will not be passed on to your children, I will allow you to keep it. You will now be known as 'Fatima Perez'. You may go."

They walked back to the Admiral's mansion without speaking. Finally, as they were entering the house, Fatima asked Isolda, "When will my hand be given away?"

She stopped suddenly. Her own words made her shudder, the very expression gave her a chill. She remembered her father's last words to her, to trust in her hands. Now, someone had asked for her hand—and it would be given to him. Isolda put her arm around Fatima.

"It can take place at any time. Unlike my cousin's wedding, your ceremony will be simple. All that is truly necessary is for him to say 'I take this woman' and for you to respond, 'I take this man.' After that, you're married. You need no witness, no priest, no celebration, nothing more."

Fatima was relieved that there was to be no ceremony. She felt hesitant enough about marrying a stranger, without doing it in front of a crowd.

"I'd like to have you by my side. I'll need you there with me."

"I would be pleased to do that, my friend." Isolda nodded. "Now, come into the house. I have a surprise for you."

Fatima followed her into the great room. Laying on the table was a psaltery.

"This is my wedding gift to you." Isolda smiled at the surprise on Fatima's face. "You will find your voice and sing again, Fatima. And I'm looking forward to hearing it."

She went over to the table and picked up the psaltery. It was a beautiful instrument, more valuable and finer crafted than her grandmother's had been. She sat on the bench and picked out a simple song on the strings.

"Thank you, Isolda," Fatima blurted out, through her tears.

"I'm so glad it pleases you." Isolda's voice broke, moved by the emotion on Fatima's face. Isolda sank down next to her on the bench and, until dark fell, watched her fingers sing.

The two women went to the market the following day. Instead of shopping for fruit or meat, that day they were looking for a man. Many bakers gathered there midweek to discuss their trade, and Isolda was told that Alonso's son would be there among them. They walked in silence, their arms linked together; Fatima was too nervous to chat. For the first time, she would see the man she was to marry. She knew that whether his appearance or his demeanor pleased her or not, she was to spend the rest of her life in his company.

As they approached the marketplace, Isolda pointed to a group of men all wearing the customary garb of woolen tights and knee-length tunics. Some wore capes against the chill in the air, and others, hats against the sun.

"Which one of these men is Carles?" Fatima's question came out in a whisper.

"He's the one in the green tunic with a knife in his belt."

From that distance Fatima could see that he was tall and well built. As they got somewhat closer, she saw, to her great relief, that he seemed to keep himself clean; unlike some of his fellows, his hair wasn't matted or oily and his tunic was unstained. Another baker called to him and he turned to wave, making it possible for her to study his face. Comely enough, she noticed his nose was slightly off-kilter, as if it had been broken and not mended properly. She was pleased by this defect. It made him human, a person with a past; he too had lived before this moment, perhaps he had suffered as well.

"Are you ready to meet him?"

"In a moment," Fatima said, turning her back to the men. She looked at Isolda with a serious expression. "But first, I'd like to ask you something."

"What's that?"

"Once I am wed, will I see you? Will we be friends?"

"Fatima, what are you saying? It would break my heart not to see you anymore. And the children—they'd be devastated. Of course, you will always be welcome in my home. And don't forget—for now, your bridegroom works at my bakery. And I suppose he will expect you to help out there."

"So, I shall learn to fashion shapes out of bread dough?" she arched an eyebrow. "I wonder if it will please me as much as clay."

"The important thing is that the bakery is right behind my house," Isolda said. "You will still be near me and you can come over whenever you like."

"Perhaps," Fatima ventured, "in the evenings, we could meet at the baths? To relax in the steam and talk about our day."

"I'd like that," Isolda answered with a smile.

With a glance at the moon and the star in Isolda's eye, Fatima smiled back.

The day after she was married, Fatima arrived to the bathhouse early. In an empty bucket, alongside her towel, soap and sponges, she carried a small hammer and a chisel. She had never done work like this before, but how different could soft stone be from hardened clay? She wanted to give Isolda a surprise. One that wouldn't go away.

Reconstruction

June 2011

After a month in Valencia, I was sitting on Hector's terrace, sifting through medieval bath images on the internet, when a long email came in from Nick. I'd heard from him several times since my arrival but usually in the form of one-line messages on Facebook: "Glad your trip was ok." "Electricity back on in the house!!!" and more recently "Making good progress here." It seemed ironic to me that this young texting generation bore such a resemblance to their terse, telegram-writing ancestors; I could almost see the STOP after each line. Today's email, however, was a proper letter.

> *Dear Mom,*
>
> *Sounds like you're having a good time. That's great that you met Marisa. Whose mother is she again? Didn't get the*

connection. When will the Baths architect be back from Dubai? I'm sorry to hear that the construction/real estate bubble has burst in Spain too. I would have loved to work there for a couple of years after graduation! I guess I'll have to go to a country that's still building stuff. China? Anyway, maybe that architect will be able to solve all the Baths' mysteries for you. After you told us about the I/F carving, we tried to figure out the meaning over a couple of beers. Allison went all Shakespeare on us with "Iago and Falstaff." The best of Erik's lame ideas was "Iggy Fop." I decided on a very stately "Icarus Falls." Mitchell was off having a much better time somewhere else.

Work on the house is moving along. We've cleaned up the bedroom and replaced the windows there, so it's almost back to normal. As for the study, we've gutted it: no more tree, damaged wood, or broken windows (leaving pretty much a gaping hole). You'll be happy to hear that some of your things—even some books!—survived the storm. The mandolin suffered a bit of abuse (the neck was cracked) but the guys at the Guitar Gallery say it can be fixed.

You know, even though we're living here under a blue-tarp shadow of tragedy, there's something really uplifting about it. It's hard to explain, but I imagine it's what the Londoners experienced during the Blitz or New Yorkers after 9-11. EVERYONE CARES. And everyone has come together—working, helping, volunteering. People are sharing their tools, kids are making PB and Js for workers, little old ladies are knitting afghans for storm victims... It's amazing! Really, we're proud to be a part of it.
Lots of Love—
Nick
PS Your neighbor Mike is a great guy. Something to keep in mind when you get home. :)

I sat back in the teak lawn chair, staring at the last line. It was topped off with a smiley-face emoticon. Was Nick suggesting I go out with someone? I thought he'd had a major problem with me dating. Or did he just not like Todd Russell? I scanned back over the message, smiling again at their attempts to decode the initials and, even more, at the idea that some of my treasures had been spared. But when I reread his description of post-tornado life in Tuscaloosa, I squirmed. I felt guilty for having skipped town, for not taking part in its recovery. Had I already forgotten the terror of the storm and the destruction left in its wake? Was the memory of those who had suffered most—the dead, injured, ruined, homeless—also beginning to fade?

Getting up to water the plants, I felt like I'd spent the last month, so pleasant and carefree, in a wrongful, reprehensible way. What had I been doing? I'd spent hours there on the terrace reading. I'd played around on photoshop, transforming white-washed bathhouse pictures into colorful collages. But I'd had the most fun, by far, going out—strolling on the beach in the late afternoon, going to galleries and museums, having a beer after a movie—with my new friend Marisa.

The day I went back to the bathhouse to take the photos, she was there talking to the tour guide, Xavi, who ended up being her son. With a head of curly, dark hair and a quick smile, Marisa Flores was about my age, and also divorced with a grown son. As the bathhouse was tourist-free at the time, the three of us sat down to chat. In a matter of minutes, we discovered that not only did Marisa and I own the exact same reflex camera, but that, at that moment, we were both reading the same Paul Auster novel. To top it off, she lived on the same street where I was staying. In fact, Marisa—a translator for museum catalogs—had been friends with Fergal for years. Coincidence was proclaimed destiny. I decided to forego my photo shoot that day and we went out for coffee instead. We'd seen each other several times since then and today she was coming over for an early lunch on the terrace.

When Marisa arrived, I already had the table set under the parasol, with pasta, olives, cheese and salad.

"I hope you're hungry," I said, as we sat down at the small table, brimming with food. "I think I went overboard."

"I'm sure Xavi would be happy to take care of any leftovers. You know boys; they're always starving."

"Speaking of starving boys, I heard from Nick today." I paused, struggling with the corkscrew and trying to avoid thoughts of Todd. The cork finally popped and I poured us each a glass of chilled white wine. "It seems not *every*thing in my study was lost. In fact, my old mandolin even made it through the storm. I'm really happy about that. It's been in my family for generations."

"Do you play?" Marisa asked.

"No, but Nick does. Well, sort of. He strums it like a ukulele and sings songs like "California Girls" and "Surfin' USA.""

"Your ancestors must be so proud." Marisa grinned.

"Well," I countered, "the first Americans in my family did live in California. They came up from Mexico during the Gold Rush, back when borders were hazy. So, maybe he's being true to his roots."

"Mexico, huh?" She scrutinized my face. "You don't look it. I mean, you're paler than I am. And I wonder where you got those light green eyes?"

"Who knows?" I shrugged. "I don't really know much about my family history. My father's father, the one who gave me the mandolin, was from San Francisco. His name was Lawrence Cardon, but everyone called him Law—not that he was on the straight and narrow. Far from it! He was a big-talking gambler, a real card shark. He used to tell me all about his youthful adventures, but he never mentioned family. I have no idea what his parents did—or *their* parents, back in Mexico. It's funny to think that we come from a long line of people that we don't know a damn thing about."

"Spaniards move around a lot less than Americans, but even when a family lives in the same place for a century or two, you don't necessarily know anything about them," Marisa said. "Both sides of my family come from a village near Cuenca, but all I know about the ones before my grandparents are their names and dates. No good stories. And, it doesn't help that Spaniards have the tradition of naming their children after themselves." Marisa rolled her eyes. "I come from an endless line of Maria Luisas and Miguels. Generations of them! How could anyone hope to stand out?"

I laughed. "Yeah, it seems Spaniards put all their creativity into nicknames, which don't even survive."

"Another thing," she added. "Although this has been a Catholic country since 1492—yes, yes, very exclusive of us, I know—if you go back far enough on anyone's family tree, there's a Muslim or a Jew peeking through the leaves. Now, I'm sure *those* ancestors could tell some fascinating tales."

"Each family must have thousands of lost stories. The unclaimed baggage of their past," I said. "It's sad, isn't it? I mean, my grandfather's gold-hungry relatives must have been some real characters. And the women! Those are the stories that have really fallen into the dark pit of oblivion. People think that, before the twentieth century, women were just busy raising children, keeping house, feeding a family or whatever, when they must have been doing incredible things."

"But think, Rachel. Back then, trying to feed a family was probably an adventure in itself."

"No doubt. But, I do wonder what my grandmother got up to while ole Grandpa Law was off bear hunting." I jiggled my eyebrows for effect. "Hey, let's give a toast to the old rascal's mandolin. Now, that's a hearty survivor if there ever was one."

We clinked glasses and took a long sip.

"It's funny how our favorite possessions become part of us," Marisa said. "Our houses aren't just sheltering structures, but windows into our souls. No, wait a minute. That's our eyes. Well, you get it."

"Of course. This morning I started thinking again about the people in Tuscaloosa. Those who lost everything they owned."

"It's so hard to imagine," Marisa agreed. "I mean, how do you up and replace a whole house?"

I nodded. "You know, my mother's mother, who came from an endless line of southern farmers, lived to be a hundred. Unfortunately, though, for about the last ten years of her life, she was completely senile. She had to move in with us, a city about a hundred and fifty miles from her small town. For years, she wanted to run away from our house and go back to hers. Neighbors would find her, walking down the street, with a few dresses thrown over her shoulder, dangling from hangers. They'd bring her home, but the next day, she'd be at it again. 'My house,' she'd say. 'I want to be in my house.'"

"It's true. The pull of one's home is very strong."

"Well, a few years later, her condition got worse. She forgot who all of us were. Hell, she forgot who *she* was. She fixated on the word 'house' and started calling herself that. Like, when my mother would lift her up to dress her or bathe her, she'd say 'What are you doing to the house?' or 'Be careful with the house!' The last year or so, she didn't speak at all. But, you know what? The day after she died, her house—the one in the country, where she'd lived with her family? It mysteriously burnt to the ground."

"You're kidding!" Marisa cried. "My god, that sounds like something García Márquez might have written—way too good to be true."

"I swear, it happened." I laughed, crossing my heart. "But, seriously, it does show you how attached we humans are to our houses. In fact, I bet Hector and Fergal are missing theirs right now." I cast an appreciative gaze around the terrace, on the lush plants and the rooftop view of the old city. "Hmm, I wonder if Nick would be able to attach a little deck on to my study?"

"I think you should just aim for having your windows on straight," Marisa joked. "By the way, Rachel, when are you meeting that architect, Paco Nogales?"

"I've got an appointment with him tomorrow morning at eleven o'clock. Though I haven't really thought about what to ask him. You know him, don't you?"

"Not well. I've run into him at a few openings and museum events, but I've never had a real conversation with him. He's well respected in the field—he's done original work as well as restoring historical monuments—and, I must say, he's very attractive."

"After my last romance," I said, "I can't say I'm interested."

Sitting in the window-lined, minimalistic office, I had to admit that Marisa was right. At fifty or so, Paco Nogales was still a remarkably good-looking man. When I walked in, he was casually propped on the corner of his large, designer desk, empty except for the latest Mac computer. He was wearing faded jeans and an impeccable white shirt which contrasted with his skin, lightly browned by the desert.

"Rachel Cardon?" He showed me to a table next to the window; once seated, I brought out my notebook. "So, you're interested in the Admiral's Baths." Paco gave me a self-assured smile. "That was an interesting project."

"The restoration is really beautiful," I said. "It has a medieval feel, yet it's clean and airy. I imagine that's what it was like when it just opened."

"That was the idea," he said, clearly pleased. "Now, you said on the phone that you're writing an article about the bathhouse? What's it about?"

"Basically, I'm comparing Spanish bathing customs with other European countries. We know that, contrary to what people think, during the Middle Ages bathing was very popular all over the Continent: in Germany, France, Russia, Finland. The methods varied, of course, from steam, to saunas, to tubs. But, I wanted to determine the Muslim influence on bathing here in the peninsula."

"That is unquestionable. Daily ablutions are one of the most important Muslim rituals. Here in Spain, bathhouses were an integral part of a Muslim neighborhood. You see, they built their cities in separate, independent communities. Each had its own mosque, bakery, market—and public bath. When James I conquered Valencia from the Moors in 1238, there were as many as twenty-five bathhouses here in the city."

"Well, a lot of European cities could boast a couple dozen public bathhouses back then." I shrugged.

"But for what reasons?" he asked, raising an eyebrow. "The Germans and Eastern Europeans thought of baths as therapeutic or medicinal. That was never the case here. And in Paris and many other cities, bathhouses were just glorified brothels."

"I know." I smiled. "I'm sure you've seen those Gothic miniatures of bathhouses from France and Italy: the ones of women attending male clients or couples together in large tubs, eating and listening to musicians. Some even show men blatantly groping the women."

"Exactly! But here it wasn't like that. In fact, there is almost no Spanish iconography of bathing—it wasn't even considered an erotic subject. Spanish baths weren't places of debauchery for two reasons. For one, they were collective spaces, for groups. There were no private rooms or big tubs to play around in. But mainly, because men and women were never at the baths at the same time."

"I know the custom of bathing on alternative days. But, don't you think people would occasionally bend the rules? To meet up for a tryst?"

"No way. In fact, if a man went into the baths on the women's day—even just to sneak a peek—it was punishable by death. And if a woman dared go in on the men's day, it was open season on her. They could do with her whatever they pleased. Those were the laws, but, really, it seems that each sex enjoyed being there on their own. The women used the bathhouse to get together with their friends and sisters, away from dominant men, and the men used it to discuss business and—"

"Football?"

He laughed. "Maybe. Who knows?"

"Even so, don't you think it's naïve to imagine those customs would completely prevent sexual activity?"

"Oh, like Spanish bathhouses were medieval sex clubs for gay orgies?" He laughed again. "Sorry to disappoint you, Rachel, but I'm afraid they were really just places where people went to get clean. And gossip—that was *very* important too."

I looked down at my notes with a small smile, wondering what Hector would make of this guy. Paco had an attentive gaze and a soft, husky voice which, surely, had seduced a fair share of women over the years. He was good-natured, though, and charmingly intelligent.

"Let's see..." My voice trailed off. As we'd been talking about sex for the past five minutes, I'd lost my focus. "Oh, yes. According to my research, the popularity of the public baths began to wane all over Europe around 1500?"

"That happened even earlier here." Paco nodded. "At the time of James II—when the Admiral's Baths were built—it was still considered a good business. There were fourteen or fifteen bathhouses in the city: one in the Jewish Quarter, one in the Moorish Quarter, and a dozen or so in the Christian town. A hundred years later, that is around 1425, there were only about five in the whole city."

"According to what I've read, baths closed in sixteenth century Paris because of the spread of syphilis," I said. "And in Germany, the numbers dramatically dropped because the Protestant church, which of course was brand-new at the time, opposed them. If they weren't considered sinful in Valencia, why did they begin shutting down?"

"Well, the *hammam* is a fragile system—you can imagine the stress on the structure caused by those extreme temperatures—and it's rather expensive to maintain. If the owner wasn't making a good profit, I'm sure he'd close it up in no time. And, as a historian, you must remember that, in Spain, the Renaissance—if you could even call it that—was different than in the rest of Europe. The Inquisition was burning books and persecuting New Christians; the great monarch of the time, Philip II, was famous for austerity and piety; and the artists here weren't reveling in the human body—they were busily painting religious scenes or well-dressed noblemen. So," he concluded, "it probably wasn't the greatest time for public nudity."

"Of course," I said, almost blushing. I knew all that! Hell, I'd been teaching graduate level courses on Spanish history for years. I suppose I just hadn't thought of it in terms of bathhouses. Or something was distracting me. "Oh, another thing. I've been wondering about that little carving on the pillar in the warm room. The **I i F**. What do you make of that?"

"Not much," he said with a small shrug. "It dates back to the fourteenth century. It was probably either someone's initials—something akin to scratching "I was here" on your school desk—or a small declaration of affection. You know, like 'you + me = love'."

As he said it, smiling playfully, he looked me in the eye. I nearly blushed again.

"Really, we found a much more interesting mystery when we were doing the restoration," he said, going over to his desk to open a drawer. "We found these, in the storeroom wall, hidden in a crevice in the plaster. They're centuries old as well."

He handed me a pair of dice made from bone. I studied them in my outstretched hand: the cubes were imperfect, the carved dots, dyed with reddish ink, were now mostly faded. Staring at them, in my mind I could hear Indiana Jones' voice: *That belongs in a museum!*

"Wow," I whispered, tilting my open palm to make them move. "Do you know anything about them?"

"Not really," he said. "From the wear around the hole—which was near the floor, and probably behind some shelves—it seems that it was a regular hiding place. Gambling was illegal at the time, but extremely popular. We don't know if this person—maybe an owner? a client?—just kept his dice at the bathhouse, or actually played there as well."

Unable to resist any longer, I tossed the dice onto the desk.

"Double sixes." I grinned.

"Yeah, you'll get that a lot." He laughed. "These dice are loaded."

"No way!" I cried, trying again. In a half-dozen rolls, I got sixes three times. "So, maybe the Spanish Renaissance wasn't as pious and austere as all that?"

A few minutes later, I was at the door, shaking Paco's hand.

"Thanks so much for meeting with me," I said. "You've been a lot of help."

"Maybe now you could do something for me," he said, still holding my hand. "How about dinner tonight? Nine o'clock?"

THE DICE

1530-1535

*We live in such difficult times that
it is dangerous to speak or be silent.*

LUIS VIVES IN A LETTER TO ERASMUS

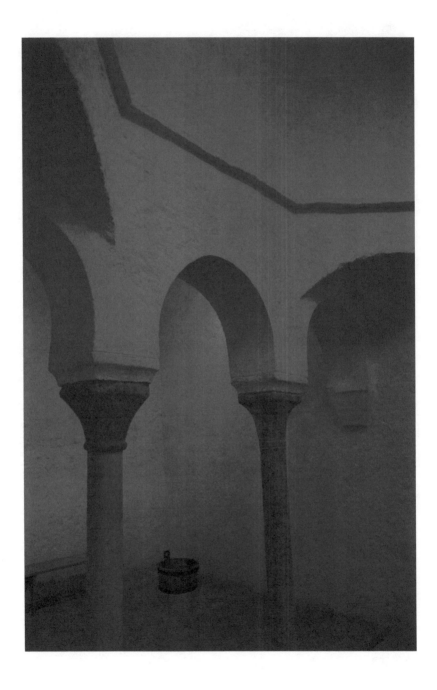

Angels Bonafé stood at the altar waiting to marry a man she barely knew. Wearing a black lace mantilla and a gray silk gown—items borrowed from her mother's trunk and dating from much better times—she was overly warm, but stood motionless in the stale air, the smell of incense still lingering from mass. At four o'clock on a June afternoon, the church was empty except for the meager wedding party. The groom, Bernat Flequer, having no remaining relatives, had asked his journeyman Luis to be his witness; Angels was attended by her mother Consuelo and brother Ricard. They were all watching as the priest walked towards them, tying his sash with a yawn, his siesta cut short; the sound of his slow footsteps was accompanied by the buzz of a vagrant fly.

"Good afternoon, Father Servando," Bernat said, stepping forward to give him his hand.

"This is the young lady, is it, Bernat?" the priest asked, appraising her sluggishly, then awarding her a smile. Angels' unusual fair hair, delicate features, and the inviting curves beneath the silk, did not leave even the craggy parish priest indifferent. "Shall we begin?"

Angels bit her lip with a glance towards her mother, and nodded.

"Now, what is your full name, miss?" the priest asked.

"Angels María Bonafé Ruiz," she said quietly, looking down at the floor.

"Bonafé?" he asked sharply, his expression towards the young woman immediately transforming, his eyes filling with distrust. "Are you related to that Bonafé woman who was arrested for Judaizing a few years back? The one who made such a spectacle of herself at the auto-da-fe?"

Angels went cold. She stared into his face, already twisting with undisguised loathing, unable to respond. The event he mentioned so effortlessly was one of the worst moments of her life. Was this priest going to question her faith too? Was he going to call the Holy Office? Bernat took a step forward.

"That was her aunt, Father," Bernat said in a low voice, "but the whole family had been on bad terms with her for more than a decade before it happened."

"Come here, young man."

The priest pulled Bernat to the side of the altar for a private conference, but everyone could hear what he said.

"What are you thinking, Bernat? You're from an old family! Why contaminate your blood by marrying into a filthy family of Jew-lovers?"

"Just look at her," he murmured, casting a glance back at his beautiful bride.

"You don't have to marry her to enjoy those pleasures. The Jewess," the priest proclaimed knowingly, "is notoriously weak of flesh."

"She is *not* a Jew, Father," Bernat whispered loudly. "And I want to take her lawfully. I want to marry her."

"Your parents would have never allowed it. You could ruin your reputation. Think of the bakery. Generations of hard work which, overnight, could—"

Angels stopped listening. Her family's public disgrace some four years ago had had so many tragic outcomes that being rendered almost unmarriageable seemed rather benign. She was sure that Bernat had heard these same arguments before, warnings about the possible consequences of marrying her. It astonished her that they did nothing to change his resolve.

Had she been able to choose, however, she would *not* be marrying Bernat Flequer. Although he was agreeable and handsome—with a striking face featuring light green eyes—he was a bungler, a risk-taker. This was, perhaps, the very reason he was willing to marry a woman from a family of converted Jews. Especially one who'd had an aunt judged guilty by the Inquisition.

Bernat's own background was rather humble (before the scandal, *her* father had owned one of the few printing presses in the city): he could barely read and was useless with accounts. But, he was an Old Christian. He had inherited the family bakery and, not bothered by gossip or genealogy, he bet his odds on marrying a woman of refinement and rare beauty. And, although Angels neither loved him or respected him, she reasoned that marrying a man of clean blood would give any future children a chance to earn a decent living and a reputation of their own making. She also thought that Bernat was probably the only option she would ever have.

"Are you sure?" she heard the incredulous priest bark out.

Bernat nodded and regained his place by Angels' side. With a long sigh, Father Servando mumbled, "You are either very brave or very foolish. Now then," he resumed, his head bobbing from one face to the other. "We shall proceed."

After the short ceremony—vows and rings rapidly exchanged, the registry dutifully signed—the priest returned to his chambers, unbuttoning the cassock as he walked away, and the journeyman ran back to the bakery. No further celebrations were planned. Angels stood in the sun in front of the church, turning the braided silver band around on her finger. She could think of nothing to say.

"Do you want to come round today and collect Angels' things?" Consuelo asked Bernat.

Angels turned to her mother with a creased brow. Relieved as she was that the ceremony had been performed as required, she had forgotten that she would now be moving to Bernat's house over the bakery. Although a fully grown woman of twenty, she was nervous about leaving her family home and becoming the mistress of her own.

"Yes, I've borrowed a friend's cart," he said. "Though I'd like to take Angels on a ride first."

"Come when you like," she said, giving Bernat's hand a formal shake. "We'll be there."

Ricard kissed his sister's cheek then turned to Bernat. As Angels embraced her mother, she heard her brother's voice, low and serious.

"Mind that you treat her well," he said. "Old Christian or not."

Bernat led Angels to the mule cart and helped her up. Sitting next to him, she realized that, although they were in a city street, it was the first time they'd ever been alone together. With a similar thought undoubtedly in his mind, he picked up her hand and kissed it.

"Shall we go outside the walls, wife?" He smiled.

"Wherever you like, Bernat," she said, in no mood for playing the happy bride and calling him 'husband.'

With a flick of the reins, the cart heaved forward with a jerk, and they began to roll down the street. Angels let the mantilla fall onto her shoulders and undid the small buttons fastening her collar; she would have liked to have changed into a simpler, cooler dress before being paraded about. Proud of his wife's beauty, he deliberately weaved through the marketplace to call out to his friends—other bakers and tradesman—who clapped and whistled as they went by. She sat next to him, silently stewing. How would they react if they knew her family name? The idea that she should feel grateful to Bernat Flequer for marrying her made her cross. Four years ago she would have never considered accepting his hand.

Determined to impress her, he headed toward the gates to show her how an important man like himself did business. Outside the city, he drove over to the Penyarroja mill in Mont Olivet where he had his grain ground into flour.

An enormous place on the Na Rovella canal, it had six working millstones. These were surrounded by farmers, bakers, and more than a dozen millers, tending to the clients, the mechanisms, and the donkeys, which tread round the stones, a thin layer of white powder covering their fur. It was a chaotic place: men were shouting, accusing the millers of swindling them while packing the sacks onto squeaky carts; the animals, braying; the wheels, grinding—and in the middle of it all, the owner was quietly surveying the scene. Bernat pointed him out to Angels.

"That's the man I deal with, don Filibert Penyarroja," he said. "Not only does his family own this mill—one of the biggest in the city—but they've also got a number of bakeries in town. They say his ancestors were at King James's side when they ousted the Moors from Valencia." He leaned closer to her and lowered his voice, despite the din around them. "A few years back, he married a noblewoman, Salvadora de Hurtado. She's older than him and thin as a rail—but I can say that one of my fellow guildsman dines at the Viceroy's Palace."

While Bernat was talking about don Filibert, maneuvering the mule cart closer, Angels was studying him. A big man, he was elegantly dressed, wearing a brocade doublet and velvet cap even in early summer. His features were regular and pleasing, framed by a well-trimmed reddish beard, and his bearing commanded respect. Bernat reined the animals and jumped down from the cart, eager to boast his acquaintance.

"Good afternoon, don Filibert," he said cheerfully, shaking hands.

Filibert turned his gaze on Angels, still seated in the cart. Without taking his eyes off her, he murmured, "It seems you've brought something other than grain today, Bernat."

"This is my new wife," he said, presenting her with a sweep of the hand while thrusting out his chest. "Angels, come down and meet the owner of the mills, don Filibert Penyarroja."

Bernat took a step to help her down, but Filibert was closer. As he took her hand, they got a shock, making them each draw back their hands back and laugh. She slid her fingers down her silk skirts, then offered him her hand again.

On the ground, Filibert's gray eyes found hers; she was attracted to their serene power, their unfaltering confidence.

"Don Filibert, this is Angels Bonafé," Bernat said, taking her arm. "I thought I'd show her where I get my flour."

"It's a pleasure to receive such a visit, but this is really no place for a lady." Filibert reproached the baker. "Especially one so beautifully dressed. After a few moments here, Madame, you'll find yourself covered in flour dust."

"Oh, don't worry about that," said Angels, her eyes twinkling. "It's become quite fashionable for ladies to brush on a touch of white powder before going out into the street."

"Quite so, Madame," he returned, "but you seem in no need of artificial aids for beauty."

"Hear, hear!" Bernat chimed in, delighted with his wife's wit and courtly manners. An able match for don Filibert. "But today there'll be no powder for you, Angels. We still need to move your things."

"Well, I hope to see you again," Filibert said, holding fast to her hand as he helped her back into the cart.

He patted the mule and waved at Bernat. "See you next week. That is, unless you are taking nuptial holidays?"

"No such luck," he said. "I'll be here."

It took very little time to collect Angels' few possessions: a trunk of clothing and linens, some crockery, a half-dozen books and a carved box full of quills, a long-ago present from her father. While Bernat was packing it all onto the cart, she went to her parents' room and took off the wedding dress. She stood in silence, surrounded by the vestiges of her childhood: the heavy, worn furniture, the wall hangings, her grandmother's chipped washbasin, painted with the golden glaze. Her eyes wandered fondly around the room, then came to a stop on her father's library. It had not seen a new volume since the family had lost the press. She was suddenly engulfed by an overwhelming sadness. How had it come to this?

Before their Aunt Esther was arrested, their father's print shop had prospered, especially since the university—a place requiring multiple volumes of a great many texts—had been built on the top of the razed Jewish Quarter. At that time, Ricard, then eighteen, had his own notions about expanding the business while Angels, two years younger, was looking at bright marriage prospects. All of that changed in a few hours. It didn't seem to matter to anyone that they'd been estranged from their aunt for years. Was that fact seen, perhaps, as a sign that they knew of her deceit? Complicity through silence? After the auto-da-fe, her family lost everything: their good name, their livelihood, and shortly thereafter, their father, Jesús. They had been interrogated by the Head Inquisitor himself and finally released. But ever since, they'd lived in fear that, one day, they would be brought back in and tortured into confessions.

Breathing deeply, Angels put on a simple dress and lay the silk and lace on the bed, making a wedding ghost. With a last glimpse round, she returned to the salon.

"Oh, Angels." Her mother sighed. "You looked so lovely in that dress. You don't want to take it with you?"

"I'd have nowhere to wear it."

She put her arms around her mother and brother, and pulled them close. Since the family's ruin and the death of Jesús, the three of them had been inseparable.

"Everything's tied onto the cart," Bernat called from the doorway.

"I'll come by tomorrow," Angels promised. "And probably every day after that."

When they had brought her things up the stairs of her new home, Bernat smiled at her.

"Remember, this is your house now. Make what changes please you. I'll be back in a few minutes. I have to take Felipe back his cart."

Angels looked around, fanning herself with both hands; above the bakery oven, the room was uncomfortably warm. A moment was all that was needed to take in the sparse decoration: a few simple pieces of furniture and whitewashed walls. These were unadorned except for a large plate hanging over the fireplace featuring two coats of arms, glazed green. She shook her head and plopped down on a wooden stool. How gloomy and colorless this was compared to her family home. Even after they'd been forced to sell their nicest things—the buyers slipping in to make their purchases in secret, paying a fraction of the worth—their house had a certain elegance. And how might Bernat's place, perched precariously over a bakery, compare to the estate of don Filibert Penyarroja?

With a sigh of resignation, Angels began unpacking her trunk. She'd been born with a practical nature, hardened by circumstance, and always tried to take advantage of limited opportunities even when the choices seemed bleak. In that respect, she was like her grandmother.

Grandmother Judith had lived with her family when she was growing up and the older people in the community often told Angels that she took after her. As a girl, she never liked being compared to a wrinkled old woman, but she gradually saw the truth in it. Not only had Judith been fair-haired and pretty in her youth, but they had a similar character. She remembered her grandmother talking about the difficult decisions she'd had to make with her own husband, Samuel, an impractical dreamer much like Bernat. And more than once, Judith had told Angels and Ricard about the painful choice she'd made in the spring of 1492.

Pregnant with Jesús and Esther just three, Judith had been spinning one day when Samuel rushed into the house with the news: the Jews were being expelled from Spain. Isabella and Ferdinand, the Catholic Monarchs, had allotted them only four months to settle their affairs, but would not allow any gold or silver to be taken out of the country. Wringing his hands, Samuel had begun spouting out different options—Turkey, Portugal, Italy?—while interrupting himself with his worries about the task at hand: what of the printing press? And the library? Judith had watched and listened, and then finally, very softly, said, "I'm not going anywhere."

More pragmatic than religious, Judith wanted security for her children, not aimless wandering. On this matter she was firm. They would convert to Christianity and stay in Valencia. Her husband was less sure and suffered greatly over the idea of losing his religion, his culture, his family ties. But, in the end, Judith persuaded him to stay. The three of them, Samuel, Judith and little Esther, converted to Christianity; their surname, Barouk, was replaced with Bonafé, meaning 'good faith.'

In the next few months they watched as their loved ones readied themselves for the move. The market was completely flooded as the Spanish Jews were forced to sell their possessions—properties that had been in families for generations—for next to nothing: a house for a sack of lentils, a workshop for a jar of honey, a vineyard for a handkerchief. At the end of July, the last Jews left Spain, leaving the peninsula on uncertain voyages to distant lands. At the same time, Judith gave birth to Angels' father, a handsome, healthy baby. Eager to prove themselves good Christians, they baptized him Jesús.

Some months after the exodus, the *converso* community began hearing rumors and reports about the fates of their families, friends, and neighbors, those who had left Spain. After loading onto boats at Valencia's port, paying high fares for lowly conditions, they'd had all sorts of misadventures at sea. Some were attacked by pirates who knew the Jews would be carrying all their finest possessions with them. Others were victims of unscrupulous captains, who abandoned them on beaches, sold them into slavery or simply murdered them on board. Many of those who reached their destinations, Lisbon, Naples or Fez, had been stricken with cholera or dysentery on their journeys and died shortly after their arrival.

Judith, although devastated by the tragic news, felt an intense relief that she had made the decision not to go. Samuel, on the other hand, felt guilty about having stayed, about his comfortable lifestyle and fraudulent status. He felt that, by forsaking the God of Israel, by abandoning his fellow Jews, he had somehow conspired to let such suffering happen. Had her grandfather spoken to Esther of his feelings? Had he impressed his shame upon her as a very small child?

Those who stayed, however, found that the life of the converted ones, the *conversos,* would also prove difficult. Spaniards became obsessed with lineage. Blood had to be old, pure and clean, untainted by a Muslim or Jewish ancestor. Elaborate genealogies were made, showing Christian lines that went back for generations, and shields and heraldry took on new meaning. Those who could not prove that their blood was clean, that their lineage was old and pure, were suspect. They were not allowed to take public office or religious orders and were barred from the army and the university. It was assumed that these New Christians were secretly practicing the rites of the infidels—shunning pork and praying in foreign tongues—and encouraging others to do the same. Therefore, the Holy Office, the Inquisition, became necessary to oust false converts, to keep Spain solely Catholic. Clean.

Angels looked up again at the coat of arms over the fireplace. Even without riches, special skills, studies, Old Christians could boast of their ancestors. Thinking back on hers, she shuddered, thinking what they had endured. But, skillful at discretion and visible humility, Angels had, up to now, kept Inquisitors away. And she had even managed to find a husband, such as he was.

After a simple supper—Bernat insisted on making the fried eggs and sausages himself—Angels went into the bed chamber to prepare for her wedding night. She pulled her linen dressing gown out of the trunk, and, before slipping it on, examined it; years ago she had put it away, starched and ironed, for this occasion. With a sigh, she ran her fingertips over the white-on-white embroidery, done at age thirteen, when she still enjoyed foolish daydreams about a future husband. Although the needlework around the neckline was delicate, the gown was cut like a sack and, where her legs came together, there was a slot in the fabric. Not only was it considered improper for a man to distinguish the outline of the body he would bed, but the woman was expected to wear the costume throughout the carnal act. With a shiver of fear, she put it on over her head. Looking down, trying to make out the effect, she saw the hole in the middle and was ashamed. Angels jumped into bed and, although it was a warm evening, pulled the curtains closed.

"Can I come in now?" Bernat called through the door, already peeling off his shirt.

Beside her in bed, eager to touch his beautiful wife, he pulled at the thin linen dressing gown. Overly-starched years before, it was brittle, and immediately tore in his hands.

"Bernat," she cried, but he closed her mouth with a kiss and ripped the homely gown in half.

Angels braced herself for the worst: unpleasantness, pain, brutality. For years, she had caught fragments of women's conversations, disgruntled complaints about the nighttime rituals when husbands employed their bodies for pleasure. However, surprise soon replaced her nerves. Despite her shredded clothing, Bernat's caresses began slowly and in the most unlikely places: he kneaded her shoulders, nipped an earlobe, licked her neck. Her body, as stiff as the starched linen, gradually began to relax, to respond. By the time his hands grazed her nipples, she was aroused and anxious for him to continue. As his hands and mouth explored her body—slow and rough, fast and gentle—she moaned in delight. As she squirmed with desire, however, it was not her husband she was imagining touching her. Tightly closing her eyes, she was in the commanding arms of Filibert Penyarroja.

✥

Filibert was distracted at dinner. Glancing down at his fingers as he sopped his bread in gravy, he was suddenly reminded of the small spark he'd received when he touched Angels Bonafé. When he saw her, riding into the mill on the mule cart, he couldn't believe that a man like Bernat Flequer had been able to capture such a prize. She was graceful, refined and such a beauty! He was immediately reminded of the tales of Tirant lo Blanc, the knight who had won battles all over Europe, but lost his heart to a fair princess:

You know that in all my jousts, no knight has ever bested me, yet this damsel, with one glance, has vanquished my defenseless soul. If she has caused my ills, what doctor can cure me?

Filibert had never been much for reading, preferring the satisfying symmetry of numbers instead, but had loved that book since he was a boy. And now, he felt he understood Tirant's anguish over his love, Carmesina. In fact, Flequer's new wife was what he imagined the princess would look like, with her *shimmering golden tresses,* her eyes *shining like twin gemlike stars,* her face, *the color of the whitest lilies and roses.* How was it that this buffoon, this man he had seen lose so many times at dice that he was always a favorite to play, was able to wed a lady that other men could only read about in romantic tales?

When the last dinner plates had been taken away, Filibert decided to go to a tavern and make some discreet inquiries about her. Before leaving, he peeked into his wife's dressing room. After her last miscarriage a few weeks before, frail and still prone to tears, she had been keeping to her rooms. She looked up from a book, her face worn and lined.

"Salvadora, I'll be out for a few hours," he said. "Don't wait up for me. I'll sleep in my own quarters tonight."

She nodded in response, seemingly grateful.

A wide-brimmed hat aslant on his head and a light cape hanging off one shoulder, he quickened his pace out on the street. Although he rarely frequented the taverns, Filibert knew where his workers drank their wine and was confident they could tell him what he wanted to know. These men were always kept abreast of everything that went on in Valencia through their spouses: millers' wives were notorious gossips.

"Don Filibert!" one called out in surprise as he walked through the open door. Three of his men were sitting at a battered table in the corner. "To what do we owe this pleasure?"

"A jug of wine," he said to the barman and pulled up a stool to sit with the millers—Pep, Enric and Rafa—who all revealed their profession by the traces of flour on their hair and clothes.

After a few minutes' talk about work, Filibert casually mentioned Bernat's appearance that day at the mill.

"Did you see Flequer today, flaunting his new wife?" he said with a smile.

"Yeah, I did. Can you believe he married her?" Pep shook his head and the others followed suit.

"What do you mean?" asked Filibert. "It seemed to me the lady outranked him in every way."

"Oh, she's a beauty, alright," Rafa agreed, "but marrying into that family is just asking for trouble. Surely, you've heard the story of Esther Bonafé."

"No." Filibert shook his head. "That must have been when I was at war. Pray, what happened?"

"Ah, it's true," nodded Enric, the oldest among them, who had worked for Filibert's father as well. "You were off fighting in Italy at the time. Well, Esther Bonafé—and she would have been just as pretty as Bernat's wife if she hadn't had that crazy look in her eyes—got caught in a secret synagogue."

Filibert whistled. Many converted Jews were taken in by Inquisitors for dubious causes. He himself knew corrupt businessmen who accused *conversos* of Judaizing merely to get their hands on the victims' possessions. But this? This sounded like hard fact.

"There were about twenty of them, worshiping in Hebrew," Pep said with a little snort. "They even had their own rabbi. The auto-da-fe was a few weeks later. I saw the whole thing."

"I went too," Enric said. "They set up a scaffold in front of the cathedral so the tribunal could sit up high, for all to see. There was a huge crowd; people came in from the villages to watch."

Filibert shifted on his stool. He'd never been to a public display of that kind: the crowd heckling the condemned while snacking on nuts and wine. He found it vulgar, beneath him.

"There were fifty or sixty prisoners that day," Pep continued. "All wearing those pointed yellow hats. There were charges of bigamy, sodomy, heresy—but most of them were Jews."

"And none of those Jews from the synagogue would re-pent. Not one of them would convert to Christ, although they knew what was in store." Enric shook his head in wonder. "They took them on mules down to the riverbed, where the stakes were waiting."

"You should have seen them." Pep laughed. "They were filthy, with torn beards, and dressed in smocks painted with devils and flames—and still the pointed hats. They looked ridiculous!"

"To make them look even funnier, the guards put them on the burros backwards, two by two, with their hands tied behind them. Bouncing against each other, they looked like cheap, yel-low puppets."

Filibert could imagine the ghoulish mob, laughing delight-edly at the sight of the miserable prisoners, then rushing down to the dry riverbed to get as close to the flames as possible.

"So," he asked quietly, "the Bonafé woman was burnt?"

"No," Enric said. "Esther Bonafé was not sentenced to the pyre. She was to wear the San Benito. For life."

Filibert raised his eyebrows with a nod, grasping Angels' situation. The San Benito, or sacred sack, was perhaps even crueler than the relatively quick death by burning and brought terrible shame to the families. The accused had to wear the pointed cap and a yellow, sleeveless smock, painted with the Cross of Saint Andrew, a giant red X, every time he went out in public, to be insulted and spit on by those in the street. When the offender died, the smock was hung in the local church with his name written on it, for all eternity; if the cloth began to disintegrate, to decompose, a new one would be made. In this way, the sin and the shame was passed down from one generation to the next, forever. For a society obsessed with family lineage, with pride and honor, this was far worse than death.

"But, don Filibert, it did not end there," Enric said, wiping his mouth after a long sip of wine.

"What do you mean?" he asked.

"After the mass and the sentencing at the cathedral, she was allowed to go, wearing the San Benito," Enric explained. "Everyone was in the riverbed, waiting for the fires to be lit, when we saw her on the San José bridge. She'd climbed up the side of it, onto the rail." He put out his arms in demonstration of her keeping her balance.

"And she was grinning," Pep said. "Like a lunatic!"

"By now, everyone in the river had noticed her. They were looking up and pointing, waiting to see what she would do. All those people who'd been shouting all day suddenly went silent. Esther looked down at the crowd—at her family standing among them: Angels with her parents and her brother—and threw off the pointed cap and screamed, 'I am a Jew! And I will die a Jew, but on my own terms,' or something like that. And with that, she jumped! She jumped into the riverbed, the San Benito flying behind her."

Filibert's mouth dropped open.

"But she *didn't* die. She was maimed, but she didn't die. They took her off to the hospital for madmen and simpletons."

"She's still there," Rafa said, finally able to add something.

"And, you know," Pep said, a trickle of wine spilling out the side of his mouth with his laughter, "the nuns hate false converts. I bet they take their time to change her stinking bedding—if they ever do."

They told Filibert about the resulting consequences of the scandal: Angels' father's death, the loss of the printing press, and the family's financial ruin. He then understood why she had married the baker. In fact, for the first time ever, he was impressed by Bernat Flequer; it had taken real nerve to marry the beauty.

"She must truly love Bernat, after all he's done for her," Filibert ventured, as if he were completely indifferent.

"Oh, I don't know about that." Rafa shrugged. "My wife says she's a cold one. Seems the only people she has a real fondness for are her mother and her brother, Ricard."

"Yeah, Bernat's a real dolt." Pep sneered. "Though, I must say, I wouldn't mind sharing a bed with her."

At this turn of the conversation, Filibert got up to go. He bid the millers goodnight and paid for the wine. Walking home, he imagined scenes from the auto-da-fe: the carnival atmosphere, the yellow hats and smocks, the flames, the figure on the bridge. Poor Angels! It was not her fault that her father's sister lost her mind. Of course, he could not risk seeking her out but, perhaps, in some small way, he could find a way to help the young lady. After all, she'd been through so much.

⚬➲⚬

Angels was too ashamed to look Bernat in the eye when they awoke. She was relieved when he made no mention of her abandonment in bed, but merely suggested showing her the bakery. It was understood that she would begin working alongside her husband, though, growing up she would have never imagined her future would consist of kneading dough and manning hot ovens.

She followed him down the stairs to the San Roque Bakery. A modest establishment, it enjoyed a marginal success due to the fanciful designs of its bread: depending on the grain, the loaves were stamped, cut or molded in different ways. Angels had often come in to buy the cheap rye shaped like a cat's head or occasionally the sugar-bread spiral. In fact, that was how she'd met Bernat.

"All these details seem unimportant," he said, swiftly turning a white loaf into an eye-shape, then cutting lines down the sides. "But it's been done in exactly the same way for generations. Family legend has it that, after the Black Death swept through Valencia, when the city was just beginning to come back to life, an ancestor married a green-eyed beauty from the north. They bought these ovens and christened them San Roque, for the patron saint of healing, one that could combat the plague. It was thanks to her arts, they say, that we began making bread this way. Our customers have always liked it. In days of epidemics, this loaf is even considered lucky. It's said to ward off the evil eye."

Angels took a piece of dough in her smooth, white hands. In imitation of Bernat, she made an oblong shape and twisted the ends. The result somewhat resembled a pear.

"How do you *do* that?" she asked, wondering if she would ever learn this unwanted craft.

By the end of summer, however, she had mastered the shapes of all the different breads and her bedtime embarrassment as well. Dough and sex became the two main elements of her new married life. In those first few months, Angels also learned all about her new husband, who was not a complicated man. Apart from his talent as a lover, his cheerful demeanor, and his rich singing voice—to the delight of his clients, Bernat would occasionally burst into song at the bakery—she was disappointed by almost everything else.

He was so untidy that Angels usually greeted the day by stumbling over his boots or kicking a plate or cup. Moreover, his outlook on reality was completely askew: he didn't sense danger, was a poor judge of character and often bent the truth past all recognition. But what infuriated her most by far was his passion for games of chance.

Bernat seemed drawn to them, as if he had no will of his own, convinced each time that he would win largely. The games he liked required no skill whatsoever; he would merely play a card to see whose was highest, or cast a die upon a chessboard and bet on what color square it would land. Since gambling was prohibited and punished by substantial fines, Bernat could usually be found playing in dark taverns, under a bridge, or in some stranger's kitchen after curfew. He invariably seemed to lose. This careless attitude towards their scant savings vexed Angels, who worried that one day he might bet the bakery or the house. Having lost so much already, she could not bear the notion of losing to folly what little her husband had.

Nearly every day, when the bakery closed, Angels walked over to her family home to pay a call on her loved ones. A big X, the Cross of St Andrew, crudely carved on their front door after the auto-da-fe, was still visible on the wood, despite repaintings.

Before opening the door, she ran her finger down its groove; the very wood was tainted with the family shame.

"Hello?" she called as she walked in. "Mama? Ricard?"

"We're in the drawing room," her mother called back, "where it's coolest."

Feeling far more comfortable here than in her husband's home, she came in and curled up on her father's big oaken chair.

"How are things at the San Roque?" her mother asked, looking up from her needlework.

"Well, Bernat slipped out at mid-morning and came back without his belt." Angels sighed, shaking her head. "And a pocketful of money was undoubtedly lost before that."

"He's too trusting," said Ricard. "I'm sure all the rogues in Valencia test their marked cards on Bernat."

Although Angels usually didn't mind discussing his failures, today she was tired and cross, and wanted distraction.

"And how about you two?" she asked. "Any news?"

"I started work this morning on a new place on Caballeros street," Ricard said, showing her his broken palms. "Just working the pulleys, but they pay weekly."

Angels smiled sadly at her brother. After the auto-da-fe and their father's death, Ricard tried for a full year to keep up the family business. With the scandal, all the commissions they'd had been working on were immediately cancelled. A few of their more humble clients had come in saying that they would take their printed material if Ricard would be so kind as to remove the name Bonafé Printers from the frontispiece. Ostracism and debt finally forced him to sell the printing press for a scant sum.

Ricard told himself that—with the Inquisition's Index, censorship, and repression—it wasn't a good time for books, anyway. He would find a new craft, something that he liked even better. In the three years since the business had collapsed, however, he had only managed to find work in construction as a common laborer. For such lowly jobs, they didn't bother asking him for his full name.

"I'm sure something will come along soon," Angels managed.

"Yes," Ricard nodded. "Of course."

She was tempted to make a joking remark about how *he* should marry, but decided it inopportune. Ricard Bonafé was every bit as attractive as his sister and, having spent the last few years working construction, had a sculpted body: a broad chest, a slim waist, muscular legs. His looks, combined with his cultivated mind, would have made him a favorite for marriage, even outside the *converso* community, had it not been for the scandal. As it was, with neither financial stability or clean blood to offer, Ricard was still a bachelor with no prospects.

Crossing the plaza on her way home, Angels saw Filibert Penyarroja letting his horse drink at the fountain. After their playful exchange on her wedding day, she'd been hoping to see him again and was vaguely disappointed that he'd never come into the San Roque on miller business. But, she assumed that he must have learned her family history. Since they met, she'd glimpsed him only once, escorting his wife out of church. At first, Angels had seen the woman at his side and thought it was his mother, so gingerly he touched her, so hesitant her steps.

She watched him for a moment—his wide hand stroked the sweaty horse, then he took off his hat to drink himself, a strand of wavy hair flopping into the stream—pleased to have material to fortify her bedtime fantasies. Suddenly, Filibert looked over, catching her gaze. He raised his hand in greeting and led his horse over to her. She was taken aback that he would acknowledge her in public; not wanting to attract attention, she scanned the plaza, relieved to find only a couple of gypsies sitting in the shade. Those people didn't meddle in the affairs of others.

"Good afternoon, don Filibert," she said, bowing her head slightly.

"Greetings, Señora de Flequer." He smiled, giving her hand a light shake. "I see your touch is gentler today. Married life must agree with you."

"As a married man yourself, you must be keenly aware of all the benefits of having a spouse. 'The bone of my bone, the flesh of my flesh,' as the Bible says."

"Does it, then?" He raised his eyebrows, amused. "Well, it must be so."

Despite their words, each of them suspected the other was completely ill-suited for their respective partner.

"It's a beautiful horse you have," Angels said, searching for a topic beyond Bernat and Filibert's noble wife. "A strong, powerful animal, by the looks of him."

"Yes, he's an excellent sire," Filibert said.

They stood for a moment in silent conversation, merely looking at the other, until the horse interrupted with a whinny.

"A pleasure to see you again," she said. With a lick of her lips, she walked away.

⬥

Throughout the rest of the day, Filibert's thoughts wandered back to Angels Bonafé, her fair hair and sensual lips, her rounded figure and poised demeanor, and the mundane words they'd exchanged: *benefits, flesh, bone, beautiful, strong, powerful, animal, sire...* By nightfall, Filibert found himself at the gates of the city brothel, in spite of himself.

The *bordell* was a walled section of city, a town within a town, and bigger than both the Jewish and Moorish Quarters had been— *combined*—back before the expulsion. The only gate leading inside had a noose hanging from it, inciting visitors to behave. He walked in, past taverns where men were drinking and rolling dice, and houses where women sat under ornamental lamps, waiting for clients. He could hear tambourines and pipes being played and men howling with laughter, but felt uneasy and out of place. Filibert covered his face with the brim of his hat, hoping not to be recognized, but in dire need of finding a blond. He was aching with desire for Angels, and his imagination was not fanciful enough to allow him to simply go home and bed his wife, a plain, graying woman whom he had married solely for her station and title.

Prostitutes were confined to the *bordell*, an excellent city business, well-organized, protected and carefully watched. There seemed to be hundreds of women to choose from in the various taverns and brothels, extravagantly dressed in velvet and silk, and some were even good-looking. Filibert finally made the decision to go into one of the houses, and found it well-decorated and sweet smelling. The man at the door, even taller and broader than himself, welcomed him and asked what his pleasure would be.

"I'm looking for a pretty, fair-haired girl," Filibert replied, his voice flat and stern, as if he were there on serious business.

"Catalina!" called out the man, and a dark-eyed blond approached.

She had an attractive face and a pleasing figure, and she wore her hair down, something respectable women never did. Filibert could see that her hair was dyed with saffron, but it was wavy and long, hanging down to her elbows. He was aroused at the sight of it. She reached for his hand and led him to her bedroom. He had his pleasure with her, burying his face in her thick, musky hair, using the tips of it to gently brush her nipples, digging his hands into it as her well-trained mouth made his whole body tremble. Finally, he mounted her, grasping her hair like reins. All the while, he was imagining that he was not with a common whore, but with Angels, his Princess Carmesina. Filibert was never to forget that night.

It was made all the more memorable two weeks later, when he discovered a chancre sore the size of a fava bean on the left side of his penis. His concern was heightened still when, a fortnight later, he was laid up in bed with debilitating headaches and fever. His wife called her doctor—the best in Valencia—but, during the consultation, Filibert failed to mention the lesions oozing around his groin.

❧

Angels and Bernat had been married about a year and a half and were expecting their first child. She had long since reconciled herself to being a baker's wife and their business was doing quite well. Then, one chilly fall day, he came strutting into the bakery announcing an entrepreneurial victory. Exhilarated and triumphant, he boasted that he had bought a nobleman's bathhouse.

"The widow of the Baron of Alaqùas, Doña Damiata Montagut, has just sold me the Admiral's Bath and Bakery," he said, pronouncing the names with care. "What a feat, Angels! Up until now, all the owners have been noble. As of today, it belongs to us."

She looked up from the long wooden table where she'd been braiding pastry dough, and stared at him in disbelief.

"The 'Admiral's Baths!' 'Nobles!'" She spat out angrily. "How grand you make it sound! I've seen that rundown old bathhouse at the end of the alleyway. Don't you know? No one is using the public baths anymore; they've done nothing but close down." She walked over to the big adobe oven, warming her back while protectively holding her immense belly. "A feat! I'm sure the Montagut widow was delighted for you to buy them—you took a bad business off her hands."

"There's the bakery as well," he said quickly, "which gives us a chance to branch out."

"Another bakery? But we can't be two places at once. How will we manage?"

"We can work it out. Luis can work at the new place and I can go back and forth," he said confidently. "The ovens there are magnificent. And you'll like the baths once you've seen them."

"Even so, who will come to them? Certainly not the nobles, who are changing their clothes regularly, and no longer have any need to bathe. You yourself have three shirts to rotate. Nowadays, people wash their clothes, not their bodies. Only paupers clean themselves in public. How will the dirty bodies of the poor pay for the kindling to fire the ovens?" Angels let out a long sigh, softened by the expression on her husband's face. One of hopeful excitement. "Oh, Bernat," she finished quietly, "I do wish you'd asked my opinion."

The next morning, Bernat took her to see his new property. Angels walked slowly and heavily, her baby turning inside her. The night before, after much quibbling and stalling, he had finally admitted to the price of his new acquisition. He'd only been able to pay a fraction of the cost and had taken on a loan with high interest. The debt frightened Angels, but Bernat, always the gambler, was delighted with himself for buying the baths from a well-dressed lady from Caballeros street.

When they walked into the baths, she pulled her shawl tightly around her. It was musty and dark and, without the boiler working, the thick walls were keeping the chill of a rainy autumn inside the building.

"A cold bathhouse seems a bad omen, Bernat."

"The widow shut it down a day or two ago so that we could make a few general repairs. Honestly, Angels, I was here last week, and the baths still work beautifully."

"Beautifully." She sighed, trying to see around her.

The glass over the skylights was covered in such a thick layer of dust and soot, it barely let the light through. Examining the walls and arches—splotched with patches of mold—Angels thought it ironic that a place for washing oneself could look so filthy. They walked from the vestibule into the three bathing chambers, usually referred to as the cold, warm and hot rooms, though that day, they were all cool and damp. Angels found it a dismal place, old and bare, with uneven columns and splintery wooden benches.

She sat on one of them and, looking up at a large crack in the archway over the vestibule, she shook her head. "The first common people to own it," she said, repeating her husband's words.

From the bench, she watched Bernat poke around the place, his face glowing with a child's enthusiasm. Did he think now, with three commercial properties, he was going to join ranks of the elite tradesman in Valencia? Harboring misplaced ambitions and taking on impossible debt, Bernat had no head for business. Again, she was reminded of Filibert Penyarroja—a princely man of affairs with a veritable empire—and wondered what her life might have been like had she married a man like him. Comparing him to Bernat, she frowned in frustration, envisioning inaccessible leisure, finery, repose.

As if her thoughts had conjured him up, they ran into Filibert as they were coming out of the alleyway. He was going into the Admiral of Aragon's stone mansion, to pay a call on his old friend. Angels was initially embarrassed to be seen in her condition, with bloated features and a cumbersome frame, but when she saw the change in Filibert's appearance, she quickly forgot her own. He was much thinner—his hose sagging on narrow thighs—and his deep, ringed eyes made his exhaustion obvious. Clearly, he'd been gravely ill.

"How have you been?" Filibert smiled as he took her hand. "It's been months since our paths have crossed." He took a swift inventory of her body. "Ah, I see you are with child. Congratulations to you both. " He finally acknowledged Bernat.

"Thank you," she said, blushing down at her belly. "And you? Are you well?"

He shook his head and shrugged, as if this were a matter of little importance, and went on to ask about her brother, Ricard.

"I've heard that he has had difficulty finding proper work. What's he doing at the moment?" he asked, staring into Angels' face, with his mind seemingly on other things besides her older brother.

Angels looked him steadily in the eye, answering his question with a slight smile, which was rather out of context.

"He's been working construction these last few years. He wasn't trained to do any such thing. My father always assumed he'd take over the family printing press. He is such a knowledgeable man. But, I'm afraid at the moment he's working the pulleys. Not a very noble profession."

"I thought perhaps I could introduce him to my cousin, Miquel Sanchis. He's an established silk merchant and is looking for a new assistant. He's always done quite well."

"Don Filibert, that would be wonderful!" Angels exclaimed. "Ricard is good at both numbers and letters. He's refined and well-spoken. I'm sure that your cousin would be pleased with him."

"I will be happy to make the introductions, Angels. God be with you."

"God be with you, don Filibert," she said with a low bow. "And thank you."

When Filibert had gone into the Admiral's mansion, Bernat looked at his wife eagerly.

"Angels, this is marvelous. Filibert Penyarroja seems to have taken a liking to us. And so willing to help! Should we ask him to be our child's godfather? It would be useful for him to have such a powerful kinsman."

Angels shook her head, looking at her husband, perplexed. How was he able to forget her family's precarious situation? Did he never feel anxious when he saw inquisitors or priests walking with decision down their street? Did he think everyone had forgotten her Aunt Esther's dramatic performance? She didn't know whether to applaud his optimism or pity his blindness.

"Oh, Bernat, what are you saying?" Angels' tone was gentle. "Don't you understand what an awkward position that would put him in? He would have to refuse, of course. The Bonafé name would bring shame on him and could even put him under suspicion. Don't you remember the warnings you were given before we married?"

"Things have worked out fine," he said with a shrug. "No one has ever come knocking, wanting to question us or make arrests."

"Not yet," she said, "but it would take almost nothing to provoke them." She stopped suddenly and grabbed his arm. "I wonder... Bernat, what if the Church considers the bathhouse immoral? It *is* a place of nakedness, there's no denying that. Or maybe too...unchristian?"

"I'm sure the Holy Office has no interest in the Admiral's Baths. They've been around forever. Don't worry about it," he grumbled, a glint of unwanted concern in his own eyes. "And just forget what I said about Penyarroja."

"I must admit, I am surprised he is even willing to make informal introductions on Ricard's behalf. That's much more than I would have ever imagined from him. But, truly, it would be impossible for him to have an official connection to us. That would only cause him embarrassment."

Angels knew these things to be true, but could also read desire in the eyes of Filibert. Even in her condition, that look of longing was still there. She smiled to herself, thinking that, perhaps, she had a trace of influence left in this world.

❦

Filibert sat quietly in the Admiral's study, waiting for him to move a chess piece. He was playing poorly, thinking about Angels rather than pawns and bishops. She seemed pleased about her brother's new opportunities. Mildly aroused, he wondered how she might show her gratitude. He had always found her attractive but *now*—with a swollen belly, breasts increased twofold, lips riper than ever—he'd had to restrain himself from reaching out and touching that smooth skin stretched to bursting. His wife had never gotten past the third month of pregnancy, had never become round. How he would have liked to suck those milk-filled teats, grab those hips and take her right there on the street! Although he was still weak from his illness, the rash and sores had subsided, allowing him to return to his conjugal duties. But he would trade a lifetime of bedding his crisp, rigid wife for one night with the full-blown Angels Bonafé, be she Christian, *converso* or Jew.

He crossed his legs, staring down at the chessboard unseeing. If Angels' aunt had been arrested for witchcraft, he would believe it to run in the family. This inordinate desire—he slowly breathed out—felt as if a spell had been cast upon him.

Uncomfortable with his thoughts, he glanced around the study, his eyes jumping from the floor tiles to the painted ceiling, from the tapestries to the furniture. Everything in the room was adorned with the Admiral's heraldry, his arms, the family shield. A testimony to the fact an Old Christian lived within those walls.

Filibert Penyarroja's own house was covered with similar proof; his grandfather had designed their coat of arms as a young man: red, with six stylized millstones, and the motto *constancia en todo*, Constancy in all things. Filibert had had it painted on everything, down to the chamber pots. He thought of Angels' wretched ancestry—New Christians, Judaizers, lunatics—and wondered, in passing, what her house must look like with no shields or mottoes to decorate it.

When the Admiral finally called check-mate—which he could have done an hour earlier had he not deliberated so—Filibert made his excuses to leave. During the silent game, he had decided to go to the *Hospital de Folls i Innocents*, Valencia's madhouse, to see Esther Bonafé with his own eyes.

He'd passed the large building on numerous occasions—had even heard an occasional howl from its windows—but had never ventured inside. He loped slowly down the street towards the hospital—ever since the appearance of those first open sores, his joints had ached as if predicting perpetual rains—wondering what to expect. Was she indeed beautiful, like her niece? Could her survival be due to sorcery?

Inside the doorway, he stopped the first nun he saw, her black habit exposing only two small hands and a prune face.

"Excuse me, Mother," he asked, "can you tell me where to find Esther Bonafé?"

"Family, are you?" she asked, stroking her rosary and giving him a sharp look.

"Heavens, no! I... just wanted to see the Jewess for myself."

She nodded slowly.

"No family has ever visited, of course. Who would claim her? After the auto-da-fe we had dozens of curiosity-seekers come in to take a look, but not in recent years. You'll never see another like her," she said, pointing up at the ceiling with her thumb. "All women patients are on the second floor. Her bed is to the far left."

As he made his way up the stairs, Filibert could hear the patients' wails, screams, and cries for pity. The whole place reeked of urine and other odors, unidentifiable but equally unpleasant. On the second floor, he passed a woman in a cage who, in the unheated hallway, was wearing only a dirty shift, her hair cropped short. She bared her teeth at him and growled. Others patients sat limply on stools, or curled up on the floor. Some had metal chains on their arms or legs, eating into the flesh and smelling of rot; they were all filthy, with greasy hair, open sores, mucus making trails on dirty faces. Glancing at the pus-filled lesions around one woman's mouth, he told himself that they were completely unlike his own.

Approaching the narrow cot at the end of the corridor, he studied the form which had lain fallow there for over five years. Her legs, which no one had bothered to set with splints after the fall, were mangled and useless. Her arms were folded over her crossed garment: instead of the threadbare shifts worn by the other patients, Esther was still dressed in a San Benito, the yellow stained a dark ochre. The pointed cap was crumpled on the floor. Filibert could see that Esther Bonafé had certainly been handsome: her nose and jaw were straight, her long hair, blond swirled with gray, was thick but now matted. A sly smile wavered on her lips. Although she looked helpless and weak, Filibert dared not to get within an arm's reach of her.

"You there, Jew," he called "You are Esther Bonafé?"

There was no answer; her stare was blank though the smile remained. He didn't know what conversation he wanted from this woman; he expected to gain no knowledge or insight. Suddenly, however, a dark stain began to grow on the thin sheet underneath her, the smell of excrement filled the air. Filibert gawked a moment at the thin body producing this rude response to his inquiry, then shivered in repugnance.

"My God," he said, in disgust. "Filthy lunatic."

He examined her face for mirth or triumph, but saw nothing. Perhaps the Devil was working his magic here? In a panic, he quickly turned to go, barely believing this low animal— unspeaking, unmoving, unashamed—was related to his Angels. As he passed the woman in the cage, she began calling to him, her eyes shining.

"You! You think *you* are free? Think again!" she cried, grabbing the bars of the cage, her scrawny hands like claws. "Here, no one controls *my* thoughts. *I* can say what I please. You think *you* are free?" With that, she lifted her dress and exposed herself, shrieking with laughter.

Outside once more, Filibert wrapped his cape around him and walked quickly away from the hospital, unmindful of the pains in his legs, breathing the relatively fresh street air in great gulps. A shrewd, rational man, he found the hospital upsetting, and the lunatics, outside his grasp of understanding. Shivering in the fall breeze, he thought again of Esther: her pretty features ruined by the crafty smile, the vacant eyes, the soiled San Benito. It was no wonder she'd left such an impression on the crowd.

∽

Angels went to see Ricard, to tell him the news. She walked in the door, called out, and found him in the kitchen in front of the fireplace, pouring a trickle of olive oil on a slice of bread.

"Hello, little sister," he said with a grin, looking pointedly at her enormous belly.

"Today, Ricard, you have every reason to smile."

"Why's that?" His brow wrinkled with curiosity.

"I've just seen Filibert Penyarroja, the owner of the Mont Olivet mill. It seems that his cousin, a silk merchant named Miquel Sanchis, is looking for an assistant. Ricard, he's going to suggest you for the post."

"Really? That would be marvelous! How I would love to leave the fine art of pulling pulleys to boys—or to monkeys." He laughed, tossing the bread on the table to embrace his sister. "But, Angels, why would Penyarroja suggest me? I don't understand. Do you know him well?"

"Not really," began Angels, surprising herself by blushing.

"Oh, I see," he said, giving her a smile of complicity. "I won't ask any more questions. But, I do appreciate it. Silks! I should like to learn such a trade."

"I'm sure you'll do well. And, by the by, there is nothing between Filibert Penyarroja and me." She tried not to smile back at her brother. "But, listen, I have more to tell you, though this news is *not* good. Bernat has just bought the Admiral's Baths. You know, that dingy little place behind the cathedral. He's gotten us into terrible debt, and for what? A ramshackle old bathhouse—I swear it was built before the Flood—that no one even uses anymore."

"Oh, Angels, come now. I've always liked those old bathhouses. They have their charms. And the steam, it feels so good."

About to make a retort, Angels, with her mouth still open, suddenly felt a surprising stream running down her leg. She looked at her brother in panic.

"Ricard, my waters have broken," she cried. "Where's Mama?"

"She's gone to the cemetery," he said, already grabbing his hat, "Listen, you lay down and I'll go get her. I'll try to find the midwife as well."

"Tell Bernat too," she said. "He should be at our place. Though, Lord knows, maybe he's gone back to that worthless bathhouse."

Angels gathered some clean rags to soak up the waters and lumbered into her parents' bedroom to sink down onto the bed she'd been born in. Hugging her unborn child, she began to tremble, petrified at the idea of giving birth. She looked around the room, still filled with her father's presence, wishing he were there. Jesús Bonafé had always been able to set everything to rights: catching a stray kitten or mending a toy, tending a cut or whispering brave words. How different their lives would be now if he hadn't been killed.

Lying on the bed, she thought back on the days following the auto-da-fe. Terrified then too, she and her mother had stayed in the house, haunting it like ghosts. They were afraid of encountering vicious crowds and even uneasy about running into their neighbors; they no longer had any friends or acquaintances, as dishonor was more contagious than plague. When they finally ducked out to get food, Jesús accompanied them. Going to his workshop every day, he was getting used to being insulted on the street.

They were leaving the marketplace, toting bags of legumes, rice and salted cod—easily preserved foods, to avoid going out again until the crowds had found new game—when suddenly they heard a shout.

"Ha! It's the family of that witch that jumped off the bridge," cried a man. "That's her brother." He pointed at Jesús.

All of the people within earshot suddenly turned to stare, turnips and pears dropping from hands. The misfits on the margins came closer to gloat and curse, always delighted when others fell lower than they.

"Bonafé—what a name! It should be Malafé." crowed an old woman, pleased with her own wit. "I bet you're a bunch of Jew-lovers too."

"Smell them! What a stench. Just like Jews!" shouted a group of youths with varying degrees of beard, from the first down on the upper lip to a full set of whiskers. Trying to look menacing, they picked up rocks and feigned throwing them. "Get out of here, swine! They should have burnt the lot of you."

Jesús was standing in front of the women, trying to steer them away from the young roughs, when a sharp stone slipped from the hand of the bearded boy. It hit Jesús hard in the skull—crack!

Both their mouths, the boy's and the man's, popped open in astonishment. Blood began streaming down his cheek, his arms still weighted down with the bags of lentils and chick peas. At the sight of it—bold, red, running—all of the other boys let their rocks fly at once, pelting him as hard as they could.

Weeping, Angels curled up on the mattress, warm water leaking from her womb. She and Consuelo had stood watching, stupidly clutching their stores of food, unable to move. When the boys finally ran away, Jesús was dying in the dirty market square.

"Angels!"

To her vast relief, she heard her mother coming through the house. Consuelo burst into the bedroom and held her child.

"You're going to be fine," she whispered, wiping Angels' tears with her thumb. "Have the labor pains begun?"

"Not yet," she said. "Mama, I'm scared."

"I'm right here," her mother said, giving her hand a squeeze.

Ricard shortly returned with the midwife and left again; Bernat wasn't as easy to find. After trying the house, the baths and the bakeries, he began searching the gaming taverns. Late that evening, when they walked into the bedroom, Bernat was still trying to explain to his brother-in-law his eagerness to pay off the baths' debt.

"My wedding band isn't gone for good. I'd started winning again, for Christ sake!"

But he was immediately cut off by Angels' scream. Her pains had begun in earnest. The baby, however, would not be born for another eighteen hours. When she finally had him in her arms, euphoric and exhausted, Angels allowed her husband to name their son after himself.

Little Bernat was born in November, the same week that his father bought the Admiral's Baths. For several weeks Angels stayed at her mother's house and left the business affairs entirely to her husband; occupied with their newborn, she forgot to fret about his propensity to blunder. Bernat came by in the evenings, reeking of dry sweat, to see his son and give his wife news. In the afternoons when the bakery was closed, he'd been hard at work repairing the bathhouse, fixing the vaulted roof and replastering cracks. Ricard helped him at first, but soon went to work for Filibert's cousin; his presence became rare after that.

While Bernat barely slept, working harder than he had in his life, Angels lounged in her mother's feather bed with her baby. The overwhelming tenderness she felt towards her son, the outpouring of pure love, surprised even her. She spent the days cuddling him, fingering his scant curls as he nursed, staring at him, marveling at his tiny ears, his perfect nose. Her mother brought her rich broths for strength and sat by her bed, entertaining her with the tales of when she and Ricard were small, omitting all talk of the pregnancies she'd lost.

"Oh, how I wish Papa could see little Bernat." Angels sighed when the baby was a few days old. "I've been thinking about him ever since I lay down on this bed, wishing he were here. Look, he has Papa's chin."

"He does at that," her mother said, reaching down to gather the baby in her arms. "A grandson. He would have been so pleased."

From the bed, Angels watched her mother unwrap the newborn to bathe him, smiling at his little limbs. She tossed the soiled swaddling bands to the floor and gently dipped him into the old washbasin.

"Ah, Angels, he is beautiful."

Holding his head carefully, Consuelo began to clean him. The baby soon relaxed in the warm water, occasionally giving it a twitchy slap. As she washed her grandson, her smile was gradually replaced by a frown.

"Did you ever wonder," she asked, her eyes on the baby, "what came between your father and Esther?"

"I never really thought about it. Somehow I knew better than to ask why she never came here." Suddenly uneasy, Angels stared at her baby's determined little fists held above the water. "Did something happen, Mama? Did Papa know she was a practicing Jew?"

"We found out," Consuelo uttered tightly. "But, unfortunately for your brother, we found out too late."

"What do you mean?"

"She came by one day and asked Jesús if she could take Ricard to the livestock market. He had not yet turned two and I was heavy with you. I still remember Esther that day, using her charms to convince him. 'Tell me, brother, has he ever held a piglet in his arms?'" Consuelo mimicked the voice Angels had never known, then pursed her lips with fresh indignation. "She persuaded him. And Jesús let her take our son."

Her voice cracked, breaking the narrative; her eyes clamped down, still angry, twenty years later.

"When they finally returned to the house, Ricard wouldn't stop crying. Jesús took him and found his clothes were stained with blood. I grabbed my baby. 'What have you done?'

"Esther was so pleased with herself. Her eyes were already showing the madness within. 'I have honored your son with the ancient ritual,' she said. We were horrified, filled with rage, but terrified too. Just one year old and our son's life was ruined. Jesús wanted to shout but kept his voice low, anxious about being heard. 'You have given our baby the death sentence,' he said. Esther looked at him—so calm, so cool—and said she wanted to bring Ricard up in their parents' faith. Jesús told her to leave, that he never wanted to see her again.

"During that time, all those years we didn't see Esther, we clung to the hope that she'd come to her senses. That her fervor for being a Jew was just a passing fancy. We were deeply afraid, of course, that one day she would be caught and that the whole family would be made to suffer. God, how many times we wished she'd go off to the Promised Land and leave us in peace."

"Poor Ricard," whispered Angels, reaching out for her baby, needing to hold him immediately, naked, without his swaddling bands. "Poor Ricard."

She offered a breast to little Bernat and caressed his silky skin. She'd had no idea about her brother's circumcision; they'd never played naked as children, no one had ever hinted at it. Since her marriage, Angels had sometimes wondered if her brother had ever been with a woman. She could not imagine him frequenting the *bordell*, but supposed he'd had lovers. Now she knew that if the wrong woman saw his naked groin, he would surely be arrested.

Newfound concern for her brother and the enjoyment of her mother's care kept Angels with them longer than she'd intended. The days passed with talk of family—comic and bittersweet memories intermingling with the tragic—and Ricard's enthusiastic praise of Miquel Sanchis and the silk trade. In complete repose with her newborn in her arms, she was disinclined to move back in with her husband. She was dreading the awaiting chores at the bakery and bathhouse and found she rarely missed Bernat's company.

Filibert's illness never went entirely away. Whenever he thought he was getting better, he would relapse again, with fevers or headaches or terrible pains in his bowels. Sleep and appetite were both so rare, that his clothes hung on his once robust frame and his face was gray and hollow.

At Christmastime, more than a year after that first chancre had already disappeared, he decided to pay a visit on Andreu Llopis. A physician, he was one of the few Old Christians in the field. They had been neighbors as children, and he couldn't remember a time when he hadn't known him. As boys, they used to go down to the dry riverbed, pretending they were knights. Filibert always demanded the part of Tirant lo Blanc. Sometimes they would fight, brandishing sticks, and Filibert would defend his fair Carmesina, usually played by a watery log or a spindly tree. Filibert and Andreu rarely saw each other as adults but having spent a childhood together, they maintained a trusting friendship.

The moment he walked in the door, Andreu could see that his old friend was ill. He bade him sit down, drink a glass of wine, and tell him his symptoms.

"I feel like I've been poisoned," Filibert said in despair, after having listed his various ailments. "If I had any real enemies, I would swear to it."

"Yes, you have a terrible collection of complaints. And all of this within the year?" Andreu sat quietly for a moment, considering what could be causing his friend such pain, then looked at Filibert with a serious expression. "Let me ask you this, have you also had a rash? Bumps on the torso, the limbs, even on the palms?"

Filibert looked at him in surprise. "Yes, some months ago, I did. Although the bumps were unsightly, they didn't bother me—they neither itched nor hurt. I didn't worry about it, and they went away. But, how did you know? What does it mean?"

"My next question is not so easy, Filibert. But you can trust that your answer stays here, with me."

"Yes, yes, what do you need to know?"

"Have you lain with another woman? A prostitute, perhaps?"

"Andreu, you frighten me." Filibert's eyes were wide with alarm. "How do you know these things? Yes, I went to the *bordell* about a year ago. Don't ask me why—"

"And after taking the whore, did you do anything to protect yourself? Did you wrap yourself—your manhood—in a wine-soaked cloth?"

Filibert looked at his glass in distaste and rested it on the table, shaking his head.

"I'm very sorry to tell you this, old friend, but I think you have the great pox. You'd be surprised how many men do these days. Nearly all the men at the siege of Naples got it." He looked at Filibert's despondent face and frowned in empathy. "But, there is a cure that will help."

"What is it?" Filibert asked eagerly.

"Quicksilver."

On his way home, Filibert was feeling worse than he had when he'd arrived at his physician's. To take his pains away, Andreu mixed liquid mercury with henna and herbs, and heated it over coals. He had Filibert undress, then put a large cloak over him, and had him sit over the pot, breathing in the fumes. The quicksilver gave him an insatiable thirst but, at the same time, made him salivate uncontrollably. It was a maddening experience. When he could finally control his glands, when his mouth had stopped gushing like a broken pipe, he shakily put his clothes back on. As he looked into the mirror to put on his hat, he noticed that his skin had a bluish tinge. It was then he caught a scent like fried dough coming from his own pores. The whole episode horrified him; he didn't know if he would be able to continue the cure.

As Filibert was crossing the plaza in front of the market, walking slowly and feeling dizzy, he ran into his cousin. With a full head of silver hair, Miquel, who was several years older than him, now actually seemed the younger of the two. Well-built and energetic, he patted Filibert on the back, beaming.

"You found me an excellent man, dear cousin," he said. "Ricard's intelligent and well-spoken—and the ladies love him. And you know, he was honest enough to bring up the old family scandal, determined to warn me of the risks of our collaboration." Miquel shrugged. "But, even if I were worried about such infamy, most of our business is done in trade fairs outside of Valencia. The madwoman's notoriety does not pass the city walls."

Filibert, immensely tired, nodded in response, anxious to be on his way.

"Thanks again, Filibert," he said. "And a most happy Christmas to you and Salvadora."

He gave his cousin a half-wave and began his slow trek home. Again he wondered how thankful Angels might be about her brother's prospects. But, for the moment, the idea of coupling with her had lost all its attraction.

At New Year, Angels finally returned to her husband's house, which was unusually tidy. In her absence, Bernat had engaged a maid, Josefa, to help with the chores and the baby. Angels, still not ready to go back to work, was pleased by his generosity and immediately took to the maid. Tall, thin and stooped, Josefa had a hawkish nose which was unable to hide the thin black moustache growing beneath it. In spite of this imposing appearance, she was kindhearted and shy. She took care of everything, allowing Angels to pass the day with little Bernat.

That May, when their son was six months old, Bernat stoked the ovens and reopened the bathhouse for business. In spite of its scrubbed walls and skylights, the fresh paint, sturdy benches, and a new supply of oils and soaps, hardly anyone noticed. Bernat tried to encourage the customers from the bakeries to come bathe, but only succeeded in offending them. In the first week, a few people trickled in, but like his wife had warned him, they were all commoners.

"Angels," he slowly began, "I need you to help work in the bathhouse. For now, I just have Luis's little sister Maria keeping watch there, but it's no good. I think other woman would be encouraged to frequent the place if they knew a woman like you—"

"Like me!" She snorted. "Surely you must be kidding! Your Old Christians—be they dirty or poor—would not want me in their midst. I'll bake your bread but I will not be in the bathhouse, washing feet or oiling hair."

"I'm not asking that. I just need you to pop in, collect the earnings, check the place—"

"Oh, that I *will* do, Bernat." She smiled at him and stroked his face. "I'll mind the Baths' purse strings for you."

The next morning, Angels was finally drawn outside by a brilliant blue sky; the first, it seemed, since Bernat bought the baths. She decided to take her son on his first outing and made herself ready to leave the house. Josefa gently brushed Angels' hair, so long unattended, and twisted it into a plaited bun. She helped her out of her chemise, soiled with the dried rings of her own milk, and into her nicest dress; she had already regained her waist, though her breasts and hips were still exaggerated from pregnancy. Angels tied a fine lace bonnet under Bernat's chin and wrapped him in a small silk blanket; both were gifts from Ricard, already enjoying the benefits of his new post. She held her baby in her arms, smiled at their reflection in the mirror, then stepped into the sunshine.

Josefa accompanied them to the market and both women were delighted to watch the infant stare with grave intensity at all the colors and shapes on display. Angels gave him different things to touch—a clove of garlic, a walnut, a lemon—and laughed as he immediately brought each item to his mouth to try and suck it. He soon fell asleep, however, and the women began shopping in earnest.

Filibert Penyarroja had already finished conducting his affairs with the flour merchants and was leaving the marketplace when he caught sight of the two women buying fruit: a tall dark figure with a large beak, loaded down with baskets, stood next to a lovely fair one carrying a bundle of silk. What a peculiar pair they made, he was thinking, half amused, when he realized it was Angels Bonafé, out with her maid and son. He looked her over carefully, envying the intimacy the little suckling shared with that body, those astounding curves.

After making her purchases, Angels turned and saw Filibert watching her. They exchanged glances and smiled at one another. He looked healthier than when they'd last met, less thin, and his forest green cloak flattered him, his complexion and ruddy beard.

She quickly scanned the nearby stalls—she recognized none of the shoppers, all thoroughly preoccupied with meat and produce—then handed the baby to Josefa, who was able to balance both him and the baskets in her long arms. Angels sent them off to fetch a loaf of bread and slowly walked over to greet him. Filibert's eyes sparkled and he smiled to himself; the absurdity of a baker's wife buying bread made it clear that she wanted to be alone with him, that the attraction was mutual.

Watching her approach, he wondered if she would consent to becoming his mistress. Could something be arranged? The nun at the hospital said that it'd been years since anyone had shown interest in Esther Bonafé, which surely meant most everyone—including the Holy Office?—had forgotten that old story. At any rate, his own reputation was so solid, so indisputable, that he could have relations with whomever he pleased. Filibert Penyarroja had nothing to fear.

"Don Filibert, how happy I am to see you." She beamed. "I've been wanting to thank you again for recommending Ricard to your cousin. He loves the trade and says Señor Sanchis is a marvelous man."

"Yes, and Miquel is more than satisfied with your brother. I'm pleased it's worked out so well for them both. Now, tell me, how are you faring? I see you've had your child."

"Yes," she said, gesturing to the baby in Josefa's arms. "Little Bernat is a joy."

"And, already in his very short life, he has managed to perform an almost impossible feat. It seems he has made you even more beautiful."

Angels' mouth fell open. He would compliment her here in the marketplace. Again, she glanced around to see if anyone was watching, if they were attracting attention. Although she delighted in his praise, she could not afford to be the subject of gossip.

"I've been thinking," he continued, "you and I should spend more time together, Angels."

She stood smiling stupidly, unsure of how to respond. What was he suggesting? Was he doubting her respectability? Surely he wasn't yet another Old Christian who thought the Jewess 'weak of flesh'?

"Our meetings are always a pleasure," she said finally, clearing her throat, "but we are so rarely at the same places."

"True," he said jovially, "and we need to rectify that. Where can I find you?"

"Well, don Filibert," she said slowly, her eyes darting nervously around the marketplace, "if you should need me, I am nearly always at home or at the San Roque. And now, it seems, I'll often be at the Admiral's Baths as well."

"Oh, yes." Filibert shook his head in amusement. "I heard that Bernat had bought the old bathhouse. I wonder why?"

"With all the soap and steam," she said quietly, looking him in the eye, "maybe he thinks the Bonafé blood will become clean."

He'd professed an interest in her company; she would test his forbearance. Filibert raised an eyebrow, impressed.

"Perhaps it will, if you scrub hard enough," he said with a smile. "I have every faith in you, Angels." He pressed her hand; she shivered. "I should like to visit Bernat's bathhouse. I hope to see you there soon."

Cradling her baby in her arms, Angels swept quickly out of the plaza, Josefa following her closely behind. She was utterly flattered by Filibert's attentions—her ideal partner wanted to be with her too—but terrified by them just the same.

That June, around the time of her second anniversary, Angels began working again. While Bernat ran the San Roque, she was in charge of the Admiral's Bakery; Josefa took care of the baby, carrying him to his mother at feeding times. Since the bakery shared a wall with the bathhouse, on women's days, she would go in every few hours, to check on Maria, verify everything was in working order, and collect the money. On the men's days to bathe, Ignasi, their young hireling, would bring her the earnings at the end of the day. Very few people went in, however, and she had yet to see Filibert there.

After a few weeks of monitoring the baths, only ever catching the odd woman shyly washing herself or a chemise, one day Angels was surprised to hear a lengthy conversation coming from a handful of women in the warm room.

The women who came to the baths rarely spoke at all; there was no empathy or solidarity among them. Angels assumed this solemn silence came from fear of saying something wrong, something that could be misinterpreted. When people were taken away by the Holy Office, it was never revealed who had turned in their names. The accusers remained anonymous, which made people wary about talking in front of strangers. This was an ignorant lot. These women were of very low station and had almost no education. But they were not stupid.

As Angels walked in and out of the warm room, surveying the boiler, the fountain, the stock of soap and buckets, she caught snatches of their discussion. That small group, wrapped tightly in bathing sheets and trying to wash themselves without disclosing their nudity, was talking about being women:

"Last Sunday at mass, the priest said that we're all the daughters of Eve. He said that, by nature, we women are wicked."

"No, there are *two* kinds of women in the world, the Marys and the Eves, the good and the bad."

"They say that Eve was dark, with black hair and eyes, but that Mary was fair," said one, sadly looking around the room at her fellow brunets.

"We should always try to be like the Virgin, modest and obedient, and not to tempt men—"

"Men are weak enough as it is."

"Women shouldn't try to be pretty with fine clothes, perfumes and powders..."

"My confessor says that a woman's body is the cause of sin. I am proud to say that I have never touched myself between the legs, not even to wash."

"Oh, heavens no! I would never touch myself there."

Angels slipped back into the vestibule, shaking her head. These virtuous ladies were literally unclean. She wondered if they really believed the things they were saying, or if they were merely repeating the words of the clergymen. Safe conversation to keep the inquisitive away. Surely, these poor, humble women didn't think themselves wicked. What thoughts did they really have in their heads?

Of course, according to the Church, even thought could be sin. Acts, words, thoughts: these were all to be divulged to one's priest at the moment of confession. Angels, however, was of the belief that her thoughts, ideas and desires, were hers alone, not something to be divulged to a black-robed man. Within her mind, she could freely enjoy thoughts that could put her on the pyre.

Recalling the women's description of the two models of women, she realized for the first time that, having inherited her grandmother's blond hair and blue eyes, she had the physical type of the Virgin. What an irony, she thought, for a *converso* to resemble the Mother of God.

As Angels came out into the street, moist from the steam, she saw Filibert walking towards the bathhouse. She wondered if *he* thought she resembled the Virgin Mary. Or did he think of other things when he saw her? She quickly smoothed her hair into place and waved back at him. They were alone in the alleyway.

"I've finally made it to your baths," he said. "I'm ready to cleanse my soul."

Beside her now, he shook her hand lightly. Although he had not regained the color and strength he'd had before his illness, she still found him attractive and was delighted by his attentions. Especially there, alone, in a windowless cul-de-sac.

"I'm afraid you can't do it today." She laughed, her stomach aflutter. "It's the women's day to bathe. You'll have to come back tomorrow."

"What a shame. I don't know if that will be possible. It seems I'm always so busy. Where are you off to now?"

"Back to the bakery," she said, still smiling at him. "I don't suppose you need a few loaves?"

"That I don't. But I will walk with you. For a moment or two."

⚭

Although Filibert's agenda was indeed full with meetings with guild members and accountants, the next day he stole away to return to the baths. Not only did he hope to see Angels again, but he also thought the hot steam would relieve the pain in his joints. He walked into the quiet vestibule and took off his hat and cloak. The place was less squalid than he'd been expecting—the hefty walls had recently been whitewashed and the place smelled clean—but the other man in the room, pulling his woolen socks up to a stained pair of baggy breeches, was obviously a peasant. Straining up to remove the lace ruff from around his neck, he realized how difficult it was to undress without his valet. And if he and Angels did have a tryst? Did one take one's servants along for the disrobing? Would she do the honors?

In no humor to fight with his clothes, Filibert quickly gathered his things and left the bathhouse. Peeking into the bakery, he saw Angels sitting down, breastfeeding the plump baby, the maid towering over them possessively. Bernat was there too, joking around with a few other men, laughing his loathsome donkey's bray. Filibert made his way out of the street, determined to find moments when he could meet with Angels alone.

In the weeks to come, he ignored his wife and his duties to the mill, and concentrated on discovering the routines and whereabouts of Angels Bonafé. Now entirely indifferent to rumors of ill-repute, he rose early in the mornings to watch her house, followed her movements, and even shadowed Bernat in the evenings, locating his favorite taverns and gaming spots.

Filibert learnt when she went to market, in what church she attended mass, and at which times Bernat was absent from the bakeries. With a few carefully chosen words in the street one morning, he also ingratiated himself to her maid Josefa, making an important ally. In the evenings when the family was tucked into their house, Filibert made appearances at the most fashionable palaces and soirées, arming himself with ample provisions of anecdotes and gossip about court and fashion. As the weather cooled at summer's end, he was ready to begin his campaign. He was determined to have Angels Bonafé, the most beautiful woman in Valencia, as his lover.

Filibert was amused at her astonishment when he first began to make his presence known to her: near the noisy fishmongers, in the shadow of a vacant confessional, leaning against the bathhouse wall. 'Oh, don Filibert,' she'd nervously breathe, 'it was as if you were but waiting for me.' He knew that, despite her modesty and bashfulness, she wanted to be with him.

In their brief interviews—at first never longer than a few minutes, but gradually increasing—she would sometimes allow him to gently touch her: her sleeve, a lock of hair, her hand. Josefa, discreet and faithful, made it possible for them to have a few moments alone, stepping aside with little Bernat, now a toddler, to call his attention to something on the street: a one-armed beggar playing the pipes or clouds shaped like hats.

Filibert Penyarroja took pains to speak to her like a knight to his lady, Tirant lo Blanc to Carmesina, sure that Bernat was incapable of such speech. He provided Angels with details about the festivities he attended at the Viceroy of Valencia's palace, always lamenting the fact that she could not accompany him. He painted her pictures of elegant evenings of chamber music, theatre and poetry, or strolls through the palace grounds, where exotic animals and plants from the New World abounded.

Rapt, her blue eyes glowing with attention, it was clear that Angels loved these encounters, which left so little to chance. However, as the months went by, she continued the farce of not understanding what he wanted, making it impossible to plan a meeting alone, in his rooms. Although it was frustrating, he would have expected nothing less of his lady. He could wait.

⤛⤜

A sunny morning that spring, from behind the counter of the Admiral's Bakery, Angels saw Ricard and Miquel coming from the direction of the bathhouse. She jumped from her stool to go outside to greet them.

"Jaume!" she called out to their new apprentice from the doorway. "I'm going out for a bit. Keep a watch on the front, will you?"

She ran out to the street to give her brother a hug.

"Good morning, you two," she said, shaking hands with Miquel. "Have you been back in town long?"

"We pulled in early this morning covered in dust and grime from the journey," Ricard said. "I suggested to Miquel that we come here and take a proper bath."

"Quite luxurious, I must say." Miquel nodded. "I feel like a new man."

"Splendid! It's nice to hear that someone is actually using it for bathing." She rolled her eyes. "Would you believe that I caught Bernat and his mates in the vestibule last week, crouched down in the middle of the floor, shooting dice? It finally made sense to me why he wanted to buy the place—to have his own gaming rooms! Even though it was a man's day, I stormed in there and kicked them out. Imagine what could have happened if they were discovered? I know Inquisitors don't make a point of going after gamers, but in our case, who knows?"

"Well, have no fear, this morning there were no cards or dice." Ricard laughed at his sister's temper. "Just our sweaty bodies, hot water, soap and a couple of sponges."

Angels blushed, remembering not only her brother's lack of foreskin—had Miquel noticed?—but herself.

"Forgive me, don Miquel. I suppose I shouldn't talk about these things outside of family."

"You pay me the compliment of intimacy, Angels," he said with a slight bow. "I'm flattered."

"Let's forget the bathhouse," she said, linking arms with them both. "Now, tell me, how was your journey?"

"Seville is lovely," Ricard said. "And, of course, as the only port allowed to do trade with the Americas, it's bustling with business. At the market we bought some of the strange produce from the New World, but it was nearly inedible—all of it either tasteless, bitter or spicy. Oh, and we even saw some savages—"

"They're beautiful in their way," Miquel added. "Dark and hairless."

"And the fair was excellent. You should have seen Miquel at the bargaining table. His negotiations were all shrewd, his deals, all profitable—"

"And Ricard has learnt the trade every bit as well." Miquel laughed. "He's a natural merchant."

"Angels," Ricard continued, beaming at his mentor's praise, "Miquel and I have been invited to show our silks at the Court of Charles the Fifth. Next month, we'll be traveling the Camino Real to Toledo."

"That's magnificent," Angels cried. "Perhaps one day your nephew can join you in the trade."

"Barely walking, yet you have made plans for the lad." Ricard squeezed his sister's arm playfully. "You never know, he might like to follow his father's footsteps. Bernat's prospects could take a upward turn and—"

"Yes," Angels retorted, "and Aunt Esther could be beatified by the Church."

"Hey," Ricard said, slowing down as they reached their front door, the great X almost worn off. "You know I'll always be here for your son."

"Yes, I know. Bernat does try, but I can't help worrying. Listen, I should go back to the bakery, but I'll come back this afternoon. I want to hear all about your adventures."

Turning back on her steps, Angels was unamazed to see Filibert Penyarroja not ten paces away, pretending to look at a potter's wares. After her initial reluctance about talking to him in public, she'd come to realize—to her great surprise—how infrequently other people watched her, how unconcerned they were about what she did or who she spoke with.

With a small smile, she walked towards him. The square was rather crowded, but she could risk a short exchange. No longer wary or embarrassed, she now looked forward to these interludes; his appreciative gaze and charming words made her feel noble.

"Good morning," she said to him softly, picking up a dish painted with the hand of Fatima. "Nice work," she said in a serious tone, playfully mocking his feint. "Are you in need of crockery, don Filibert?"

"Angels!" He gave her a broad smile. "How nice it is to see you."

"And you," she said, her eyes shining. "I've just been with your cousin and Ricard. They returned from Seville this morning."

"Excellent," he said, leading her away from the vendors. "I'll pay a call on him soon to hear an account of his journey. Now, how are you?"

"Fine," she said. Scanning his face she noticed again that odd bluish tint. "And you? I haven't seen you for a day or two. Pray, how have you been keeping?"

As they made their way down the street, Angels still took care to walk an arm's length away from him, her hands held primly together.

"Very well," he said, "In fact, I went to the Viceroy's last night. He was entertaining some French dignitaries. And I thought Valencians were vain." He smiled with false modesty, stopping in the street to take in her keen expression. "These men, to appear more manly, padded their doublets with hay until their chests were nearly a yard across! Yet they reek of sweet perfume and, in their fingertips, they clutch the daintiest little handkerchiefs imaginable."

"And the women?" Angels asked breathlessly. Her interest in fashion and fine clothing had not been lost with her prospects.

"They pluck their hairlines, cover their faces in white paint, and then spend the evenings hiding behind their folding fans." He laughed.

"It's no wonder," she said with a giggle. "So, you cannot tell me, then, if they were beautiful?"

"None to match you." His voice was sincere. "But they do use their fans to a strange advantage. It's a new court language I have yet to master. The fan's location, movement, the way it's opened or closed, it all has meaning—though I have not discovered what." He pulled something out of his sleeve and handed it to her: a fan of ivory and lace. "This is for you. Perhaps, as a woman, you can uncover the mystery for me."

"Oh, Filibert." She gasped. "It's beautiful."

Opening the delicate fan, she looked into his eyes, wondering if they could risk a kiss. She contented herself with a meaningful hand squeeze, but so much emotion could hardly be contained in a gesture so small. Angels fluttered the fan in front of her face and sighed, wishing again that her relationship to Filibert had been sanctified by the Church. These moments with him, away from chores and finances, were dreamlike, and just as fleeting.

Regretfully, she turned down the street towards the San Roque, knowing he would accompany her to the corner, then take his leave.

"Oh, and last night," he said speaking quickly, also aware their time was near its end. "We were served something completely new. A smooth, brown drink from Mexico, sweetened with sugar and spiced with cinnamon. Xocolatl, they called it. It is so heavenly, I'm sure the Holy Office will forbid it." He gave her a smile of complicity. "I must try and get you some. Although I have heard it makes one desire love. Or love desire, I cannot remember which."

She blushed, savoring the look in Filibert's gray eyes, covering her mouth with the open fan.

"I'd like that," she whispered. "Now, I must go."

She felt his eyes on her as she climbed the stairs to her house, too excited to go straight back to work. She sat on a stool gazing down at his generous gift, fingering the fine lace, the sculpted ivory. The fan made a faint ripple as she opened and closed it, first slowly, then faster and faster.

Though Filibert's attentions made Angels feel attractive and alive, she was not so naïve as to think he was satisfied with this game. He wanted her as his mistress, that was clear. Angels was fairly certain that Bernat had been with other women since they'd wed—especially during the long weeks she'd spent with her mother, after the baby was born. She considered the possibilities, the clandestine meetings, the potential rewards, the risks. How might her fortunes change?

Weighing the consequences—what if they were caught?—she concluded, once again, that she was unwilling to add adultery to her family's disgrace. His delightful descriptions of life at court also made her keenly aware of the distance that separated them. Though he seemed unconcerned about being seen with her, she knew that he could never take her out in society. To many, her family was lower still than the slaves shipped in from Hispaniola. No, she would not give the Inquisitors a valid reason to condemn her. Angels would not discourage Filibert, but she would not let him have her. And perhaps, by not giving in and becoming his lover, she would also keep his interest.

She put the fan in the box with her quills—there would be no occasion ever to use it—and went back to the bakery.

Hours later, in her dark bed with Bernat, she held Filibert's body in her imagination, the only place where they could meet. Feeling the pressure of his heavy, ringed fingers on her body, a hint of cinnamon on his breath, she was overcome with passion.

Even though Angels resented the baths, their ill-repute and financial failure, she would go once a month, during her cycle, to stand in the hot steam and let it soothe the dull ache in her womb. Relaxing in the warm room, often alone, she amused herself with the notion of how horrified the men would be if they knew that, on alternate days, women bled on those benches, that they used the buckets to rinse out their rags. Nothing was as unclean to them as menstrual blood. Women on their periods were considered vile—they were certainly not allowed in churches—so frightening and awe-inspiring was it to men that, from a woman's sex, blood was shed without pain.

Without pain, thought Angels, was saying much.

She sat thinking about the Christian obsession with blood: pure and old—but not from a woman. Pondering the notion of clean blood, she reckoned fewer people came to the baths now because they associated them with the tainted races, the Jews and Muslims. The Muslims' had their daily ablutions before prayers and the Jews, their rituals of purification. For over a hundred years, it had been against the law for the three races to bathe together. As if Christians bathed! Clean blood, but dirty bodies.

She wondered if Christian men ever fantasized about the infidel baths of Granada, the ones in the Alhambra palace. Boabdil's wives would gather to wash in the tiled Hall of Beds with its horseshoe arches and center fountain. Angels imagined them scrubbing each other's backs, dancing, laughing softly. A harem of women each with thick black hair down to their waists, mysterious dark eyes painted with kohl, and green and purple jewels inexplicably grasped in belly buttons. They say that, from the gallery up above, the Islamic king would look down upon his naked wives and throw an apple to the one he wanted to bed that night. Oh, no, Christian men, the Inquisitors themselves, would not like *that*.

She glanced up again at the carving on the pillar: **I i F.** The grime trapped in the stone made it plain to see. It was clear to her that an over-zealous patriot had chiseled it there in honor of Isabella and Ferdinand, the obsessive Catholic Monarchs who had fought their Crusades at home. In 1491, they defeated Boabdil and Granada fell, and the next year, they expelled the Jews. When exactly did they create their ingenious Inquisition? I and F: Insanity and Fanaticism. If she weren't so relaxed, she would scratch out that carving herself.

Angels sighed, squeezing the water out of her rags. She threw a bucket of hot water on the bench where she'd been sitting, picked up her bath sheet and walked through the double doors, back to the vestibule, to get dressed and go home.

⁂

Filibert, visiting at the Admiral's mansion, saw Angels leaving the alleyway through the window. He resisted the urge to rush down to the street, contenting himself with observing her unseen. Today her blond hair was covered by netting; it looked a shade darker and he assumed it must be wet. He imagined her bathing, pouring buckets of water over her breasts, onto her lap, and got aroused at the idea. He fancied her dancing like Salome under the star-shaped skylights, her milky thighs exposed as she played with her seven veils, spinning around him. Just the idea made him dizzy. He would like to take her in the baths. Maybe sex with a beautiful Jewess could cure his ills?

He watched her backside until she disappeared from view. Filibert looked back into the room and found his friend speaking to him. The Admiral wore the same questioning expression, of misgiving and curiosity, that he'd seen on the face of his confessor this past year. Filibert, retracing his thoughts, suddenly had the vision of his own head on a platter.

THE ADMIRAL'S BATHS

Filibert hadn't been able to keep his mind on work for months. Before, his business affairs had thoroughly consumed him during the day and, at night, he had often focused his attentions on producing a noble heir. Now, he was interested in neither endeavor. He was too restless to oversee the mill activity, he was bored by the bakeries, and found touching his wife repellent. Remiss in all his other duties, he still kept his appointments with his physician.

As his condition was still delicate, twice a week, Andreu Llopis administered the treatments. Desperately wanting to appear the virile lover in front of Angels, he endured the thirst and spit, the nausea and dizziness, that the mercury brought on. However, he was not improving; in fact, his list of complaints seemed to be growing. Now, suffering also from gastric distress, tremors, hair loss, and rotting teeth, he was beginning to wonder if some of his problems were caused by the cure itself. With Angels, he tried to feign robustness, unheedful calm, total control. He did not use his walking stick and combed his hair carefully to hide its lack; he never mentioned ill health, but the charmed pursuits of a well-made man.

Nonetheless, he himself felt his weakness before her: not the frailty caused by the pox, but the one she herself imposed upon him. So fixated he was that, depending on her attitude, affection or words, he found himself at the height of euphoria or the depths of depression. Filibert was beginning to doubt if he would ever have her alone. And, if so, would he be strong enough to perform?

When crestfallen—a rainy day spent without a sighting; a glimpse of Bernat grabbing her waist; a moment when she seemed indifferent or rushed—he sometimes remembered her aunt's twitchy grin and, shuddering with agony, dared wonder if he *were* a victim of sorcery. Perhaps he should discuss witchcraft with his priest?

⌘

By the harvest of 1533, Bernat now two, Angels had grown wary of her chance meetings with Filibert. She could not leave her house without seeing him; he was lurking at every turn. However, he had not only grown careless, but unpredictable.

Although he could still be amusing, engaging her in playful banter, more often than not he seemed annoyed, suspicious, or bedeviled by her. At first she assumed that, after being thwarted for over a year, Filibert had become fed up with the chase. But, to her bafflement and frustration, he persevered.

He was no longer the man, so commanding and distinguished, that she had met on her wedding day. Not only was he losing his attractive mien—he had rapidly aged in the last few years—but he had become temperamental, vulgar, even frightening.

Once, outside the bathhouse, he had forgotten himself and backed her against the wall, his hands held fast to her waist. He'd brought his mouth to hers, had reached up to grasp a breast. She could smell him then, an unsavory combination of perfume, tooth decay, and that queer odor of fried dough. His washed-out eyes, so intent on her own, had given her a chill. With a few clever words, however, she had been able to break free, her charm intact.

Far worse than groping, however, was his recent allusion to the Grand Inquisitor. Just yesterday, he had stopped her in the marketplace and wedged her into a corner.

"You will never guess whose acquaintance I made at the Viceroy's palace last night. Don Alfonso of the Holy Office." He held her hand tightly, reveling in the effect the name had on her. "Such a pity you couldn't have been with me. He's such an enlightened man. And I'm sure he would have loved to meet *you*."

His smile was vicious; Angels turned pale, unable to come up with a retort.

"Perhaps you will give me reason to make introductions, dear Angels? Or maybe we could just have an evening to ourselves and leave don Alfonso to his own devices."

She nodded mutely, wrested her hand away, and turned to go, resisting the urge to run. This was a serious threat. Should she just sleep with the man—pay her dues and be done with it? It made her feel sick. The man she had long imagined in her bed no longer existed. She wondered what could be responsible for transforming a gentleman—her gallant knight, her ideal partner—into a bully and boor. She thought it must be drink.

Instead of giving in to his demands, offering herself up as tribute, Angels simply chose to stay close to home. She knew he would not come knocking. She invited her mother and Ricard to enjoy the warmth of the house above the oven and sent Josefa to the market alone. Dreading an encounter, she scanned the street thoroughly before going out—always in company—ever hoping he would find a new object for his affections. By the next harvest, she had become quite skilled in the strategy of avoidance. She'd not seen him alone since late summer when he flaunted the name of the Inquisitor.

Angels missed the romantic, courtly exchanges between them, the flattery and fantasy; she was even rather worried about Filibert, for his health and sound mind. But, for the first time since she married him, she realized she was better off with Bernat Flequer. Though he could be exasperating, he was, at least, consistent.

A year passed quickly. Now about to turn three, little Bernat was a handsome boy—taking after his mother but with his father's clear green eyes—and quick-witted as well. As their son prospered, however, the family businesses floundered.

Although the bakeries did a fair trade, the baths made no profits at all; in fact, much of the money made from bread was used for its upkeep alone. Bathhouses were no longer respectable, as Angels had said from the start. People were ashamed of their bodies and certainly did not want to expose them in public. Also, washing implied touching oneself, a suspect activity, a sin in the eyes of many. Bernat tried to make up these losses by playing cards and dice, confident in his luck, but his efforts were further draining the family's resources and putting them in serious debt.

Ricard, doing well in the silk trade, happily helped the family along. He brought his sister bolts of cloth and volumes of poetry, as well as high-priced items from the market. Little Bernat worshiped his uncle—his good nature and generosity—a fact which piqued his father.

That November, Bernat decided they should celebrate his son's birthday. Odd numbers were always best and three, the luckiest. He liked to bet on threes, praying to the Holy Trinity and blowing on the dice, and though he rarely won, he was never convinced that the number was without a certain magical quality.

He told Angels to invite her mother, Ricard and Miquel to spend the evening with them and specified that they needn't bring anything. That morning, he prepared a special dessert at the bakery—a large sugary bun with raisins and walnuts—and bought sweet wine at the bodega.

The guests arrived after the shops closed; nearing winter, it was cold and already dark.

"How are you keeping, Bernat?" Consuelo asked.

"I can't complain," he said, affable as always.

Angels smiled at her husband and squeezed his hand, delighted with him for making these arrangements.

"And here's young Bernat, already three," called his grandmother, whisking him off the floor.

Consuelo sat down on a stool in front of the fireplace and put Bernat on her knee. Ricard knelt down next to them and pulled a box out of his cloak.

"I've brought you a surprise," he said to the boy, both of their eyes shining at the idea.

"You know, Bernat, this beautiful cloth"—he gestured to the silk lining of his cape—"is made by beastly little worms. These worms, in fact."

He whipped the lid off the box to expose a half-dozen chubby gray silkworms, chewing on a bed of leaves. Bernat shrunk back, momentarily startled. He shyly reached in, poked one, then picked it up. He put it on his hand to stroke it.

"It's smooth," he informed the others. "And its feet tickle."

"As fat as he is, you may be surprised to hear that silkworms are picky eaters," Ricard told the boy. "These little fellows only eat one kind of leaf, that of the white mulberry tree. These here," he said, picking up a leaf from the box, to find another worm feeding on its underside. "That was a secret the Chinese guarded for centuries, so no one else would be able to make silk."

"The Chinese? Are they like Jews?" Bernat wrinkled his nose, proud of the new vocabulary he'd learnt at the marketplace.

"No," Ricard said, with a sigh. "They're wise men from the Orient. But, let me finish. These worms, after eating many, many mulberry leaves, will want to take a siesta—just like Miquel after a big meal," he joked, winking at his friend. "Before going to sleep, they make themselves a blanket from one, long thread. You'll see them do it. They wrap themselves up, warm as can be, and they fall asleep, dreaming of wings."

"Will they fly away?" he asked, gently closing his small hand around the worm.

"No, their wings are too weak. To get the thread, the silk farmers put the cocoons into a pot of boiling water and—"

Bernat made a horrified face, opening his hand again to stare at the worm.

"But these silkworms are yours," he said quickly. "You can do what you want with them."

Little Bernat smiled down at his new playthings. He watched them systematically munch leaves and let them creep and curl on his hands. The others sat down to enjoy the refreshments and admire the child.

"I'm going to be a silk merchant too," Bernat decided happily.

"Oh, no, little man!" said his father, frowning in the direction of Ricard. "A real man of affairs has his own place of business, his name boldly written on a property deed. That's why I bought the Admiral's Baths and Bakery when your mother was carrying you. To have an important legacy to hand down. To you, my heir."

Even if that meant getting tangled in debt, thought Angels, saddened by her husband's speech. Bernat beamed at his son, who sat on the rug with his worms, confused. He hadn't understood half of what his father said.

She gave her husband a kiss on the cheek. He was as well-meaning as he was misguided.

⌘

It had been ages since Filibert had seen Angels alone. Could it be that the lunatic's niece, that *converso,* thought she was too good for *him,* a Penyarroja? An upstanding member of the community with an impeccable family tree? Surely that was impossible. Was her husband guarding her for himself? Had Bernat become possessive? Wise to her affection for him?

Although he had not seen her—except through doorways or heavily accompanied—she still plagued his thoughts and prevented him from carrying out his duties. He had even begun to wonder if perhaps she'd been in league with that blond whore to poison him. Had they been plotting against him from the start? Was Bernat involved too? The mother, the brother? The repulsive witch-aunt? He considered discussing the matter with don Alfonso.

Since Angels had become so scarce, he had taken to following her husband. Watching him from behind, alone or with a friend or two, Filibert imagined the bedtime liberties he took with his spouse. Did they laugh about him under the covers? Did they assume his penis small? His heart pounded with the indignity of it, but he was unable to stay away.

Around Christmastime, Filibert was standing watch in the shadows, his fingers raw with cold, when he saw Bernat leave the bathhouse. Whistling a tune, the fool! Weighing heavily on his stick, Filibert walked slowly behind him, a man so simple and trusting he never noticed he was being trailed. Tonight, it seemed he was heading home.

As Bernat turned the corner onto his street, Filibert heard him call out to neighbor and stopped to watch.

"Hey there, Tomás."

Filibert saw a broad-shouldered man adjusting his hat outside a door. The two shook hands.

"Good evening to you. How will you spend it, Bernat?"

"I was on my way home. And yourself, Tomás? Where are you off to?"

"I'm on my way to that tavern run by the skinny Catalan with all the dogs."

"Jordi," Bernat said with a smile. "Will there be gaming there tonight?"

"A group of us are meeting to play some cards, though I'm sure others will be playing dice. Who knows, there might even be a cockfight in the plaza when it gets late. You want to come?"

Bernat's head bobbed down the street in the direction of his house, then back at Tomás.

"Why not?" He shrugged.

When Filibert slipped into the bar a minute or two after Bernat, no one paid him any heed. To the sound of barking dogs and the reedy groan of a hurdy gurdy—expertly played by a drunk with his eyes closed—Bernat was in the middle of the room, clapping his hands and dancing. He sang a couple of lines of the song: *Have pity on my sorry heart, you that so put it to the proof.* He burst into laughter and greeted the others in the bar. His tuneful voice surprised Filibert, as well as some of his acquaintances.

"Sing, Bernat!" called out his old friend Felipe. "Sing us a ballad."

He shook his head. "I've come to play, not sing, you old sod." He laughed, gesturing to the barmaid for some wine.

As Bernat sat down amongst a dozen men perched around tables clustered to one side, Filibert quietly ordered a glass of wine and fell onto a stool in a dark corner nearby.

"So, tell us, Bernat," said one with a wink. "How goes the bathhouse?"

"Yeah!" Another laughed, raising his eyebrows and nudging a friend's side. "By now, you must be bored of spying on naked ladies—all the noble beauties you've got bathing in there."

"Nice one." Bernat chuckled. "I would surely make the triple if I carved a hole in the wall and charged scoundrels like you for a peek."

"Seriously, man," said Felipe, rubbing together hands encrusted with dirt. "Do people really go in there? It's been so cold and damp lately, I can't imagine taking off my clothes and splashing in water." He shivered at the thought.

"It was summer that was really slow," Bernat said. "Being so hot, people weren't much attracted to the steam. One day last August, I was rather pleased to have a group of men pay to go in but, after a while, I got nervous. I thought that maybe a group of false converts had discovered my empty bathhouse and were using it to perform their rituals." Bernat looked around at his friends, a gleam in his eyes. "I started to panic. You know, what with my wife's history and all, the last thing I need is troubles with the Holy Office. I ran into the warm room, expecting to catch them slaughtering a goat. But there they were, wrapped in towels, soaking their dirty feet in buckets of hot water. Innocent as babes. I don't know *what* brought them in there."

"Couldn't have been to clean themselves," cried one, laughing.

"Well," Bernat said, "it seems that the main patrons we've had so far this winter are people who can't afford a fire in their own hearth. Or, even worse, those sad buggers who just run in for a moment to warm themselves before going back out to the street. You know the ones: the simpletons and drunkards, the widows and street kids. Just yesterday, I found three men passed out on benches, still in their boots and clothes, and reeking of wine."

"It's too bad your wife found out about the gaming," Felipe said, with a nostalgic air. "It made a cozy place to throw dice. And in summer, the cold water basin kept the wine so cool."

"Yeah, it was nice while it lasted. But Angels was right. No reason to go asking for trouble when you've already got plenty. Perhaps I should never have bought the old place. But, hell, I don't know. It seemed like such a good idea."

"Ah, forget it, Bernat," said Tomás. "We didn't come here to talk about your business woes—entertaining as they may be. Let's play."

As Tomás and three others settled down to cards, Jordi came over to Bernat's table.

"Bernat, you've always enjoyed a good game of dice. Let me show you what I got today." He put a ceramic chessboard in a wooden frame down on the table in front of him. "A peddler brought it in and was selling it for almost nothing. Curious, isn't it? Have you ever seen a board made of clay? And painted green and white?"

"It was probably made in Paterna," remarked Felipe. "The potters there use that glaze. It looks old, though. Even looks like it's been in a fire."

"Can we play on it, Jordi?" asked Bernat. "If it survived a fire, perhaps it's lucky."

"Of course. Why do you think I got it?"

For hours, Filibert slumped in the corner with the brim of his hat down low, watching Bernat, while his rival sat chatting and drinking with the other men of the tavern. Filibert listened carefully for more talk of Angels, but she was not mentioned again. Mostly, the duffers were just betting on which color the dice would land. For once, not only did Bernat still have his earnings in his pocket, but he was winning. The other men teased him that his good fortune came from the chessboard, whose green squares were the same color as his eyes.

"The damn thing *has* brought him luck."

"Either that, or he's put the evil eye on *us*." They laughed, though they did not look amused.

An hour or so before dawn, most of the men were ready to quit gaming. At different states of drunkenness, everyone except the winners had become peevish. Tonight, however, Bernat was one of the privileged few. Filibert, who rarely slept much anymore, put down his glass—finally empty—and snuck out as they all bid good night to Jordi. With a great yawn, he bolted the door behind them and they scattered into the night.

The streets were still dark. Filibert, unenthusiastic about the idea of going back to his house, decided to follow the two men to theirs. They'd had too much drink to mind the man shuffling a few paces behind them. Perhaps he would even get a glimpse of a glowering Angels, vexed with her husband for coming home at daybreak. Too bad his winnings would soften her anger.

During their walk home, Tomás didn't speak; he had done extremely poorly at cards and was in a foul mood. Bernat, however, couldn't resist humming in satisfaction. As they were about to turn into their narrow street, a loud cracking noise startled them, all three. Bernat looked up towards the sound when a large piece of balcony crumbled down, striking him on the head. He staggered for an instant then collapsed. A pot of rosemary, teetering on the edge of the balcony, dropped, following the broken mortar onto Bernat's skull. The crash, shock, and blood nearly caused Filibert to fall over himself, but he managed to press himself into the black shadows of the nearest wall.

"My God!" Tomás screamed. "Bernat!"

Tomás knelt down next to his friend, skirting the blood and the crushed brow, to see if he were still breathing, if he had anything to say. He knew at once Bernat was dead. He crossed himself sadly, glanced around, then plunged his hand into Bernat's coat and helped himself to the money pouch inside. Tomás scrambled up and quickly skipped home, clutching the small fortune to his chest.

Filibert crept over to the awkwardly splayed body, dirt and rosemary sprigs littering its hair. An expression of surprise—his eyes wide, his mouth a great O—was fixed on the dead man's face. The noise and Tomás's cry would bring a neighbor to the street as soon as he'd slipped on his shoes. Filibert looked around, wondering if he should be found here, at the side of his rival's corpse. Should he himself deliver the news to Angels? How would she take it? Surely she would not feign grief?

Filibert decided to flee—if a skinny, stooped man making off with baby steps could be considered taking flight—and leave the responsibility of informing the widow to a stranger. He could not bear it if Angels displayed remorse or sorrow. He would wait a few weeks to see her. Surely, by then, he thought, his face twisting with glee, she would be ready for him.

⥤⥢

Angels, sweltering in black mourning attire, sat down on a bench in the vestibule. She'd been taking count of all the cracks that needed plastering in the hot room, incredulous that Bernat had renovated the place just three years before. After reaching an unaffordable number, she was beginning to wonder if whitewashing would keep the walls together. Maria interrupted her thoughts.

"Today's earnings, ma'am," she mumbled, taking the burlap pouch from around her belt and handing it to the widow.

"Thank you." Angels nodded at her. Normally a lively girl, Maria had become reverently quiet around her in the days since Bernat died.

Angels began counting the money. A smattering of change, it did not take long. Sighing, she put the thin, dirty coins back into the pouch, one by one. Had Bernat been gone a week? Angels pushed the damp hair away from her face, trying to make sense of this jumble of days. It seemed like either much more or far less time had passed since that morning when Father Servando had come to her house at daybreak, shouting and beating on the door. Grabbing a blanket to put around her shoulders, she'd run out into the street to find Bernat dead. A scream caught in her throat, Angels fell onto the cold cobblestones, reliving the day in the marketplace when she'd cried over her father's broken skull.

A group of neighbors carried his body inside the house and arranged him on the table. Angels was cleaning the blood from his head when their son stumbled in from bed, still half-asleep.

"Why is Papa on the table?" he'd asked. He went round the side to take his hand and found it cold. He tried to warm his father's large rough hand with both of his small ones. "Mama, what's wrong with him?"

He'd looked at her in confusion with his large, green eyes. Bernat's eyes. "He's gone," she'd whispered, unable to say more. She'd held their son on her lap, rocking him, the two of them sobbing together. Poor, sweet Bernat—bad luck had followed him to the last.

Soon, her mother had appeared at the door. After a long embrace, they began the more practical matter of fashioning a shroud. Consuelo stitched an old sheet, while Angels took off her husband's clothes. In his coat, although there was no money pouch, she found a pair of dice. Chuckling sadly to herself, she held them warmly in her hand, then opened the carved box of quills from her father. She put the dice in her treasure box, next to the pens and the dainty folding fan Filibert had given her, back before he had changed. Angels closed the box with a trembling chin and went back to his body, wondering how many more pairs of dice he had stashed around.

Later that day, in front of Bernat's meager family and numerous friends, the slab was removed from the tomb. His relatives' bones were swept towards the back, and the shrouded corpse lain inside. Eyeing Angels suspiciously still, Father Servando had said a prayer for the bereaved. As they were filing out of the cemetery—the shock had rendered them all silent, except for Felipe, who was crying openly—the priest caught her by the sleeve.

"I think the best we can hope for," he'd said, glaring at her though half-closed eyes, "is purgatory."

She still had no idea what Father Servando meant by that. Was it because he'd died without the last rites? Or because of his gaming? Or, more likely, because he'd married *her*? Angels rose from the wooden bench. How many days had passed since then? Four, five? It was all a blur of condolences, strangeness, worry and grief.

"Come on, Maria. Let's go."

As she walked home—still expecting to find him there, ready to greet her with a wink and a grin—Angels wondered again how she was going to pull little Bernat and herself out of this hole. Although she too had worked hard these last few years—running the Admiral's side of the affairs and doing the dismal bookkeeping for all three places—she had depended heavily on Bernat, the driving force behind it all. His energy and good cheer were what held everything together. Although relieved that no more money would be lost to the gaming tables, she was unsure of her ability to manage alone. Would she be able to keep the businesses afloat until Bernat came of age? She knew that the public—and even more importantly, their creditors—preferred their shopkeepers to be men. Remembering Bernat's easy laugh and incurable optimism, she bit her lip to keep away the tears. She would have never guessed how much she'd miss him.

When she got back to the house over the bakery, her mother was cooking. They had decided to live together, two widows helping and supporting one another, and had reluctantly let Josefa go. Also, it was time Ricard had a house of his own to share with someone, to settle down and start a family.

"Bernat's taking a nap," Consuelo greeted Angels, who always wanted reports on her son straightaway. It was difficult, though, to hear the name that had belonged to his father as well. "So, tell me, what state is the old bathhouse in?"

"There's the usual cracks," Angels said. "What I'm really worried about, though, is the heating system. It doesn't get as hot as it used to. There's rubble in the chamber below the hot room. Perhaps part of a wall has fallen? I'm almost afraid to call a mason." Her eyes filled with tears. "I don't know what I'm going to do. God, I wish Bernat were here. I can't believe... There was a time..."

Her face crumpled; she couldn't continue. Consuelo put down the spoon to hug her daughter.

"I suppose every wife finishes a widow," she whispered into her hair. "It's been almost a decade since I lost Jesús."

"How did you stand it?" Angels managed through her tears.

"I had you," Consuelo said simply. "You know, your Grandmother Judith lost Samuel when she was quite young too. He died leaving her with the printing press to run and two children to feed. She managed and did well. Angels, you will too.

"I'm not nearly as strong as Grandmother was."

"But you have me," her mother said, "and your brother. You can do it."

Filibert could not contain his frustration. Here he was in the prime of life, but his body was aging with such swiftness that he felt he would be an old man before the year was out. In spite of the mercury treatments, he was still in pain, and the outward signs of his illness were almost more than his vanity could take. He was losing his hearing *and* his hair; he walked with a shuffle and talked with a stammer. But worst of all, his manhood seemed particularly unresponsive. It had been months since Filibert had been able to pay the conjugal debt. Even after filling his imagination with visions of Princess Carmesina, completely nude, her long, golden tresses flowing down to her round behind, he was unable to get an erection. Hell! He could hardly take a piss.

The day before, he'd had his tailor fashion him a new codpiece, hard, upright and generously padded. Filibert fastened it on under his doublet, over his slack groin, and looked in the mirror admiringly. Feeling a bit better, he put on his cloak and hat, slamming the front door behind him.

Two months had passed since Bernat had died. A prudent timeframe, he calculated, before seeking out his widow. He was sure that, with her, his carnal prowess would rapidly return, that she would make a man of him again. He had thought of a new way to make her beholden to him, or at the very least, to ensure her gratitude. The week before, Filibert had met with his accountants and a contract of sale had already been drawn up. It was time to find Angels Bonafé; he had a business proposition for the widow.

⌘

Angels was buying sausages at the market when she glimpsed Filibert on the street. She hadn't seen him for months and, assuming he'd found a new lady friend to flatter, had stopped worrying about him when she went out. Rather, as Bernat's long-time miller and fellow guildsman, she'd found it somewhat remiss that he had not bothered to come to his burial or pay his respects.

From the safety of the butcher's, she gave him a long look. Supporting himself with a cane, his gait made a zigzag pattern in the dirt. He was dressed in a garish suit of yellow silk—making his complexion appear bluer, sicklier—with an exaggerated crotch. She shook her head in disbelief. How had this man transfixed her so?

As she walked out of the shop, he immediately spotted her and, waving his hand above his head, called out. She looked around; others had noticed the gentleman in yellow, hailing her too.

"Angels, I've been looking for you."

He approached her there next to the butcher's stall, the smell of offal and slaughter mixing with his own strong perfume. Uncomfortable, she shook his hand loosely and glanced up at his eyes. The pupils had all but disappeared and the gray was cold and foreboding, a rainy winter sky.

"Hello, don Filibert," she replied, smiling nervously. "What do you need of me?"

"I have heard tell of Bernat's accident, Angels. A terrible blow," he said, looking down. Was he resisting the urge to laugh? "I'm sure that now, alone, you must have grave concerns about the businesses. I can only imagine the debt he has left you in. Angels, *I* would like to help," he said, filled with self-satisfaction.

He paused dramatically, his eyes reflecting the morning light, and stepped closer to her.

"Yes?" she asked, taking a step back, her smile failing.

"I'm going to buy the bathhouse and bakeries from you. I'll give you a good price for them—despite their real worth—as well as some peace of mind. I'll take care of it all and you needn't worry about a thing." He smiled magnanimously, awaiting her most ardent thanks.

She looked at him in surprise. In the after-haze of Bernat's death, she had considered trying to sell the shops, to take whatever was offered and live off the money until it ran out. But, after another week or two, she had rejected the idea. She appreciated Bernat's desire to leave his son property, a deed, a legacy in stone—even if the faulty construction was more solid than the business itself. She also remembered her father's pride in his own business and how fate and his early death had taken it away from them. She had thought about selling the bakeries and that cursed bathhouse, but had since changed her mind.

"I don't know, Filibert. I was planning on keeping them."

"What do you mean? What will you do with them?"

"Well, Bernat wanted his son to have an inheritance. I would like to respect his wishes."

"Respect that fool's wishes," he cried, his loud voice ringing like that of an indignant drunk. "As if you ever loved him. We both know that is a lie. So, Angels, you want to play the part of the grieving widow, then?"

Angels looked around to find that they were being stared at by the passers-by, an old couple at the fountain, the women buying mutton and pork. She looked back at Filibert, and saw that he was furious.

"For years," he snarled in a shaky whisper, "I have compromised my honor to speak with you in public, hoping that one day you would grant me that private interview." As he spoke, his head began to bob, in a sharp, rhythmic twitch. "Now, I had thought to do you yet another favor. But, it seems that you are no longer interested in favors from me. Do you have another man doing your bidding now? Who is your lover? A richer man, a noble, perhaps?"

"Don't be ridiculous, Filibert. I was shamed by my aunt, but I have never dishonored myself."

"Such virtue!" His voice sputtered sarcastically. With a menacing stare, his hand grasped at his cane – did he mean to strike her? When suddenly, a shrill, unearthly squeal startled them both: a pig being slaughtered behind the butcher shop. Surprised into movement, Angels picked up her skirts to flee.

Filibert, who could no longer run, shouted at her retreating form, stammering the words out with difficulty. She heard him plainly enough:

"I will have your shops! And I will have you, Angels Bonafé!"

She did not stop running until she arrived to Ricard's house, the family home. She let herself in and bolted the big wooden door behind her, safe in the darkened hall. Shaking, near tears, she tried to catch her breath. What was wrong with that man? Had he gone completely mad?

When she had collected herself, she began looking for her brother. He was neither in the drawing room nor in the kitchen. Perhaps he was still in bed. With no trade fairs that month, they were busy organizing their stocks, making plans for an ambitious journey up to the Low Countries.

She went quietly to his room and pushed open the door. Through his open bed curtains, she could see her sleeping brother. His naked body was curled around that of his mentor, Miquel Sanchis.

Angels gasped, pulled the door closed with an unintentional bang, and quickly made her way downstairs. She found a chair and fell into it, trying to make sense out of what she'd seen. Nude men locked in embrace? What were they doing? A few minutes later, Ricard was leaning over her, his strong arm around her shoulders.

"I wasn't expecting you. Miquel and I…" his voice trailed off as he searched for something to add.

She stood up and studied his face. Was he too mad? She looked him in the eyes, but saw no change.

"What?" she asked, knitting her brow, trying to understand. "He isn't your lover, is he, Ricard?"

"He's my partner. In everything."

Angels was on the verge of tears, unable to believe it possible.

"Do you trust, him, Ricard? Has he seen your...deformity?" she asked, awkwardly pointing to the midsection of his robe.

"For Christ's sake, Angels!" he cried, astonished.

"Mother told me what Aunt Esther did to you," she said, her face plastered with worry.

"Miquel would never have me arrested for being a Jew."

"But, Ricard," she cried, still perplexed, her gestures nonsensical. "Aren't you afraid of going to Hell?"

"Hell?" he asked her with raised eyebrows. "I'll tell you what Hell is. It's the gruesome spectacle of the auto-da-fe. It's having your father stoned in the marketplace because his sister felt the need—yes, the need—to jump off a bridge. It's losing a prosperous business to fear and cowardice. It's filth, death, greed, hate... Angels, how can I be afraid of Hell? I grew up in it."

She stood there speechless. He returned her gaze, his vexation quickly disappearing.

"I have found love, Angels," he said gently. "And contentment. I hope that one day you will too."

Tumbling back into the chair, she burst into tears. She felt a terrible, sudden loss. She wept for the men in her life: for her loving father, viciously killed before her eyes; for her good-natured husband, another victim of fate; for her persistent suitor, somehow transformed into a savage beast; and her brother, risking the pyre, foolishly giving his love to a man. She did not forget to cry for herself as well.

When she had calmed down, Ricard's handkerchief rolled into a tiny ball, she saw that Miquel was sitting there too. His silver hair was disheveled from sleep but his intelligent, brown eyes were filled with concern. He smiled at her, lightly grazing her hand, and, with false formality, said, "To what do we owe the pleasure of your visit?"

Angels stared at Miquel, still unsure of how she felt. Had this older man corrupted her brother? Was he responsible for this unnatural relationship? She took a long breath—truly, she needed them both, their friendship and support—and decided to speak.

"It's Filibert," she whispered.

When Angels had told them what had happened outside the butcher shop—Filibert's offer, her hesitation and his resulting rage—Miquel nodded, serious.

"I have seen a great change in him these last few years. Filibert had always been my favorite cousin, a dignified, clever man, but since he fell ill—the gout, epilepsy, or whatever he has—he has not been the same man. What I don't understand, though, is that it has affected his mind as well. I have seen him overjoyed, aggressive, indignant, downtrodden—all in the same short visit."

"He frightens me," said Angels. "He boasts of his association with the Grand Inquisitor. I don't know what he means to do."

"He frightens me, too," Miquel replied. "He's become so volatile, he could put us all in danger one day, without even wanting to. The Holy Office is not known for its scruples. The wealthier the offender, the more likely he will be found guilty. Once charges have been made— "

"You think Filibert capable of such of thing?" Angels asked.

"I don't know what he's capable of nowadays."

It was June, 1535, and Bernat had been dead for nearly six months. Angels, who had recently turned twenty-five, had become wasted and thin, using all her energy to run the businesses. As well as managing the bakeries, she was trying to make her peace with the old bathhouse; after all, it was not to blame for her misfortunes. After having it repaired and cleaned, she found herself using it much more often. She would stand in the steam until she could hardly breathe, trying to make sense of the dangerous, irrational times they were living in. Ricard had called it Hell; in the hot room, she could believe it so.

When Angels had time, she taught her son all she could, about numbers and letters, the classic tales, but also about her own family history—from the expulsion of the Jews to the notion of Old Christians, from the sacred sack to the hospital for the mad—to try to explain to him who he was and what it all meant.

The rainy spring turned warm and Angels was glad for the celebration of the Corpus Christi, to have a day off, to take her mind off her worries. She had always loved the Corpus procession which, unlike most things associated with the Church, was colorful and lively, fanciful and fun. She and her mother walked the boy over to the cathedral where they met Miquel and Ricard. They all settled into the shade of the immense bell tower to wait for the parade. A sunny morning, many people were lining the narrow lane, snacking on nuts and fruit and chatting with one another. Bright cloths hung from all the balconies, and herbs and flowers covered the procession path. Suddenly, they heard the sound of the drums and the *dolçaina*, the reedy pipe typical in Valencia. As everyone got to his feet in anticipation, Ricard swept his nephew up onto his shoulders.

The procession was led by a group of soldiers, dressed in red velvet, looking anything but threatening as they smiled and waved at the crowds. They were followed by groups of children:

girls carrying hoops of flowers, boys dressed as shepherds, others wearing pasteboard horses around their waists. Every few yards, these small performers fell into circles and did charming dances. During one of these interludes, Angels noticed Filibert, who had taken a place in the crowd opposite her, on the other side of the lane.

He was dressed in youthful finery which contrasted sharply with his withered, dilapidated body. Again, he was wearing that ridiculous codpiece, which reminded Angels of an engraving she'd once seen in her father's bestiary, an animal called rhinoceros. Filibert seemed oblivious to the music and the children skipping about right in front of him. He had his eye on Angels, watching her with longing and hatred.

"Here come the *Rocas!*"shouted a tall youth hanging onto the base of the bell tower.

The Rocas, exquisitely carved wooden carriages led by beautifully adorned horses, were the highlights of the procession. Huge, they barely fit the streets; the excited crowd backed up, pressing themselves against the buildings. The first one, pulled by white horses, their manes braided with red ribbons, was the Roca of the Final Judgment. The Archangel Saint Michael stood in the center, carrying his shield and his sword, and on one side of him was a soul going to Hell, and on the other side, to Heaven.

"I wish I had wings... and a sword," said Bernat, leaning down to talk into his uncle's ear.

His mother smiled at him, then looked nervously across the street where Filibert was standing. He was leaning against the building behind him, steadying himself with both hands. He looked confused.

Two more Rocas lumbered by, one representing San Vicente Ferrer, the local saint who had zealously tried to make

Christians of Jews, terrifying them into conversion; the other, depicting Faith, where a sculpture of a blind-folded woman carried a chalice with the Holy Wafer. Angels sighed to herself, thinking that it was true that Faith was blind—it could not see reason.

Finally, the last Roca was approaching. The horses were magnificent, with mirrors and glass in their headdresses, as was the carriage, carved all around with devils and demons. The boy cried out from his lofty height: "The *Moma*! The *Moma*!"

Inside the last carriage were the players. Dressed all in white, with a mask and veil, the Moma stood tall in a golden crown, representing Good. The Momos, seven men depicting the Capital Sins, had black veils covering their faces and carried big wooden poles. The Roca stopped right in front of them and, to the music of drums and *dolçaina*, they began their dance of Good triumphing over Evil.

The Momos fought rhythmically, crisscrossing their poles, stepping in circles around the Moma. Finally, she reached out with her golden scepter, dramatically pointing it at each man, defeating them in turn. However, as she got to the last one, she lost her footing and dropped her scepter onto the street. The music stopped and was immediately replaced by a hysterical fit of laughter.

Filibert, his eyes gleaming, cried out, "So, Evil has won over Virtue? And which Deadly Sin has vanquished her?"

Everyone turned to stare at the extravagantly dressed man with the crazy grin, though he was looking only at Angels and her family.

"Was it the sin of Pride? Or Avarice—the sin of the Jews? Or was it Lust? The favorite of whores and sodomites!"

He was weaving about, his speech slurred, his head bobbing, as if he'd spent the whole morning drinking. Oddly though, he didn't smell of wine, but of fried dough.

"Look at the sinners!" he shouted, pointing at them, his hand wrought with tremors. "Look at them!"

"He's been taken by the devil, that man," Consuelo murmured, making the sign of the cross.

Unable to look at him, Angels stared at the ground, but little Bernat, still perched on top of Ricard's shoulders, couldn't take his eyes off him. He was trying to decide if the grotesque man with the bright clothes and the bulging crotch was funny or frightening. Taking her brother's hand, Angels nervously scanned the crowd. Would these people turn on them and stone them, as others had stoned their father? She felt dizzy; her heart was racing. Were the soldiers of the Holy Office already on their way?

"Look at the sinners!" he continued shouting, his voice a long slur. "Sssinners!"

She watched as the people around Filibert began edging as far away from him as they could. The men were giving him looks of contempt, and the women, visibly disgusted, were whispering about him behind their gloved hands and folding fans. They were all taking glimpses at Angels and her family, the objects of his assaults. However, their looks were not filled with disdain, but sympathy.

It was then Angels realized that he was harmless. Whatever wrongdoing Filibert Penyarroja, in anger or in folly, could accuse them of—being Jews, sodomites, witches or whatever else—he could not be taken seriously. Though he was an Old Christian, with clean blood and an influential family name, not even the

Holy Office would take testimony from him now. His illness had rendered him completely impotent.

The last Roca finally passed, and the crowd began to follow it, becoming part of the procession themselves. Bernat liked the idea of being in the parade but Angels wanted to go home. Filibert was still just across the lane, but his face had lost that look of hilarity, giving way to a brooding sorrow.

"Perhaps I should go talk to him," Angels heard Miquel whisper to Ricard. "Help him home, or sit with him until he's stable."

"Do as you wish," Ricard murmured with a shrug, but Miquel didn't move.

"Oh." He sighed. "There's nothing I can say to him when he's like this."

Suddenly, Filibert wailed so loudly his cries were heard distinctly above the crowd.

"Carmesina!" Filibert cried, his voice cracking. "My princess! Why do you torment me? Good lady, do you not see it is me, your knight?"

He made a few steps towards her, then stumbled, and fell to his knees. He did not try to get up, but stayed in the dirt street and began to weep.

"Mama?" Bernat looked at his mother, in wide-eyed amazement, "Is that old man really Tirant lo Blanc? The knight from the tales? Is it him, Mama, is it him?"

Angels looked down at Filibert, the near-noble who had wooed her for years, the man she'd longed to marry. His red face was streaked with tears and dirt, his whole body heaved with sobs. His arms were wrapped tightly around his torso, as if they were trying to comfort him.

"No, Bernat, he's not a knight," she replied softly, all fear now turned to pity. "He's a pathetic soul who has lost his mind."

"Will they take him to the hospital for the mad? Like your aunt?"

"I don't know." She shrugged, unable to imagine the two under the same roof.

Angels took her mother and brother by the arm, and began walking away, Miquel a few paces behind them, a safeguard. Little Bernat, however, could not resist squirming around on his uncle's shoulders to steal one last glimpse of the man on the street. He was still trying to tell if he were a clown or a monster.

Reconstruction

July 2011

"Tell me, Rachel," Marisa began immediately after our cursory kisses, "how's it going with Paco?"

"I don't know." I smiled, adjusting my sunglasses. "God, it's bright out here. Let's cross."

"What do you mean you don't know?" she insisted, following me into the shady side of the street. "I've always said that the best cure for a failed romance is a new one. But, hey, don't listen to me. I'm a disaster when it comes to relationships."

"Well," I laughed. "I like Paco fine. He's charming, smart, handsome... I just don't know him very well."

Since that dinner, six weeks ago, I'd gleaned bits and pieces about his background, his interests. Paco was twice divorced with children from each of his relatively short marriages: twenty-three-year-old twins from the first, an eleven-year-old son from the second. (Did this recommend him? Todd, at forty-two, had never been married. Was that a warning sign?) Paco supported the leftist party and the Barça soccer club. He read insatiably, spoke several languages, and had an apartment at the beach. He was funny, generous and a good kisser. I'd discovered these things, but it wasn't near enough to sort out my feelings.

"Don't know him? But I thought you'd been seeing a lot of each other."

"More or less." I gave her a noncommittal shrug, knowing that this was an understatement; we'd been together up to three times a week in the last month and a half. At this stage, however, it still seemed important to keep expectations low. "I haven't seen him for almost a whole week," I added as proof. "He's at the beach with his kids. We're meeting on Saturday morning, though. He's taking me to see the mansion of the Admiral of Aragon, where the Baths' original owners lived. Nowadays it houses the Regional Ministry of Economy and Taxes."

"A terrible fate for an old palace, wouldn't you say?"

"Absolutely! Oh, and since you mentioned failed romance—I heard from Todd yesterday."

"Really?" Marisa looked up from the sidewalk, where she'd been skirting around a clump of dog poo. "That's a first, isn't it?"

"Yep," I said, with a brisk nod. "He didn't even call after the tornado. I mean, my street was on prime-time news, but he didn't bother to see if I was ok. And now, two and a half months after he walks out, he sends me a one-line message."

"What did it say? Wait, let me guess. 'I can't live without you.'"

"Nooo. It said: 'Do you miss me?' It was all I could do not to spit at the screen."

"Well, maybe that's a good thing. Makes you realize how much better off you are without him. The jerk."

"And I must say, he makes Paco look fabulous." I smiled. "Now, where is this bookshop anyway?"

"It's by the train station." She pointed to the far end of the square. "You're looking for a facsimile of an old book, right?"

"Right. A nineteenth century tourist guide to Valencia, or something like that. It was written by the Frenchman Alexander de Laborde. He was one of the Baths' most distinguished visitors."

"Never heard of him," Marisa said flatly.

"Nobody has! That's why I'd like to learn more about him. He was a writer and an artist. He made some beautiful engravings of the bathhouse around 1805."

"Ah, the creative type." She winked. "Alluring, yet dangerous."

"Oh, this guy wasn't so easy to peg. He was a scholar, known for his curiosity and zest for knowledge, but also a military man and a political attaché."

"A Renaissance man, then?"

"More like the Enlightenment, actually."

"Damn historians," Marisa muttered, "always splitting hairs."

I had spent the previous night researching Alexandre Laborde, finding as much information about this obscure historical figure as the internet would provide. Evidently, he had come to Spain around 1800 with a team of writers and illustrators to produce an exhaustive travel book, to be jointly financed by the French government and the Spanish King. It was to include hundreds of copper-plate engravings, some of which he would draw personally. However, after Napoleon invaded Spain, Laborde was left with the cost of publishing it himself. It nearly ruined him. He continued writing, but also became involved in politics. Napoleon must have liked him; Laborde was made Knight of the Legion of Honor in 1809.

On the screen, I'd stared at the engraving of Alexandre de Laborde, the only available image, repeated time and again in the different articles dedicated to him. I liked his looks: his wavy hair, his straight nose, his neck wrapped to the chin in muslin. He sort of reminded me of Alan Rickman, irresistible in *Sense and Sensibility*. From the confines of his portrait, he looked at the viewer as if pleased with the content of their dialogue. His lips were on the verge of smiling; above his heavy-lidded, almost sleepy eyes, his eyebrows showed just a hint of surprise. What might our conversation be about? History, travel, art... or perhaps a public bathhouse?

"Here we are," Marisa said. "Let's see if they have what you're looking for."

The shop didn't have a facsimile edition of Laborde's first book, the one chock-full of illustrations, his *Picturesque and Historic Voyage of Spain*. However, they did have the original Spanish translation of the Valencia chapter taken from his *Descriptive Itinerary of Spain*, a massive opus he'd worked on later, when he'd returned to Spain in 1826.

"Laborde, eh?" The bookseller smiled as I paid for the book.

"You know him?"

"Sure. As dry as this seems now, it caused quite a sensation back in the day. It put Spain on the Grand Tour. After Laborde published this, French writers came down in droves to experience our quaintness for themselves. Stendhal, Georges Sand, Dumas, Flaubert—all the big names. They'd all read this," he said, holding up the slim facsimile. "Or the *Voyage Pittoresque*."

"That's the one I was really looking for. Do you know where I might be able to find a copy?"

"E-bay or antique shops," he said, "but be prepared to pay thousands. Tens of thousands, maybe. They're collectors' items. But, you know, you might be able to find some of the engravings sold individually. There's a great antique shop down by the Santa Catalina church. It specializes in all things paper: posters, photos, books—you name it. Try there."

After a quick ice coffee, Marisa and I made our way to the antiquarian's. Struck by most everything in there, we spent a good hour browsing through old advertisements, comic strips, Civil War propaganda, bullfighting posters, large photographs of a bygone Valencia —before we even thought to ask about the engravings.

"Laborde? Yes, we've got a few of his pieces here," the shopkeeper immediately answered, turning towards a cabinet next to the wall.

"Come to find out this guy's a household name," Marisa whispered with a smile. "Who knew?"

"Maybe they'll have one of the Baths," I said, watching the man opening the long, thin drawers. "That would be amazing."

The clerk came back with three prints, all landscapes in black and white. None of them was as striking as the architectural engravings he'd made of the bathhouse, but one caught my eye: Vista of the Alameda. These were the fashionable strolling grounds of nineteenth century Valencia, across the river from the old town. In this engraving, people on horseback, in carriages or chatting in small groups were dwarfed by tall trees—palms, poplars and pines—swaying far over their heads. The clouded sky, rippled like damask silk, cast shadows on the dirt road. I liked the Lilliputian Valencians in their traditional hats, skirts and cloaks, but even more, the suggestion of movement in the piece despite the stiff medium of engraving. I peeked at the price, penciled lightly on the corner.

"I'll take it," I said, almost giddy.

When I got back to Hector's flat, I propped my new acquisition up on the bookshelf in the living room. I stared at it, delighted to have a piece made by the Parisian gentleman, the influential traveler, the attractive man who had drawn the Admiral's Baths so long ago. I laughed at myself then, remembering that when Alexandre de Laborde had visited the bathhouse, it was almost five hundred years old.

That Saturday morning, when Paco buzzed from downstairs, I asked him to come up to the flat.

"I want to show you something," I said.

This was the first time I had invited him up; until now, I'd always answered his call with a "I'll be right down!" or we'd just meet at specified rendezvous places: his studio, in front of the cinema, outside a restaurant. I'd been leery about meeting him in private, reasoning that being alone in close quarters would only encourage us to rush things. But, after nearly a week without seeing him (and with a new purchase to share), that no longer seemed so important. I listened to his quick tread on the four flights of stairs and hoped he wasn't expecting to be seduced. I opened the door and looked down the stairwell.

"Hey there," I called down. He looked up and gave me a small wave and a brilliant smile.

On the top floor, though he was panting from the climb, he kissed me warmly on the mouth. "What? You don't want to see the palace anymore?" He sounded vaguely optimistic.

"Of course I do." I took him by the hand. "But first, I want you to see something." I pointed him to Laborde's representation of the Alameda.

"Isn't it great?" I gushed. "What do you think?"

He looked at it, then back at me.

"Are you serious?" he asked, raising an eyebrow.

"Yes, I'm serious. I bought this a couple of days ago at an antique shop. I was drawn to it because it was made by the same guy who did the engravings of the Baths. Alexandre Laborde?"

"Oh, yeah?" he said, taking a step closer. "I remember those. Especially his floor plan—really top notch. So, this is the Alameda? Huh. Hard to imagine it with no traffic. And look at those trees."

"You don't like it." I gave him a mock pout.

"Well, I usually associate this kind of artwork with my grand-mother's teacups," he said with an innocent shrug, "but it's not bad. I just prefer paintings that move me. The Expressionists, Francis Bacon, *Guernica*—"

"You're not comparing my poor little engraving to *Guernica*!" I laughed. "But, you're right. I guess it was the historian in me that bought it, the part of me that always wants to touch the past, to hold it in my hand."

"If this lets you do that," he said, looking into my eyes, "then it was worth every cent."

"Thanks, Paco," I said slowly, staring back at him. I'd missed him this past week. After Todd's impromptu departure, I was nervous about the idea of being with another man, though I couldn't help but feel Paco's pull. The attraction between us was certainly solid, if nothing else was. After a few seconds, I shook my head and began gathering things into my bag—camera, notebook, phone—asking myself if I could actually be ready for a new relationship. "We should be going, no?"

As we went down the narrow street, Paco reached for my hand. I smiled to myself; I couldn't remember the last time I'd walked along holding hands.

"I'm a little surprised that you're so interested in the Admiral's palace. You know, the palace and the bathhouse parted ways around 1425 when the last Vilarasa owner died. In the fifteenth century, the palace went through major renovations—almost an entire reconstruction. That's when the Borgia family owned it."

My mouth dropped open and it took me a second to put it back. "You don't mean the crazy, incestuous, power-hungry Borgias?"

"The same." Paco laughed. "Hey, they were one of Valencia's most renowned families. Two Popes, loads of cardinals and, yes, intrigue, sex, poison and all that." They passed the loud boys skateboarding in the plaza then paused outside the mansion's great wooden door. "Alexander the Sixth's sister lived here."

I reached out and grazed the stone doorway with my fingers, impressed, touching history with my bare hands again.

"Did you do the restoration here as well?" I asked, taking in the austere façade, the clean lines of its rectangular windows, the simple balconies.

"That was done in the mid-eighties, when the regional government had just bought it. At that time, I'd only been out of Architecture School for a year or two and was still scrounging for jobs. I knew some of the people who worked on it, though, and I came by to observe a couple of times." I pulled out my camera as I listened. "While they were working, they found the remains of the old Moorish complex underneath it. Really, in this part of Valencia, anytime you dig a hole, you come across your ancestors' bones."

"I love that." I sighed. "Where I'm from, you might be able to find a broken arrowhead. *If* you're lucky."

I took a few photos of the façade and zoomed in on the stone coat of arms over the door.

"Is this the Vilarasa shield? Or the Borgia?"

"No, this one was added much later, in the eighteenth century maybe. I think it belongs to the Palafox i Cardona family, but I'm not really sure."

"Wow—that's like my name, Cardon." I enlarged the image of the shield on my camera. "Hey, are these artichokes?"

"In Spanish, 'cardo' means 'thistle.' But"—he squinted down at the small screen—"you're right, those look more like artichokes."

"Thistle? I didn't know. Maybe that's why I have so many prickly family members. I wonder what our family crest would look like? A bunch of thorns, probably." I looked back at the photo. "I love the artichokes, though. If I could chose, my crest would have a few artichokes, some manchego cheese, and a bottle of wine. Hey, I wonder what medieval corkscrews looked like?"

"Stop, Rachel, you're making me hungry. Come on, let's take a look inside then I'll treat you to lunch."

We walked in the door, through a wide Gothic arch, and out into the courtyard. From the arcaded patio, I looked up at the great stone staircase leading up to the top floors, the dainty columns separating the archways, the slim windows carved with clovers. "It's beautiful."

"Yes." Paco nodded in agreement.

"So, tell me, how was the household arranged?" I asked between photo shots.

"Well, down here was the public area, mostly for domestic service. There were stables and storerooms, wine cellars, rooms for the stable boys and maids. The next floor, a mezzanine, was where the lord did business. It had his administrative offices, study and library. And the top floor, or the noble floor, was private. It had the bed chambers, chapel, drawing room and the great dining hall for receiving friends and family."

"Three spaces," I said, making connections. "Just like the baths, you know. From the vestibule to the steam room, they sort of went from public to private too."

"I guess it's like anything," he said softly. "The further in you go, the more intimate it gets."

We spent another thirty minutes going through all of the spaces open to tourists, but found most of the stone rooms stripped of any decoration except for the ceilings. The old wooden beams, however, were carved then painted with the heraldic symbols of all the families who had lived there.

"Amazing." I took dozens of pictures of the cross work of the beams and the intricate patterns painted in rich colors: the deep red and yellow of Aragon, forest green, navy blues, gold gilt. There would be no need to alter these; they were figurative abstracts, unrecognizable as ceilings.

Leaving the mansion, we couldn't resist taking the small alleyway alongside it, which led to the bathhouse. Outside, we found Xavi, smoking a cigarette.

"Hi there!" Xavi and I exchanged two quick pecks. "I think you've met Paco Nogales." I paused for them to shake hands. "We've just been to visit the Admiral's palace. I've never seen such impressive ceilings. I'm sure their guests got cricks in their necks admiring them."

"Well, back then, the rugs, tapestries and furniture would have given them some competition." Xavi smiled. "The funny thing to me is that, after a hundred years or so, everyone had already forgotten the connection between the palace and the bathhouse. The baths' origins became so muddled that, finally, its history was completely reinvented. Until recently, even scholars were convinced they were real Arab baths, built when city still belonged to the Moors."

"Most people in Valencia still think that," Paco said. "I think they prefer it. Old and exotic—it's much more romantic that way."

A group of German tourists suddenly appeared in the alleyway, maps in hand, looking expectantly at the Arabesque doorway.

"Ciao, Xavi," I whispered and turned to Paco, taking his hand. "So, what would you like for lunch? Do you want to go out? Or I could cook something. Nothing fancy, mind you, but—"

Paco pulled me into his arms and kissed me. "Your cooking. Definitely."

In the end, I didn't cook anything. Rather, he helped me fill a large tray with pâté, cheese and bread, I tossed a quick salad, he uncorked some wine, and we carried it all out to the table on the terrace. We huddled together in the slim shade of the parasol, chairs touching, elbows occasionally colliding. I could smell his cologne. I breathed in and stole a long glance at him as he drizzled olive oil on his bread. I did like this man. What was I so afraid of? Another natural disaster—a twisted relationship, a stormy affair, a torrential breakup? Even though we had spent so much time together, our conversation had seldom moved into the personal; although we often discussed history, it was rarely our own. I decided it was time to open up. To see what would happen.

"You know, the week before I came here was a doozy," I began, deciding on a lighthearted approach. "It all started Easter Sunday."

I told him about Todd, the ensuing tornado, and how my previously-mentioned, almost-architect son was overseeing the reconstruction of my house. Fascinated by it all, he kept stopping me to ask questions. While talking to Paco, I realized that many of the things that had seemed so horrible before, now made me smile. Well, mostly Todd.

The whole time I was speaking, though, I couldn't get past his nearness—his elegant hands, inches away; his smell; his mouth, that one slightly chipped tooth—and the seclusion of the terrace. It was the first time we were alone together, without chaperons, unobserved.

"I'd love to see Nick's handiwork," Paco said, reaching out to brush a crumb from my face; I tingled at his touch. "What a challenging project for a student."

"You can visit anytime you like." I smiled calmly, though my heartbeat quickened. "Really, I'm not just saying that."

"I love your smile," he said suddenly. "It goes perfectly with your eyes. Hey, Rachel; let's go inside. Out of the sun."

We took our wine glasses into the living room which, out of the afternoon glare, seemed almost dark. We'd been perched on the couch for only a moment, time for a half-sip of wine, when I made up my mind. I took his hand and led him to the bedroom.

An hour later, although we were both sweaty and satisfied, he had not stopped touching me. Gently stroking my arm, he said, "This has been really great," his voice slow and languid.

"What do you mean?" I asked, bristling despite myself.

"Being with you, silly." He leaned over for another kiss. "*This*. It's been great. I'm going to miss you."

"I'm not leaving yet," I said, with a relieved laugh.

"Didn't I tell you?" His brow creased. "I have to go back to the Emirates for a few weeks. I'm leaving on Monday morning."

"No, you didn't mention it." I sat up and pulled the sheet over myself. "When will you be back?"

"August fifth."

"I'm leaving the fourth," I managed with a small frown, already beginning to feel a gentle wave of rejection.

"You're not staying the month of August?" he asked, genuinely surprised. "I thought everyone was on holiday in August."

"Not in the States." I sighed, reaching for my bathrobe, disillusioned. Why was I so unprepared for this? Was it his impeccable timing, this talk of leaving just minutes after the first time we'd had sex? I knew it was irrational—I was leaving soon enough myself—but I couldn't help it.

"I just assumed…" he started but his voice immediately petered out. I stood there looking at him, the covers up to his waist, his hand absently smoothing the sheet. I waited a few seconds for more but when nothing else came, I ducked into the bathroom. He was already dressed when I came out.

"I have a million things to do before I go," he said. "But, hey, I'd really like to keep in touch. Can I have your email address?"

We awkwardly exchanged business cards; our lips barely touched as we kissed good-bye. What had just happened? I stood at the door in silence, listening to his feet triple down the four flights. As soon as I closed the door, I began foraging through Hector's CDs, looking for some Leonard Cohen. He'd accompanied me through every sentimental disappointment since the age of thirteen. I put one on and settled into the sofa. *I'm your man*, he crooned. I was singing along with that whisky-and-cigarette voice but my throat soon caught, feeling swollen and barbed. Maybe I was exaggerating, putting a summer fling up to the Cohen heights of juvenile love—the intense school crushes, the unrequited infatuations—and, even more, those of Jeff and Todd. But I'd really liked Paco, his warmth, his humor, and I thought the relationship had potential. Then again, maybe all women felt that way about him. When the CD was over, I sat there, waiting for night to fall. However, at this latitude, in this apartment, summer daylight lingered until after ten-pm. I'd always loved that; today I craved darkness.

I looked around the room, the wine glasses half-empty on the table, Fergal's paintings laughing on the wall, Laborde's passionless promenade. Alexandre de Laborde. I hadn't even cracked that book I'd gone searching for, the Valencia segment of his *Descriptive Itinerary* from 1826. I found it on the bedside table and flopped back down on the sofa. I began flipping through it, plucking sentences off of pages, random facts nearly two hundred years old:

> *A quarter of the people in Valencia work in the silk industry [...]*
> *Valencia was the first city in Spain to have a printing press[...]*
> *Its foodstuffs are good and easily digested, rice being the most*
> *common ingredient[...] Its women are lovely and tall. Their skin*
> *is whiter here than in the rest of Spain...*

I skipped around in the text for a good forty minutes with nothing really sinking in. My eyes then landed on Laborde's description of the Valencian character: *They are friendly and most attentive to foreigners. Vivacious and clever, they are also rather fickle.* Seriously, had nothing changed since the early 1800s? I tossed the book aside, curled up on the couch and closed my eyes. I hadn't felt so adrift since the night of the tornado.

LE VOYAGE PITTORESQUE...

1805

Humanity is never perfect in good or evil.
Scoundrels have their virtues just as men
of honor have their failings.

PIERRE DE LACLOS IN *LES LIAISONS DANGEREUSES*

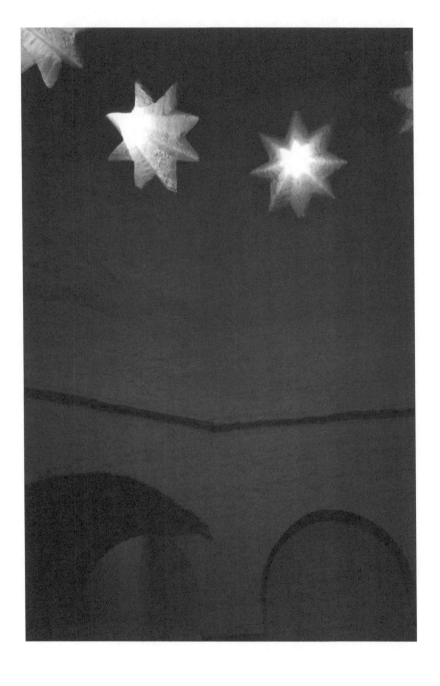

I n the center of the baked-dirt courtyard behind the house, Clara Ventura was cooking paella. Bent over the large shallow pan, she was singing an old children's song, softening it, drawing out the vowels, turning it into a sophisticated ballad. She added beans to the meat, and with a long, metal spatula, she mixed it all together. The pan—more than two feet in diameter—was set on an iron tripod over a low fire. She bunched her skirts up between her legs to keep them away from the embers, making it look as if she were wearing red linen trousers. Her legs were thin and lanky, and under them, her long, narrow feet were bare. Suddenly, one of their chickens quickly strutted past, startled, and a nervous thumping came from the rabbit hutch. She looked at the doorway and saw a stranger.

Clara immediately stopped singing and, with her eyes on him still, stood up straight, loosening her skirts and smoothing them into place. An elegant man was standing in the open doorframe consulting some written directions, his walking stick held carelessly in one hand. His clothes, fashionable yet not new, made it obvious that he was from abroad. Probably French. Visitors were rare enough in the back courtyard, but a well-dressed foreigner was unheard of.

"Yes?" Clara asked with open curiosity, taking in the details of his dark suit and silver-tipped cane. He was handsome and refined, with the dignified bearing which comes naturally after years in the military. He was probably around her age, she guessed, in his early thirties. "Can I help you?"

He stepped into the courtyard and removed his hat. "Good morning. I am Alexandre de Laborde. I am looking for Señor Vicente Plancha." He spoke slowly, with correct Spanish, but a marked accent.

"Yes, Vicente lives here, but he's not in at the moment," she replied. "I'm his niece, Clara. Could I help you with something?"

"Pleased to make your acquaintance, Señorita," he said with a minuscule bow. "I do have an inquiry. They tell me Señor Plancha owns the old Moorish baths here in Valencia."

"Yes, that's right," Clara said, looking at him even closer. She had been working in the bathhouse since her uncle bought it five years earlier and, in all that time, not a single nobleman had expressed interest in it.

"I have visited the baths of Gerona and Barcelona," continued Monsieur de Laborde, "and I've been told this one is even older. I wanted to ask him about its history."

"Well, I could tell you about the bathhouse as easily as my uncle could," she said with a smile, "but I'm sure he would enjoy giving you the details himself."

She had a lopsided smile which, as it went up on one side, revealed the tip of a white, jagged tooth. He returned her homely smile with his own polished one. Flustered, she looked down at the pan and gave the meat and vegetables another stir. With a peek back at him, she picked up a jug of water and carefully poured it into the shallow pan, until it reached the brim. It sizzled a moment, releasing an aroma of rich broth.

"Listen, why don't you come back at half-past five?" she boldly suggested.

Clara knew that if it were up to Uncle Vicente, he would probably arrange to meet with this man at his club—his refuge away from the house—to have a smoke, introduce him to his cronies, and talk importantly about his business. But, she reasoned, an outsider would provide the whole family with a change of pace; after the siesta, Sunday afternoons often dragged on interminably—either that, or her aunt found her unnecessary chores to do.

"You can join us for liqueur and fruit," she added. "I'm sure my aunt and uncle would be delighted to have you here, to tell you about the baths and anything else you might want to know about Valencia."

"Thank you for your invitation. I would be pleased to join you all this afternoon," he replied, in his well-practiced, courteous tone.

As he turned to leave, she said softly, "You're French, aren't you?"

"Yes, I am." He smiled again.

"You *do* know," she said, looking at him quite seriously, "that for many Valencian people, the French seem like the wolves in fairy tales. Clever, but untrustworthy."

Laborde opened his mouth, hesitated, and closed it again.

"Oh, don't worry," she said quickly, regretting his embarrassment. "My family and I have no hard feelings towards the French."

Monsieur Laborde was putting away his pocket watch as Irene, the servant girl, ushered him into the salon where he found a group of people with round, ruddy faces, staring up at him with curiosity and expectation. An older man with a large red nose and an old-fashioned powdered wig quickly rose, offering his hand in greeting.

"Good afternoon. I am Vicente Plancha," he said, his voice loud and jovial. "You must be the French gentleman my niece has told us all about."

Laborde located her face towards the back of the room, nodded amiably, and introduced himself to the attentive group tucked into yellow sofas and overstuffed pink chairs.

"I am Alexandre de Laborde," he said, with a bow. "Thank you so much for having me in your home."

Vicente, in turn, introduced him to the others in the room, beginning with his wife Rosa. A small, perfectly round woman with heavily rouged cheeks, Rosa gave him a pleasant smile despite the fact her armchair seemed to be holding her hostage. On the sofa sat their daughter, Silvia, who had recently turned twenty-three, her infant son Juanito in her lap. Her plunging neckline showed her fashionably plump body to great advantage and the baby grasped her enormous breasts protectively. Silvia's husband Juan looked as if he were longing to go back to his siesta, his large brown eyes on the verge of closing, while Silvia's younger brother Antonio, although somewhat cross-eyed, stared at the foreigner with shameless fascination.

"And you have already met Clara Ventura, my niece."

They exchanged smiles. Clara had been watching Laborde studying the group. She knew that in her uncle's family, all distinguished by voluminous curves, her tall, bony frame seemed even more exaggerated. But unlike the others, she had unusual green eyes, a gift from her father's side of the family.

Monsieur Laborde was given the best armchair and when he was settled with a glass of anisette, Vicente apologized for the meager offering.

"I scolded Clara for not having invited you to eat with us. I hate to tell you, but her paella was excellent today, as usual." He smiled fondly at his niece.

"A bit salty, wouldn't you say?" asked Silvia.

"Not at all," Vicente said, his tone friendly and unbothered. "Now, Monsieur, could I offer you some oranges? They are from my cousin's orchard and, although summer is nearly here, they're still delicious."

Laborde held up his hand. "No, thank you, I have eaten well myself. The anisette is very refreshing, though," he said, raising his glass to his host. "I am eager to hear about these Moorish baths of yours. Tell me, how did you come to purchase them? Have you had them long?"

"I bought them a half-dozen years ago from a nobleman by the name of Gaspar de Peñarroja. They'd been in his family for generations, for centuries."

"Peñarroja... The name sounds familiar," Laborde said.

"It is well-known name in Valencia, a very old family," Vicente said knowingly, as if his were too. "I believe they originally made their fortune with flour mills. You see, the old baths used to have a bakery attached to them. It's said that, back when the Inquisition was at its height, one of Gaspar's ancestors bought the bathhouse and bakery for the love of an enchanting Jewess. To save her from ruin. Or prison. Was it execution? Something like that."

"Ah, a romantic tale," said Laborde appreciatively.

"And a tale it probably is," said Vicente. "But Gaspar had no such romantic notions about the bathhouse. In fact, he had no interest in them at all. You should have seen the state they were in when I first bought them. Gaspar was delighted to rid himself of what he considered to be the dead weight of the family patrimony. But, now these baths are not only profitable, we have made them fashionable."

"Fashionable? What do you mean?" Laborde looked at him suspiciously. "Is it no longer a Moorish steam bath? A *hammam*?"

"Why no," Vicente cried. He looked pleased with himself while absent-mindedly scratching around the wig he was unaccustomed to wearing. "We've made great renovations in the old bathhouse. We've turned the place around and brought it into the nineteenth century!"

Laborde nodded politely, unable to hide his disappointment. He took out his snuff box, ceremoniously tapped the elegant ivory lid, took a small pinch with his fingertips, and delicately sniffed the grains into each nostril. He offered the box around to the other men who, unpracticed, snorted noisily. Antonio let out a tremendous sneeze and, lacking a handkerchief, quickly excused himself from the room.

"Tell me about these renovations. The old Arab baths I saw in Catalonia had a large vestibule and three chambers, the cold, warm and hot rooms. Do your baths have the same structure?"

"Originally, yes, they did. They were built to work with the old Roman heating system, the hypocaust. That is, a steam-filled chamber under the floor. But, with time, the pipes broke and the chamber filled with rubble. It hadn't worked for a hundred years. Like I said, the Peñarrojas couldn't be bothered with the upkeep of the baths. During that time, the bathers, and I don't think there were many, washed in wooden tubs."

Clara took a small sip of anisette and looked up into the large wall mirror which reflected everyone in the room. She was amused to see that, during this exhaustive review of the bathhouse, Juan and Juanito had both dozed off using Silvia's soft body as a cushion. Her cousin was looking down at her sleeping son, lightly tracing his faint eyebrows with her fingertip, looking far kinder than she really was. Aunt Rosa was smiling vacantly from the grips of her chair, obviously thinking of other things; Clara could not begin to speculate what. Laborde suddenly glanced up into the mirror to give his hair a quick inspection. He caught the reflection of Clara's gaze, which smiled at him.

"My uncle has made great improvements to the baths," she said, turning to look Laborde in the face. "Really, they're lovely now. I think you'll agree when you see them."

Vicente beamed at his niece. "I must say, it's true. The baths are very popular. People these days want to be clean—you know, your fellow countryman, Diderot, discussed the importance of the bathtub in his *Encyclopædia*—but they also need their privacy. That's why we've built partitions in the baths—sixteen cubicles in all—each one with its own bathtub."

"And the bathtubs"–Rosa, smiling proudly, spoke for the first time—"are made of the finest pink marble."

At that moment, Irene came back into the room, accompanying an attractive gentleman in a tall feathered hat, a silver toothpick jutting out of the side of his mouth. As he walked in, Laborde caught a whiff of *l'eau divine*, a perfume popular in Paris when he was a boy.

"Good afternoon," the newcomer cheerfully addressed the room, sweeping his hat off with a flourish. His entrance awoke the entire family who, smiling broadly, immediately sat up straighter and began arranging their skirts, shirts, hair and wig. Clara awarded him a casual grin.

"Lorenzo!" the men stood, as everyone greeted him at the same time. "Come in, come in! How are you?"

"Alexandre de Laborde," Vicente stated formally, "allow me to introduce you to Lorenzo Palafox i Cardona, the son of the Admiral of Aragon, who honors us with his friendship. Monsieur de Laborde is a distinguished visitor from Paris."

Laborde shook hands with Lorenzo, who bowed politely, removing his toothpick and storing it in his pocket. Laborde looked rather surprised to find a provincial dandy visiting the bath owner's home, while Lorenzo regarded the Frenchman with undisguised suspicion.

When they were all seated again, Lorenzo settling himself comfortably next to Clara, anisette in hand, the conversation resumed.

"We were discussing the Moorish bathhouse," explained Vicente. "In fact, Monsieur Laborde, Lorenzo's family lives in the palace right next to the baths."

"Yes, that's so," Lorenzo said, looking over at the foreigner. "Although my father's house is very old—the original foundations were laid just fifty years after James I and his Christian army took Valencia back from the Moors—the baths are even older. They were built by the Moors themselves."

"In those times, when this city was known as Balansiya, they were called the Baths of cAbd al-Malik," Clara added, her accent convincing as she pronounced the Arab names. "But now, they are simply referred to as the Admiral's Baths because of their proximity to the Admiral's Palace, Lorenzo's home." She gave her friend her crooked smile.

"During the renovations, we decided to give the baths some Arab touches, to give it back some of its original character,"

Vicente continued. "Since the walls are no longer hindered by steam, we decided to decorate them. We replastered them in ochre and put up red geometric tiles. Oh, and we also repaved the floor—well, *that* we had to do, to install the new drainage system for the tubs."

"Oh!" cried Clara, "And you wouldn't believe what I found. One day, when the old floor was being taken out and the pipes fixed, I went in there to bring the workers some lunch. I was looking around, up at the starry skylights, at the awkward old pillars, at the pebbles under the floor—you know, trying to imagine what it must have been like, long ago—when all of a sudden, something golden caught my eye. It was half-buried in a pipe, where one of the men had been digging. I bent down and uncovered the most exquisite ceramic horse you could imagine. It was made in the Moorish style with the golden glaze of the Paterna potters. It's a beautiful piece."

"I would love to see it," said Laborde, with genuine interest.

Clara returned to the room a few minutes later, carrying the horse, and handed it to Laborde. It had a few chips and a broken tail, but it was clearly the work of a master craftsman.

"It's one of my treasures," Clara said, ignoring Silvia's scornful expression.

"It looks quite old. You are indeed fortunate to have found it," he said, handing it back to her. "It makes you wonder who made it, and how it came to rest in a bath pipe."

"I know," she said. "I've imagined a hundred different stories, but I suppose it will always remain a mystery."

"Another mystery to *me*," said Lorenzo, with a hint of sarcasm in his voice, "is why a Parisian gentleman has taken such interest in an old Spanish bathhouse."

"Lorenzo," chided Clara, as if he were a naughty child, which earned her a boyish grin.

"I agree, it must seem curious," acknowledged Laborde. "The fact is, I'm writing a book about Spain and, at the moment, I'm traveling around the country gathering information. I will also provide some of the illustrations. I am making the drawings here, which I'll use as models for the engravings once I've returned to Paris. The work will be called *Le Voyage historique et pittoresque en Espagne*." He said the title with an almost theatrical tone.

"I understand that," said Silvia brightly, "It means 'Historic and Picturesque Voyage in Spain.'"

"Exactly so, Madame." Laborde smiled and clapped his hands.

Lorenzo and Clara exchanged a quick look, amused at both the facile translation and the Frenchman's exaggerated acclaim.

"Why have you decided to embark on such an endeavor, Monsieur? And why Spain?" inquired Vicente, seemingly flattered by the idea.

"Ever since I was a boy, I have been fascinated by the great explorers. My favorite was Captain James Cook. An amazing man! He spent twelve years sailing in the South Seas, discovering new lands and unimaginable tribes of people. But, alas, I get seasick." He smiled sheepishly, in playful self-reproach. "Last year, when I heard about those two Americans, Lewis and Clark, setting off across that wild new land, filled with savage Indians and dangerous animals, looking for passage to the Pacific, I was inspired—in my own way. During my career in the military I went all over the Continent, from Austria to Holland to Italy, but I decided to write about Spain, whose history, to my mind, is the most interesting in all of Europe." He concluded with a slight bow to all present.

Everyone began speaking at once, how splendid, how admirable, how delightful this book promised to be! Clara, who had the feeling he made that very same spontaneous speech to anyone who asked, remained quiet, a small smile playing on her lips.

Lorenzo's face, however, became serious, and suddenly his voice was heard above the others: "Picturesque are we? You French have always tried to make Spaniards look ridiculous. You exaggerate our habits and customs, making them sound amusing or backward to the people in Paris, then you congratulate yourselves on your culture and refinement. I don't think a Spaniard could possibly recognize himself in anything written by a Frenchman."

"It is certainly not my intention to make a mockery of Spanish culture," retorted Laborde, suddenly on his feet. He was indignant, but trying to remain calm. "In fact, my father was Spanish. He was born in a village in Aragon, in the Pyrenees. He went to France as a young man and made his fortune there. Too vast a fortune, I'm afraid. He was guillotined during the revolution because of it."

The room fell silent. Vicente bit his lip, not wishing to offend either gentleman. The mantle clock was plainly heard for a second or two, when Clara stood up and looked their guest in the face.

"I'm terribly sorry, Monsieur Laborde. I'm afraid we're a bit sensitive here, having such powerful, ambitious neighbors. Please, sit down. Can I get you anything? Some sweet wine, perhaps?"

"No, I must be leaving now. It has become quite late. But, I would like to see the baths and make some drawings, if that won't be a problem," he said, looking over at Vicente.

"Of course, you may make as many drawings as you like. We would be honored to have our humble baths included in your book."

Alexandre de Laborde took leave of everyone, paying them compliments and expressing his thanks. He and Lorenzo, however, shook hands without a word.

When the dawn Angelus bells rang out from the scores of church towers, convents and monasteries around the city, Clara was still in bed, awake with her eyes closed. She mumbled a Hail Mary under her breath and, as the last toll faded into silence, got up and opened the shutters, illuminating her room. It was simple and clean, like a nun's cell, the only adornment a crucifix, hanging slightly askew over her cot. She quickly made her bed then put on a freshly washed skirt and blouse. She laced her espadrilles up to mid-calf, thinking that was one advantage of no longer being of marriageable age: she didn't have to cram her big feet into dainty shoes but could wear the same kind the men wore when working in the fields.

When she was in her early twenties and there was still a remote possibility of finding her a husband, her aunt had once insisted she wear a lace-up corset. It was not to make her slimmer—impossible—but to give her straight torso a waist, a semblance of curves. Clara had tried it, willing herself to be beautiful. At that time, she still thought Honorato Ramos would one day propose. How naïve she was then. But even Rosa could see that the only curves the corset had brought out were her ribs and her hip bones, making her look like a comical skeleton rather than a buxom potential bride.

She splashed her face with water, washing away any more thoughts of Honorato, and quickly wound her light brown hair into a knot. Although it was rather long, it was so fine that it made a bun no bigger than a green plum. She sighed into the mirror, covered her hair with a dark blue kerchief, put on an apron, and went downstairs.

"Good morning," Clara said.

Irene was in the kitchen, toasting yesterday's bread on the fire. They were always the first to rise and had breakfast together. Clara cut some cheese and dried sausage and they sat down to eat in silence. After sharing an orange, Irene began tidying the kitchen and Clara picked up two supple baskets made from rushes.

"What do you need from the market?" she asked.

"Get some pork ribs and potatoes for the soup," Irene said. "And see if you can find any fava beans. The smaller the better."

"Very well. See you in a little bit." She went out the door, heading for the Central Market, a hectic hub on the other side of the cathedral.

Clara had never minded doing the morning's shopping. At her uncle's house, she was usually lonely since, straddling the line between family and servant, she was accepted by neither. She preferred being out in the lively street, chatting with neighbors and vendors, exchanging greetings and catching up on the latest gossip. In the market, she took her time; she slowly strolled through the narrow aisles between stalls, past red and orange towers of paprika; past lifeless newborn pigs with their small, doleful eyes; past the freshly-caught octopuses, curling around one another like lovers. She breathed deeply, taking in all the smells: cured ham, olive brine, farmhands.

When her baskets were filled, Clara left the market to head back to her neighborhood. On the corner, she greeted Paloma, a young gypsy girl with honey-colored skin and shiny black hair, who sold licorice root. When she caught sight of Clara, she gave her a wide, gap-tooth smile, and pulled a slender piece of licorice out of her bundle. Clara placed a coin in her small hand, then put the root in the side of her mouth and began to chew.

"So, Clara, shall I read your palm this morning?"

"Oh, Paloma, why do you insist? You know I always say no."

"Come now, who knows what your future has in store for you? It could be your lucky day—perhaps you'll finally find love."

Clara laughed at the young girl, waving her hand in a mixture of good-natured dismissal and goodbye. On the way back to the house, she stopped to buy Vicente the *Diario de Valencia* from Domingo, who had been a dear friend of her father's.

Domingo Lopez held court in the square, seated on a short stool with his ankles crossed, a stack of newspapers piled high on the crate in front of him. He was bald, though his thick, gray eyebrows nearly compensated for the lack on his head, and protected his scalp with a bright yellow kerchief, tied in such a way that it stood up like a pointed hat. With one hand, he pulled on a short, bone pipe, a habit which had dyed his front teeth the color of tobacco, and with the other, he held on to a long stick.

He gave Clara a brown grin, squinting up at her. "Lovely morning, ain't it, my dear?"

"Lovely, indeed, old friend. So, Domingo, tell me, what's new in the world?"

"How would I know?" he replied in a cantankerous tone, taking her coin and handing her a paper. "I just sell the damn things, I don't read them."

She smiled at him affectionately, then hurried through the square, making her way around a burly man pushing a wheelbarrow full of melons and a noblewoman being carried in an elegant covered chair by two red-faced men in silken breeches.

Clara walked into the house, baskets in her hands, the newspaper under her arm, and the licorice sticking out of her mouth. Her uncle was up and dressed and sitting at the table, waiting to be served breakfast.

"Here's your newspaper," she said cheerfully, removing the licorice stick to give him a kiss on the cheek.

Vicente, her mother's brother, was her favorite member of the household. Pity he spent so little time there. Maybe he too felt more comfortable out in the street.

Clara went to the kitchen and gave the groceries to Irene. She checked the clock: it was almost nine. Time to be at the baths. Every day but Sunday, she supervised the young women who worked there, making sure the tubs were clean and functioning properly. Still sucking on the root, she headed out the door once more.

At the ringing of the noontime bells, Clara stepped out the door to sweep the bit of street in front of the bathhouse, a preventive measure to keep customers from tracking in dirt. As she whisked between the cobblestones with her broom, she began to sing in a rich, clear voice:

> *Since you looked at me*
> *I have a thorn in my chest*
> *That doesn't let me rest*
> *By night, or by day*

She swayed slightly to the tune remembering how, after Honorato had asked Francisca to marry him, she'd been unable to sing that song, or anything for that matter, for months. Talk about thorns in your chest. She had been so sure that he felt the same

attraction for her as she did for him, that they had an understanding. What had those meaningful glances at church been
about, then? She gave a long sigh and, with the tip of the broom,
viciously attacked a bit of straw stuck between the cobblestones.
Why was she thinking about Honorato all of sudden? That story
was almost a decade old.

She straightened up and, holding the broom at arm's length,
began the song again: "Since you looked at me, I have a thorn
in my chest…" When suddenly there was a step behind her accompanied by a voice.

"Good morning, Clara."

Immediately silenced, she swung around to find Alexandre
de Laborde, grinning at her. How long had he been standing
there?

"Oh, hello," she said, blushing deeply.

She couldn't believe he'd caught her singing—and nearly
waltzing—in the street. In fact, he probably thought that she and
the broom made a well-matched pair—if only it had been wearing a powered wig.

"I didn't expect to find you here," he said jovially. "Do you
work at the baths?"

"Oh, yes. I have always earned my keep at my uncle's house,"
she replied, wiping her hands on her apron, regarding Laborde.
Dressed casually today, but not without style, he held his cane in
one hand, a portfolio in the other.

"Have you lived with his family long?" His interest seemed
sincere.

"Since I was orphaned at the age of six," she answered. His
sympathetic gaze inspired confidence in her, the confidence
that comes when talking to a stranger. "I suppose that in the
beginning there was the understanding that, one day, my uncle

would pay my dowry. But now I think we both know that, at my age, I will not be collecting on that debt." Her smile this time was straight and her lips nearly disappeared.

He seemed rather taken aback by her directness, and gave her gaunt frame and plain face a look of tenderness.

"Oh, don't misunderstand me," she corrected, "My Uncle Vicente has always treated me kindly."

"I could see that for myself yesterday. It's clear that he's very fond of you." Laborde gave her a teasing smile, "And he is not the only one. Your friend Lorenzo seemed protective of you as well. You may need that dowry yet, Clara."

"Lorenzo!" she cried, her eyes shining with mirth. "Oh, my heavens, no."

Although the tone of her voice made the idea sound preposterous, as children, she and Lorenzo had often played games of make-believe, pretending to be a couple: a prince and a princess, a pair of pirates, a mother and a father. Sometimes, Lorenzo's little mutt Pinto would allow them to hold and cuddle him, becoming their makeshift child. Back then, before Clara had learned such concepts as high birth or social standing, she had assumed that they would grow up to marry. However, since early adolescence, she'd contented herself with the special friendship they shared.

"You see," she continued, smiling still, "we've lived on the same square since childhood and have always been good friends. My aunt was his wet nurse. She was a widow when she married my uncle and already had children of her own." She paused a moment, wondering, as always, what had inspired her Uncle Vicente to marry an older woman, a widow with two daughters of her own. "Lorenzo, it seems, has had a special fondness for my family ever since."

"I believe your uncle said that he was the heir to the Admiral of Aragon?"

"He is his son, but not his heir. Lorenzo is the fourth son, the youngest. His eldest brother is the heir to the title and fortune, the second one is a military officer, and the third has a promising career in the Church. I'm afraid Lorenzo has not yet found his way, although he is trying. Believe me, he's trying! I am his confidant and he tells me about all of his... endeavors."

"Then, *he* must be *your* confidant as well."

"Me?" Clara looked surprised. "Why, I have nothing to tell."

At that moment, two men came out of the baths, their faces freshly shaved, their damp hair neatly combed. One nodded to Clara as he passed, then gave the foreigner a raised eyebrow. She suddenly realized that she had been standing in the middle of the street, broom in hand, carrying on a strangely personal conversation with a Frenchman she'd met just the day before. She looked up at him, slightly embarrassed.

"But you have come here to see the baths. I'll be happy to show them to you."

Closing the door behind him, Laborde found it was like walking into a church, the thick walls keeping the interior cool and quiet. They entered the vestibule, the high-ceilinged hall; a soft glow of sunlight fell through the arched windows at the top. Cubicles had been built between the columns and they could hear the people within, washing, splashing, rinsing, whistling. The place smelled clean, like lemon, with an underlying aroma of perfumes, soaps and oils. Laborde looked around carefully, then brought out his sketchpad.

"May I see some of your drawings?" Clara asked.

"Of course," Laborde replied politely, though he seemed surprised by her interest. "I have some in here of the baths in Catalonia, if you'd like to see what they look like."

She watched him leaf through several pages of architectural details, floor plans, and drawings made with perfect perspective and painstakingly precise lines. Finally he found one of the Gerona baths, highlighting its fountain, and handed it to her.

"How well you draw," she said, looking at it closely. "It's just how the eye sees."

"Yes, it is true that my hand obeys my eye, though perhaps my drawings are lacking a bit in spirit. In the future they will probably invent a machine that can do what I do," he said, smiling at the idea.

"I also like to draw," she said with certain shyness. "Perhaps one day I will show you my pictures. They can't compare to your work—I am far too impatient for that. I mostly make portraits. I think I've drawn all the people on the square: the vendors, the children, the gypsies—even some of the dogs and cats."

Laborde looked at Clara with wonder. Provincial spinsters were rarely interesting, and never surprising.

"Well, I should get back to work. The tubs must be cleaned after each bath, and after certain clients, those who visit us less frequently, they require quite a scrubbing."

This time, when she gave him her crooked smile, he looked expectantly for the tip of the white tooth. Finding it, he smiled back.

That evening, Clara and Lorenzo pulled cane chairs out to the courtyard, to enjoy the fresh air, lightly scented with jasmine, and to talk without interruptions. He had just come from having hot chocolate with the Vidal widow, which was obvious by the attention he'd spent on his toilette. By now, however, his long hair, powdered, scented and curled, was rather mussed, and the velvet beauty mark he had put on the side of his mouth was in danger of falling off.

Lorenzo was telling her the story of Manon Lescaut, the last novel he'd read. Like *Les Liasons Dangereuses* and the works of Voltaire, it had also been banned by the Inquisition for depravity and immorality, making it highly popular, easily available, and eagerly discussed in all the salons and *chocolaterías*. Lorenzo read all the forbidden books, some in French, some in translation, and afterwards, he would tell the stories to Clara. He was a talented raconteur, always including rich details and descriptions, and she listened with fascination. She would pick up her mandolin, the only keepsake she had from her father, and strum on it as Lorenzo was talking, improvising along with the story. Sometimes she would produce a melodramatic chord at a sad moment or a jaunty strand during an exciting part, which would make them both laugh.

Lorenzo had just got to the part of the story where Manon, a fallen woman, was being deported to the penal colony of New Orleans, when Clara interrupted.

"I don't understand this character at all," she said, throwing up her hands. "A handsome young nobleman adores her, yet, because he cannot afford to cover her in jewels and finery, she sells herself to a rich old coot? Who would do that? It's completely unrealistic."

"How innocent you are, Clara." Lorenzo smiled. "I think most women prefer luxury and riches to love. Lord knows, I've met my share. Money and pleasure, that's what they want."

"Well, I don't understand it," she said stubbornly, putting her mandolin on the table. "You'd think anyone would be overjoyed to be loved like the Chevalier loves Manon."

Lorenzo picked up the worn instrument. "Speaking of love, Clara," he said, "I've written a song. I'd like for you to tell me what you think."

He gave her a wink, strummed a chord, and began to half-sing, half-recite his composition. It spoke of his passion for an exciting lady with sparkling eyes and the voice of an angel. When he was finished, he looked at her expectantly.

She gave him a small shrug and a quizzical expression, not knowing exactly what he wanted from her. Help with his mandolin playing? Her opinion about the sentimental lyrics? A moment of awkward silence passed, until Lorenzo barked out with laughter.

"You're a hard one, Clara," he cried. "I've seduced a dozen women with that song." He took out his shiny brass snuff box which, Clara noticed, matched the buttons on his coat. "The funny thing is," he said with an affected sigh, "each one thinks it was written for her."

"Lorenzo, you're incorrigible. Really, how can you lie to these women, making them believe in your love, when all you want is pleasure?"

"But, I don't lie to them." Lorenzo brought his hand to his heart, mockingly offended by this injustice. "When I'm at my lady's side, I *am* in love. Every word I say is true. But, once I leave her company, my love slowly begins to fade, like a dream upon waking until, finally, I have quite forgotten the whole thing."

He shook some snuff onto the back of his hand, snorted it up, and dabbed his nose with a flowered handkerchief.

"And as for pleasure," he continued, "they desire it as much as I do—sometimes more. I have been with women who have cried in gratitude. Like the Countess I told you about. Dear thing, she was old enough to be my mother. When I woke the next morning, she was holding me in her arms and I was suckling her like a newborn."

Clara rolled her eyes as he chuckled at the memory. He considered another pinch of snuff, decided against it, and put the box back in his pocket.

"Or the poor Centelles girl. What a beauty she was before she got small pox. Now, she's so scarred her own family is ashamed for her to be seen in public. She was thankful to be in my arms, I'll tell you that. That is my gift, Clara, to see the beauty in every woman and to give her love. For a little while anyway."

"Ah, my dear Lorenzo, lover of all women," she said bitingly. "How noble of you."

She stood up and, with her back to him, began picking dead leaves off the lemon tree. For a moment Lorenzo was worried that she was truly irritated with him; finally, she turned around and smiled sadly.

"Let's have a glass of *mistela*, shall we?"

Clara came back to the patio carrying a tray with two glasses of sweet wine and a small plate of olives.

"Oh, by the way, I saw Monsieur de Laborde this morning at the baths. He showed me some of his drawings. He's very talented."

"That fraud?" Lorenzo reached for his glass with an exasperated expression. "Comparing himself to Captain Cook, indeed. I suppose that makes us Spaniards wild tattooed savages. I thought him an insufferable prig."

"It is very curious to me, Lorenzo," said Clara, selecting an olive with a playful smile, "how you love all things French: novels, clothes, dances—even hairdos—and yet you hate the French themselves. How can you explain that?"

"It's true, I love French style. But Frenchmen are so pompous, so arrogant, so superior... You're right. I can't abide them." He picked the beauty mark from the side of his mouth and flicked it onto the plate with the olive pits. "And now Napoleon has crowned himself Emperor—Imagine! That cocky little commoner thinks he owns the world. Mark my words, he'll be sending troops across the Pyrenees soon enough."

"Do you really think so?" Clara had heard him make this prediction before. "I thought Spain and France were allies."

"The French are capable of anything. Don't you remember, Clara? They murdered their own king."

"Of course I remember," she said, half-annoyed. "How could I forget? What a riot that caused. Everyone was so furious, so indignant that—"

"Yes, the people completely lost their heads. So to speak." Lorenzo smiled unpleasantly.

"It wasn't funny. Those French people lost everything—their shops looted, their houses burned. You could smell the smoke all over the city." Clara shivered at the memory. "It was terrifying, all of it."

"Yes, until they were finally expelled, sent off on ships back to France. And rightly so," Lorenzo said with a wave of his hand.

"You know, I later heard that almost all those families had been living in Valencia for generations before the revolution. Most of them didn't even speak French. The only foreign thing about them was their last names."

Dusk had slowly settled in the courtyard, and when Clara looked over at her friend, she couldn't make out the expression on his face.

"Clara?" she heard her aunt call from inside the house. "Clara! Where are you? My corns need shaving."

Clara looked look down, embarrassed, and sighed.

Lorenzo took her hand and whispered, "I'll be back soon to tell you more about Manon Lescault. And you can be sure that she shaved a few corns in her day."

He smiled at her, kissed her forehead, and went through the door in the courtyard, out into the black street.

A few days later, Clara saw Alexandre de Laborde at the baths again. He had already finished a few detailed drawings of the vestibule and the warm room, which he readily shared with her.

"Monsieur, why have you not drawn the partitions and cubicles? And these horseshoe arches? Where are they?" she asked, looking around the room.

"Don't tell your uncle, Clara, but I find that his renovations—although practical and modern—have disfigured the integrity of the baths. I am trying to depict them as they were originally."

"Excuse me for saying so, but don't you think that's deceptive? You pretend to show them as they were in the past, but we have no idea what they really looked like then."

"Deceptive? On the contrary, Clara, I am trying to be faithful." Laborde smiled at her confusion. "But, I must agree that, although they don't date from the time of the Moors, these marble bathtubs are marvelous. I took a bath here myself this morning, and it was quite luxurious. So much nicer than the old copper tub at my father's house," he said, sliding the drawings back into the leather portfolio where he kept his papers.

"Yes, they're large and comfortable," Clara agreed. "They've been a great success."

"In Paris, near the Pont Royal, there is an elegant bath boat on the Seine. The water is pumped directly from the river, then filtered to fill the tubs. For three *sous* you can take a wonderfully refreshing bath," Laborde said, with a slightly nostalgic air. "Of course, there are some men who can't be bothered with the formality of the boat—or perhaps they lack the *sous*—and just take off their clothes and jump in the river. More than one lady has been quite shocked by these artless bathers during her evening stroll along the quay, believe me."

"You must miss Paris," Clara said, looking up into his face.

"Actually, when the revolution broke out, my father sent me to Vienna, to join the Austrian army. I was seventeen at the time. I have scarcely lived in Paris since. Indeed, when I go there now, I feel a bit lost. All my fellows seem to be either frivolous or cynical. That's why I have come to Spain," he said, smiling again, "in search of Don Quixote."

"Well," Clara said, smiling back, "I hope you find him."

Sunday was drearier than usual. Not only was it a gray day but, without the presence of either Lorenzo or the French gentleman, Silvia was bossy, boastful, and altogether unpleasant. During her weekly visit to her parents' home, she expected to be treated as returning royalty, wanting her family to gush over her, her baby and her husband Juan as if they were their superiors. Her mother was happy to comply. Her older daughters hadn't married well and still were living in her first husband's village, working in the fields. Rosa was extremely proud of Silvia and her son-in-law, the court clerk.

"Isn't he just adorable?" Silvia cooed, looking down at her son.

Her mother nodded, "Just like you, when you were a baby. Rosy cheeks, dimples, and big fat legs—I could just eat him up!"

She took her grandson's little arm and pretended to give it a bite, then covered it with loud kisses.

When the baby's appearance and accomplishments had been duly praised, he was put down for a nap. The company was called in for dinner and, as they ate, conversation went from Silvia's new frock to Juan's important acquaintances.

"Señor Blasco Sanchez?" Clara asked, remembering him as a client from the bathhouse. "The one with round glasses?"

"Oh, Clara." Her cousin laughed. "You couldn't possibly know who we're talking about."

"Of course not," she replied with a stiff smile.

Throughout the remainder of the meal, Clara did not listen to another word they said. Instead, she thought of how she might draw her cousin and her husband in caricature, highlighting, respectively, a spoiled pout and turned-up nose and a set of bleary eyes.

After they'd finished lunch that day, Vicente sat back and smiled at his niece.

"I must say, Sundays—when Clara cooks—are my favorite days at table. Today your rabbit in garlic sauce was just delicious."

"Papa." Silvia scowled. She'd been jealous of her father's fondness for Clara ever since she was a toddler and her older cousin, a teenager. "How you exaggerate Clara's culinary gifts. Now, *our* cook is truly fine, wouldn't you say, Juan?"

"Yes, she's excellent. In her hands, even simple dishes are exceptional. I don't know how she does it."

"How lucky you are," Rosa smiled at her daughter, delighting again at Silvia's situation, a grandiose reflection on herself. "Here, we make do."

"I'm off to my club," said Vicente, coughing into his napkin. "See you all this evening."

After he had left, Rosa retired to her room, Antonio went out for a smoke, and Juan stretched out on the sofa to sleep off the large portions of second-rate rabbit he had indulged in. Silvia looked over at her cousin with an innocent smile.

"Although we are blessed with a good cook, I'm afraid the maid isn't very good at ironing. Clara, you wouldn't mind doing a little ironing for me this afternoon, would you? There's a basket there in the hall"—she cocked her ear to one side—"Is that the baby already waking up? You'll excuse me."

As always in her uncle's house, Clara did as she was asked.

Clara was in the kitchen, beating egg whites with sugar. She'd seen Monsieur de Laborde at the baths the day before, and he'd asked her to meet him there that afternoon. He wanted her to help him measure the rooms to make an accurate floor plan but also claimed to be curious about her sketches. When she got up that morning, she decided to surprise him with a batch of Spanish sweets. As she mixed the toasted almonds into the meringue, Clara began to sing. Irene looked up from the pot over the stove and raised her eyebrows.

"You're in good spirits this morning," she said with a smile. "And making *besos de novia?* Are they for someone special?"

Clara looked into the bowl and blushed. *Bride's kisses.* The name of the sweets had slipped her mind. How ridiculous, she thought, how truly pathetic that a plain-faced spinster should be making romantically-named sweets for a handsome gentleman. Hopefully, he wouldn't have any idea what they were called. Now embarrassed, she asked Irene to take them to the bakery to be fired, not wanting to hear any more amusing comments about them.

After lunch, siestas, and an overly-long session of brushing her aunt's thinning hair, Clara got up to leave. She carefully put her sketches, collected in a cardboard folder, and the meringues inside a basket. When she arrived to the baths, Laborde was already there, waiting for her outside the door. In one hand, he was holding the thin rope that he used for measuring, ten times the length from his elbow to the tip of his finger, and in the other, he had his own portfolio.

"Ah, Clara, thank you for coming," he said, gallantly taking her basket in his free hand. "Let's take the measurements first, then we can sit down and have a good look at your drawings."

For nearly half an hour, Clara helped by simply holding the opposite end of the rope from various walls, corners, pillars, and doorways; Laborde jotted numbers down on a quickly drawn plan of the baths. Not wanting to disturb him, she watched him in silence from her side of the rope, taking in the way he sometimes pursed his lips in concentration, or ran his hand through his hair as he looked up in a pensive half-squint. She was wondering if she would be able to draw him later from memory, when he suddenly looked up and caught her staring at him. He smiled at her blush. He probably had plenty of experience with admiring girls.

"I think that's everything," he said finally. "Now, let's enjoy ourselves."

They sat down on the bench in the middle of the vestibule, where the sounds of bathing poured out from the occupied stalls: various tunes hummed around them as water splashed. Clara brought out her basket and shyly offered him a cookie.

"How thoughtful of you, Clara." His smile was dashing. "Although, I must say, I am the one who owes you a treat for helping me." He ate half of one, declared it delicious, then pulled out his pocket handkerchief and carefully wiped his hands. "Now, may I see those sketches? I've been wondering about them since you mentioned them last week."

She handed him the cardboard folder and he opened it on his lap. He found a few dozen sketches inside, some done quickly, others with care; he studied each one.

Clara, he found, was skillful at portraiture. Not only were her models faithfully represented, the drawings also seemed to convey a great deal about who each person was. There was Domingo, the newspaper vendor, his pipe in his hand and an expression of affected ill-temper on his face; Clara's cousin Antonio, finely dressed but looking unavoidably simple; the gypsy girl who sold licorice root in the square, barefoot with a gap-toothed grin. Her street scenes captured movement; one could almost see them unfolding before one's eyes: stray cats stretching in the sun, boisterous children playing leapfrog, well-dressed ladies shielding themselves with their parasols, nuns walking briskly through the square.

"I've always thought they looked like flocks of crows," said Clara, interrupting Laborde's thoughts. He gazed up at her and she smiled at the look of wonder on his face.

"Clara, you have surprised me more than once with your frankness and originality," he said. "I'm pleased to see those traits are reflected in your artwork. These sketches are very good."

"Thank you, Monsieur," Clara replied, genuinely pleased. She was often praised by her neighbors for her talents, but she took a special delight in Laborde's compliments, he, who had seen the world and drew so well himself. "I do love sketching. It's a shame one has to work too."

He continued looking through them and she watched his face as he went from one drawing to the next, from the formal full-length portrait of her wigged uncle, to the detailed study of Lorenzo, holding the mandolin.

"Ah, your friend is also a musician?" he asked.

"No, he's just posing with it." She smiled at the picture. "He didn't know what to do with his hands while I was drawing him, so he picked up my mandolin."

"*Your* mandolin? Tell me, Clara," he demanded, laughing, "what *can't* you do?"

"Many, many things," she replied, almost saddened. "You'd be surprised how many things I can't do."

Laborde leafed through the next few drawings, until he got to the last one: a self-portrait which froze in his hands. It instantly reminded him of Pope Innocent X's legendary comment when he saw the painting Velazquez had made of him: *troppo vero.* Too real.

Clara had depicted herself as accurately as she could, without attempting to soften her features or round out her lines. Her face stared out at the viewer with a serious look of concentration, while in her hands she held the golden ceramic horse. The portrait showed an indisputably plain woman who, at the same time, was able to attract her audience with her clear, unflinching gaze, her fine-spun hands, and the tilt of her chin. It was a powerful piece.

"May I have this one, Clara?" Laborde asked, studying now the face of the model, who was, perhaps, prettier in person. "In turn, you can choose one of my drawings for yourself."

"Of course, you may have it," she said, flattered that he would ask for one of her drawings but, even more, that he wanted her own likeness as a keepsake. "But I think the trade is too much in my favor. Here, why don't you choose a drawing for me?"

He opened up his portfolio and, after rummaging for a few minutes through his sketches, he handed her a drawing of the partitionless warm room, the star-shaped skylights twinkling above arabesque archways.

"Please, Clara, I'd like for you to have this one. My *faithful* representation of the how the baths used to be." He grinned. "And, I think you are wrong. I have won this barter."

She slowly traced the lines of the arches with a finger, admiring their symmetry and precision. Clara carefully thought out her next words and turned back to him.

"Thank you, Monsieur. But, looking at the excellence of the craftsmanship, I'm inclined to think that you're working too hard." She gave him her clumsy smile. "Perhaps tomorrow you could take the day off, and my aunt and I could show you some places of interest here in Valencia."

"It would be an honor, Clara," he said formally, with a slight bow of his head.

"Lovely." She smiled nervously at her success. "Shall we meet at my uncle's house in the evening, around five? When it has cooled down a bit?"

"Fine! I'll see you then," he said, standing. "Now, I think I'll try to make a decent copy of this floor plan."

She picked up her basket to leave, casting a quick look of mild disappointment at the nearly ignored meringues inside. "See you tomorrow," she said brightly, though his back was already turned.

As she walked home, she realized she had not thought the invitation through. Grown bold by the exchange of the drawings, the nearness of him on the bench, Clara had forgotten that Alexandre de Laborde had already been in the city for two months. He had probably seen–and drawn—every possible monument, church, and square within its walls. Also, she had overheard him speaking to some of their more prominent bathers, and gathered that, at the very outset of his sojourn, he had been formally presented to Valencian society. Since then, he had dined in all the best homes, had hot chocolate with all the most fashionable ladies, and taken rides along the Alameda in all the finest carriages. He had been to picnics in the country and seen private performances of operettas. Truly, what could she and Rosa, two dowdy ladies of the lower bourgeoisie, show him that he had not seen?

She briskly scraped her shoes on the jute doormat and went inside. Now she would have to convince Aunt Rosa to accompany them and even more importantly, come up with a plan that would be new.

She found her cousin Antonio in the salon chatting with Silvia's husband, Juan.

"Good evening, you two," she said pleasantly, then reached into her basket and brought out the bundle of sweets. "I made some meringues today, if you'd like some."

"Thank you, cousin," they replied, taking a handful each.

Climbing the stairs to her room, she could clearly hear their laughter.

"Besos de novia?" Antonio snorted. "What would old Clara know about kisses?"

"Or brides!" responded Juan, smacking his leg with glee.

With a heavy sigh, she lit a candle in her room and took Laborde's drawing out of her folder, propping it up behind the Moorish horse on the narrow table by the cot. She gazed at the picture, imagining his full lips pursing in concentration as he made the perfect arches, him tousling his thick hair as he gazed up at the stars. She lay on the bed and closed her eyes. A languid smile slowly spread across her face.

Clara went upstairs for her siesta, but couldn't relax. Her aunt had gladly accepted the invitation to accompany her and the dignified Frenchman on a stroll through the city, and Laborde was to be there in little more than an hour.

She picked up her hand mirror and, stretching her arm as far as she could, looked at herself with a critical eye. She tried pulling her blouse down to where Silvia and the other women wore theirs but, upon careful observation, found that exposing her bony chest was far worse than defying fashion and wearing it up to her collar bones. She put the mirror down and tied her nicest scarf around her hair, the one of green silk that brought out her eyes. Looking at her reflection again, she considered putting on rouge.

Opening the little pot, Clara thought back on the circus she'd seen at Portal Nou when she was five or six. It was one of the few clear memories she had of her parents. They'd seen camels and a crocodile that day, and a man breathing fire. But, the moment that really stuck in her mind was when a cat was sent up in one of those newfangled hot-air balloons. Her father, as excited as a child, clapped his hands, while her mother, her laugh rich and warm, knelt down next to her and pointed out the clowns holding on to the ropes. They had bright red circles painted on their cheeks.

Clara closed the rouge pot with decision. She took another look at her reflection: from various angles, serious, smiling, at her teeth, her long nose, her pointy chin. Frustrated, she set the mirror face down on the bed, got up and went downstairs. No matter what she looked like, at least she had come up with a good plan for their outing.

When Alexandre de Laborde arrived, Clara was pleased to see that he was elegantly dressed and carrying his walking stick as if he were truly escorting two fine ladies around town. For her part, Rosa had outdone herself applying her rouge and was wearing her most extravagant bonnet, one with blue ribbons and green feathers coming out from all sides. Her face looked like an unusual tropical flower, picked for its enormous size, then left to wither in the sun.

When they had walked only as far as the cathedral, Clara threw her head back to behold the top of the Micalet and looked back at Laborde.

"I thought I would show you the whole city at once. Shall we climb up to the top of the bell tower? There's a wonderful view from up there, from the mountains to the sea."

Rosa looked at her niece in disbelief. "Surely you're not serious," she cried, letting out a loud puff of air just at the idea. "What a terrible climb that would be. The bell ringers themselves wouldn't go up there if they didn't have to."

Laborde smiled at the older woman, then at Clara. "You know, I have drawn this tower at least three times, and passed beneath it dozens more, but it has never occurred to me to actually climb to the top of it. With apologies to Madame, I think I should like to do it."

"I will certainly not prevent you from doing so, but I cannot join you," Rosa said, folding her hands daintily across her broad belly. "I will take this opportunity to go to confession. I'll see you two when you're back on *terra firma*."

Rosa turned and entered the cathedral through the Door of the Apostles, pointedly ignoring the blind beggar sitting on the top step.

Clara led the way up the long spiral staircase, her skirt in one hand, while Laborde followed carrying his walking stick, useless for such a climb. They watched their footing carefully, as the faint light inside grew and faded with each rotation; the tower's tall, thin windows were only on one side. About half-way up they passed the bell ringer's dark, simple lodgings, then, towards the top, the floor with eleven massive bells. At this point, each step became steeper and narrower than the one before; they balanced themselves by sliding their palms along the center column. Finally, they reached the terrace of the octagonal tower, with the huge bell, named for Saint Michael, hanging in the middle.

They made their way to the edge and looked down upon a labyrinth of twisted streets and flat-roofed houses while a forest of church towers, spires and domes came rising up from beneath them. Laborde, to his delight, was able to identify many of the buildings he'd drawn during his stay in the city: the Silk Exchange, the city gates, various palaces, the convent which took up a large portion of the former Moorish Quarter. They made their way around the tower, pausing on the eight different sides. On the south, they could make out the Albufera—the large fresh-water lake separated from the sea by just a finger of land—and its surrounding rice fields, a brilliant green this time of year. To the north, they saw little farming hamlets and wheat fields. On the horizon were the mountains and the coast.

"You can even see the ships' masts at the port. But, from here"—Laborde shaded his eyes as he looked out—"you can barely distinguish them from the palm trees. Don Hugo de Moncada took me to the beach last week in his carriage. It was so peaceful there, with such a pleasant breeze. Do you ever go to the shore, Clara?" he inquired politely, turning to face her.

"Actually, I used to live on the sea—at the port—until my parents died. They drowned, both of them."

"Oh, I'm sorry, Clara," he said gently. "Did your father have a seafaring trade? Fisherman? Ship builder?"

"I suppose he did some of those things. My uncle would probably tell you that he was a sailor of some kind or another." She looked Laborde in the face. "But the truth is, my parents were *contrabandistas*."

"Smugglers?" Laborde asked, raising his eyebrows in surprise.

"Of course they didn't talk about it in front of me. I was just a child," she continued. "But, Domingo—do you know the man who sells newspapers in the square? Well, he was a close friend of theirs and has told me about it. Evidently, the night it happened, they were waiting offshore for a silk shipment from France. The sea was so rough, it pitched them right out of their boat."

Laborde was so taken aback by this matter-of-fact disclosure that he was left speechless. He put his hand on her shoulder, gave it a light pat, then brought out his snuff box and took a few well-mannered sniffs.

"The irony is that before the great war a hundred years ago, my father's family were successful silk merchants," she said. "But, in the battle for the Spanish crown, like most Valencians, they supported the Habsburgs. When, in the end, a French prince sat on our throne, they were sent into exile with the rest. They went to Naples, having lost everything. My father's father finally returned to Valencia, a humble fisherman. And my father, well,"— Clara shrugged limply with one shoulder—"he went back into the silk trade."

Laborde brought out his handkerchief and dabbed at his nose, visibly uncomfortable. These topics, from her parents' dishonorable profession to the Valencians' humiliating—and unforgotten—defeat to the French in the War of the Spanish Succession the century before, were hardly the typical drawing-room conversations Laborde was accustomed to having with ladies. He mumbled a sympathetic apology of sorts.

"Oh, every family has its history, Monsieur. This is simply mine."

She looked into his face, its awkward rigidity and guileless compassion, and felt moved. She smiled at him, longing to reach out and touch his hand.

"Wait!" Clara cried suddenly, "What time is it?"

Laborde pulled out his pocket watch. "It's about to strike six."

"Indeed it is," she said with a laugh, pointing to the enormous bell. She took him by the hand and rushed to the stairs.

As they arrived at the landing where the other bells were, the first deafening peal of the evening Angelus rang out. They could only see one of the bell ringers, a wiry, extremely pale man—it was impossible to tell if he were young or old—who was pushing a great bell, ducking as it swung round, then pulling its rope as hard as he could, flinging himself up onto the walls. Clara looked at Laborde's wide-eyed amazement, at the incredible volume of the bells combined with the spectacle of the ghostly bell ringer, and tried not to laugh as she recited the Hail Mary. After a moment, she nodded her head toward the stairwell, motioning him to descend, her hands covering her ears. The bells were still ringing loudly as they spiraled down the stairs, arriving at the bottom of the tower breathless and dizzy.

"Heavens me," Laborde puffed out, as he tried to catch his breath. "That was extraordinary! Thank you so much for showing me the view."

"And letting you hear it as well," she said in jest. "Now, shall we go find my aunt? She should be finished with the priest by now. Surely, she doesn't have that many sins to confess."

They walked toward the nave of the cathedral, looking for Rosa in the somber half-light. Laborde's gaze lingered over the uniquely Spanish feature of the church: the row of ageing San Benitos hanging against the wall, threadbare and yellowish-gray with mold. Passing by, he read the faded names of those condemned to wear the sacred sack, stitched in black over the now-pink sideways crosses: Perez, Diez, Marín, Bonafé... He tried to imagine what these people—long since dead—might have done to so offend the Holy Office.

"Come," Clara said, growing impatient with his dawdling. "I'd like to show you something."

Unlike the listless ladies of the court, Clara walked swiftly. Laborde left the Inquisition's old clothes behind and followed her thin frame.

She hurried past a glass case, encrusted with jewels, holding the mummified arm of Saint Vincent, and passed an enormous gold-gilt altar dedicated to the Virgin. When she came to a large, dark canvas, hung high upon the wall, she stopped and turned to Laborde.

"Ah, Monsieur, have you seen this?" she asked, pointing up at the picture.

In it, a bluish corpse lay miserably on a bed while winged demons smiled gaily behind it. A priest brandished a crucifix which squirted blood at the rigid body.

"I watched him paint it."

"Who?" he asked, straining his neck to get a good look at it.

"Master Goya," she said, turning around to look at the oil painting herself.

He stood there a moment, staring into the back of her head.

"Clara," he began. "You astonish me. How do you know about Señor Goya? None of the Valencian nobles I have met, not one of the rich merchants has ever heard of him."

"So, you know him too?" She turned back around and smiled at him.

"Know him? Well, no, we haven't met. But, I admire him. I first saw his work in Madrid, at the Duke of Osuna's house. He's a friend and patron of the painter and owns several impressive canvases. After that, I bought a copy of Goya's *Caprichos*. Have you seen them?" Verifying Clara's shake of the head with slight relief, he continued. "It's a collection of engravings depicting the follies, the weaknesses of mankind. It's outstanding! I'll have to show it to you."

"I'd love to see it."

"You know, I was beginning to wonder if, outside Madrid, anyone knew his name."

"This canvas," Clara said, pleased at having impressed her companion, "he painted here in Valencia, in a rented atelier nearby. It was summer and he used to leave the door open for the breeze. One day, I peeked inside and saw him at work. After that, I made a point of going by on my way home from market. I'd just stand in the doorway and watch. He didn't mind. Sometimes he'd notice me there and invite me in to have a closer look. I was only fifteen or sixteen at the time. I'd usually find him a snack in my basket, an apple or some bread. It was fascinating to see him work, to see the painting take form, change and come alive."

"Did you speak much to him?" Laborde inquired.

"Not really. He is quite deaf, as you may know, but always quick to smile," she said. "One day, though, he left the atelier early. He wiped his hands clean, put on his hat and said: 'Today, Pedro Romero is in the bullring. These ghouls can wait.'"

Laborde laughed out loud at Clara's imitation of the great painter.

"Oh, and I'll never forget. When he walked past me, giving me a friendly tip of his hat, I noticed that his clothes, even his hair, gave off the distinct odor of fried dough," Clara remarked. "You know, like the big vats at fair, where they fry *churros* in boiling oil. A strange smell for an artist, I've always thought."

Suddenly Rosa appeared. "There you are," she said pleasantly, but when she noticed which canvas they were discussing, she frowned. "Oh, Clara, with all the beautiful paintings in this cathedral, why are you looking at this? Demons, blood and cadavers! What were you thinking?"

She looked at Laborde in exasperation, as if to disassociate herself from her niece's poor judgment.

"Aunt Rosa," Clara said, unaffected by her aunt's seeming embarrassment, "shall we treat our guest to a glass of *horchata*?"

"Splendid idea," exclaimed the fat little woman.

Crossing the square, Laborde confessed that, since his arrival to Valencia, he'd had countless glasses of wine, dozens of cups of chocolate, and even a few rare cupfuls of coffee, but he didn't know what *horchata* was.

"It looks like milk, but has a sweet, earthy taste," Clara explained. "It's served icy cold—a perfect drink for summer."

They sat down at a table under the Santa Catalina tower with its swirling columns, and ordered three *horchatas de chufa*. Clara watched Laborde taste it and couldn't help but notice his slight grimace.

"I suppose it takes getting used to," Clara said with apologetic eyes.

"It is interesting," he said, putting his glass aside. "But awfully sugary."

Clara sat back, sipping her own, wondering if one could really trust a man without a sweet tooth. As they rested in the shade, Rosa began to tell them, between intermittent slurps, a long tale of provincial gossip that she had heard in the confession line. Clara, however, was far more interested in a group of scruffy boys playing with tops in the street. She listened to their laughter—she was sure they would love to drink Monsieur's *horchata*—and ignored her aunt prattling on about their neighbors' misfortunes.

Finishing her drink, she reached over to put her glass on the table. It was then she noticed that Laborde also seemed completely unaware of what her aunt was saying. But, instead of watching the children, he was staring at her. She smiled at him, wondering what he saw. The look in his eyes was not one she was accustomed to. If she didn't know any better, she'd say it was desire.

When they returned to Vicente Plancha's house, Rosa went straight to her room, ready to lie down after the exertion of the outing. Clara stood hesitantly on the doorstep, with Laborde on the street, at eye-level. She knew her cousin Antonio and uncle would be out and, although she wanted to prolong their time together, she didn't know if it were seemly for her to entertain the French gentleman on her own.

"Would you like to come in?" she asked nonetheless. "This time of day, it's quite nice out in the courtyard. I'm sure I could find you a drink more to your liking than *horchata*."

"No, thank you, Clara," he said with a smile. "I must be going."

His refusal was mildly disappointing, but to be expected. Not only would his visit be improper, but surely she was not alluring enough to demand any more of his time.

"But, before I go," he added, "I wanted to tell you, well, what a special person you are."

She looked at him, dumbfounded. Not even Honorato, back when he was wooing her (at least she thought he was) all those years ago, had gone so far as to call her 'special.'

"I mean it," he said more confidently, nodding his head. "You have a rare combination of natural intelligence, artistic sensibility and innocent honesty. It is really quite refreshing."

"Oh," she murmured, blushing deeply. She held her palm against her belly, but was unable to feel the flutter from the outside. "Thank you, Monsieur."

Clara imagined that Alexandre de Laborde's experience with women was vast, but what she could not know was that all of his women had been rather similar. High-bred courtiers, stylish and pretty, who were practiced in the fine arts of flattery, flirtation and vanity, intent on collecting hearts, while giving theirs to no one. His last mistress, Alexandrine de Bleschamp, was so beautiful that Lucien Bonaparte had wanted her. Laborde, his mere attaché, was obviously outranked by Napoleon's younger brother and she'd gladly left him for a man of higher position and greater wealth. Although Clara did not know the details about his past romances and paramours, she did know that a smuggler's daughter with a bony frame and lopsided grin would be an unacceptable companion for such a man. And completely unpresentable at court.

"I've enjoyed your company as well," she said.

He gave her his stellar smile. "I'm sure I'll see you again, Clara. And thank *you* for a memorable afternoon."

When Clara went to the baths late the next morning, her basket was filled with towels, soap and oil. After taking a quick survey of the place, satisfied that everything was in order, she slipped into one of the cubicles and locked the door. This was the most private space she knew. It had no equivalent in her uncle's house; her bedroom door had no lock and her aunt and cousins felt free to go in when they pleased. Sitting on the edge of the tub, she began removing her clothes. She filled the tub halfway and got inside, the warm water immediately relaxing her body.

She closed her eyes, breathing deeply, and began to imagine Monsieur de Laborde as if he were a character in one of the French novels Lorenzo recited to her. She pictured him leading her by the hand into his elegant chambers, the brocade curtains blocking out the sunlight, and laying her on his soft feather bed. He would look at her, his handsome brown eyes filled with wonder and longing, and leisurely disrobe her. First he would unwind the scarf tied around her head, letting her hair fall down her back, then untwist the black strands of her espadrilles, rubbing his hands up and down her calf. When she was completely nude he would appreciatively gaze upon her; his finger on her skin would draw lines from one mole to the next, charting the different constellations they formed: the archer, the scales, the ram.

Clara poured some sweet almond oil into her palm and began, eyes closed, to lightly graze her body, her shoulders, her little breasts, her inner thigh, then to stroke herself harder, imagining his hands all over her, his kisses, his declarations of love. She touched her mouth with a finger, his tongue. She lazily moved her longest finger down her neck in a straight line to her belly button, and down between her legs. With one hand, she began touching herself, imagining it was him. A few moments later, she was already digging her nails into the palm of her other hand, holding her breath, her back arched. The stars glanced blandly at Clara quivering beneath; for centuries, the baths had failed to astonish the heavens.

After slowly breathing out, her body now slack, she stayed absolutely still for several minutes, marveling at that intense sensation. Clara opened her eyes and poured a jug of warm water over herself, sighing in relief.

Once she had washed herself and dried off, she put her clothes on again. Clara had understood for years how to touch herself, to satisfy that longing. Though it was probably a sin, she kept it to herself; and her confessor, well, he never asked. Perhaps he couldn't imagine it of a woman.

As she was leaving the cubicle, Clara nearly ran into Laborde, coming out of what had once been the hot room, carrying a book on top of his portfolio.

"Ah, Clara," he said, visibly delighted. "I was hoping to find you here today. I've brought Goya's *Caprichos*.

"The *Caprichos*, why, thank you," she stammered. Smiling stupidly, her eyes shining still, she wondered if he could possibly know what she'd been doing; her face, she thought, must be flushed. She quickly glanced at the cover of the book before putting it in her basket with a trembling hand. Fumbling for ordinary words, she added, "I look forward to leafing through it."

"Keep it for a day or two. If you like the painting in the cathedral, I'm sure you'll enjoy these: there are monsters, executions, scenes from the Inquisition—"

"What must you think of me." She laughed, already recovering herself.

"I think you are a woman with a curious mind," he said, his eyes twinkling at her good nature. "And a clean one, I see."

He gestured to her basketful of bath products, making her wince at the idea of her earlier thoughts, far from clean.

"Yes, yes," she said quickly. "And you? What are you doing here today?"

"I've just finished my last drawing." He smiled. "My 'Admiral's Baths' series is now complete."

"Congratulations," she managed brightly, despite her disappointment. This would mean she would no longer be running into him. "You have certainly shown our humble old bathhouse in the most positive light." She paused as he carried out an elegant bow of thanks and decided to tempt fate by issuing yet another invitation. "Perhaps you will allow us to celebrate with you?" she asked. "Tomorrow evening, Silvia, Juan, Lorenzo and I are going to the Portal Nou where three *novillos* will be let loose in the streets. Although they aren't full-grown bulls, they are dangerous," she explained. "Men like to show how brave they are, chasing and dodging them. It can be quite a show."

"Yes, of course, I'd love to join you. However, I can't make any promises about my bravery with bulls. Maybe you could teach me a few lessons?"

She slipped quietly back into the house, hoping to enjoy some time to herself before the mid-day meal. If Aunt Rosa knew Clara was home, she would undoubtedly require some unsavory service. Back in her room, she hung her towel on a peg and sat on her bed to look at the book of Goya's etchings.

As she turned the pages, each piece, striking and strong, made an impression on her: the grotesque images of disfigured people, hobgoblins, and witches; the negative commentary on the clergy and the Inquisition; the pictures of monkeys and asses, ridiculing professors and lords. Clara was especially interested in the painter's depiction of women. Not only did he show them as vain or flighty, but as victims of bad marriages, abuse and treachery. In one, a beautiful dancing girl was surrounded by winged monsters. It was entitled *You will not escape.* With a small shudder, she put down the book. It was too dark, too bleak.

She gathered a charcoal stick and a fresh sheet of paper from her folder and made a quick sketch of herself waltzing with the broom. Her limbs, face, hands and shoes were all long and skinny: her whole body a veritable collection of horizontal and vertical lines. She made it smile—one not unlike the maniacal grins from the Goya prints—and then, with difficulty (and not without error) she wrote beneath it: *The Happy Spinster.* Truly, she thought, this drawing isn't even ironic; compared to the young brides betrothed to old ghouls in the *Caprichos*, being unmarried was not such a harsh sentence.

"Clara!" her aunt called from the foot of the stairs, disinclined to climb them. "Are you up there? I need you *here!*"

"Yes, *tía*," Clara called, scooping up the pages and putting them away. "I'll be right down."

Laborde surprised them all—even Lorenzo—by arriving at the Plancha house in his friend Hugo de Moncada's elegant carriage to take them to see the *novillos*. All of the neighbors came out to the square to see the Berlin coach, ornately carved and painted with cupids and roses. There was such enthusiasm that, finally, the coachman had to threaten the grimy children with his whip to stop them from climbing on it. Rosa, seemingly even shorter next to the large back wheel, watched with pride as her daughter climbed inside, while Vicente went over to admire the handsome pair of white Andalusian horses leading the coach. The four Valencians seated themselves in the back, while Laborde ceremoniously took his place on the box with the driver.

"My, my." Silvia giggled. "How marvelous that our French friend has procured this coach for the evening. Look, the inside is every bit as elegant as the outside. Why the seats are upholstered in satin."

"So, my man." Juan winked at Lorenzo. "Are you happy *now* that Laborde is joining us?"

"It is quite agreeable in here," Lorenzo said. "Especially with our host out there."

"Come now," Clara said to the two men. "Let's do try to be pleasant."

"Look who's giving orders tonight." Silvia snorted. "My, my."

With a sharp jerk, the carriage pulled away from the square. Silvia thrust open the red curtains and waved to everyone in sight. "Adios, adios!" she cried, as if she were finally being carried away to her rightful place in life and would be gone forever.

After driving down a series of cramped streets, the carriage barely squeezing through, they arrived to the Portal Nou. The large square backed up against the city wall, with impressive gates on one side and houses and shops on the others. There were already scores of people milling around, waiting for the arrival of the *novillos*. The owners of the buildings around the plaza were putting up crude wooden barricades and sheaves of moldy hay to protect their windows, doors, and shop-fronts from the bulls, who, when trying to break away from the aggressive people, used their bulk and horns, even against walls.

At their arrival, the expectant crowd, already grown restless, turned its attention to the carriage. Silvia, delighted at the occasion for making such an elegant display of herself, scrambled over to the door and opened it, first exposing one small shoe. Smiling coyly at the spectators, she lowered herself to the ground. As she alit, however, her heel got caught between the cobblestones and she tripped, twisting her ankle. The crowd—most of them common folks who would never see the inside of a carriage—began to laugh, enjoying the lady's comeuppance.

"Being driven around, one forgets how to walk!" a man in the crowd called out.

"What do you mean?" cried another. "Those baby shoes aren't meant for walking!"

"Maybe she should crawl!"

Juan jumped out of the carriage and held her as she wept, partly in pain. Surrounded by hoots and jeers, Laborde, feeling responsible, was immediately at their side, trying to remedy the situation.

"*Can* you walk, Silvia?" he asked, "Should we find a doctor?"

"Just take me home," she blurted out among sobs, her face still pressed against the front of her husband's jacket.

At that moment the big closed cart carrying the young bulls came lumbering into the square, and the crowd quickly lost interest in the beautiful carriage and its clumsy passenger.

"It would be a shame for you to miss the *novillos*," Juan said, turning to Laborde. "If you don't mind, perhaps your driver could take us home. He'll have to move the carriage out of the square anyway. The bulls would tear it apart, and the horses too."

As they were leaving, anyone peeking through the half-drawn curtains could have seen Silvia's disconsolate face streaked with rouge, powder and tears, and Juan holding her hand, looking gravely disappointed. Laborde bid the driver to return to the Portal Nou once the couple was safely back home, and to stay with the carriage on the northern side street.

After they left, Lorenzo shrugged and said, "Perhaps it's better this way. Silvia wouldn't have been able to run away from a bull to save her life." He looked over at Laborde and added, "Here in Spain, there are two ages of women: married and unmarried. After they marry and start having children, they spread out and begin to age at a tremendous rate." Lorenzo laughed, making a gesture of an ever-widening woman. "In another year or so, you won't be able to tell Silvia from her mother."

"Perhaps that's why Clara looks like a young girl," Laborde replied with a smile, making her glow and Lorenzo frown.

The men from the cart were now setting up barriers in the narrow streets leading away from the plaza, to prevent the bulls from leaving the square and causing havoc in other parts of town. Lorenzo took out his snuffbox and offered some to Laborde.

"So, tell me, how goes the *Voyage Pittoresque*? What are you including in your book besides Moorish baths?"

After a sniff of tobacco and a graceful wipe of his nose, Laborde answered, "Oh, a little bit of everything, really. From history to commerce, laws to fiestas."

"It sounds wonderful," Clara said, regarding the handsome Frenchman warmly, still basking in the compliment from minutes before.

"And for each important town," he continued, "I discuss the agriculture and industry, the population, its best artwork... I'm even making maps to show the best routes for future travelers."

Lorenzo's eyes narrowed. "What are you saying exactly?" His voice was steady, but cold.

Laborde cocked his head to one side, making a weak attempt at a smile. "What do you mean?"

"Information, routes, *maps*?" Lorenzo stole a look at Clara, before turning back to Laborde. "Sounds like this charming little travel book of yours will prove highly useful to Napoleon when he decides to bring in his troops. They'll even know where to steal our artwork. It's the perfect guidebook for sacking and pillaging!" He spat on the ground, furious.

Laborde lifted his chin slightly and looked Lorenzo in the eye. "That is a very serious accusation. Calm yourself, friend, or this could get ugly indeed."

"Come, Clara," he said through his teeth, refusing to look at Laborde. "I won't be in the presence of such a man. I'll take you home."

"Lorenzo, you're being ridiculous. Monsieur de Laborde is a writer, an artist, not a spy. What's wrong with you?" she reached out for his arm, but he shook her off and went running through the square, past the barriers and out of sight.

"Monsieur, I don't know what to say. I do apologize for his frightful insults." Clara was wringing her hands, clearly distressed. "I don't know what's gotten into him."

Suddenly a loud roar went up from the crowd as the bulls were goaded out of the cart. The powerful brown beasts, stunned and anxious, stood scanning the plaza for a way out, while adolescent boys, armed with sticks, immediately began taunting them. They darted their massive heads back and forth and grumbled, but did not yet move. Laborde and Clara, Lorenzo now forgotten, moved in closer to see. The air around them reeked of sweat, wine, urine, and sheer excitement.

A dwarf, with a large cigar jutting out from his lips, swaggered up to one of the bulls. He straightened out a red bandanna, squinting to keep the smoke out of his eyes, and started making slow, elegant passes with it. He stood erect, his hat on par with the animal's head, and they looked each other in the eyes. Watching the dwarf, the crowd was appreciatively silent, erupting into *Olés!* following each sweeping pass of the scarf. Even the other two beasts stood staring at him, unblinking, until a mischievous youngster pulled the bull's tail. It dashed forward and crushed the dwarf's foot. His piercing cries were heard plainly above the laughter of the mob as he was carried to the side of the square and dumped onto some hay.

Now all three bulls were moving around the plaza, pawing the ground and panting; each one had a ring of people around it, shouting boldly, poking it nervously, then running a few feet away to safety. A few of the braver men were using rags or scraps like quixotic toreadors, but each time the bull charged, or even moved a step or two, the entire crowd would scatter, screaming in joyful fear. Clara and Laborde stood in the back of one group, more spectators than participants, watching in fascination and disgust.

As it got dark, a few of the men lit torches, and, dancing in front of the bulls, they waved them in their faces. The light from the flames cast shadows on both the men and the beasts creating hideous masks of monsters and minotaurs. Feeling the heat from the torches, the bulls panicked; one, blinded, began to run wildly through the crowd. It headed straight for Laborde and Clara, who turned and ran, the hooves pounding on the cobblestones behind them. Clara quickly ducked behind a pile of scrap lumber, falling to the ground as she pulled Laborde in behind her. The beast charged past.

Lying next to each other on the cobblestones, their chests heaving, they tried to catch their breath. Staring into the other's face, their noses almost touching, they were wide-eyed, flushed, unspeaking. They both began to smile. He took her face in his hand and with his thumb, gently rubbed the tip of her jagged tooth. His heart still pounding from the chase, from the thrill of danger, he pulled her towards him and kissed her. His warm lips were on hers, nuzzling them, kneading them, then—to her surprise—they slid opened and his tongue found hers.

Besides closed-mouth pecks from family or friends, usually deposited on the cheek, forehead or hand, Clara had never been kissed. Honorato had never been so bold even to clasp her waist or thread her fingers through his. Exhilarated, she let her tongue roll and play and felt their faces meld into one.

He held her and whispered into her hair, "Mmm, Clara, how you thrill me."

She pulled away, breathless, and searched his face, unable to believe he was serious. He stared back into her clear green eyes, panting still, and kissed her again.

"Come," he said. "Let's go back to the carriage."

They stood up, quickly brushing off the dirt and hay from their clothes, and he took her hand and led her down the narrow street to the coach, both of them now oblivious to the skittish bulls and the frenzied crowd.

"Halloo," Laborde called to the driver. "Make your way down to the Glorieta and stop there. And take your time," he added, smiling at Clara. "We're in no hurry."

In that light, Clara's blush went unnoticed. Although she didn't dare peek up at the driver, she knew he'd be smirking. Laborde guided her into the carriage—her hand was trembling—and leapt in behind her. She watched him draw the curtains, nervous but excited. Stroking the satin seat with one hand, she thought back on her fantasy in the bathhouse, the beautiful bedchamber, the languid disrobing. Filled with anticipation, she sat back with a sigh as the horses began treading through the rough street, the coach lurching behind them. Laborde kissed her again in the darkness pulling her body to his. He wrapped her in his arms; her torso was so slight, his hands nearly found their way back to him.

"Your body feels so fragile. Like a girl's," he murmured.

Terribly aroused, he quickly unbuttoned his pants, then grasped Clara's hand and plunged it inside. At the touch of the hot, smooth skin, she pulled her hand away.

"Don't be afraid, Clara," he said, earnestly lifting her skirts.

Bouncing with the coach, his hand fumbled through her undergarments and quickly found what it was looking for. With a knee on either side of her hips, he mounted her. At the moment she cried out, astonished by the sharp pain, his entire body trembled in orgasm. He collapsed on top of her, gasping, as the horses arrived to the Glorieta. Trying to breathe under his weight, she felt a thin stream of blood run down her leg. At least she thought it was blood.

"Ah, Clara," Laborde sighed, as he heaved himself off her. He cleaned his groin with a large cotton handkerchief, buttoned his trousers, and awarded her his winning smile. Suddenly, they heard voices outside the carriage.

"Everything in order here, sir?" the night watchman called up to the driver.

"Better for some than for others," he responded.

As she heard them laugh, Clara could imagine the driver's winking gesture to the interior of the carriage, and her face grew hot with shame.

As the watchman walked off, they heard his monotonous cry: "Ave Maria! Half past eleven! *Sereno!*"

"It's late," Clara whispered. "I must be going."

Laborde called out to the driver, and the carriage began its bump and roll towards her uncle's house. For the first time since she'd met him, Clara had nothing to say to the French traveler. She sat next to him looking at the floor, bewildered at how *quickly* one could lose her virginity.

When the coach stopped at the big wooden door leading to their courtyard, Laborde gently touched her cheek. "Can I see you tomorrow? Shall we meet at the baths? Before lunch?" he asked. "How about noon?"

Clara looked at him briefly and nodded. "Good night, Monsieur."

She went up to her small bedroom, took off her clothes and washed herself carefully. Rinsing the cloth in the small basin, she was interested to see how faint the color was; she expected this blood to be darker, for all the importance it was given. She put on a light shift and lay on her bed on top of the sheets. There was no breeze. Clara absentmindedly picked up the ceramic horse from her nightstand and began to finger its lines. Was this love? The most celebrated, the most sublime of all emotions? Of all acts?

She had not been opposed to becoming Laborde's mistress—she was certainly no longer saving herself for a husband—but it was not how she'd imagined it would be. When Lorenzo talked to her about sensuality, love, pleasure—about his own adventures or stories from the forbidden books—was *this* what he talking about? She remembered that in Laclos' novel the notorious rake the Vicomte de Valmont seduces a prim young virgin, turning her into a libertine mad for pleasure.

Pleasure? This Frenchman had not kissed her neck in rapture, caressed her breasts, tasted her—he had not even bothered to take her clothes off. Would he have behaved differently with a woman of the court? Would he have taken his time, determined to prove his skill as a lover? Unable to sleep, she tried to recall his hands, the lines of his face, his voice. She desired him still.

As Clara breathed out her first Hail Mary in accompaniment to the dawn Angelus bells, it struck her that she was no longer a virgin. The buzz of prayer immediately stopped as her mouth fell open. She could hardly believe it. Although she'd always considered herself a good person, when comparing herself to Mother Mary—so demure, and ladylike—up to now, virginity had been their main point in common. Feeling the blood rise to her cheeks, she touched one, felt its heat, then let her fingertips wander to her lips, remembering his kisses. It was time to get out of bed.

Her bare feet quickly moved around the cool tile floor as Clara got dressed, made her bed, tied up her hair. While carrying out her morning routine, her eyes kept darting from the crucifix over her bed to Laborde's drawing of the Moorish baths. Clara knew that someone in her position should feel terribly ashamed—she was a fallen woman, she thought in awe—and would be expected to go straight to confession. But, somehow, Clara was feeling no regret, no guilt. A grown woman, unmarried yet hungry for love, she didn't think it unnatural to lay with a man. It was wicked, she supposed, but it was not cruel or deceitful; no one was being harmed. No, she would not visit the parish priest that morning, but would meet her lover instead.

Before going downstairs, she picked up the drawing and studied every line. She imagined Laborde's fingers at work, the look of determination on his face as his hair fell forward. Lifting it to her nose, she breathed in deeply. Could she detect a mannish scent here? Or was it her imagination?

Far too restless to sit at breakfast with Irene, Clara gathered up the baskets.

"I'm going straight out today," she mumbled, overly aware that this would be considered odd. "Is there anything you need from the market?"

Irene turned around in surprise.

"You're not hungry?"

Clara hesitated and shrugged. "I don't feel altogether myself," she said, acknowledging that it was true. "I need some air."

"Of course," Irene said with a nod, which did nothing to hide the suspicion in her eyes. "While you're out, get some chard. I'm making *potaje* today."

Once in the street, Clara crossed the plaza and sat down next to Domingo.

"Out early, are we?" he said, with a pull on his pipe. "Surely your uncle isn't waiting for his newspaper at this hour."

"No, no. I just thought I'd sit with you in the sun for a while. See how you're doing."

"Me? Same as I ever was." He gave her a careful look. "Now, tell me about you."

Clara looked up at her father's friend, a man she'd known as long as she could remember. She knew that he cared for her deeply and out of no sense of obligation; she trusted him as she did no one else. She had the urge to tell him everything about the night before—the bulls, the carriage, Laborde—but couldn't. She didn't want him to think her a silly fool. Or worse.

"Domingo," she started slowly, "why didn't you ever marry?"

His large, bushy eyebrows shot up to his hairline, but his eyes remained locked on hers. His snarl softened almost immediately as he scrutinized the sincere look of confusion on her face.

"Well," he huffed, "two things. No money and no woman."

"I know all about that." She sighed. "But my father, he didn't have much money either, did he?"

"No, but he had something far more important," Domingo said. "Your mother."

"They were in love, weren't they?" she whispered, unusually emotional.

"Of course!" He laughed with a snort, patting her on the back. "No one *arranges* marriages like that."

She fell silent and, lifting her chin to the sun, closed her eyes. She knew better than to imagine anything formal would come out of her relationship with Alexandre de Laborde, even though he claimed to admire her. This folly she carried out, not for any hopes of a future, but for her own satisfaction: her curiosity, her need for affection, but also, the rare opportunity of being desired.

When she returned from the market, she found her cousin Silvia installed in the drawing room. Her ankle, wrapped daintily in a pink silk ribbon, was held aloft on a footstool while the rest of her, all her weighty curves, lounged on the sofa. Juanito's crib was placed in one corner, her vanity in the other. It looked as though she would be staying for quite some time.

"There you are, Clara," she said, by way of welcome. "Mama insisted that I come here while indisposed. She thinks that you and she are better suited to administer to my needs than mere servants."

"I'm so sorry to see that your ankle is still bothering you," Clara said, the words heartfelt.

"*Bothering* me! I have never felt such pain." She wiped her brow. "Now, be kind enough to bring me something to eat. Hot chocolate and honeyed toast. I haven't had a bite all day."

After preparing a tray for Silvia, Clara ate a few plums, relieved she would be out for the rest of the morning. Whether Monsieur Laborde was paying her a call or not, she still had to work. She put her favorite scarf around her hair and slid the Goya book into her basket. With her heart pounding, she went off to the baths.

At noon, as the church bells pealed, Clara stepped nervously out into the street, thankful the bathhouse had no windows. She hated the idea of being observed. To her embarrassment, she found no one. She turned around to go back inside, in search of her broom; she would rather sweep than stand idly in the street, waiting there like a child for the Magi. But before she got to the door, she heard Laborde call her name.

"Clara!"

She waved, squinting in his direction as he approached, and offered him her snaggletoothed smile.

"What a lovely day," he said, returning her smile as he took her arm. "Do you mind a bit of a walk? You know, the carriage doesn't fit back here and was so conspicuous on the square. I left it down by the gates."

"That's fine," she said, walking with him in stride, feeling the weight of his hand on her arm. Did they look like a couple? Old friends, out for a stroll? What might she say if she bumped into a neighbor? Or, far worse, Lorenzo? Turning her head slightly and breathing in, she could detect the smell of his hair, his perfume. She glanced shyly at his face.

"I've brought the *Caprichos*," she said.

Really though, her rendezvous with him seemed much more capricious than any of Goya's engravings. She didn't even know how to address the French gentleman at her side: 'Alexandre' seemed too presumptuous, plain 'Laborde' too manly, and 'Monsieur,' at this stage of the game, ridiculous.

"I so appreciate you lending it to me," she continued, without calling him anything at all. "His work is impressive, but these engravings are almost too black for me." She handed him the book. "Some of the images made me shiver. Like, the one of the woman stealing the tooth from the hanged man or…"

A tingle ran down her spine, making her voice fade. From the memory of the engraving? Or Laborde's eyes on her now?

"I daresay you have a brighter outlook on the world, Clara." He smiled at her again. "I can see that from your pictures."

"I suppose so," she murmured, shrugging lightly. "Have you done any drawing today?"

"No, I've had a lazy morning and done next to nothing," he said. "And yourself?"

"The same."

She didn't want to bore him with her list of chores, or indeed, turn their talk to Silvia and how she'd usurped command of their household. As insufferable as her cousin was, Clara didn't want to plant another woman's image—and one so much younger and more attractive—in his mind. Nearing the carriage, their conversation was becoming lighter and lighter until, at the coach door, it had dwindled to nothing.

With a quick look around, he bundled her in and told the driver to take the long promenade toward the port. She swallowed deeply, watching Laborde climb inside and toss the book onto the seat. When he had closed the curtains, it became surprisingly dark.

"We're alone again, Clara," he whispered.

The horse-tread jostled them together and he pulled her to him. One long kiss completed, he gathered up her skirts and got on top of her. Having found the narrow opening between her legs, his hands explored no further afield, but held hard to her shoulders. As the carriage wobbled down the lane, he jerked inside her. At an awkward angle, her left buttock digging into the *Caprichos*, Clara tried to keep time with him, to find pleasure in the trotting ache. What would a woman of the court do? But, again, after a few minutes his task was finished.

"Ahh," he sighed, then cleaned himself off. Clara wondered if a gentleman—one who would readily offer his handkerchief to a lady in tears—should present it to her in this situation. Or should a gentleman be in this situation?

"Let's open the curtains, shall we?" he said jovially. "It *is* such a lovely day."

He embarked upon vague, polite topics of conversation: the landscape, the weather, the carriage itself. He did not indulge in sweet talk; there was no praise of her merits or appearance, no new expressions of admiration. In fact, after being inside her, he barely looked at her, but rather kept his eyes trained on the view. As for Clara, though she often peeked over at her lover, she said almost nothing. In just thirty minutes—the bells were chiming the half-hour—they were back at the gates.

"Clara, you don't mind if I let you off here, do you? I must get the carriage back to Señor de Moncada. You understand, don't you?"

"Of course," she said. "It's not far."

"Shall we meet again tomorrow? At the same time?"

Clara nodded, grateful that he desired her still.

When everyone had sat down to dinner (Silvia at the head, where she could enjoy more leg room), Vicente turned to Clara.

"You remember José Pla? The man from my club whose hand got caught in the olive press when he was a boy?"

"The owner of that small bodega near the market?" she asked.

"That's right. He saw you today," her uncle continued, eyeing his niece carefully.

An image of the fiftyish, one-armed man formed in her mind. Clara breathed in, hoping Señor Pla had not recently become a widower and was looking for a replacement. *You will not escape* the Goya engraving had read.

"Oh?" Clara smiled pleasantly.

"He said he saw you getting out of a gentleman's carriage. I told him he must have been mistaken, but he seemed so convinced that—"

"Oh, Papa." Silvia produced an affected laugh. "*Our* Clara?"

Clara felt the blush rise to her face and cleared her throat.

"Actually, that *was* me, uncle," she began slowly, her mind racing with half-truths. "Monsieur Laborde came by the bathhouse this morning and asked me to accompany him to the port. You see, I'd mentioned to him once that I lived there as a child. He thought it would make for a more amusing outing if I could show him areas of interest..."

Her voice trailed off and she looked around the table, awaiting her family's fury. For a woman to go unchaperoned in the company of a man—and in a carriage no less—could bring ruin to her and disgrace to her relatives. Apart from José Pla, a dozen other neighbors had probably witnessed the fact. Were they all gossiping about it now, assuming the worst? Would her uncle banish her from the house? Where could she go?

"Clara," her uncle said, swallowing the bite he'd been chewing, "how kind of you. I'm sure Monsieur Laborde truly appreciated your company."

"Did you go in that same beautiful carriage we took to the *novillos*?" Silvia asked, a mixture of jealousy and fondness in her voice. Fondness, not for her cousin, but for the memory of riding around Valencia in that elegant coach.

"Yes, we did," Clara managed, with a small cough.

"Well, it was the perfect day for it," her aunt added, then noticed her son's plate. "Antonio, have some more meat. You've hardly eaten a thing. Aren't you feeling well?"

"My poor foot is killing me." Silvia reminded the table, lest her brother try to steal her thunder.

The family quickly forgot Clara's excursion with Laborde and went on with their usual fare of dinnertime conversation. Staring into her plate, Clara felt surprisingly slighted. Of course, it was a relief that no terrible row had ensued and that she would not be ousted from her uncle's house. But, this obviously meant that her family saw her as too unappealing to cause a scandal, a woman so undesirable that she was virtually sexless. No one here doubted the French gentleman's motives, nor thought it remotely possible that he would try to seduce her. If they only knew! A warmth rising from her thighs, to her belly, up to her breasts, she picked up her wine and took a long sip.

Clara couldn't wait to get to the baths the following morning. Juanito had begun crying after dinner and had remained inconsolable throughout most of the night. Silvia could not be burdened with her son, and in turn, cried out for her cousin's assistance. The baby only quieted down when Clara vigorously bounced him at a right angle from her torso, which she did, up and down the hallway. While jiggling the chubby baby with a bored coo, she tormented herself, wondering what Laborde was doing: if he were thinking of her, if he had met someone else, if her imaginary rivals were beautiful courtiers. When she awoke the next day, her arms were sore and her heart was heavy. Gray doubt clouded the prospect of their next outing.

Although it was a busy morning at the bathhouse—a score of people had come in from the country, wanting a city bath—at a quarter to twelve, she sidled out the door and walked down to the gates. She held her sketchbook under her arm. In the case he was detained—or unable to come at all—she would have something to keep her occupied. Clara was trying to be rational about this—whatever *this* was—but, after spending the morning replaying his kisses (and improving his caresses) in her mind, she knew she would be hurt now if he didn't appear. Really, she was still astonished by her own good fortune. Just the idea that such an attractive, worldly, talented man—a man worthy of any lady in Valencia—had chosen *her*.

"Alexandre," she whispered to herself; her belly tingled in response.

Finding a bench in the shade, she sat down, pulled out a piece of paper, and made a rapid sketch of the pigeon scouting for food at her feet. However, she couldn't keep her hand from shaking; she was too nervous, too restless to continue. She put down her sketchbook and scoured the square for acquaintances, wondering if Señor Pla was lurking nearby. Near the fountain, standing alone, she spotted the slim frame of Honorato Ramos. She took a sharp breath and turned away. Although they lived on the same side of the city, Clara almost never ran into her former sweetheart. She peeked at the fountain again; he was taking great gulps of water and splashing his sweaty face.

Suddenly, she heard the clopping of Señor Moncada's white Andalusian horses. Laborde had come! As the Berlin coach pulled into the square, Clara stood up to meet it, but stopped when she noticed Honorato examining it from his place at the spigot. Part of her wanted him to see her stepping into the beautiful carriage on the arm of the handsome French gentleman. He would see that she'd gone up in the world since the days when they'd flirted at mass. Would he be jealous? Might he be the only one capable of imagining that the Frenchman had designs on her? Would he suspect she'd become his lover? Would he think her a common whore?

That nasty thought made her shiver. What was she doing? She leaned against the bench to steady herself, unsure what to do. She watched as Honorato ogled the horses once more, then turned and walked out of the square. She breathed out in one long gust—surely, Honorato would have shared her family's view, that she was too old and skinny to attract a scarecrow—and stepped out of the shade. When she approached the carriage, the door opened from inside.

"Hello, Clara," Laborde called from the darkened interior. "Please, let me help you."

She took his outstretched hand, relishing the sharp tug, pulling her in. It was not Laborde's charms or finery that had seduced her; it was the thrill of being wanted. By his side, she felt more alive.

"Good morning," she said simply.

After a few perfunctory kisses and before the horses had pulled out of the square, he was reaching for her skirts. Desperately wanting to slow down the process, Clara grabbed his hand; she wanted to rub it all over her body and through her hair, but instead she kissed its palm and began clumsily sucking a finger. With a look of distaste, he quickly shook her lips off him, regained her skirts, and took her. When he was through, they sat for a few moments in silence, side-by-side, catching their breath to the canter of the horses. His desires appeased, he threw open the curtains.

"The weather certainly is good in Valencia this time of year."

She saw that the coach was still in the city, merely driving along the street on the inside of the walls. When it got to the square in front of the cathedral—a short walk to the bathhouse from the opposite direction—Laborde called to the driver to stop. Their third sexual encounter, remarkably similar to the first, had evidently come to an end. They had been together for less than ten minutes.

Clearing his throat, he finally looked at her.

"Clara, I'm going to be away for the next several days. I've been invited to the monastery of San Miguel de los Reyes. I'll make a series of drawings there, while collecting information about the buildings. Though its brief history can't compare to your uncle's baths," he said with a smile.

"I hope you enjoy yourself," she murmured, wondering if this was already the end of their affair. Brightening, she remembered an upcoming fiesta and, for the third time, made a proposal to the French visitor. "Will you be back to Valencia by next Saturday? There will be a *Baile del Candil* that night in the Alameda gardens. Really, the whole town will be there."

"A candlelit ball? That sounds wonderful. I'll see you then."

Pleased, she swiftly kissed his lips. He opened the carriage door and, from inside, helped her down.

"*Au revoir*, Clara."

The week of his absence passed with excruciating slowness. Clara tried to keep herself busy, but was unusually clumsy and unable to concentrate on her tasks. While waiting on Silvia, she knocked over a pitcher of water, dousing her cousin and the baby. "Get away from me, you idiot!" she'd shrieked. The next day, Silvia moved back to her own house to surround herself with efficient servants.

Clara was pleased that misfortune had taken such a positive turn, but was unable to take advantage of the free time it allowed her; she was too jumpy to draw or play the mandolin. Having lost her appetite, her strolls through the market had also lost their appeal. When she wasn't working in the bathhouse or helping Irene, she stayed in her room, alone with her thoughts.

She revisited all the moments spent with Alexandre de Laborde. Had their entire relationship only taken place in a matter of weeks? She thought back on the first time she saw him, peeking into their courtyard: his figure cut fine in fashionable visiting attire and his rich voice, a tad hesitant in Spanish. Clara tried to remember the expression on his face when he saw her—cooking paella barefoot and singing a silly song—wondering what impression she might have made. She reexamined his visit to the family home: his exquisite manners, his exposition of his project, his quarrel with Lorenzo. How improperly her old friend had behaved towards their guest.

After silently scolding Lorenzo in her mind, she went chronologically ahead, to their meetings at the bathhouse, their inspection of one another's drawings, their outing to the bell tower. She tried to remember his exact words as he teased her about Lorenzo, requested her self-portrait and complimented her sensibilities. With even greater detail if possible, she relived the night of the *novillos*. She could see the look on his face right before he first kissed her, his lips partially open, his admiring gaze. Then, she, Clara Ventura, had made him quake with desire. It was still hard to believe.

The next two days she had met him willingly, falling into his arms and letting him inside, but those encounters were less satisfying. So hurried and distracted, he had seemed less interested in her and only intent on his moment of pleasure. She had begun to doubt his admiration for her and question her feelings for him. Was she merely besotted with the dashing Frenchman? Or was this love? Her feelings now—intense and all-consuming—were so much stronger than the bashful, inarticulate emotion brought out by Honorato.

While musing on love and desire, she came to realize to what extent Alexandre de Laborde had changed her; their secret made her feel special and important, but, at the same time, terribly insecure.

During this time apart, she often studied Laborde's architectural sketch of the baths, a lover's keepsake. Fingering the picture, the straight lines made with a ruler, she imagined him busily using his string to make a floor plan of the San Miguel monastery, drawing the building, inside and out. It was reassuring to know that Laborde was spending his time surrounded by monks.

Although she was lonely, Clara was relieved that Lorenzo didn't visit that week. A keen observer, he would have surely noticed something awry and may have very well guessed that a man was the cause. And on her own, she could indulge herself, undistracted, on a steady diet of Alexandre de Laborde: memories of their short past together, meditations on what he was doing at present, the imagining of future encounters. At the end of seven days, she found herself even thinner than before.

When Saturday arrived, Clara became truly anxious. She was thrilled at the prospect of seeing her lover again, but didn't know when he might arrive. She wondered if he would come to meet her at the baths that morning and, unable to work, she kept looking towards the door, hoping to see him appear in the soft light of the vestibule. Surely he would want to show her his new drawings and tell her about his trip. After lunch, barely touched, she thought perhaps he would arrive unexpectedly with the carriage, impatient to take her on a stroll before the ball. She went to her room, as if for a siesta and, checking herself in the mirror, thought about what they would say to one another. Wary of being tongue-tied again, she tried to think of anecdotes to amuse him. As day turned to dusk, she tried desperately to remember what they had actually said when he left. Had they made plans to go together or to simply meet at the ball?

It was getting late and she began looking, uninspired, through her trunk of clothes. Contemplating various sashes and scarves, old but intact and smelling of lavender, she remembered that old French tale Lorenzo used to tell her when they were children, about a downtrodden girl meeting her prince at a ball. Clara smiled, thinking that, although she already had her prince, she could still use a fairy godmother's help with what to wear.

The *Baile del Candil*, the nighttime ball celebrating the feast of San Juan, was held in the gardened promenade of the Alameda, lit with candelabras for the occasion. It was one of the few events in Valencia that everyone attended, from the nobility and bourgeoisie to the commoners and *campesinos*. The center was filled with couples dancing while the shadowy fringes were perfect for passing secret notes and fondling paramours.

Although the lighting was faint, everyone was dressed with great care. Many flaunted the fashionable French style while others wore traditional Spanish outfits; for some this was an intentional choice, a protest against Northern politics. The latter, the *majos*, with jackets cut short and brightly colored vests and sashes, found the imitation Frenchmen effeminate, ridiculous. These, dressed in embroidered coats, cascading cravats, curly wigs and long, perfumed ponytails, were mostly of the upper classes, or those who wished to appear so.

The women also dressed in their finest attire and, perched atop their puffy coiffures, wore fanciful hats or mantillas on golden combs. Many women, and some men, powdered their faces with rice flour and attached satin beauty marks to different areas of their faces, each location conveying its own specific message.

Clara had always loved the San Juan celebration. She was a good dancer and a favorite partner. Singing along, she danced lively jotas and fandangos with elderly neighbors, making them feel young again and, with sophisticated formality, she did the minuet with little boys, who then fancied themselves grown men. She usually went with her uncle and his family, all of them crossing the bridge together in their relative finery before parting company at the ball to dance and chat with friends and acquaintances.

This year, however, Aunt Rosa decided to spend the evening with Silvia, to attend to her housebound daughter—those tasks which could be done from the confines of an armchair, that is— and to coddle her grandson. When Vicente, Juan and Antonio, all three sporting tall hats and walking sticks, were leaving for the Alameda, Clara told them not to wait. She was too edgy for pleasantries and light conversation. After they'd gone, their loud voices and laughter already faded, she went out the back of the house to calm her nerves in the courtyard.

Softly greeting the rabbits and sleepy chickens, she went round the patio grazing the plants with her fingertips, breathing in the jasmine. Slowly, humming an old love song, she made her way over to the hibiscus tree and, smiling at the large red flowers, broke one off and fixed it under her green scarf. Not bothering to look at herself again in the mirror, she pushed the heavy door and went out onto the street.

As she was crossing the square, she heard a familiar voice call her name; Domingo appeared out of the semi-darkness. He had put on a velvet vest and had a long fringed cloak thrown over one shoulder. She knew that these were probably both made of deep, rich colors, but in that light they were variations of gray.

"Are you on your way to the ball, my dear?" he asked, blowing a puff of smoke out of the side of his mouth. "I'll walk with you."

"Your company is always a pleasure."

They walked along in silence and, in his presence, Clara began to feel less tense and more herself than she had in days. They quit the city through the stately Porta del Real and, crossing the bridge towards the Alameda, they paused to take in the scene before them. They could hear the music and the murmur of voices coming from the pale glow on the other side of the river: Chinese shadows in the palm trees. Clara looked up at the night—a thin sliver of a moon was hanging low in a royal blue sky—and exhaled.

As they arrived to the *Baile*, she recognized many people, and nodded pleasantly to neighbors, clients from the baths and vendors from the market. She saw Irene, charming in a bright red skirt and a black lace mantilla, laughing with a young *majo*. With a piece of meat, they were making a small dog dance. She also noticed the gypsy girl Paloma, alone on the outer edge of the sandy promenade, doing a few hesitant steps in shoes that were far too big for her.

"Are you looking for your uncle?" Domingo asked. "I believe I see him over there, near the orchestra."

"No, I was hoping to meet a friend," she replied shyly.

Domingo looked her in the face and raised his bushy eyebrows with a smile.

Avoiding his eyes, she looked up and down the promenade, wondering yet again if Laborde had already arrived to Valencia. Had he been detained at the monastery? Had he met with ill fortune? Then, there, not ten yards away, she spotted him. Elegantly dressed in a light blue coat and skintight golden breeches, he was chatting with a group of young noblewomen, not one of them older than twenty. She smiled broadly and started to wave, then stopped herself, watching him with these stylish ladies, covered in ribbons and curls. Contemplating his leisurely gestures and perfect smile, she realized it was the first time she'd seen him in his element, with his peers.

In the dim light, unobserved, she watched as he laughed delightedly at the prettiest one's unheard comment, gazing upon her as if she were the most fascinating creature he had ever encountered. He stepped behind that lovely girl, whispering into her ear, breathing onto her neck. He took his fingertip and lightly touched her earlobe, playing a moment with a dangling pearl, then moved his finger slowly down her neck and across her plump shoulder, and rested his hand on her elbow. Murmuring something that made her smile, he gently slid his hand down her forearm, where it swooped onto her hand, clutching it to her waist. Clara blinked. In the three times he had taken her in his carriage, Laborde had never touched her with such delicate deliberateness.

Standing next to her, Domingo followed her frozen gaze to the French dandy. He looked at Clara with great affection and said in his grumpy tone, "Any imbecile can find beauty in that woman. Your beauty, Clarita, is just as striking. It only requires a cleverer, more original observer. One day you will find the man who can see it properly. And when you do, believe me, he won't let you out of his sight."

Clara reached up, took the hibiscus out of her hair, and handed it to him.

"Thank you," she said, kissing him on the cheek. "I think I'll be going now."

Declining his offers to accompany her home, Clara turned away from the Alameda and back towards town. In the shadows far from the candles, she made out the figure of Lorenzo, sitting under a palm tree, clutching a wineskin. She hadn't seen him since that night he'd left in anger, the night the bulls were let loose—*that* night. She slowed down until she was standing just a few paces away from him. He had abandoned his French fashions and was wearing a new outfit, in the style of the *majos*. He did not seem to be enjoying himself, however; his eyes were nearly closed and his face wore a surly expression.

She had seen him like that on a few different occasions, when his dissatisfaction with his frivolous life, usually hidden under layers of bravado, rose dangerously close to the surface. The summer before she had found him lying in the center of the plaza, gazing up at a shower of shooting stars, drinking and weeping.

"Clara," he'd cried, "You know what they call these falling stars? San Lorenzo's tears. Even the heavens cry for me."

He had gone on to bemoan his fate, damning his lot: his brothers' arrogance, his father's displeasure with him, his lack of inheritance. She had knelt down next to him and tried to console him, but he only began repeating himself, cursing again his miserly father and self-satisfied brothers, the words tripping awkwardly over his tongue. He seemed so contented with his misery, she'd stiffened and gotten to her feet.

"I cannot help you, Lorenzo. I have no knowledge of family or fortune." She had turned and left him there, silenced, stretched out on the cobblestones.

Tonight she couldn't bear to hear his complaints. She could offer him no affection or encouragement, needing all she had for herself. She moved to pass him but, as he recognized her, his expression changed to a smile.

"Clara, my dear. How lovely to see you." He raised the wineskin in salute. "But, you're alone? Where're you going?"

"Good evening, Lorenzo." She weakly returned his smile. "I'm pleased to see you too, old friend, but I'm going home. Tonight, I'm not well."

He looked at her with drunken concern. "Shall I walk you home?" he asked, with a slight slur. Clara shook her head, already heading off. "I'll come by tomorrow," he called after her, "see how you are."

As she left the ball, she could hear the first fireworks being let off behind her. She didn't turn to look at them but continued on towards the other side of the river. She would not run, she thought wryly, nor would she lose a shoe.

When Clara was returning home from mass the following morning, Paloma came to meet her in the street, her bare feet red and blistered.

"A gentleman gave me a letter for you, Clara," Paloma said, handing her a neatly folded note, her dark eyes shining with curiosity. Clara peered down at it, her heart racing.

"Shall I tell your fortune today?"

"Perhaps you already have," Clara said, displaying the note with a smile. She quickly made her way through the square.

Taking off her mantilla with one hand, Clara rushed up to her room to open the letter. She unfolded it carefully and gazed at the writing. Unlike his drawing, architectural in its precision, Laborde's calligraphy was an affected assortment of curlicues, his signature ending in a long sweeping flourish. Clara was entranced by its beauty but, never a strong reader, could not make out the intricate script except for his name and her own. She sat staring at it, lightly passing her finger over the words, as if she were writing them herself. She brought it to her face and breathed in, but found no trace of him; here, there was only paper and ink. She hid the letter behind his drawing, deciding to confide in Lorenzo.

He showed up in the early evening in his new, short-cut jacket and with dark circles under his eyes. For over an hour, Lorenzo sat in the salon, listening to Vicente and Antonio talk about the ball, trying to conceal the fact that he didn't remember too much about it. Finally, Vicente went out to meet his friends to lightly discuss politics while playing a serious game of dominos, and Antonio, who had also overindulged the night before, went to lie down. Clara was then able to usher Lorenzo out into the courtyard.

"I have something I want you to read to me," she said, once they were seated. "It's not a novel or a play..." her voice trailed off as she handed him the note, her hand trembling slightly.

He took the letter in his hand, but looked at her, not it. His regard was surprised and questioning, but lacked the teasing flippancy she'd been expecting.

"Did you receive this last night?" he asked, his eyes still on her. "Is this why you left?"

"No, it was delivered this morning," she replied, her voice steady. "I believe it's from Monsieur de Laborde."

Lorenzo clenched his eyes shut, rubbing his brow with his hand. "Oh, Clara," he began, then stopped, deciding to first read her the letter. He unfolded it, scanned it quickly, and, in a tired voice, recited:

> *My Dear Clara,*
>> *I want to thank you for sharing with me Valencia's most delightful attributes, of which you are certainly one. I will not be returning now as I am required in Paris. I wish you peace, love and joy.*
>
>> *Sincerely yours,*
>> *Alexandre de Laborde*

Lorenzo looked up at Clara; she sat unblinking, biting her lip.

"He wishes me love and joy," she said quietly, "I suppose that means he will be providing me with neither."

"And peace." Lorenzo scowled. "What does a Frenchman know of peace?"

He moved his chair next to hers, and patted her gently on the back as she started to sob, her head in her hands, almost buried in her lap. Lorenzo, unable to remember having ever seen his old friend cry even as a young girl, was taken aback, unsure of what to do. Stroking her shoulder, he began muttering to himself, the word *French* repeatedly spit out like the worst of insults.

The day after she received the letter, she went into the salon, where her uncle was reading the newspaper.

"Vicente, I almost forgot," she said, her smile faltering at intervals. "You remember Monsieur de Laborde? He's gone back to Paris, but he left this drawing for you as a token of his appreciation."

She handed her uncle the picture of the warm room, its perfect lines depicting arches that could not be seen.

"Very kind of him," Vicente said, looking at the drawing. "And it's very well done at that. But, did you notice how he left out our modern advances and concentrated on the stars? What a romantic that man is." He smiled to himself.

He rose and put the drawing between the pages of his atlas for safekeeping. When the large book was closed and returned to the shelf, Clara went back upstairs. She sat on the edge of the bed and sighed, pleased to have erased the last physical trace of Monsieur Laborde from her room. She had burned the letter that morning.

After the initial hurt, the overriding sensation Clara was left with was foolishness. She had known from the start their relationship had no future and that the word 'lover' rarely indicated love, yet she had not expected it to end so abruptly, with a few pleasant lines elegantly written on half a sheet of drawing paper.

When he'd been gone a week or two, she came to realize how little she knew about him. Even his drawings, so analytical and carefully measured, revealed nothing about the man who had made them. Having shared so much of herself with him, she'd just assumed that he'd done the same. Now Clara understood that she had invented him. His sensitivity, kindness, sincerity, knowledge—these were traits that she herself had bestowed upon him. Like her sketches and playful wanderings on the mandolin, he was her creation, perhaps the most elaborate, most polished product her imagination had ever produced. Laborde had come to Spain in search of Don Quixote; well, Clara mused, he had found her. Someone capable of turning a common windmill into a fantastic giant.

Thinking back, she supposed that the stranger she saw at the ball was probably the man he really was. She imagined him in Paris, at parties and literary salons, impressing the ladies with his picturesque engravings and narrating charming anecdotes: the fiestas, the bulls, the dowdy fashions. He would be surrounded by young women looking at him with ardent devotion and bursting out of their corsets. He would gaze at each of them in turn, his regard seductive but shallow, his compliments familiar with overuse. Reflecting deeper upon the flattering words he had awarded *her*—special, intelligent, honest, curious—she found them decidedly more suitable for a manservant or a hound than an object of desire. She had never really appealed to him.

Clara, who had always been strong and practical, would reason to herself that one could not miss something that did not exist, nor be nostalgic about something that never was. Then her lip would involuntarily curl and she would begin crying again, crying and cursing herself for doing do, for her own weakness, her own folly.

In the month following Laborde's departure, Clara slept. She had lost interest in what the day might bring—every day was the same as the next, for God's sake—and, for the first time in her life, she was slow, lethargic, drowsy. The Angelus bells could not wake her, she was yawning by mid-morning, her siestas were heavy and dreamless. During the next few months, Clara slept and ate. Dates and figs on the way home from the market, handfuls of almonds in the kitchen, second helpings of paella. She found she needed to eat, if not, she felt weak, or sleepier still. She no longer drew or played music and was rarely up for a chat with Domingo or Lorenzo.

Late one morning towards the end of a long summer, after a few hours cleaning in the baths, she went into a cubicle. Hot and tired, she locked the door. She had neither soap nor a towel with her, but decided to rinse the sweat off and rest a while. She took off her clothes and, sitting on the edge of the tub, the marble cool beneath her, examined herself. She saw her body was becoming rounded, her belly, hips, thighs. She felt her breasts; filled out, they were swollen and tender. Clara would have been delighted at these changes, had she not realized that, since before San Juan, she hadn't had her monthly cycle.

She bathed herself slowly—her hands moving gently, old friends trying to offer comfort—as she imagined her uncle's reaction to her pregnancy. She could almost see the shock in his face. That she, plain-faced old Clara, had been with a man and was expecting his child. She knew he considered himself enlightened, a progressive thinker, an avid reader of the *Diario de Valencia* and the *Encyclopædia*. However, he would feel he had no choice; Clara would be sent to a convent. She splashed warm water over her face, cooling her cheeks, hot and distorted from crying.

One evening, autumn already begun, Lorenzo came over to tell Clara the story of *Paul et Virginie*, a novel not banned by the Inquisition, but which he liked nonetheless.

It was still warm enough to sit in the courtyard and, after they'd taken their places, she picked up her mandolin, doing her best to smile at her old friend.

"Clara," he said, looking at her carefully, "you've changed these past few months. Your face has become softer and you finally have some meat on those bones. Really, you have never looked so pretty." His gaze was tender, but curious.

She looked at him, studying his face, but saying nothing. Finally, she closed her eyes tiredly, took a deep breath, and opened them again.

"I'm expecting a child, Lorenzo."

"Mother of God, Clara," he exclaimed under his breath. He jumped up from his chair, tossing the book aside, and began pacing around the patio. After a few minutes, he looked over at her, accusing, angry. "It was that Frenchman, wasn't it? Damn him!"

"I'm a fool." She shrugged sadly, her eyes filling with tears.

"Oh, Clara," he said softly, shaking his head. He knelt in front of her, taking her hands in his. "And now what? Does your uncle know?"

"Heavens, no. I don't know how to tell them, but I do know what they'll say. Lorenzo, they'll put in me in a convent. What else can they do?"

"A convent?" he shouted in a low whisper. "You're much too alive to be locked away."

Again, he got up to pace. Sighing, she began to play a melancholic tune on the mandolin, a folksong about telling lies:

The hare races through the sea,
The sardine, through the mountains...

She sang slowly, making a dirge of the old song, and watched her friend move around the courtyard. Lost in thought, he plucked a ripe lemon from the tree in the corner, rubbed the skin and brought it to his face. Lorenzo, she smiled to herself, had always loved the smell of lemon.

"Clara." Lorenzo looked at her, suddenly inspired. "And if we left Valencia?"

"To go where?" she asked, frowning at his growing enthusiasm.

"We could go to America." His voice was hushed, wondering at itself.

"You think I should go to America like your Manon Lescaut?" she asked, raising her eyebrows, her voice serious. "But I have not been unfaithful to anyone but myself. I'm not fickle or frivolous. You would have me go to New Orleans to die of disease? I am *not* a whore, Lorenzo."

"Christ, Clara, I know that! I'm not talking about punishment, I'm talking about opportunity." Lorenzo's eyes were gleaming. "Think about it. What do we have here? In Valencia, I am nothing but my father's unworthy son, an embarrassment to him. And you—"

"Yes, I know. I am nothing at all."

"Nothing!" He grabbed her hands. "After twenty odd years together, you have never failed to delight me. Why do you think I've spent so many hours in this house? Clara, you are the only woman I've never grown tired of. You make me laugh, make me *think;* you constantly surprise me. Your friendship is the only meaningful thing I've ever had."

"Lorenzo," she whispered, moved by his words.

"When we arrive to the New World—Mexico, Cuba, wherever we land—we can tell people that I am your brother or your husband. I would be proud to be either one." His expression became unusually shy. "But, I must say, Clarita, I'd rather you be my wife."

Her mouth fell open as she tried to grasp what he was saying. Moving to the Americas? Getting married? It seemed too far-fetched, like joining a band of pirates in search of El Dorado. A game they would have played as children.

"What you say is impossible." She would not let herself get caught up in another fantasy. "The crossing itself would be expensive—and dangerous too. I've heard Napoleon's fleet is battling the British at sea. Anything could happen."

"And anything will." He knelt beside her. "Damn Napoleon and his fleet. As for the expense, that won't be a problem." He smiled at her sheepishly. "I have amassed a small fortune over the years. An inheritance of sorts, from grateful widows."

They looked at one another for a long moment, then he kissed her softly on the lips. "I *am* serious," he whispered. "Think about it. We'll talk tomorrow." He rose and put on his hat. From the door leading out to the dark, he turned. "Clara," he called softly, "I love you. I always have."

Curled up in bed, her knees nearly touching her chin, Clara thought about Lorenzo's proposal. She had been dreading the idea of going to a convent, of leaving her uncle's house in shame, rude remarks and insults hurled from Silvia and... everyone else. To live within cloistered walls—forever?—bearing the nuns' contemptuous stares. But she was also doubtful about this scheme to steal away from Valencia, to start a new life in a strange land. It was so difficult to envision; Clara had always lived in the city—surrounded by neighbors, markets, church bells—how would she fare in the wilderness of the New World?

She thought of who she would truly miss, and found the list to be quite short. Her Uncle Vicente, good-natured but usually absent, was her last link to her mother. And Domingo... Picturing his friendly scowl and tobacco-stained smile, she got a painful lump in her throat. Then, she considered Lorenzo.

She knew him well—both his laughter and his temper—and had loved him since childhood, settling on friendship when she'd realized their stations in life were far too different for anything more. Had he always loved her too? In their twenties, she'd watched sadly as her sensitive friend, never able to please his harsh father, began to throw his life away. Maybe if he were to leave his family home, he would finally grow up and become a man; as a father himself, he could be more than just a son. Perhaps, far from Valencia, they could have a life together. Lorenzo, Clara and the baby.

She stretched, filling her small bed with the length of her body. Her hands found her belly and, drawing circles around it with one long finger, she thought about the new life inside her. Could it survive in that unknown land? Although she knew that, at thirty-three, she was frightfully old to be giving birth, Clara dearly wanted this baby. Despite everything, she longed to hold it in her arms. She doubted the nuns would let her keep it. What would become of her child?

Clara tried to imagine the difficult crossing, the long voyage, but shook her head, and concentrated instead on what she might pack. She had very few things worth taking to the other side of the world. A few changes of clothes, her father's mandolin, and the golden ceramic horse. Clara would give her drawings away before she left. To each person, his portrait. They would understand, only later, that it was a token of remembrance, for they would not be seeing her again.

Thinking of her sketches brought back the day she had shared them with the Frenchman, Alexandre de Laborde, the unlikely father of her unborn child. She wondered if he would ever come back to Valencia, and if so, would he try to find her? Clara sighed, reproaching herself with a little snort. She had been under the spell of a fairy tale of her own making. She now knew that Laborde was neither a charming prince nor a bad wolf, but just a passing traveler. And, in their story, there was no enchanted forest, no magic castle—only a Moorish bathhouse, re-fitted with all the modern conveniences.

Clara imagined again her flight with Lorenzo, how they would walk to the port at dawn, hand in hand, smiling excitedly at one another. They would cross the gangplank, the morning crisp and misty and, as the ship quit the harbor, sailing over the waters where her parents had drowned, they would look back at the city. They would make out the walls, the gates, the Micalet. Then together they would turn and face the West.

As she lay in bed, her decision made, she suddenly felt the quickening. Her child was turning, turning inside her. Clara reached down to stroke her belly and, feeling the tickle within, laughed.

Reconstruction

August 2011

I looked at my watch again; Hector and Fergal were expected back from Tangier any minute. I was eager to see them—for the past two weeks, I'd been holed up in the apartment, finishing the article—and spend my last days in Valencia in the company of old friends. Dusting, mopping, wiping windows, I'd finally gotten the flat back up to the boys' high standards and had also stocked the fridge; I took care to buy plenty of wine and beer, bacon and ham, assuming that during their summer in Morocco they hadn't been indulging much in alcohol or pork. I couldn't wait to hear about their adventures. Our electronic correspondence had been rare due to technical problems, though they had sent a few picturesque postcards: the Sultan's palace, the souk, the Strait of Gibraltar. Finally, around four in the afternoon, they buzzed from downstairs.

"Rachel, we're back!" they called into the intercom.

I ran to the balcony, waved at them with an unabashed grin, and called down to the street: "You need any help?" surprised at the number of bags they had.

"No, just buzz open the door, would you?"

They made their way up, groaning and bumping their suitcases against the steps, and spilled into the flat.

"Welcome!" I hugged them both at once. Hearing their voices, Molly the cat, who had spent an asocial summer keeping cool among the flower pots, came sauntering in, accepted a quick stroke from Fergal and began sniffing all the bags. "We're both thrilled to see you."

"It's great to see you too." Hector smiled, eyeing me up and down: I was barefoot, in a thin cotton shift and had my hair up in a clip. "You look like a kid."

"That's good to hear. I feel like an old hag. Now, who wants a beer?"

After we were all served up, Fergal opened the first bag.

"I couldn't resist the crafts down there," he said, uncovering a ceramic tagine used for stewing couscous, three hooded djellabas, and some pointed leather slippers. "They use such simple lines, but it's all so elegant." He peeked into another bag and handed me a small box. "We didn't forget you, of course."

"Yes, love, thanks for minding the flat," added Hector. "Everything looks great."

I opened the box and pulled out a necklace. At the end of a thin golden chain was a pendant, an airy filigree of the hand of Fatima.

"It's beautiful," I said, admiring it closely before sliding the long chain over my head. "Thanks, you two. You didn't have to get me anything, but, hey, I'm really glad you did."

"It's to ward off the evil eye," Fergal said.

"So, it's practical too?" I looked back down at the pendant and kissed them both. "Excellent. I really needed something like that."

"We can show you the rest of the shopping later," said Hector. "I'm so sick of carrying it that I can't even look at it. Let's sit out on the terrace."

"Ah, you mean my office," I said, as we filed out the French windows and on to the patio. "It's been the best work space I've ever had. Really, I should be the one buying you presents."

"How's your article going?" Hector asked.

"It's done. I finished it a couple of days ago."

"Would you like me to take a look at it before you submit it?"

"You know, I thought about that," I said and took a swig. "The luxury of having you read it, your comments, your feedback… But then I realized that could only result in rewrites for me. So, I sent it off yesterday."

"Well done." Hector laughed. "I'm sure it's fine."

"You know what?" I peeked over at him with a sheepish smile. "I think it's better than fine. It may be the best piece I've ever written. In the end, I felt a connection to that old bathhouse. It's hard to explain. Oh, and guess what? Along with the article, I submitted some photos—straight ones, altered ones—but I think they really captured the place. Who knows what they'll make of *that*, but I wanted to give it a shot. Maybe one of these years I'll be able to give up the day job."

"A history slut like you?" Hector rolled his eyes. "You could never do anything else."

"Well, how about you two?" I grinned back at them. "Did you get any work done? Or was this just a three-month shopping spree?"

Fergal brought out a sketchbook filled with studies and notes made in pencil, charcoal, and pastel. Street scenes for the most part, he'd drawn a variety of beggars, women's shapes obscured by tunics and scarves, vendors' stalls and outdoor cafés, cats in archways.

"They're wonderful, Fergal." I handed him back the sketchbook, brimming with life. "I can almost smell the spices."

"My next series of paintings will be based on this," he said. "Maybe that's why I went overboard at the market. I wanted to remember the richness of the place, the colors and textures."

"And how about you, Hector?" I prodded his knee with my toe. "Have you just been lounging around smoking kif this whole time?"

"I started writing a new book, I'll have you know," he said, feigning offense.

"Oh, Hector, that's fabulous! What's it about?"

"It's a double biography, a *bi*-biography as it were," he said, his eyes flashing. "It's on two fin de siècle writers, two Europeans who went exploring in the Maghreb: Isabelle Eberhardt and Michel Vieuchange. The interesting thing is that they each felt the need to cross-dress down there. To enjoy complete freedom, she always dressed as a man, whereas he, on his journey to Smara, tried to pass himself off as a Berber tribeswoman. They're both utterly fascinating and, needless to say, neither one of them made it to the age of thirty."

"Hmm." I sniffed. "A new series of paintings, a *book*? Compared to you two, I feel like I've just wasted my summer in Valencia. How dull and lazy I am."

"Well, you know what they say about all work and no play," Hector joked. "So, tell us, what else have you been doing?"

After a short account of my friendship with Marisa Flores, our immediate bonding and various outings, I confessed my short-lived affair with Paco Nogales. In fact, I'd been dying to talk to them about it for weeks.

"Paco Nogales?" Fergal nodded in appreciation. "He's like a train."

I laughed at his literal translation of the Spanish expression for gorgeous but Hector gave him a weary look.

"Right." Hector said, taking over. "So, basically, things were going wonderfully well when he had to leave town on business. Well, have you heard from him?"

"Yes, we've exchanged a few emails." I blushed slightly. "Well, actually, more than a few. More like dozens. But, I don't know..."

"What?" Hector said.

"It just seems so unlikely." My voice sounded surprisingly matter-of-fact. "A cross-Atlantic romance? At this point in my life? And after the Todd thing... I just don't know if it's worth it."

"You mean, you're afraid of it not working out? Or of being hurt again?"

"Not just that." I absentmindedly fingered the pendant, protection against the evil eye. "I'm afraid of losing Nick again. After the tornado, I realized how stupid I was, to ever put a man ahead of my son."

"Nick's an adult now, Rachel," Hector said softly. "He's going to have to get over it one day. He has a girlfriend. Why can't you be with someone too?"

"I know. But we've had some really nice talks this summer. About the reconstruction mostly, but about our experiences too. I'm just so happy to have him back in my life." I paused a moment to chase away tears. "And he's so excited about me seeing the house. They've even lined one of my study walls with new bookshelves. Of course, there's no other furniture in there. He knew I'd want to pick all that out myself but—"

"Did you mention Paco to him?" Fergal asked.

"No." I sighed. "I just didn't want to go down that road again."

"Listen, Rachel, it sounds like he's happy to have you back too," Hector said. "Maybe things will be different next time."

I nodded, unsure of my voice. I'd found the correspondence with Paco exciting but troubling too. It had begun with a quirky apology about his untimely departure, but had quickly moved on to colorful travel anecdotes combined with flirtatious banter. He confessed his immediate attraction to me ("When you were talking about sexy medieval miniatures, it was all I could do to stay in my chair!") and expressed serious regrets about the fact I was leaving. I had cautiously revealed that I was interested in him too. Then, in his last email, Paco announced that he'd applied to work on some projects in the States. I didn't know how to react. Did that make it real? Could it actually happen? I had to admit, every time I saw his name in my inbox, my heart started pounding, my face flushed, my breath faltered. Although I recognized the delicious thrill of falling in love, I had to remind myself that those were also the symptoms of fear.

Talk on the terrace drifted back to Tangier—life in the city as well as their excursions to villages, veritable trips back in time—and over a light supper, we chalked out plans for the following day, my last full day in Valencia.

I got up with the church bells and began packing my suitcase. With the loathsome new weight restrictions, I worried about it being too heavy and had to periodically test it on the scales. I lined the bottom with books, put the tube with Laborde's engraving safely to the side, then filled the rest of it with unironed clothes.

I added the gifts: red and yellow t-shirts proclaiming Spain 2010 World Cup champions for my construction crew of four, plus a small leather backpack for Allison and a book on Valencian architecture for Nick. I hadn't forgotten his request for Spanish ham and on the top stored a half-kilo of exquisite black-hoofed, acorn-fed *jamón,* pre-sliced and vacuumed-packed. I made a quick plea to my old buddy Saint Joseph of Cupertino—the patron saint of air travelers—for the customs officials not to confiscate it. I zipped up the bag. It was just barely under the weight limit. I sat back and sighed. I was getting nervous about the trip. Not so much the flight, as the landing. What would I find? How would they be, my town, my house, my son?

After breakfast, I took a long walk with Hector and Fergal, down through the riverbed park and up through the old town.

"Hey Rachel," Fergal said, as we were nearing the cathedral. "Why don't you show me your bathhouse? I've never been."

"I'd love to. I was thinking I should go say good-bye to it anyway."

On the half-hour, Xavi peeked out of the door to see if anyone was waiting.

"Hey, I've brought you some customers. Xavi, these are my old friends Hector and Fergal. This is Marisa's son."

They shook hands, and we entered the cool bathhouse, leaving the warm, dusty street behind. To the tune of medieval melodies, we watched the short video, then began the tour of the cold, warm, and hot rooms. Fergal took a small sketchbook out of his bag and began drawing the arches and pillars.

"You know, we went to a bathhouse when we were in Istanbul a few years ago," he said. "But it had more of a Roman feel: a huge dome, Corinthian capitals, marble and mosaics. Don't get me wrong—it was fabulous, not New Agey or twee—and we got massages and the works. But this place," he said, turning to the next page and making a few more quick strokes, "it feels like the real deal. We saw some buildings like this in Morocco, the same massive walls, rustic lines, this timelessness. I love it."

"I know. And look at this." I pointed to the little carving, remembering with a flutter how Paco had said 'you + me = love.' "It's one of the baths' little mysteries."

"Well, the F must surely stand for Fergal," he said with playful seriousness. "But the rest of it?"

"Let's see, let's see," Hector said. "I know: Icon *is* Fergal."

"C'mon, boys." I laughed. "Let's look at the roof."

We climbed the short staircase to look down on the white roof; glass knobs covered the skylights dotting the vaults and dome like uniform soap bubbles.

"It's a stocky little thing, isn't it?" Fergal sighed. "Homely, really."

"Hard to believe it's still here," Hector added.

"Thank god *some* things last," I said. "Makes me wonder what Tuscaloosa is going to look like now. It's been nearly three and a half months since the tornado."

Before we left, I gave Xavi a hug—"Thanks for everything. Come and visit me in Alabama!"—and the three of us went to the market. We'd invited Marisa to join us for a farewell dinner.

Back at the house, we unloaded armfuls of products hard to come by in the States: octopus, periwinkles and pickled anchovies, *morcilla* and *longaniza* sausages, baby fava beans and seriously good bread. Since we all wanted to eat a variety of Spanish foods—Hector and Fergal, upon returning, and me, before leaving—we were planning a tapas menu. As the boys were rearranging the fridge, I decided to check my email, something I'd been doing a lot more frequently lately.

I popped open my laptop and saw that, since last night, I'd only received two new messages. Mildly disappointed that the name Paco Nogales wasn't there (but unsurprised, since I hadn't responded to his last letter, the rather serious one about the possibility of us living on the same continent), I was pleased to find one from Nick. I opened the other message first—a dull reminder of an upcoming faculty meeting from my department head—then clicked on Nick's with a ready smile.

Dear Mom,

We're completely stoked that you'll be back tomorrow! Can't wait for you to see the house! Erik and Mitchell have gone back to Auburn, but Allison and I will be there to pick you up at the airport. Oh—be prepared: the yard still looks like a barren wasteland. Allison planted some flowers in the front beds, but they look like the sole survivors on a battle field. You'll have to use your green-thumb magic on the place when you get back. Let's plant some new trees this winter (I know a guy who runs a nursery in Auburn). That would definitely help.

Tuscaloosa itself is looking much better than when you left, but it's still going to take time—decades?—to get it back together. Now there's a big debate going on about how to re-build: to improve on the past (with parks, bike lanes, etc) or to go back to the way it was. Lots of pros and cons… I'll let you figure it out when you get here.

Listen, the main reason I'm writing is that I've been wanting to talk to you about something, but I haven't really known how. And thinking about you coming home tomor-row… I don't know. I just want to get this over with. And maybe this is the kind of thing best told from a distance, with a long flight in between. It's about Todd. I know that my reaction to you dating him must have seemed like a total ex-aggeration, like I was being a spoiled brat. But, I want you to know two things: I don't care if you date and I wasn't just being a jerk. There was a reason I left that day during the game and why I didn't come back. At halftime, Todd followed me into the bathroom. When I asked what he wanted, he said "you know" and reached between my legs and tried to kiss me. It was all I could do not to clock his ass.

I guess I should have told you—warned you about him—but I was too freaked out to talk about it. I just wanted you to automatically understand, to trust me. I'm sorry, Mom.
Love,
Nick

I sat immobile, staring at the screen, my hands suddenly frozen in the warm attic apartment. When he started hedging around for words, my mind had begun to race: Had he gone way over budget? Was Allison pregnant? But I'd been totally unprepared for *that*. I read those lines again and again, going back over my relationship with Todd, the near-year we had spent together: the dates and din-ners, the lazy Sunday mornings, sex in the shower… How dare he touch my son. Controlling a gag, I finally shouted: "Hector!"

Back on the plane, thirty-five thousand feet up, I was feeling something similar to safe, another nameless sheep caught in the present tense. The evening before had not gone as planned. I had wept and raged, threatening to call Todd long distance, to call the FBI. I felt dirty, guilty. Despite the unfestive mood,

Marisa had joined us for dinner anyway. Picking at our food, jabbing it, tossing it, throwing bits to the cat, we had all taken part in a hearty, scathing analysis of Todd Russell. In the end, it was the most cathartic meal I'd ever had.

The flight—a less-than-comfortable cocoon-stage before facing reality—was a long, undefined drone lasting from snack to dinner to breakfast. I tried to distract myself. I drank two Bloody Marys, half-watched a movie, leafed through the Sky Mall magazine, ever astounded by the bizarre items on sale. But I always came back to the image of Todd groping my son in the bathroom—the same tiny room that had been my refuge when, alone, I faced that EF-4 tornado. On the last flight, they'd mistaken me for a blind person. It seemed I really was.

I scanned Nick's message, fuming again, then tentatively scrolled down to reread Paco's emails. I opened them one by one, from the first—the brief apology—to the last—his determination to meet in the States. Paco... So intelligent and sweet, successful and funny. Would he too be attracted to my handsome young son? Would he also be tempted, after a few beers, to make a pass at him?

I considered the idea but, after a few moments, declared it groundless fear. During last night's dinner, we had discussed various incidents I'd had with Todd, red-flag moments. Even his way of breaking up—*I can't do this anymore*—said far more about him than it did about me.

I still didn't know what I'd say to Nick when I got home, how I could begin to apologize. *I just wanted you to automatically understand, to trust me,* he'd written. How had I been so thick? I fiddled with my new pendant, the Hand of Fatima, said to keep bad luck at bay. If only I'd gotten it earlier.

When I walked out of baggage claim at the Birmingham airport, I immediately saw Nick, tall and lean, his arm draped carelessly around Allison's shoulders. They were smiling together, sharing a Coke, both exuding the artless confidence of youth. Had he been affected by the experience with Todd? Had it changed him in any way? Or more likely, had I done the damage by not putting my faith in him? Looking up, he caught my eye and quickly rushed over.

"Hey!" he called with a grin.

As I hugged him close, I whispered in his ear, "I'm so sorry."

"Don't be," he said into my hair, then pulled back to look into my eyes. "It's not your fault." He grabbed my suitcase. "Now, are you ready to see the house?"

On the drive home, Nick and Allison gave me some details about life in Tuscaloosa after the storm: survivors' tales and the rising death toll figures, the political arguments and the selfless acts of kindness. Beyond fixing my house, they had also spent some time volunteering; Nick, whose Spanish was quite good, was especially helpful working with immigrant families. I looked at their glowing faces. They radiated that same air of satisfaction and enrichment that people had after a summer of NGO work in Africa. Tuscaloosa had become the third world overnight.

As we drove into town, I saw that, although the eerie, treeless light was still there, most of the debris was gone. How many tons of wood, metal, brick and concrete had been hauled away? The figures were impossible to imagine. Nick pulled into my street, almost unrecognizable without the oaks and pines, and parked in front of my house. For a moment, I just sat in the car, staring at it. It looked like it had been set down in a 1950s housing development, back when they used to clear-cut the land before building.

There were no plants and even the grass had bald spots. I had just gotten out of the car when I noticed the marigolds—smelly, ordinary plants with weedy leaves and drab orange blooms—in a newly dug bed near the front door. I felt extremely moved.

"Thank you, Allison." Near tears, I pulled her into a tight hug. "For the flowers. And for taking care of Nick."

"Nick?" Allison said, peeking at him as he yanked the suitcase out of the trunk. "He's fine. Seriously, Rachel. He's just been worried about you."

"Well?" he joined us, gesturing towards the house. "What do you think?"

Suddenly remembering that part of my house was also new, I looked up at the bedroom and study. The roof, the walls, the windows: it was almost the same as it used to be, before the storm.

"Wow," I whispered, trying to recall exactly how it had been before I left: the pecan tree rammed into the study, squirrels in the bedroom, the turquoise tarp covering the hole.

"We enlarged the windows a bit," said Nick, "mainly because those were the only frames we could find. And shingles that exact color gray were hard to come by. We finally got some in Montgomery."

"It's perfect." I hugged them both again. "You did a beautiful job."

"Let's go inside," Nick said, "I want to show you the stuff we salvaged."

Hesitantly, I walked into the house where I'd lived for nearly ten years, taking everything in as if it were new. The downstairs was clean and orderly, much as it had been when I left in May. There was the TV that had announced the storm, the sofa where I'd slept, the fruit bowl, now filled with peaches. And there was the half-bath. I paused as I passed it, peeking inside. I would have liked to discuss what happened there with Nick but knew that now was not the time. Maybe it never would be.

I followed them up the stairs and he ushered me into the bedroom.

"As you can see, most of the furniture in here is fine. We had to replace the mattress, though," he said, sitting on it and bouncing lightly. "The other one was water-logged. So, I hope you weren't too attached to any of your dust mites."

I looked around, pleased with how much had survived. The curtains, fan, lamps, and some baubles were missing, but besides that, this room hadn't changed too dramatically. "And the study?" I asked with a grimace.

Nick stood up and led the way. The vacant room smelled new, of wood, varnish and paint. Was it bigger or smaller than I remembered? Light beamed through the windows; the view was so open, I could see straight into the neighbors' houses. I turned to the bookshelves, the only piece of furniture. Most of the shelves were empty, but a few held a scattering of trinkets and scruffy books.

"This is what's left." Nick shrugged. "Everything else flew away, broke or was ruined by water."

I approached the first shelf and, with a sad smile, looked at the random collection of books left from my library: a Tom Robbins novel that Jeff had left behind, a Latin textbook from college, long-abandoned books by Lacan and Derrida, Hector's signed book on Molly houses.

"*Ferdinand the Bull* made it, I'm happy to say." Nick smiled at his mother, pointing out his favorite book from childhood, then picked up the mandolin. "And they were able to fix it," he said with a strum. "Sounds like new."

"I'm so glad." I studied the instrument in his hands. "Your grandfather would have turned over in his grave if that had been lost. What else do we have?"

I made my way to the next shelf. I peered down at the framed daguerreotype of my grandmother, precious at age seven, ninety long years before she turned into a house. I reached out to touch a wooden devil mask from Mexico, a conch shell, a nautilus fossil...

"Ah," I cried softly, reaching out. My ceramic horse had survived. My father had given it to me before memory; it had stood guard in my nursery. With patches of missing glaze and an eroded tail, it had always looked as if a thousand children had held it, had sought comfort in its perfect lines. The old golden horse was now missing a leg.

"I found that out in the yard, believe it or not," Nick said, "near the roots of the pecan tree. It's broken but if you set it up on this rock"—he took the horse, balanced it, and gently moved his hands away—"it doesn't look too bad. I was glad it made it through the storm."

"You and me both, kid." I reached up to pull his head down, to kiss him on the crown like I used to do when he was a boy.

"Well, that's about it," he said. "I hope you're not too disappointed—"

"Are you kidding? I'm thrilled!" I beamed at them both, wiping away a happy tear; the storm-season already seemed part of the past. "You guys did a great job on the reconstruction and, on top of it, you found all of my favorite things."

"Alright, then!" Allison laughed. "I guess we can go on down and pop that homecoming champagne."

"Great! There's plenty of *jamón* to go with it."

Back in the kitchen, I noticed a pile of mail on the old sideboard. As Nick and Allison began preparing a snack, I started sorting through it: bills, solicitations, catalogs, magazines, a postcard from a former student.

"Nothing very interesting here." I sighed.

"Oh, you got a package this morning," Nick said, pointing with the cheese knife to a smallish box next to the front door, "overnight service."

I picked it up and saw my address printed out in block letters, the typical handwriting of architects. Inside, there was a card and a small white box. My hand shaking slightly, I opened the envelope and found a short note.

Rachel—
In two weeks I have a job interview in Nashville. Please meet
me there.
Take a chance!
Besos,
Paco

I took the lid off the box and found the old bone dice, the ones belonging to the furtive gambler a few centuries back. I rolled them in my right hand—would I win largely this time?—and threw them on the table with a grin. Even before looking, I knew. Double sixes.

Author's Note And Acknowedgements

The first time I ever saw the Admiral's Baths was from Tim O'Grady's balcony. It was around 1999 and he and his family had just moved into a house in the old quarter of Valencia which, from a side window, overlooked the bathhouse. It was a squat little place crammed between taller buildings and it didn't look like much. It was still being renovated and its strange roof—vaults and a dome dotted with little glass pots—hadn't been cleaned yet. However, Tim—the author of *I Could Read the Sky* and *Light*—was curious and enthusiastic about his new neighbor, as he is about most things. That night, my husband Carlos mentioned that, although he'd never been to the old bathhouse himself, his father had occasionally taken baths there as a university student in the 1940s. "Huh!" I probably said.

The bathhouse wouldn't open as a museum for several years, as the careful restoration job took a surprisingly long time. After it did open—around 2005?— our dear friends and fellow translators Agustin Nieto and Brendan Lambe, who in days of plenty used to give me jobs they thought I'd enjoy, asked me to translate the new website. The long, detailed texts about the baths, taken from the book by Concha Camps and Josep Torró, took a few months to translate into English; during that time, I became an amateur expert on the bathhouse: its history, how it worked, its architecture and restoration.

One day, I was working on the article about the families who owned the baths and, before lunch, translated the following (paraphrased) paragraphs about its owner from 1531 to 1541.

Joan Salvaterra was a flequer, *a baker, and owned a bakery near San Cristobal. He and his wife Maria, both from humble backgrounds, bought the bathhouse and bakery in 1531. They could only afford to pay less than a fifth of the cost up front and agreed to pay off the remaining debt in payments with annual interest. However, Joan died in 1536.*

Unable to settle the debt, Maria was forced to give up ownership of the property. In 1541 a member of the extensive Penyarroja family line named Filibert acquired the property. It is worth mentioning that the deceased baker and his wife had had a relationship with Filibert's father, probably because of his flour mills. Evidently, Filibert Penyarroja also bought the other bakery from Maria in the same transaction.

Although this text is rather dry (the original is worse, including all the financial and contractual details), it played with my imagination. What kind of person, with already one business, would take a risk like that? What did his wife think about taking on such debt? And after her husband died (were they in love?), how did she manage? And this Filibert character—was he an opportunist? Or her hero? Or something else entirely?

My husband took me out to lunch and I told him about poor Maria de Salvaterra. "Can't you just imagine it?" I asked him.

"There's a story there." Those paragraphs were the seed for this novel. But, by that time I had already fallen in love with the bathhouse itself, its history, its incredible longevity. *That's* the story, I decided.

Although it is sheer fiction, *The Admiral's Baths* is based on the real story of the bathhouse; whenever possible, I used the historical information available, about the baths and their owners, and the city of Valencia itself: its fine tradition in ceramics, its walled red-light district, its spectacular cuisine, its early mental hospital, its booming silk trade, its long history of gambling, its fiestas, its distinguished visitor, Alexandre de Laborde... In fact, some historians even believe that it was in Valencia that the chess queen came into being—but at least a century later than in this story.

I raise my glass to all the scholars, living and dead, who instructed and inspired me. Among the many, many sources I read while doing research for the novel, I would like to single out a few excellent references which were especially helpful: on the history of Valencia, Manuel Sanchis Guarner in his epic *La Ciutat de València*; on medieval pottery, Mercedes Mesquida Garcia in *La Cerámica de Paterna: Reflejos del Mediterráneo*; on the plague, *The Black Death* by Philip Ziegler; on syphilis, Deborah Hayden in her entertaining and informative *Pox: Genius, Madness, and the Mysteries of Syphilis*; on the expulsion, *conversos* and the Holy Office, Henry Kamen in *The Spanish Inquisition* and Jane S. Gerber in *The Jews of Spain: A History of the Sephardic Experience*; and the incomparable Robert Hughes on *Goya*. I am also indebted to Begoña Olavide and the group Mudéjar for their beautiful songs and in-depth research into medieval Spanish music, Arab, Jewish and Christian. The songs Fatima sings were taken from their CD "Al-Son"; the lyrics were translated into English by Xander Fraser.

I would also like to offer my fond affection to the people of Tuscaloosa, Alabama—my college town—who suffered through the devastating tornado in 2011. Big thanks go out to Frannie James, my wonderful friend and technical adviser on the April 27th MoFo. Anything in the text regarding the tornado and its aftermath that is false or unrealistic is due to my blatant disregard of her excellent advice. Roll tide, Frannie!

Gracias mil to the ceramic artist, Rafaela Pareja, my pottery instructor. Her classes, hugs and incredible effervescence have greatly added to my life these last few years. Thanks too to Irina Perez and Pepe Royo, other ceramists I've had the good fortune to take lessons from as I try to channel my inner Fatima.

Since this book has been over ten years in the making, there are many, many friends and family members who have read various drafts of the novel, thus providing me with invaluable feedback. From my Valencia Brits, Robert Dean, Richard Barrett, Tim Davies, and Hayley Burch (bless her), who read the very first draft of Fatima's story; to Charles Harmon, Peggy Stelpflug, Luisa Carrillo, James King, Amy Sevcik, Susan Prygoski, Rafa Higón, and Jose Luis Machancoses, who read an early draft of the manuscript; to my then-colleagues at American Institute—Meredith Kershaw, Xaq Frohlich, Stan Grammenos, Natalia Pavlovic, and Declan Lehande—who read a much later version of the book; to Chick and Rita Wells who read the final edits—and, of course, to anyone else I've forgotten. But my heart really goes out to Mary Dansak and Lizzie Hudson who put up with countless emails regarding the lives of Fatima, Angels and Clara—not to mention mine. A world of thanks, my Friends 4-Ever.

The end-product owes a great debt to Peter Cooper, graphic designer extraordinaire, for the cover (and so much more!) and to my sister Lynn Gynther, a literary genius, for the copyediting. As for the audio book, it wouldn't have been possible without the expertise of my awesome sound man, Gustavo Ibañez, my chauffer Carlos Abarca, and the person who convinced me to do it in the first place, Ricardo Gonzalez Torres.

My family has also provided me with great support and encouragement. Big kisses go out to my mother Ruth and father Malcolm, who also read a draft or two before he passed away in 2009, my brother Larry, sisters Lynn and Lisa. Most special thanks to my husband, Carlos and my daughters Claudia and Lulu, all three Valencians born and bred. This is my love song to your city, my adopted hometown.

Made in United States
Troutdale, OR
08/05/2023

11840662R00217